THE MINSTREL'S GIRL

A Novel of the 15th century

by

Lizzie Jones

**Grosvenor House
Publishing Limited**

This book is published by
Grosvenor House Publishing Ltd
28-30 High Street, Guildford, Surrey, GU1 3EL.
www.grosvenorhousepublishing.co.uk

A CIP record for this book
is available from the British Library

ISBN 978-1-78148-966-6

Also by Lizzie Jones

Mr. Shakespeare's Whore – the story of Aemilia Bassano

The Tangled Knot – A novel of the English Civil War

On Wings of Eagles – The story of Ferdinando Stanley and Alice Spencer

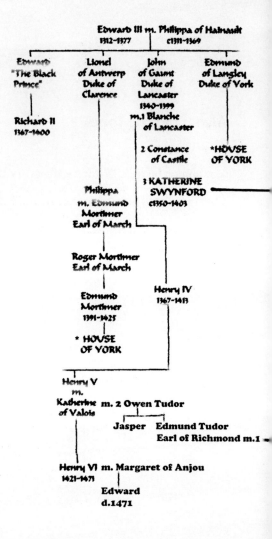

Edward III m. Philippa of Hainault
1312-1377   c1311-1369

Edward
"The Black
Prince"

Lionel
of Antwerp
Duke of
Clarence

John
of Gaunt
Duke of
Lancaster
1340-1399
m.1 Blanche
of Lancaster

Edmund
of Langley
Duke of York

Richard II
1367-1400

2 Constance
of Castile

*HOUSE
OF YORK

Philippa
m. Edmund
Mortimer
Earl of March

3 KATHERINE
SWYNFORD
c1350-1403

Roger Mortimer
Earl of March

Edmund
Mortimer
1391-1425

Henry IV
1367-1413

* HOUSE
OF YORK

Henry V
m.
Katherine
of Valois

m. 2 Owen Tudor

Jasper   Edmund Tudor
Earl of Richmond m.1

Henry VI m. Margaret of Anjou
1421-1471

Edward
d.1471

Simplified genealogical chart of the characters mentioned in the book.

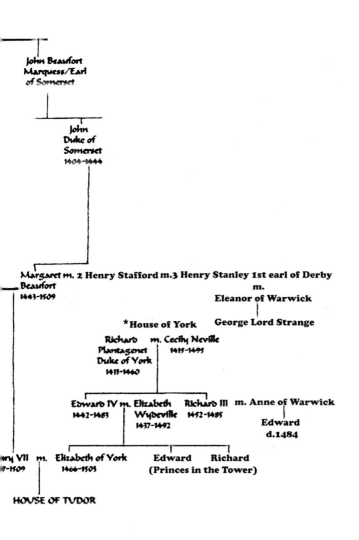

John Beaufort
Marquess/Earl
of Somerset

John
Duke of
Somerset
1404-1444

Margaret m. 2 Henry Stafford m.3 Henry Stanley 1st earl of Derby
Beaufort
1443-1509

m.
Eleanor of Warwick

*House of York

George Lord Strange

Richard   m. Cecily Neville
Plantagenet   1415-1495
Duke of York
1411-1460

Edward IV m. Elizabeth   Richard III m. Anne of Warwick
1442-1483   Wydeville   1452-1485
1437-1492

Edward
d.1484

Henry VII   m. Elizabeth of York   Edward   Richard
1457-1509   1466-1503   (Princes in the Tower)

HOUSE OF TUDOR

Chapter 1

Reims

She heard the stream gurgling over the stones before she could see it, the yellowing light of early evening melting the monotony of small brown fields into a bland haze. The birds in their twittering flight had been swept away by the approaching twilight and when the eerie near-silence was pierced by the music of running water she stopped to get her bearings. Then she began to run towards a line of alders threading the flat landscape after the forest had straggled to its close before the hills rose in the distance. There she found the stream.

She knelt down on the pebbly bank and scooping up handfuls of water splashed her face, wincing at the pain as the droplets stung the cuts and bruises. Then she began to pour water frantically over her arms then her legs, rubbing furiously but it was not enough. She felt soiled and stained to the depths of her being. There was no alternative but to immerse herself completely. She was sheltered by the overhanging alders, yellowy green so that they seemed to melt into the buttermilk sky, and the place was isolated enough with only sleeping earth and sparse clumps of trees until the town raised its towers on the horizon, the irregular outline becoming smudged as the shadows lengthened. She pulled off her gown (easily done since the laces were broken and the belt lost) then her torn smock, then slipping out of her shoes she held her breath as she plunged into the water. The iciness struck her like a blow and gasping with shock she held herself rigid until she could bear the pain, though tears mingled with the moisture on her face. Eventually the hurt melted into numbness and as sensation died she felt the uncleanness dissipate.

She stepped onto the bank, shivering uncontrollably now as the water dripped from her. She looked at her discarded shift on the grass - torn and soiled and of little use so she might as well use it to dry herself. As she rubbed the rough linen over her body the friction brought some warmth to her limbs though she had to be careful with the sore places. Her gown of green wool felt comfortably warming but she knew that in a short time it would become irritating, scratching her skin and making her itch without the protection of the linen shift. She tied the broken laces as best she could though she was aware her breasts were not completely covered, but it was getting dark so perhaps it would not be noticed. Slipping into her shoes she looked at the walls of the town ahead of her and decided she must make for there. She had no further idea what to do as she had no money, but considered it a better option than wandering in the deserted countryside. Once inside the town she might be able to beg or find some menial work in exchange for food and a bed for the night.

She was weary and hurting and the walls surrounding the town were further away than she had thought, she worried that the gates might already be closed for the curfew. Making a great effort she forced herself to hurry until she reached the wall where double doors of planked wood reinforced with iron were set in the stonework of two round towers, praying the entrance to the town was not already locked for the night.

"Dépêche-toi," barked the armoured guard, his hand already on the heavy iron bars ready to push the formidable hasp into place with a resounding finality.

"Merci," she gasped, hardly able to speak the word for breathlessness but rushing through the narrowing gap to distance herself as fast as she could from the guards in case they should note her dishevelled state and inquire her business.

On the other side of the gate the portico soon spread into a confusing maze of narrow streets and as soon as she dared she paused to ease the stitch in her side and try to find some sense of direction, but after a swift survey of her surroundings she considered it not wise to linger. The clustered houses were shuttered so no lights could be seen, their upper storeys overhanging drunkenly and almost touching each other across the narrow dark passageways and evil-smelling refuse was piled in the centre runnel of the alleys. She sensed vague shadowy figures lurking at corners and watching her. She almost tripped over a bundle on the ground until closer awareness made out a movement in the dirty rags and a skeletal hand reached out to clutch at her gown. She kicked it away and increased her pace though the stitch in her side had got worse, stepping more warily now but conscious of the noise her wooden-soled shoes made on the cobbles. She tried to keep a direct line through the frustrating maze, following the tolling of a deep bell which she believed must come from some large church and hoping that perhaps this might guide her to the town square.

After what seemed like endless wanderings that appeared to be leading nowhere she suddenly came to a broader thoroughfare lined by larger well-spaced buildings, the end of the road opening out into a large cobbled square. There were flickers of light from pitch torches bracketed at intervals on the walls and from gaps in the shutters of what looked to be imposing stone houses with gables and oriel windows while in front of her loomed the tallest towers she had ever seen. At that moment the moon slid from behind an enclosing bank of cloud and revealed the most magnificent building she had ever encountered in all her journeys through France, the stone gleaming white in the moonlight. Two towers soared effortlessly to the sky, covered with hundreds of exquisitely carved statues of saints and angels, strange beasts and mythical creatures, and in prime place above the great arched doorway the virgin sat in glory surrounded with all the panoply of heaven. She had heard tell that this was the most magnificent cathedral in France, where the kings of France from the time of the great Clovis had been crowned and where nearly fifty years ago the young warrior Jeanne La Pucelle, later burnt at the stake by the English, had helped to crown King Charles VII. She knew the stories but never in her wildest imagination had she dreamt such a superb creation could be achieved by the hands of man.

But despite the unique magnificence of the cathedral fronting the square, around the sides and at the back huddled a mass of contrasting squalor - shanties of teetering planks stuffed with turf, and decrepit hovels of mud and bracken. She sensed faces peering at her through the gaps while ragged beggars were draped across the steps in attitudes of slumber, drunken stupor or disease. Suddenly, even in the contemplation of such a work of art, even within the shadow of this house of God, a wave of menace washed over her. In panic she ran to the great arched central door, fearful that it might be shut and she would be marooned in the circle of these malevolent watchers but it opened laboriously to her frantic thrust on the huge brass handle, the sanctuary handle offering safety to the seeker. She would stay the night here, within its precincts she would be safe. No-one could touch her here during the hours of darkness.

She ran into the interior, wincing at the sudden chill that enveloped her in its icy grasp as the door thudded shut. She shivered and looked around, at first seeing nothing but black shadows until her eyes became accustomed to the gloom and she became aware of the faint glimmer of candles still burning on the altars and a shaft of moonlight silvering the stones as it pierced a saint's halo in a stained glass window, creating enough light for her to discern unlimited space soaring above and around her. The symmetry of scores of perfect stone arches disappeared into the shadows while a multitude of enormous windows of painted glass tantalisingly hid their glories except for where pinpricks of light hinted at their splendour. She stood transfixed, breathing in the faint aroma of melted wax and incense. Then involuntarily she bent her knees on the cold stones and made the sign of the cross. She whispered an Ave, concluding with a fervent "Holy Virgin, help me now."

For a few moments the consciousness of such beauty had flooded her with a spontaneous warmth but now she was trembling with cold again, only her gown covering her nakedness without her smock and she wished fervently she had not left her cloak behind when she fled.

But there was no alternative for a night's shelter without money so she made her way to one of the benches placed against the outer wall for the sick and infirm and sank down on the unyielding wood, made smooth by regular use. The stone wall at her back was too cold and uneven to lean against so if she wished to sleep she would have to lie full length on the uncomfortable narrow bench, drawing up her legs and folding her arms tightly around herself to create a semblance of warmth.

Her heart had slowed its frantic hammering and she sat quietly, relishing the sensation of being alone and safe if only temporarily. She turned her head to gaze on the beautiful rose window, dimly visible above the main door through which she had entered. She had found shelter beneath the rose, the image of love. Her father had told her the story of the Divina Commedia and how the poet Dante had used the rose as the symbol of Divine love and Heavenly bliss. As she recalled him reciting parts of the narrative the joy of recollection mingled with the pain of loss and a shaft of sorrow pierced her heart as his memory overwhelmed her again.

Suddenly she was jolted by the awareness that she was not alone. A dark cowled figure had materialised from behind one of the pillars and was approaching her. For a moment she was paralysed with fear. Then the rapid beating of her heart slowed again as she realised he must be a monk of the cathedral and unlikely to harm her although he might object to her presence and ask her to leave. He came towards her and stood looking down at her, bending close as he asked, "Are you hurt?" Even in the shadows he could see the purple bruises on her face, the cut lip with the dried blood and the eye that was swollen. When she raised herself hurriedly he noted the discomfort evident as she straightened her body.

She felt suddenly embarrassed by her torn gown and tried to pull the cloth across her partly revealed breasts. His eyes were drawn to the purple contusions there and he asked, "Has someone violated you?"

She couldn't see much of him apart from discerning grey eyes but there was compassion there and she replied softly, "Yes, father. But it wasn't the first time." Comforted by his office and feeling she was in a confessional she continued, "The first time was when I was thirteen. But it doesn't become easier."

"What are you doing here? Are you hiding from someone? Where do you live?"

The run of questions unnerved her and she answered hurriedly, "I thought it would be a safe place for tonight. My purse was taken so I have no money. But tomorrow I shall try to find some temporary work so that I can eat and pay for lodgings then I shall be on my way again."

"To where?" he asked. "Where do you belong? You are not from this part of France are you?"

"I am on a journey," she said evasively, "but you are right, I am not from Reims. You won't turn me away from the church, will you, father?" she cried anxiously. "Only let me stay here tonight and I promise you I shall be on my way by daybreak."

If it had been lighter she might have seen the half-smile that flickered momentarily across his features. He hesitated then said, "I cannot let you continue the misapprehension. The truth is that I am not a religious in any sense. I must confess that I am in fact a fugitive like you."

He pulled the hood from his head and she saw the youthful features, the dark brown hair cut short and continuing into a thick fringe, the thin lips with an apologetic smile curving them upwards. He could not have been much older than she was, at most in his early twenties.

She sank down on the bench again, covering her face in embarrassment that she had revealed so much, feeling a new twinge of alarm that she was alone again with a man of whom she knew nothing. He sat beside her and turned her to face him.

"You need not be afraid of me," he assured her. "I will help you if I can."

"Who are you?" she said nervously. "Why are you here?"

"My name is Renard, I am known as Renard de Bourgonville. I have just stolen a silver cup so I decided to hide here until morning when the curfew is lifted then I shall be on my way immediately." He made the admission without any sign of shame.

"You are a thief?"

"I don't think so. I was owed some money, rightfully earned, and when they didn't pay me then I helped myself to some remuneration, more than I would have been given 'tis true but I don't like being cheated." His face tightened and his grey eyes were stormy. "Now it's your turn, tell me about yourself."

She hesitated then said, "I was travelling with my father but he died two weeks ago. I continued on my own, I am making for Calais where I intend to take ship for England. I had enough money to pay my way but yesterday I was attacked by an evil man, perhaps he was an outlaw. I know I shouldn't have been walking alone

8

through woodland, it was foolish of me, I know I should have kept to the highway but I was told this was a shortcut to the town and I was tired and anxious to get here before dark. I struggled and he got violent as you can see. I think at first he only intended to steal my purse but when I began to fight ...." She shuddered at the recollection, seeing again the brawny figure with hard-muscled arms and big strong hands, the fierce eyes, the unkempt hair and beard.

The young man put his brown hand on hers but she flinched and he withdrew it.

She remained silent for while and the candles spluttered from a draught coming somewhere from within the lofty building, wafting towards them the musky scent of incense.

Then she asked, "What were you doing when they didn't pay you?"

He said, "I'm a chanteur." Even with her swollen eye he could see an expression of what he took to be bewilderment so he elaborated, "I'm a minstrel."

Suddenly she startled him by breaking into a peal of laughter that echoed around the vast space like a sudden shower of raindrops on stone and he looked offended. "Why is that so amusing?" he said grudgingly, standing and turning away from her.

Her unexpected outburst had torn through the curtain of their quiet speech and she put her hand hastily over her mouth to stifle her mirth. "It isn't amusing," she said, shaking her head in apology, "it is so incredible." Her voice carried a bubble of happiness that she couldn't suppress. "You see my father was a travelling minstrel. They called him Gianni le chanteur. My mother and I accompanied him on his travels and after she died when

9

I was six years old he took me with him everywhere. He taught me music and songs and when I was older I would help him entertain." She began to sing softly 'Aubade de Printemps', the purity of her voice carrying like a perfectly tuned bell even in the softest notes and Renard listened with surprised pleasure. Then her happiness died away and her bruised face held an extremity of pain as she whispered, "He died whilst we were playing in Châlons."

"I'm so sorry," he said.

There was silence for a time then she spoke hesitantly. "It seems so strange that we should come from the same world and meet here in this unlikely place."

"I sing many songs about the curious workings of fate. But you haven't told me your name," he prompted her.

"It's Belfiore. My father came from Genoa, his native language was Italian."

"Beautiful flower," he murmured. Beneath the bruises, the swollen eye, the cut lip, he could discern the beauty of her face framed by a tangled mass of long black curls and the figure outlined in the torn gown was slender but shapely.

"My father always called me Bel."

He thought for a time then said, "I think we should keep to our original plan of staying here for the night then creep on our way as soon as day breaks. I am going to Amiens and as your road to Calais will pass through there we can journey together until then and I can give you some protection. It really is not safe for you to be travelling alone. What do you say, Bel?"

"That would be wonderful," she replied fervently, inwardly thanking the Virgin for answering her prayers in such an unexpected way.

He noticed that she had begun to shiver again and unfastening his chape, his hooded cloak of brown wool, he wrapped it around her shoulders and she snuggled into it thankfully, too needful of its warmth to refuse the offer. Shorn of the covering she saw he was wearing a thigh-length belted and pleated tunic of wine-red wool over hose of forest green and short brown leather boots. Into the wide belt of brown tooled leather, beside a money pouch, a flageolet and a dagger, was tucked the silver cup. Before settling down on the bench beside her he went to retrieve from behind a pillar his lute, carefully tied in a linen bag, together with a canvas travelling bag with a long strap to carry over his shoulder.

They slept only fitfully for it was cold and uncomfortable but Bel leant against him for support and she was able to doze a little though her body was beginning to ache with the discomfort. Then as the faint grey light of approaching dawn began to seep through onto the stones Renard stirred her gently.

"Let's get out of the town as soon as the gates open, I don't want to hang around here longer than necessary. As soon as we get on our way we can find something to eat."

She blinked her eyes and nodded her head sleepily, and looking at her with her gown slipping over her shoulders he began to rummage in his bag, bringing out a collarless linen shirt.

"Here, put on my spare shirt, it will make you look more respectable and draw less attention." He held it out to her, adding "I will turn my back."

She took it and pulling down her gown slipped on the linen garment. Renard was a little taller than she was so it reached below her knees and the sleeves hung over her wrists. She pulled up her gown again and with the neckties of the shirt fastened it passed as a shift. Renard helped her tie the laces at the wrists, tying them tightly so that they bunched below her elbows. The linen was cool and comforting after the scratchiness of her wool gown. He looked at her approvingly but the broken laces made it impossible to fasten the bodice properly and he said, "I think you should still wear my cloak for the moment. You can hide the cup beneath it, I don't dare put it in my bag and you will be less suspect than I."

She hesitated at the idea of carrying stolen property, especially for a stranger of whom she knew hardly anything, but he was already draping the cloak over her shoulders and removing the silver cup from his belt. "Conceal it in the folds but don't look as if you are carrying anything," he commanded.

There was movement near the altar and they supposed a mass priest had arrived and was already making preparations for the first office of the day so they crept quietly to a side door and slipped quickly outside.

As they came round the side of the cathedral the light was spreading fast, the pale rose streaks promising a fine day as the iron-grey sky silvered, and although the air was still cool there was a hint of warmth creeping along the edges that was welcome after the blanketing chill of the night. The town looked different now in the early morning with no shroud of concealing darkness and no eyes peering through menacing shadows. As they left the cathedral square they saw buildings of stone or wood and plaster with respectable townsfolk opening their shutters and smoke curling from chimneys. There was a hum of activity as tradespeople were beginning work, the shutters of shops being pulled down for counters and servants sweeping the fronts of their premises. The air was full of the buzz of conversation as neighbours greeted each other and vendors started to advertise their wares – already fresh bread and milk for sale. Renard hastened knowledgeably through crossroads and down narrow alleys with Bel scampering behind him. In a row of bakers there was an appetising smell of newly baked bread emanating through the open doors and Renard paused to go inside, stuffing the hasty purchases into his bag. Then he made his way unerringly to the west gate where people were already gathering. Bel experienced a moment of terror as they approached the towers of the gatehouse where the guards were preparing to open the gates to the day's travellers. She knew that if the stolen cup was discovered on her person she would definitely suffer a hanging and wondered if Renard would attempt to save her or not. Fortunately her doubt was not put to the test for it was market day and hardly anyone was leaving the town whereas scores of people were trying to get in – heavily laden carts pulled by mules or oxen carrying grain, fleeces, furs, fresh rushes; country people burdened with crammed panniers and backpacks of apples, pears, nuts, bacon, cheese; pedlars with their trays of laces, ribbons and geegaws; women with cans of still-warm milk on yokes across their shoulders; hens and pigeons in baskets; pigs and sheep being poked into order by boys at their masters' commands; - all shouting and pushing, wanting to be the first to tempt the customers with their produce. The gate guards were trying to impose some order on the thrusting throng so had little time to spare for the few trying to make an exit and the two passed easily beneath their casual surveillance. They squeezed through the press of people and stepped through the gate with a sigh of relief. After passing the ruins of the Roman buildings breaking through the ground like opening graves, they were soon out into the freedom of the countryside. They still kept up a good pace for they were eager to cover as much ground as they could until Reims was well behind them. Soon the town was merely a jagged outline on the horizon with the towers of the cathedral soaring above as they followed the road to Amiens.

CHAPTER 2

On the Road

The road from Reims began as a wide well-trodden trackway along the side of the river Vesle bordered by huddles of small cob and lath cottages surrounded by kitchen gardens and some animals – a cow, a pig, a few hens. The sky had lightened now with the sun peeping from behind silvery clouds, and carts and walkers were still making their way into the town with produce. After a mile or so the road became narrower and stonier, cleaving a path through vineyards interspersed with clumps of trees. Renard paused when they reached a grassy knoll and pulled Bel down to sit beside him, opening his bag to take out a chunk of rye bread and a handful of oat cakes which he divided between them. The simple breakfast was freshly baked and they munched hungrily, Bel realising she had eaten nothing for almost a day. The burgeoning sun's rays were becoming warmer now and beyond the vines green fields could be seen. Bel felt an almost uncontrollable urge to lie down and sleep on the grass, gold-speckled with buttercups and dandelions and so much softer than the hard bench where they had passed the night, but the road ahead wound interminably into the blue haze of the far distance.

"How far is it to Amiens?" she asked.

Her companion shrugged. "I suppose it must be close on a hundred miles."

Bel groaned but he continued, "We should be able to reach Soissons today and we can spend the night there. I chose this route rather than going by Lâon which is perhaps a little shorter but there are thick forests which are always dangerous whereas this road is mainly through wheat fields and is reasonably flat and easy because we are following the river most of the time. I'm sure we shall find someone to offer us a passage when we get closer to the town, I usually manage to pick up a farm cart making a delivery. It isn't much faster but it's easier on the feet and most carters are happy enough when I offer to play for them to help pass the time."

Once again Bel was grateful to have the young man as her companion for besides giving her protection he knew the way, though her comfortable thoughts were jolted when he said, "I intend selling the cup to a silversmith in Soissons."

The silver cup was now stored away in his bag and his cloak rolled on top as it was now too warm for wearing.

"Won't the silverman be suspicious as to how you came by it?" she asked nervously. She had no wish to see her saviour carried away to the gallows for theft.

He shrugged nonchanantly. "I'm a chanteur, a teller of tales, Bel, and Soissons is far enough away from Reims. We shall have some money when I sell it, at least until I can find an engagement. But first we will have to do something about your gown."

Bel knew she couldn't mix among respectable people in such a disreputable state and was well aware that her appearance was a great disadvantage to her companion but she couldn't think of an alternative. It was useless to regret leaving her travelling pack (containing a spare set of clothing and her personal necessities) in the wood, because at that time all that mattered was that she should escape her attacker and survive with her life, nothing else had been important. However she had no means to make herself another gown and it would take a tailor at least a day to make one, and even if this should be possible once they reached a town she had no money to pay for it.

"What can we do?" she uttered gloomily.

"I have a plan when we get to a village," Renard said with a smile on his lips.

They walked in companionable silence through fields of pasture where cows grazed, the river Vesle running beside them again. Although they met few people along the road – a pedlar going in the opposite direction, two monks, an official messenger on horseback - labourers in the fields greeted them and there was security in the open vistas, only occasionally broken by copses of trees, instead of the uncertain dangers of the dense forests covering most of France. There were so many things Bel wanted to ask Renard about his life as a minstrel but she knew this would mean giving away information of her own so she stayed her questions and intuited that he felt the same. Until they knew each other better it were wise not to give away too much information.

In the near distance a cluster of buildings around a tower betokened a village. As they approached they could see it was quiet, the only noise coming from the geese and pigs on the green and the barking of dogs in cottage yards for it seemed as if the villagers were at work in the fields or attending to their tasks inside the small low-roofed dwellings where smoke curled above the thatch of some of them.

"Aha!" Renard cried suddenly, "keep walking, Bel, I'll catch you soon."

She looked at him questioningly but he was gone with the swift movements she had now come to know were characteristic of him. She did as she was bid and a short way out of the village he was beside her, carrying a bundle rolled up in his arms.

"Keep walking," he said, quickening their pace a little. Then when the village was well behind them, hidden by a copse of trees and a winding path, he unrolled the bundle. "Put this on. It might be too big but it will do until we reach Soissons."

He shook out the cloth, revealing a simple gown of faded brown wool but without holes or patches and with the laces still in the sleeves and bodice.

"Did you steal it?" she asked, recrimination in her tone, but he was unabashed.

"It was drying on a hedge near one of the cottages, as I half-expected. I'm sorry I couldn't get you a smock as well, you will have to wear my shirt for the time being. Our need is greater than theirs."

"How do you know?" she countered, still accusing with a frown puckering her forehead. "They could be very poor." She didn't feel happy about stealing. "You are a thief, aren't you?"

"Only when need arises. Come on, get dressed quickly."

He turned his back to emphasize the order and reluctantly she took off her torn gown and put on the brown one, feeling it still damp.

"Hm, it doesn't flatter you," he said brusquely. The colour was too dull and it hung loosely on her slender figure. "But at least you are now respectable enough for us not to draw attention. Now we can go into the first tavern we find and have a welcome drink and something substantial to eat."

"I have no money but I will pay you back as soon as I can."

He shrugged unconcernedly.

The first tavern in the next village on the road was unprepossessing, a thatched wooden shack with earthen floor and low roof and wormy benches set at ramshackle trestle tables, but the taverner served them sweet white wine and rustled up a plate of cheese and cold bacon. They felt revived when they continued on their way and comfort made them communicative.

"Your accent is of the south, perhaps Gascony?" Renard asked. "You said your father was Italian but what of your mother?"

"My mother's family were from near Bordeaux but they moved to Bayonne and it was there that my grandmother met my grandfather who was an English knight in the garrison there when the English ruled Bayonne. When he returned to England my grandmother returned to Bordeaux with her child, my mother. My mother lived there until she was twenty when she met my father who had come from Genoa to Provence and was making his way through France as a minstrel. They travelled together after that but she died when I was six so my father and I continued together. He always told me that if anything happened to him I should try to find my mother's kinsfolk in England because they were of the nobility."

Renard looked sceptical at the tale but did not want to destroy Bel's innocence, saying instead, "I too am from Aquitaine originally, from near Poitiers, but it is a long time since I was there."

"Then that's another link between us," she cried happily. "Both Aquitaine and Gascony once belonged to England."

Renard grimaced, thinking wryly that most natives would not appreciate such a reminder but as he had no English blood, as Bel averred she had, he made no reply to her naivety. As they walked they passed the time by describing their respective journeyings and the happenings that had ensued, though Renard revealed less than Bel who chattered happily about her travels with her father.

The river began to swing away from them again and pasture gave way to fields of new green wheat but they were tiring now. However they were fortunate enough to share a farmer's cart for a short stretch of the way and though it was slow the brief respite eased their feet. Finally in the late afternoon a carter taking a load of straw into Soissons was willing to share his waggon as far as the town itself. The straw was prickly but sweet-smelling and while they travelled Renard took his flageolet from his belt and began to play, the carter appreciative of the merry airs to break the monotony of his regular journeys.

The river Aisne, a branch of the river Vesle that they had followed for most of the way, flowed through Soissons and was crossed by a rickety wooden bridge which led to the walls of the town. However before the carter led his horse across the bridge Renard dismounted and helped Bel to climb down, thanking the carter who continued on his way alone.

"He will have to pay a toll and state his business. I must locate a silversmith who will buy the cup then we shall have some money," Renard said. "I want you to stay here while I go on my own in case there are problems. Rest on the bank, I shall soon be back and then we can find an inn for the night."

"What if you don't return?" Bel asked, remembering her horrific experience of the previous day and suddenly fearful as she looked at the strange town, a large tower looming above the walls, higher than the rest of the jumble of white stone buildings visible through the gates.

"I shall return. And before very long, have no fear," he assured her.

He set off across the bridge and after watching his agile figure disappear from sight through the gates she settled down on the grassy bank. The air was warm, balmy as the shadows began to lengthen with faint streaks of purple and silver like ribbons in the sky, but it was a way from being dark and the town still seemed busy with many people crossing the bridge, labourers coming back from the fields, travellers seeking shelter for the night, merchants returning from business. She was anxious about Renard but exhausted by the long journey since daybreak following on a sleepless night and she was soon fast asleep, her arms clasped around her knees and her head sunk on her chest. It seemed but a few minutes when Renard was wakening her, a triumphant grin on his face.

"It's done," he said, "I now have money enough, though I intend to find somewhere they will let us stay the night free in return for my playing. And I found an apothecary where I bought some comfrey to put on your bruises." He knelt down beside her and taking an earthenware pot from his pouch he began gently to anoint her bruised face with the ointment and she found tears stinging her eyes, not only from the initial smart. Renard noticed and said, half-jokingly, "I can't let people think I've been beating you." Then he was pulling her to her feet and leading her across the bridge and into the bustling town.

The road led from the river straight as an arrow to where the cathedral stood sentinel in the main square. "No more churches today," Renard grimaced and Bel's thoughts were likewise, though they stood for a moment scrutinising the irregular aspect of the white stone frontage with only one tower on the left and no corresponding feature on the right. Everything in Soissons seemed to be built of white stone, giving a luminous aspect to the town despite the usual squalor of the refuse-clogged streets, at their worst now at the end of a busy day.

"I saw an inn I considered might be suitable," Renard said, leading the way from the square, and as usual Bel had to run to keep up with his quick movements. He turned down a broad street lined with substantial houses with gables and brass-studded doors, obviously one of the wealthier districts of the town inhabited by merchants and civic dignitaries. At the head of the street stood an inn with a garishly-painted sign portraying a knight and a pathetically mild feline advertising "Le Chevalier du Leon." It was a two-storey building, long and well-maintained with a stone roof and several windows with lead panes along the frontage. An archway at the side led through into a courtyard but the main door in the centre of the frontage stood open with fresh bushes hanging at each side

"It doesn't look a cheap inn," Bel murmured uneasily.

"A poor establishment isn't likely to pay for a minstrel," he retorted, "and besides I told you I have some money now."

He strode confidently into the inn and she followed him uneasily, conscious of her ill-fitting gown and bruised face. They entered a large rectangular room with a clean stone-slabbed floor, white plastered walls and high rafters hung with bunches of fresh herbs. A large stone fireplace, empty on this warm evening, was set against one wall. There were many tables and benches of solid oak and at least half the tables were occupied with men drinking and eating, the hot food on the trenchers wafting tantalising aromas.

"I would like a meal and a bed for the night," Renard said confidently when the innkeeper strode across to see to their needs.

A burly middle-aged man with a bald pate and small shrewd eyes in a red face, his knee-length green tunic and linen shirt were reasonably clean beneath his leather apron and he held out his hands in a gesture of welcome. He began to state his prices, making Bel gasp, but Renard continued imperturbably, "I also have a proposition to put to you."

The man's small eyes narrowed further and the stance of his thick-set body became more challenging. Undeterred, Renard explained that, as a travelling minstrel, he would like to pay for their night's board with entertainment. The innkeeper, who had initially introduced himself as Mâitre Jacques, was unresponsive but Renard judged this a show of not wanting to acquiesce too easily, knowing from experience that it was not an unusual occurrence, and begun to boast of his accomplishments and the many prestigious places where he had performed. Bel listened in amazement. The innkeeper was still wary but weighed up the confident young man, well-dressed, handsome and with an undeniable charm. Folding his arms and leaning his substantial frame against the board from where the wine was served he said, "Let me see then some sample of your skill. As you must realise, we have an elite manner of customers here who are very discerning, not your usual rag-tag medley."

Renard slipped the canvas bag from his shoulder and taking out his lute, a beautiful five-course lute made of beech, spruce and walnut with nine strings to provide the widest range of notes, perched himself easily on one of the tables and after tuning the instrument began to play. Bel, knowledgeable about music, was amazed at his skill as for the first time she heard him play, judging he had chosen one of the most difficult pieces in his repertoire as his long slender figures moved effortlessly along the strings in a cascade of complicated harmonies. The other inhabitants of the room stopped eating and talking to turn and listen and Renard broke into the lively lyrics of 'Canto delle parete', his voice resonant but sweet and true. When he had finished there was spontaneous applause and Bel noted the innkeeper's wife had appeared behind her husband, her hands on her ample hips and a smile of approval on her face round as a rosy apple. Her husband looked towards her and when she nodded her head said to Renard, "Very well, a meal and a night's lodging in return for entertaining my customers, all evening mind, until we close in the late hours, we have a special licence. And no money except from what you might gather as pourboires."

The innkeeper's wife then looked questioningly at Bel who had been staying in the background and keeping her bruised face averted.

"My sister," Renard announced promptly.

The woman's expression was sceptical but his eyes were unblinking.

"You will have to share a room," she said, "we have no dormitories here. But there are two pallets."

Renard nodded his acceptance and the woman led the way through a back door and into a cobbled courtyard. Along two sides of the courtyard the inn continued in a range of two-storey wood and plaster buildings with outer staircases leading to balconies on the first floor. On the other side near the archway from the road was a row of stables from which issued the sounds of horses and men. The innkeeper's wife led them up one of the outer staircases to the upper floor, Bel following as Renard commanded. She opened one of the several doors along the exterior passageway then left them.

It was a small room but by the door was a casement window with panes of horn. There were two wood-framed beds with straw mattresses covered in hemp and blankets which seemed reasonably clean. They were divided by a rough pine chest on which stood a tallow candle on a tin plate.

"No risk of stealing the silver, or even pewter," Renard remarked lightly, putting down his bag on one of the beds. "You have no objection to sharing a room have you, we spent last night together after all. I could always take the mattress and sleep on the balcony if you wish."

Bel shook her head. "You must be tired, you need your comfort as well as I."

"Well then, let's go and find ourselves a meal," he pronounced without further ado.

Downstairs they dined well on a nourishing rabbit stew in large wooden bowls with chunks of freshly baked bread placed liberally on the bare board, followed by pancakes smeared with honey. They ate with gusto and the innkeeper's wife, whom they learnt was Madame Pernel, smiled appreciatively at their compliments but when she put on the table two pewter mugs of the dry white Champagne wine she said, "No more! I don't want you too drunk to perform."

"I never get drunk when I am playing," Renard admonished her with a resentful scowl.

As soon as they had eaten and the room began to fill up Renard began an evening of playing and singing. The inn was full with travellers of the better sort and it was obvious that some of the neighbourhood also made a habit of coming in the evening for a jug of good wine and the opportunity to talk with strangers. As word got around that the "Chevalier du Leon" had an excellent entertainer the inn was packed to capacity by an appreciative audience as the evening wore on. Jacques and Pernel smiled their satisfaction as their takings increased and Renard filled his pouch gratefully with the small coins pressed upon him by his audience, though he accepted refills of his cup only to the extent of slaking his thirst.

Bel sat quietly in a corner not far away from him, listening with joy and wonder to his performance. He really was an excellent musician and she knew enough about music to realise that some of his pieces were his own compositions. Sometimes he would tell anecdotes as her father had done, accompanied only by chords on the lute. Then she suddenly found herself an object of attention by what appeared to be a group of merchants travelling on business. Fortunately the ointment had lessened the bruising on her face and the swelling under her eye was receding but she still felt embarrassed in the ugly gown.

"What about the young damsel, does she not sing?" one of them asked jovially, intending to tease her but drawing the attention of the rest of the company.

"Give us a song too," another cried, obviously having drunk his fill. Most of them were now in their cups and joined in the encouragement.

Bel hung her head in embarrassment but the innkeeper now joined in the merriment and she could see they were intent on baiting her and looking for some amusement.

Suddenly Renard made a quick movement towards her and pulling her to his side said, "Sing something to appease them, it's almost time for me to end."

She looked doubtful but night had now fallen and she was only dimly visible in the insufficient light from the tallow candles. "Do you know Douce Dame Jolie"? she asked.

"By Guillaume de Machaut, certainly," he replied and began to play the introductory notes.

The audience did not know what to expect and were prepared to laugh at her inexpertise but as her clear voice broke through the clamour, the purity of her tone, the effortless pitching of high and low notes, crystal and velvet intermingling, a silence descended and they listened in wonder. Afterwards a storm of approval rent the air but Bel was suddenly uncomfortable with the attention and she turned and ran outside to the courtyard and up the staircase to the little bedchamber.

When Renard appeared a short time later she was sitting on the narrow bed. The horn window was open and a three-quarter moon shone directly through the aperture shedding a faint glimmer of silver over the small space so that there was no need to light the candle. He laid down his lute carefully then said matter-of-factly, "That was excellent Bel. You have a voice of great beauty and a wonderful talent."

From an accomplished musician she knew that was praise indeed and said sincerely, "Thank you."

He stood in thought for a moment then said, "Tomorrow I want you to go and buy a beautiful gown, the most beautiful gown you have ever had, I have the money to pay. There will be a tailor somewhere who will have some gowns nearly completed for customers and if we offer him enough I am sure he will be persuaded to sell one to you. Don't argue, I have decided."

He removed his boots and began to unfasten his belt then he unlaced the tags of his hose stripping them swiftly from his well-shaped legs and slipped out of his tunic so that he stood in his linen shirt and short underdrawers.

His movements were without embarrassment but Bel stood uncertainly. A light cool breeze wafted through the open window. At last she said, "Do you want me to sleep with you?"

He lifted his head and fixed his eyes on her face, standing for a moment without speaking.

Then he said bluntly, "No."

She was shocked by the brutal rebuttal. "Do you think I am soiled because of what happened to me yesterday?" she whispered.

"No, I don't," he replied firmly.

"Do you think I am ugly with my face marred?"

"I think you are one of the most beautiful girls I have ever met," he said. Even in the dim light he could see her long black curls, deep blue eyes (the swelling almost gone now), the slender figure noticeable even in the shapeless gown.

A slight smile hovered on her lips but vanished as she continued, "Do you love someone?"

Renard hesitated and she thought he wasn't going to reply then he answered briefly, "No."

A shadow of puzzlement crossed her face followed by a sudden expression of realisation as she cried, "Are you one of those who prefer boys to girls?" Her tone carried a mix of disappointment and revulsion.

Renard burst into laughter, shaking his head as he gurgled, "No, I am most certainly not."

He was very conscious of her perplexity, tinged with embarrassment as she said quietly, "You have given me so much, protected me, bought me things and now you want to buy me a new gown. I want to repay you and," she hesitated, "and I thought that would be what you wanted."

Renard almost asked her if that was the way she always paid her debts, aware that many men would expect it, but surprised himself by a realisation that he did not want to know. It was the vulnerability evident in her features and her deportment that had decided his course since they had first met. He kept the pine chest between them, some flicker of self-mockery alerting him to the realisation he lacked dignity in his underclothes, as he said seriously, "That is precisely the reason I do not want to take advantage of you. I wanted to help you without any thought of repayment, especially in that way. I like and respect you too much for that, Bel."

LIZZIE JONES

Her eyes widened, for respect was not a word she had been accustomed to hearing.

"But I know a way in which you can repay me if you wish, and at the same time make enough money for you to continue on your journey," he said. "After hearing you sing tonight I have decided that until we go our separate ways you can help me entertain. We will play and sing together but you need beautiful clothes and that is the reason why tomorrow you must buy a new gown. Then with what you earn you can repay me for that, and for anything else you feel you owe me. How does that seem to you?"

When she realised the full import of what he was saying, a smile of delighted surprise animated her face. "I would like that so much," she cried, tears starting to her eyes. "You have been so kind to me, kinder than anyone except my father."

Renard climbed onto his pallet without further comment. "Get some sleep now," he commanded. "We have a busy day tomorrow."

Bel slipped off the brown gown, loose enough for her to do so without untying the laces, and hung it on one of the hooks clamped into the wall for the purpose. Then she climbed onto her own pallet, pulling the blanket around her as the night air had grown chill. A day ago she had plunged the depths of despair, bereft of her father and her living, violently abused, robbed of everything she possessed and without any hope for the future. Now in such a short space of time she was safe and with the promise of money to be able to continue her journey. She was still wearing Renard's shirt and wrapped it tightly around her, feeling its comfort as her eyelids began to droop and she fell sound asleep.

CHAPTER 3

Entertainers

The next morning Bel was awakened by sparklets of early morning sun flickering on her face like golden droplets and opening her eyes drowsily she was confused to find herself alone in a strange bed in unfamiliar surroundings. For a moment she felt a surge of panic then memory slowly surfaced. She looked around for Renard but he was nowhere to be seen. A spasm of fear lurched her heart again at the possibility that he had left her behind but then seeing his lute bag on the other pallet she realised he could not be far. She took the opportunity to put on the brown dress and her shoes, desperately wishing she had a comb to untangle her curls, then Renard appeared, looking fresh and lively with his hair plastered damply to his head.

"There's a well of spring water in the courtyard if you want to wash," he informed her, "and a garderobe too behind the stables. The innkeeper wants me to stay another night so I have agreed. I do want us to be on our way soon but this will provide us with a little more money and give us time to see to our purchases. He has volunteered to supply our breakfast so I'll wait for you downstairs."

The courtyard was already a bustle of noisy confusion with grooms and horses and departing travellers, all occupied with their own concerns, as Bel made her way across the cobbles. She splashed her face and hands in the clean water of the spring, relishing the cold freshness and already feeling the sun's warmth stroking her back and licking the cobblestones, it would be another fine day and she felt her spirits lift.

Renard was seated at a table waiting for her and when they had eaten the bread and cheese and drunk the watered white wine served by Madame Pernel he commanded her to search the town for a tailor who would sell her a ready-made gown.

"Don't worry about how much it costs, you will probably have to pay over the odds by bribing him to sell you one he has ready for a customer. Also you must buy anything else you need." He handed her some silver livres.

"This is too much," she said in dismay. "I've never had so much money."

"Then you can give me back what you don't spend," he shrugged off-handedly. "Just don't get it stolen."

"What will you be doing?" she asked.

"I shall go into the marketplace and play and sing there. Hopefully I can earn some more."

They went their separate ways and Bel felt a surge of excitement at the realisation she had so much money to spend on herself. She soon acquainted herself with where the various shops were situated and went first to the mercers' street. It was the third shop she tried before she found a tailor who was willing to risk a customer's displeasure at a neglected commission and a gown that would almost fit her. She had stopped to finger enviously the samples of silk and velvet spread out on the boards which were the folded-down shutters of the shop window. Then she espied through the open doorway a gown hanging from tenterhooks and obviously in the final stages of completion. It was the most beautiful gown she had ever seen and she knew it was meant for her. It had taken a lot of haggling, winsome smiles and a few silver coins before the merchant conceded to let her have the gown but he was captivated by the young girl's beauty and appalled by the ugliness of her present clothing. She deserved something better to show off her beauty and his creation would obviously enhance her more than the plain dumpy girl who had commissioned it. The waist needed some reduction and because Bel was taller than the prospective customer, he had agreed to stitch a wide band onto the hem and he promised to finish it for her by the afternoon. She also purchased a hooded woollen cloak of gentian blue, considering this a necessity. Her next search was to find a shoemaker with shoes to fit for she realised she couldn't wear her walking sabots to such a fine gown and eventually she located a pair of red kid slippers that were her size. A cutler was another necessity to buy a sharp knife in a sheath, mainly to eat with but also to use in emergencies. She then visited several haberdashers, buying a horn comb, two smocks – one of serviceable linen and the other of a delicate cambric – and a set of green laces for the brown gown together with a belt of green, brown and yellow weave with long fringed ties so that she could gather in the superfluous width and make it fit better. At a cordwainers she bought a leather money pouch to hang on the belt. She looked longingly at a chaplet of white silk blossoms set on a band of silk cord, conscious of how few coins she had left, but then unable to resist the temptation handed over the necessary écus. Her final purchase was a canvas bag to hold her exciting new acquisitions.

When she realised how little was left of Renard's silver she felt a moment of apprehension at facing him and was glad that he was not in the inn when she returned. However when he returned and she began to make her apologies he was unperturbed, shrugging carelessly, "It wasn't really my money, remember."

"You did earn it didn't you?" she appealed to him, not wanting to think she was clothing herself on the proceeds of theft.

"Some of it. Anyway you can pay me back sometime if it bothers you so much." He seemed not to concern himself with the expenditure saying airily, "I earned a little more in the town today."

She had worn the brown dress when they dined that evening, beautified now with new laces and the belt which made it fit reasonably well, as well as the linen shift which peeped respectably from the top of her breasts and Madame Pernel had shown her surprised approval while Renard had smiled warmly at her. Then when Renard began the evening's entertainment as arranged, she went upstairs to change into the new gown which she had collected from the tailor's workroom in the late afternoon.

She hesitated for a moment on the threshold of the room, listening to the hubbub within and dimly hearing Renard tuning his lute, her heart thumping with nervousness. Then plucking up courage she lifted the latch and stood for a moment. A stupefied silence descended on the crowd gathered in the taproom of the inn and Renard stopped his tuning to look at her, suppressing a sharp intake of breath. The gown was of cobalt blue silk with a high waist defined by a broad embroidered scarlet band. A stiffened collar of saffron yellow velvet framed her sloping shoulders and the hanging sleeves had wide turned-back cuffs of the same bright yellow. The back of the gown fell in pleats to a small train and the tailor had extended the length with a wide hem of the same scarlet as the waistband. It was a gown of fine materials and expertly made but yet not of great luxury, lacking the costly decoration a rich lady would have expected, but the simplicity emphasised Bel's slender youthfulness and the colours enhanced her clear complexion and jet black hair, combed now into a mass of curls that framed her face and tumbled to her waist. Renard joined for a moment in the universal appreciation whispering, "Well done, that is just right," and she smiled happily at his approval.

When he invited her to sing a silence fell, only broken by the sound of pewter tankards, wooden cups and horn beakers scraping the boards and the odd cough and shuffling of feet as people eased themselves into more comfortable positions to listen. Even demands to the landlord and movements to refill their cups were stayed until she had finished the haunting 'Se je souspir'. The appreciation shown by the banging of drinking vessels and stamping of feet gave back to Bel the confidence she had lost, and her obvious enjoyment of performing brought a glow to her face and increased the charisma of her presence. She looked anxiously to Renard, hoping he would not resent her popularity but he smiled encouragingly, though there was a speculative look in his eyes. When the evening was finished he counted with satisfaction the coins he had collected.

"Together with what I earned in the market place today this should give us a good start for our journey," he said. "Tomorrow we continue to Amiens but we are going to take a small detour to Courcy-le-Château-Auffrique. I heard about it today, apparently the Seigneur is very generous to entertainers, and I think now that we have combined our talents we should find a welcome there."

"You are sure you want me to entertain with you?" she asked anxiously, aware now of how excellent a musician he was.

"It's so you can pay off your debts to me," he replied but he was laughing.

They lay on their pallets separated by the pine chest and Bel fell asleep with a happy anticipation warming her heart.

Early next morning, a morning of sharp cool brightness, they set off in a northwards direction towards the castle Renard had heard about, some ten miles or so from Soissons they had been told. However, long before they reached their destination, as they were crossing the fertile valley of the River Aillette, they could see its imposing outline crowning the top of a high cliff. As they drew nearer its enormous size became ever more apparent until it seemed to dwarf their presence on the road below. The road now began to climb steeply and the final mile was a labouring ascent. The town of Courcy was itself part of the several miles of fortifications and when they arrived in the busy little ville they discovered that the main street led directly into the lower court of the castle. They stood looking up in awe at the four enormous circular towers on each corner of the ramparts with a central donjon taller than the rest. An elderly man with grizzled hair and wrinkled brown face sat weaving a basket on the cobblestones in front of his dwelling, two children sitting on the ground beside him playing at knucklebones, and seeing the strangers' expressions of astonishment he informed them proudly, "The tallest towers of any castle in France. The central tower is more than fifty metres high and the other four not much less. For two hundred and fifty years it has stood here."

"Who is the lord?" Renard asked.

The basket-weaver's expression revealed his amazement that anyone should need to ask such a stupid question as he replied, "Enguerrand de Courcy of course, the sixth of that name."

Renard thanked him and together he and Bel made their way through the outer courtyard, lined by buildings around the walls and full of day-to-day activity, servants fetching and carrying, women gossiping and horses being led. They came to the castle's main entrance - a solid iron-studded door set in a great stone arch between two of the round towers, the gateway flanked by armoured guards. Bel looked apprehensive but Renard reported their business courteously but confidently and without hesitation the constable was called from his room above the gatehouse. This important official, overseer of all the castle's organisation, appeared promptly and surveyed them carefully. Renard donned a soft felt hat with a rolled brim, of the same shade of claret as his tunic, and his pleasant smile was devoid of pretence while the girl's astonishing beauty was beguiling, even in her simple gown. The burly officer's eyes in his bearded red face were discerning and he found the two young musicians an attractive pair, noticing the lute slung on the young man's shoulder. They were obviously what they claimed to be and he directed them into the castle with the command to ask there for the steward.

Once inside the inner courtyard of the castle they found the place swarming with menials busy about their various tasks but on the word of the constable they were admitted into a vestibule and told to wait there for the steward. At last after long delays and rigorous questioning they were given permission to entertain the lord and his family after dinner.

"The Seigneur has guests this evening so he is willing to have you entertain," the steward informed them. "If he is satisfied he will pay you afterwards. You may be seated at one of the lower tables during supper and will be called upon when you are needed. Meanwhile you are at liberty to walk around the castle and the baileys until the evening meal at five."

The grounds of the castle were thronged with people, besides servants and guards there were richly-dressed men and ladies sauntering across the grassy spaces and along the ramparts which boasted panoramic views over the valley of the Aillette, so there was much to interest the musicians as they waited. During their exploration Bel took advantage of a small ante room to change into her fine gown and they were able to mingle unobtrusively with the castle's occupants, Bel particularly enjoying the experience of walking as a lady with a handsome young man beside her. Renard suggested they took the opportunity to look at the Great Hall where they were to entertain. This was situated on the third floor of the Keep, a vast rectangular space which, together with several anterooms and a garderobe, extended along the whole level. The plastered walls were covered with colourful frescoes of hunting scenes with a frieze above of squares and lozenges painted in red, blue, and gold. The crown-post roof had beams painted blue and red and the floor was of painted tiles. Set against one wall was a huge fireplace of carved and emblazoned stone gaudily painted with heraldic devices with a domed canopy for the smoke to escape. At the top of the hall was a dais with a red silk canopy on which was set a long table covered with a floor-length white cloth and a runner of red and gold brocade on which was set silver goblets and plates. Behind stood tall carved chairs, the central pair having high conical backs of gilded wood.

Consequently when they joined the company for the meal Renard and Bel were familiar with the setting, except now the top table was furnished with flagons of wine and ewers of water with napkins of fine linen. A procession of servants began to carry in serving dishes laden with all kinds of meats – capons and ducks, venison and a whole roasted pig, legs of lamb and haunches of beef, fresh pike and carp from the river together with white manchet bread and savoury tarts.

Seated at the end of one of the trestle tables set up in the lower part of the hall, in company with less noble guests and senior servants, Renard and Bel had opportunity to study the Seigneur and his family whilst waiting for their own more simple repast. Enguerrand de Courcy was in his early forties, a small wiry man whose booming voice belied his slender frame which was almost lost within the gold-embroidered scarlet velvet houppelande, whilst a huge padded velvet hat with trailing streamers sat incongruously on his small head, seemingly held in place by his big protuberant ears. His wife Lady Isabeau, who was twice his size, wore an ostentatious green brocade gown covered with a tracery of gold leaves and complemented by a heavy gold necklace of emeralds. It was impossible to see her hair for it was covered by a tall stiff hat of gold brocade with a turned-back jewelled brim and wings supported on a wire frame, but her ample white breasts were much in evidence swelling between the swathes of the folded green velvet collar. Beside her were two boys and two girls, adolescents and imitations of their parents in appearance and dress, whilst beside Enguerrand de Courcy were seated two nobles and their wives, richly clad in the same style and obviously their guests. At each end of the long table sat the Seigneur's companions and important officials, all suitably garbed either in short tunics and hose or long loose gowns, all of rich materials and fashionably cut and wearing a wide variety of ostentatious headgear.

The meal was noisy and lengthy but when baskets of fruit and bowls of nuts and figs were set upon the table the steward came to Renard and commanded him to play. Bel watched as he approached the dais and bowed to de Courcy then began to tune his lute. They aren't going to listen, she thought anxiously, the lute is a soft instrument and they are too intent on talking. And although Renard played some lively salterellos and his voice was strong and true, it took some time before the noble company were alerted to the excellence of the entertainment being offered to them and gradually began to give their full attention. Renard began to sing a song Bel had never heard before but which guaranteed the attention of everyone in the room.

"*Roi ne suis, ne Prince, ne Duc,*
Ne comte aussi,
Je suis le Sire de Courcy."

The applause was thunderous as feet were stamped and goblets raised to the host who was laughing merrily at the obviously well-known assertion that to be the Lord of Courcy was far more than being a mere king, prince or duke, and from that point Renard held them in thrall. When he called for Bel to sing she had a ready audience and her beauty and grace entranced them even before the pure clear notes of love filled the room. Then to Renard's surprise she began to dance, the soft silk of her gown shimmering and caressing her body as she moved slowly and sinuously to the music, her arms with the long floating sleeves tracing patterns in the air, her feet in the red kid slippers executing complicated little steps as she lifted up the train of her gown, moving from the elegance of an estampie to the quick tapping of a salterello. They were both tiring before their eager audience was willing to let them go and where a troupe of jugglers and acrobats were waiting for their turn.

One of the jongleurs had a drum and another a rebec and when dancing was called for Renard joined them with his flageolet. As couples began to take the floor Bel to her amazement found herself being asked to dance by the twelve year old son of de Courcy.

"I watched you dance and I want to dance with you," he said, gazing at her solemnly with the soulful brown eyes of a puppy. He took her hand, moving with serious concentration like one newly introduced to the art of dancing until his mother commanded his presence to partner his sister. Suddenly Bel was aware that a man was approaching her with the obvious intention of taking his place. She had been aware of his intense gaze following her from the top table while she was singing and dancing alone and had tried to avert her eyes from him, feeling uncomfortable by his surveillance which she felt carried something more than an appreciation of her art. He was about forty years old, tall and burly, his broad chest and muscular legs evident in his tight-waisted tunic of blue embossed velvet, barely long enough to cover his buttocks clearly-defined in the matching hose. His short leather boots had decorative flaps of blue and gold leather and toes too narrowly pointed for current fashions. His hair was raven black, cut round his head like a basin in a style now losing popularity, his eyes almost as dark in his heavy jowelled face. For some reason Bel felt afraid and running to Renard she whispered, "Please can I play your flageolet while you play the lute?"

He looked at her in surprise, saying "Can you play the pipe?"

"Yes of course. Please let me, it's important, I'll explain later."

He was confused by her request and handed her the pipe reluctantly for the lute was not really loud enough for dancing but then he recognised the fear in her eyes and when he saw the burly figure approaching her he understood enough to bow to her wishes. He went to take up his lute again and was happier when he realised Bel could play the pipe well enough, while she relaxed in the security that no-one could seek her as a partner in the dancing if she was playing. She kept her eyes averted from the frustration obvious in the stranger's face.

When the evening finally came to an end the entertainers were provided with straw pallets to sleep with the servants in the hall once the trestles and benches had been folded and stacked against the walls. Even with the noise and disturbances of so many bodies in close contact, the constant peregrinations outside to relieve over-full bladders, as well as the overwhelming odour of stale sweat and the lingering aromas of cooked food, their youth and exhaustion ensured they slept reasonably well. When the company began to stir in the early light of morning they were provided with bread and watered wine in the kitchens before departing.

"I think I should go and ask the steward about our payment," Renard said when they had packed their bags and were ready to leave. But he was pre-empted by the official coming to find him and rewarding them handsomely, saying how much Enguerrand de Courcy and his family had appreciated their entertainment and they were invited to visit again if ever they were in the vicinity.

"How did you know about the verse?" asked the steward. "The Seigneur was greatly taken by your making a song to include it."

"I keep my ears open," Renard remarked evasively with a covert smile.

On the steep road down from Courcy-le-Château-Auffrique, the pale early morning sun beginning to shimmer through the rosy clouds and bathe the valley below in a violet mist, they chortled gleefully about the generous reward they had been given.

"Well worth a detour," Renard commented, "but half of this is yours, Bel."

"You must keep it until I have paid off my debt to you," she said seriously. Then she continued, "I have seen how you often improvise songs to relate to local events wherever you happen to be. My father used to do the same. If you like I will pass onto you some of his songs. They aren't written down of course but I could sing them for you and you could learn them."

"I would appreciate that," he said warmly. "I'm always looking for new material and I'm sure that if your father was your tutor he must have been a good musician."

"Well he won't need them now," she said sadly.

Making their descent into the valley again, picking up their route to Amiens and watching the castle on its cliff shrink in size behind them while the fields and the river below began to creep from their misty curtain, they were suddenly aware of hooves clattering on the stony slope and they were overtaken by a man on horseback. It was the man who had tried to accost Bel the evening before, booted and capped and with a short fur cloak flung around his shoulders. He reined in beside them and said brusquely, pointing his gloved hand to Bel, "I want to buy her."

She gave a gasp of fear, moving involuntarily behind Renard who looked at him in astonishment then said in a tone of disbelief, "What are you talking about? You don't buy girls."

"I do, Hugo de Maurignac. I want the girl for my personal entertainment and I will pay you a price you cannot refuse."

Renard's eyes blinked involuntarily at the sum mentioned and Bel gave another gasp of fear, looking anxiously at her companion. However he placed himself resolutely before de Maurignac saying calmly, "She is not for sale. Now let that be an end of the matter."

"You are a fool," de Maurignac said scornfully. "I offered you a more than fair price and what I can't buy I take. So make your choice."

Renard looked to be considering the proposition and then to Bel's horror said, "Very well I agree, take her for the price." Then he added, "But I fear I must warn you because I am an honest man. She is diseased. You will get something more than pleasure from her as her last patron discovered to his cost. I certainly won't take the risk but I'll be only too glad to take your money if you are satisfied."

The man looked at them both, a scowl crossing his heavy features, his expression vacillating between suspicion and revulsion.

"I shall make it my business to discover more of the matter," he snarled. "Don't think you have seen the last of me," he said to Bel in a tone resonant with anger and frustration. Then without another word he turned his horse and galloped off the way he had come.

They watched him go then finally Bel, still shocked by what had happened, found her voice and whispered reproachfully, "How could you say that?"

"Would you rather he had taken you?" Renard retorted angrily. "I couldn't have protected you from a knight like that. I'm not built for fighting. I get by with cunning and guile."

"I thought at one time you were going to accept," she muttered.

"I thought about it. The money would have kept me comfortably for a long time." She looked at him angrily and he laughed, "I'm lying."

She was still angry with him. "He reminded me of the man who attacked me," she whispered and the recollection and the resurrected terror brought forth a flood of tears.

Renard put his arm around her shoulders. "It's all over now," he said softly, sorry that he had teased her as he realised her deep-seated fear.

"I think he might come after me," she whimpered.

"No he won't. We are moving on now. But you realise how I couldn't let you travel alone. You are just too much temptation to unscrupulous men."

Bel studied him carefully and asked, "Why are you going to Amiens? I thought Paris would have been a more likely destination for you, and more direct."

"I intend going on to Paris after Amiens," he replied.

With a sudden flash of intuition she said, "You weren't originally going to Amiens were you? You were going to Paris and the shortest route to Paris is from Reims. Have you come so far out of your way just to accompany me." Her blue eyes were round with astonishment and her lip quivered.

"No that isn't quite the truth, Bel. Originally I did intend going to Paris directly from Reims, but whilst I was playing at a nobleman's house on the evening I met you, I heard about a tournament at Amiens – a Pas d'Armes arranged by the city Bailli. There is always much work for musicians at tournaments, both at the events themselves and at all the banquets arranged by the participants."

"I'm glad about that. You have done so much for me, I would hate to think you were inconveniencing yourself to such a great extent just because you feel I need protecting."

"I am not so altruistic," he responded bluntly. "I really only think of myself. It's the only thing I can do."

She looked up at him from beneath her long lashes, not completely believing his assertion despite the seriousness of his expression.

"Besides I have enjoyed your company," he continued. He paused then said, "I used to have the company of my friend Jean, a fellow musician, we played together."

"What happened to him?" she asked, noting the past tense.

"He got his hand cut off. For stealing. He played a vielle amongst other things. A musician with one hand is of little use." His expression was grim but his tone unemotional and he said no more.

When Bel saw that he did not intend to elaborate further she took a deep breath and said, "I did not tell you the whole truth when I said my father had died. In fact he was murdered."

Renard stopped in his tracks and said, "Why?" adding, "But you need not tell me if it distresses you."

"It does distress me, yes, but I would like to tell you. I said he often composed songs and anecdotes about recent affairs. When we arrived in a town or a castle he would enquire about the place, about what was happening, about the rulers and seigneurs, as you did at Courcy. He wasn't always too careful in his opinions and often used satire, obliquely disguised, as indeed do many raconteurs. This particular lord took exception to the veiled criticisms of his authority and as we passed through the streets late at night sent a band of ruffians to attack him. They smashed all our instruments though I do not think they intended to kill him. But he was not young and not in the best of health and he died from the beating, I think he banged his head on the stones. I tried to help him but there was nothing I could do.

The townspeople were sympathetic, in fact grateful, and next day they buried him at their own cost. And that was why I was travelling alone. He used to tell me that if ever I was left alone I should try to get to England to find my grandfather's family, who he said were of the nobility. My mother said her father was Sir Thomas Malory who knew dukes and princes."

Renard remained silent for a time then said, "I'm very sorry about your father. I know from my own experience that a minstrel's life is not without peril. Now come, let us be on our way. We will entertain together until our paths divide and this means you will have enough money to continue your journey. Your dancing was greatly admired but I think you should have some bells on your fingers. We will buy some when we get to Amiens."

She smiled at the thought and Renard was glad to see the shadows disappearing from her face as they continued on their way. The day was dappled, sunshine and cloud, but the clouds were fluffy and white with no sign of rain and a fresh breeze made it pleasant for travelling. They were young, at that moment carefree, talented enough to earn money and Amiens promised fair opportunities. It was still a long way but distance was halved in company and Bel taught him some of her father's songs. They walked easily together through a landscape of fertile pastures, small villages, little woods and streams, to Picardie.

CHAPTER 4

Parting of the Ways

It was the afternoon of the third day when they arrived at Amiens. Now they had been so well paid at the château of Courcy they felt no need to seek employment on the way for there were no towns of note nor large hostelries. They had enough money to buy food and simple lodging, eating the homely food the small inns provided and sleeping in communal chambers where men and women travellers shared separate accommodation.

The soft May sunshine shed warm rays intermittently from fluffy white clouds caressing a sky the colour of wild hyacinths, and there was an easy companionship between them as they walked through farmlands of sprouting cereal crops interspersed with blossoming hedgerows, patches of woodland, and small hamlets. They talked about music and the places they had visited and Bel had not felt so happy in all her life, not even when travelling with her father, and the acute pain of his loss had softened into a dull ache when memories tugged at her heart strings.

As they approached Amiens in the late afternoon the fertile ground gave way to marshes and a broad river came into view. The road descended to where the town

was situated in the river basin where the Somme mingled with the streams of the River Aisne. They joined the flow of people crowding through the west gate into the narrow cobbled streets of the walled town where they were immediately struck by the noise and colour. Painted banners and vividly dyed cloth hangings were draped from windows and decorated the fronts of the houses to celebrate the tournament and welcome the participating knights. Throughout the day the knights had been arriving, individually and in groups, all with their own heralds and retinue and proudly displaying their armorial bearings on their surcoats and banners as they paraded through the streets, a riot of colour and noise as trumpets brayed and drums throbbed. This ritual was an important part of the tournament and besides entertaining the spectators gave them the opportunity to scrutinise the competitors and lay their bets on the most likely champion.

Later when the knightly groups had found themselves accommodation in the best inns or as guests of important citizens, an evening of feasting and entertainment would follow. Renard knew that it would be difficult to find accommodation in the town overflowing with visitors, although the citizens were opening their houses also to paying guests. The whole purpose of the tournament was to bring money into the town, not only by the fees the knights must pay to take part in the competition but also by the increased trade generated by the visiting crowds. Usually tournaments were arranged by great lords at their castles but sometimes the civil authorities did so. The lord of Amiens happened to be the king himself, Louis Xl. Until a few years ago Amiens had been part of Burgundy but Louis had given money to the

Burgundian Duke Philip the Good for a crusade, in exchange for the ownership of Amiens and Picardie. The crusade never took place but with the death in battle of Philip's son, Charles the Bold, the dynasty had ended and the King became lord of Amiens. His representative, or Bailli, held total authority and he had called the tournament in the name of the King, for Louis was passionate about encouraging commerce in the towns and therefore enriching the country.

Renard knew that their best chance of entertaining was in one of the high class inns with their knightly guests but reckoned this would not be easy. However he strode boldly into 'La Couronne d'Or' which appeared to be the largest and most affluent establishment in the main square. Bel was once again impressed by his confident self-promotion sweetened by his engaging manner, his pleasing appearance and his flattery of the innkeeper's wife who lapped up the honeyed words of a handsome young man. The innkeeper himself was as much influenced by Bel's obvious beauty as by Renard's persuasive tongue and finally they were given permission to stay.

"There is little sleeping room, you will have to share a crowded attic with some of the more lowly attendants," the landlord's wife said, preoccupied with her increased duties but not impervious to the young minstrel's charm.

Renard accepted but knowing the attendants would be male squires and pages he nodded towards Bel saying, "What about my sister? Is there somewhere else she could sleep?"

The hostess wiped her sweating face in exasperation, leaving streaks of flour on her ruddy complexion as the clamour of the inn rang about her, but seeing the young girl's modest demeanour and apologetic smile something made her relent and she said, "She can share a pallet with the kitchen maids on the kitchen floor but it will mean early rising."

Bel nodded her agreement, thanking the hostess who hurried off to see to the needs of her important guests. All her life travelling with her father she had been accustomed to finding lodging wherever they could, sometimes in great houses and castles but just as often in outhouses and stables and sometimes under hedges in fine weather.

In the evening Renard and Bel performed better than they had ever done. Renard had brushed his doublet and changed into a new pair of striped red and black hose. He played and sang alone at first, songs of knightly prowess - of Roland and Charlemagne and the knights of King Arthur and the Round Table - which were greatly appreciated by the knightly audience. Then he called for Belfiore, as he insisted she be called in public, and there was a gasp of admiration as she came to his side in her striking gown. She wore the chaplet of silk flowers and it seemed as if the delicate buds were scattered among her black curls. They began to sing together to the accompaniment of his lute then she began to dance, the bells which they had purchased earlier tinkling on her fingers as she moved. The audience were entranced. When they finally retired to their separate beds it was with a sense of elation, complemented by the satisfaction of a full purse.

On the second day of the tournament it was the custom for the helmets and crests of the participating knights to be laid out on display in the Citizens' Council Hall, a large stone building set beside the Bailli's imposing three-storey house, also built of stone and only rivalled in size by the cathedral. Everyone went to the Council Hall to view and admire and make note of the knights' individual insignia so they could be recognised later. There was a festive atmosphere in the town with many sellers of wares, as well as the usual shopkeepers there were itinerant merchants offering goods of every description including goods not normally available like spices, exotic fruits and rare dyes from the east. Fantastically-garbed mountebanks touted nostrums and told fortunes from their platforms curtained with occult symbols. The place was awash with travelling entertainers - bearwards, jongleurs, stilt-walkers, tumblers and acrobats as well as bands of musicians. With so much on offer in the streets Renard decided to save his talents for a prestigious venue rather than competing with other attractions so they wandered around enjoying the spectacle.

Once again the evening was filled with feasts and entertainments and there was no shortage of hosts looking for the best entertainers to please their guests. News had got around about the young musicians at 'La Couronne d'Or' and Renard and Bel found to their delight several invitations to perform elsewhere - another large inn and two private houses where knightly company was being entertained. Remuneration was generous for everyone was in high spirits, making the most of the festival and looking forward to the tournament itself. Their schedule was exhausting for after limiting themselves to a half-hour at each venue they decided they must return and finish the evening back at the inn where they were being accommodated.

The third day of the tournament was devoted to the swearing-in of the knights, a ceremony held in the cathedral square to give everyone an opportunity to watch the event so that consequently the square was packed with spectators. A canopied dais had been set up on scaffolding, draped and decorated with gold and crimson silk hangings and set with a throne-like chair for the Bailli in his ermine-trimmed robes of office and pontiff-styled hat. All the participants had to give evidence of their knightly status and their right to bear arms and joust, a lengthy procedure with heralds to read out their achievements and each knight, richly attired in heraldic surcoat and carrying his crested helmet, had to swear to the rules of the competition.

"Do you think Hugo de Maurignac might come," Bel said nervously eyeing the knights with some apprehension.

She was relieved when Renard shook his head dismissively saying, "He isn't a knight and therefore not eligible," and she settled down to enjoy the spectacle.

A 'Chevalier d'Honeur' was elected from one of the more senior knights to act as umpire and presented with a 'couvre-chef de mercy', a white cloth fastened to a lance, whereby he would touch a knight in serious peril of his life and remove him from further combat. This was no mortal combat but a test of skill and prestige.

The evening celebrations were as before, most of their time being spent at the 'Couronne d'Or' as payment for their accommodation, but Renard said, "I want to play at the house of the Bailli before we leave," a determined look on his face. He put his mind to how this could be arranged but fate intervened. A man in spruce livery arrived at the inn with a command for them to appear at the Bailli's house on the following evening at the feast for the closing of the tournament. Word had reached the Bailli of their exceptional talents and he wished to impress his important guests.

"The most prestigious event of the whole sequence," Renard said gleefully and Bel laughed too at his obvious delight.

The fourth day was the tourney itself, the climax of the event to which all other happenings had been but the prelude. This was to take the form of a Pas d'Armes set just outside the town at Dreuil-les-Amiens on the left bank of the Somme where there was a wooden bridge across the river. The name of the spectacle had been proclaimed as the 'Pas de la Dame Sauvage.' Each knight in turn, armed and mounted and drawn by lots for order of combat, attempted to cross the bridge which was guarded by the 'Chevalier de la Dame Sauvage.' The 'Damsel' was a youth with a long fair wig adorned by a coronet of leaves and clothed in a short gown of animal skins, seated in a leafy arbour on the far bank. If the challenger was overcome by the guardian knight he retired from the competition, but if he beat the knight on the bridge then he himself took his place and won the lady so long as he could hold off the new challengers. For the spectators it was a comedy but for the knights themselves it was a deadly serious matter. No longer a mortal combat as it used to be in the past but still a contest of superiority in the skilful use of arms and the necessary strength and tenacity, a ruthless exhibition of personal honour as they re-enacted in earnest the gestes of the knights of the Round Table.

Renard and Bel joined the crowd of spectators. "Today we have a holiday," he said, and they watched the spectacle with enjoyment, availing themselves of the food being sold from booths or hawked around by vendors with trays - almond biscuits and cheese-topped pancakes, specialities of Amiens. They became increasingly excited by the progression of the game as Renard had made a bet on one of the knights.

"Have you read about King Arthur and the Knights of the Round Table?" he asked Bel. "There are a lot of French books telling their stories, the most famous is Chrétien de Troyes' book of Sir Lancelot."

"My father used to sing songs about them as you do," she replied. "I haven't actually read the books though my father taught me to read."

Then watching her screaming with delight as one of the favoured contestants was hurled into the river he asked, "How old are you, Bel?"

"I'm sixteen. My father said I was born in the year 1462. Though he said it was in the month of May so I suppose I must be seventeen now."

"Don't you know the date?" he asked and when she shook her head he said, "Today is the 21st of May so let's make that your birthday. Remember this date for this is your birthday from this day forward – the sign of the Rose in the planet of Venus, the planet of love."

She laughed in delight. "So I'm seventeen now. How old are you?"

"I'm twenty-two and I was born in December, under the sign of the archer."

When the tournament was finished and the final victor made his triumphal procession around the field and then through the town, Amiens exploded into festival. Renard excused himself briefly from Bel and ran off down a side street, telling her to wait for him. When he returned a short time later he said, "A birthday present for you," and handed her a flageolet.

She looked in amazement at the beautiful instrument made of boxwood, the honey-coloured wood glowing with a warm sheen. "I've never had a birthday present before," she said, handling it reverently, moved by the surprise.

"It's so you won't have to take mine tonight," he laughed.

He allowed her to try it out at the Bailli's house later that evening. She had not his skill but could play a tune true while he embellished it with improvisations, making the notes dance and leap like acrobats in complicated twists and swirls. But most of the time he played his lute, making up stories about the tourney to fit tunes he knew which pleased the knights and lavishing praise on the generosity of the Bailli to the official's satisfaction . They sang together a love lament about Tristan and Iseult and when he played dance tunes, saltarelli, estampie and Italian basse danze and farandoles Bel danced with the bells on her fingers. The hall of the Bailli's house was like a palace with a huge vaulted ceiling embossed with gilded fleur-de-lys, the stone walls completely covered by heavy arras hangings of mythological scenes woven in brilliant colours, and huge candelabra holding hundreds of wax candles. The dais at the top of the hall was crammed by nobles and knights in fashionable doublets and gowns of vermilion, gold, purple, white samite, edged with fur of various kinds and with elaborate hats, padded and furred, with long streamers and winking jewels. Earlier it had been the scene of the presentation of the trophy and a sack of coins to the chevalier who was the winner of the tournament.

For Bel it was the most magical evening of her life and as they made their way back to their lodging she skipped with elation, her face flushed with excitement, chattering eagerly about their success in Amiens. She was surprised that Renard was uncharacteristically quiet then like a shock of drenching icy water came the realisation that it was the end of their time together – she was to journey to Calais on the morrow while he was going to Paris. Suddenly the streets seemed dark and cold, the moon had slid behind a rain-filled cloud and the stars dimmed and faded in a sky turned from black velvet to a canopy of lead.

"Do we leave Amiens tomorrow?" she asked, hoping he might decide to stay another day. "Are you now making for Paris?"

"Yes I am. I came only for the tournament and it has proved worthwhile. Do you still intend to go to England?"

"I promised my father," she said quietly.

"It seems that the wars of the past ten years are over now that King Edward has been accepted as the lawful ruler but I have heard rumours of plague there and their barons are still unsettled. The English are not a peaceful nation. Did you say your family were of the nobility?"

"My grandfather is a knight, Sir Thomas Malory. There is a manor – a place called Newbold Revel in the shire of Warwick."

"Well if you are determined to go I intend to make sure you do not travel alone. Here in Amiens there are many merchants making for Calais, which belongs to England as you know and is their wool staple. We will find some who will let you join their company."

"You have been very good to me, Renard, I shall always be grateful to you," she said, tears starting in her eyes. She realised she did not want to be parted from him and she knew that if he asked her to go to Paris with him she would accept and forget all about her father's command to go and find her family.

As if guessing her thoughts Renard said, "I have found great pleasure in our working together, Bel, and I shall miss you, but I think you are right to try and find your family in England. I cannot ask you to come to Paris with me because I do not know what will happen there in a city where there is always danger, riots and rebellion, nor what I shall do afterwards." He paused then said, "And I cannot offer you permanent protection because I am married."

For a moment the world reeled around her. "You never said," she whispered.

"You never asked," he replied. "You asked if I loved someone. The two facts are not always the same."

"But you are only twenty-two," she said, still stunned with the shock.

"Many boys marry at fourteen or fifteen."

"Boys of the nobility," she countered.

"Yes, well I didn't tell you the truth. My real name is René de Cluys and my father is a Conte. He married me off to a rich heiress on my eighteenth birthday but I didn't want that kind of life, I always wanted to be a musician, so I ran away and became a travelling minstrel."

She looked at him seriously, trying to make sense of what he was saying, and he burst out laughing. "I'm jesting. My father was a minstrel and we come from a long line of troubadours, stretching back two hundred years. I was stupid enough to be seduced by a woman older than I, a very beautiful woman might I add. When I recovered my senses I left."

"It sounds like one of the stories of King Arthur's knights," she said but he couldn't discern whether her tone was one of wonder or scepticism. "Do you have any children?"

"None that I know of. Fortunately. I'm a lone wolf. I don't like to be bound by responsibilities, I want only to think about myself."

"Do you always lie?" she asked reproachfully.

"Only when it is expedient." Now he became business-like. "We must divide the money we have earned together."

"I owe it to you for all the things you bought. I said I would pay you back when I could and I intend to do so."

"Very well you may give me some of it. But you will need money to continue on your journey. You must stay in inns and I have been thinking, the merchants will most likely be on horseback so I think you should hire a pony, or at least a mule. We will arrange these things tomorrow morning before we part."

They didn't talk any more and walked in silence through the dark streets and past shadowy buildings where sounds of festivity still lingered, each lost in their own thoughts. When they reached the 'Couronne d'Or' they bade each other a subdued goodnight and went to their separate beds.

Bel found her place in the kitchen, unbearably hot because the fires in the ovens had not completely died and with an overwhelming odour of cooking. She took off her fine dress, folding it neatly into her bag. She did not know when she would have the opportunity to wear it again. She lay down in her shift on the uncomfortable straw pallet squashed between many others on the stone floor but was insensible to the discomfort, holding her bag tightly under the rough canvas sheet as she always did, fearful someone might try to steal it. She felt empty inside. All the joy that had warmed her during the day had dissipated into a cold numbness. She told herself it was just a reaction to all the excitement. It was her birthday and it had been one of the most wonderful days of her life. As she lay in bed she relived everything in her memory – the fun they had shared at the tournament, the present Renard had bought her, entertaining with him in such a splendid place and being applauded and rewarded. Her mind travelled back over the last two weeks since she had met Renard, realising they had been the happiest she had known in her life after the utter despair of her father's murder and her rape when her life had reached its lowest ebb. Now she had to continue on her journey alone, unsure of how she could manage and not knowing what lay at the end, whether she would find her family and if indeed her mother's stories had any truth in them. Truth had suddenly become an uncertain concept. Which of Renard's accounts of his marriage was true and was he really married or telling lies again, wanting an excuse to be rid of her so that he could continue unfettered to all the opportunities the great city of Paris offered. He was a much better musician than she was and he had never shown any inclination to advance their friendship into a more intimate relationship. And yet he hadn't spoken the truth when he said he thought only of himself, not after the care he had shown towards her since they first met. She found the flageolet in her bag and clutched it tight. She had had a flute before, as well as a tambour and a gittern, all destroyed by her father's attackers, but this was special. Every time she played it she would remember him. Tears began to course down her cheeks until she was sobbing bitterly, hoping none of the kitchenmaids would hear but they were dead to the world with fatigue.

Next morning there was no breakfast offered to them. The tournament was over and the 'Couronne d'Or' returned to its inevitable daily round, shorn of the glamour of the past few days. The innkeeper and his wife were only intent on cleaning up and busying themselves with the necessary routine tasks. It was like the end of a pleasant dream. Renard and Bel were both subdued as they left the inn just after daybreak and the weather had caught their mood for the Picardie rain had resumed its habitual prominence, chasing away the spring sunshine now the festivities had ended, only a light drizzle at the moment but the sky was grey and overcast.

By questioning, Renard had located an inn popular with wool merchants, "L'Agneau," and they hurried there. They were just in time to find a group of English merchants preparing to leave for Calais and he persuaded them to take Bel into their company to the seaport from where they would take ship to Dover. Swayed by his eloquent tongue and the young girl's astonishing beauty they had no hesitation in accepting her and offered to let her ride pillion behind one of their servants.

"Take care of yourself, never travel alone and don't put yourself in danger at any time," Renard commanded her sternly. "Have you everything you need?"

She nodded wordlessly, clothed in the brown gown he had stolen for her and wrapped in the hooded blue cloak, clutching her bag with her precious possessions – her dress, her red kid slippers, her flageolet.

"I hope you find your family. I shall be thinking about you," he said.

"I shall be thinking of you too," she said, trying not to cry. "You take care of yourself and make sure you don't get your hand cut off or get into any kind of trouble because the world will be poorer without such an excellent musician."

He smiled then and kissed her gently on the cheek. Then he turned and began his first steps towards the south gate which would start him on the long journey to Paris. She stood looking after him, the merchants preparing their departure behind her in the noisy inn yard. Her eyes followed his quick-stepping figure, his hat perched jauntily on his head, carrying his lute with his bag slung on his shoulder. She hoped he might turn around and wave to her but he continued on his way. If Renard had turned around he would have seen only a vague outline of the slender cloaked figure standing in the archway of the inn's stableyard for his eyes were blurred with tears.

CHAPTER 5

Lady Margaret

Margaret Beaufort was not beautiful. She wasn't even what people called "comely." She had always known it and had become accustomed to it. She sometimes picked up the polished silver mirror edged with rubies and pearls which lay on the gilded table, painted with the Beaufort arms as was all the furniture, at the side of the regal canopied bed where even the crimson curtains carried the Beaufort monogram. She would contemplate dispassionately the long narrow face with cheekbones so prominent that her sallow cheeks appeared sunken, the small mouth with its thin lips, the receding chin. At thirty seven years old pouches were already swelling beneath the hooded grey eyes but the eyes were bright with intelligence and framed by high, perfectly-arched brows that seemed to dare anyone to question her aristocratic superiority. No-one dared to do so and the lift of the head and the erect carriage disguised the reality of her small stature and delicate bird-like frame. It had never troubled her that she did not possess beauty, in an age and society when such an attribute was an important asset for a woman, for she knew she possessed even more valuable qualities – immense wealth, a royal pedigree and intelligence. To Margaret all these things were of equal importance and she would have traded none of them for Aphrodite's attractions. She could view dispassionately the acknowledged beauty of the Queen because Elizabeth Woodville was of low birth and fundamentally stupid even though she might be cunning. Besides beauty faded sooner or later while riches and intelligence increased with age. And Margaret's lack of beauty had been no bar to finding eligible husbands for she had been married four times. She did not count the first time for she had been only a year old and the marriage to the Earl of Suffolk's son had soon been annulled when it was no longer convenient for those who had arranged it. Her second marriage at the age of twelve had been the determining factor of her life for it had given her a son, her only child.

Edmund Tudor had abused her. It was true that twelve years was the minimum and lawful age for girls to be married but it was acknowledged custom to wait a few years for consummation, especially as in her case she was so small with a childlike figure, and Edmund was no young boy but a mature man of twenty-six years. His status as a modest Welsh gentleman (though half-brother to King Henry VI) was not equal to hers and in view of past history, her first marriage being annulled easily on account of her age, he wished to waste no time in proving the validity of this marriage by consummation and, hopefully, a child as proof.

Edmund Tudor's parentage was unusual. His father, Owen Tudor, had been merely a Welsh servant at the English Court but his mother had been a queen - Catherine de Valois, daughter of the King of France and then widow to England's heroic King Henry V to whom she had born a son who had been crowned king of England at one year old upon the untimely death of his father. The young widowed queen had fallen in love with her humble Welsh squire and borne him two sons, Edmund and Jasper. In view of the unequal nature of the Dowager Queen Catherine's second marriage there were those who said that a formal union had never taken place between the two. Edmund however always insisted his parents had sworn that a legal, though secret, ceremony had been performed. Edmund's half-brother, King Henry VI, had accepted his mother's second marriage without seeming rancour, indeed it was even rumoured that he was considering naming Edmund his legal heir if he himself remained childless. Consequently he had arranged for his half-brother a match of corresponding greatness.

The young Margaret Beaufort was one of the greatest heiresses in the land, being the sole inheritor of the vast possessions of her father John Beaufort Duke of Somerset. She also had royal blood for her father was a great-grandson of King Edward III, though from an illicit union. The Beauforts had been the base-born children of King Edward's third son John of Gaunt by his mistress Katherine Swynford. Late in life, after the deaths of his two wives, Gaunt married his long-time mistress and his great wealth and power contrived to have their children legitimised, though with the proviso that they could never inherit the crown.

Edmund Tudor's position was considerably enhanced and his fortune multiplied by this union with his child bride. He wanted no risk that the match might be annulled if he should lose favour, as had been the case with Margaret's first child marriage, or that in the future there might be ambiguity about the union, as with his parents, for then he might lose his claim to his wife's great fortune. Consequently it was essential that Margaret should become pregnant as soon as possible.

At the age of thirteen Margaret had given birth to a son, Henry Tudor, but at that time the civil war between the opposing houses of Lancaster and York was in full flow. The King was the head of the house of Lancaster, a descendant of the great Duke of Lancaster John of Gaunt, son of King Edward III, with a red rose as their emblem. Ranged against them were the Yorkists of the white rose, led by Richard Duke of York and his sons. Richard was the son of John of Gaunt's younger brother, the 4th son of Edward III although he was also descended on the female side through the 2nd son Lionel. On their mother's side they were also descendants of Edward III via John of Gaunt's Beaufort progeny, the youngest Joan whose daughter Cecily had married the Duke of York. The contenders were therefore half-cousins. Although the main York claim came from a younger son of the male line they considered they had a double, even triple, claim issuing from both the male and female inheritance.

As half-brother to King Henry VI, Edmund Tudor naturally supported the Lancastrian cause, the legitimate holders of the Crown, at least for the past three generations. But during the fighting he was captured by the Yorkists and imprisoned in Camarthen castle. A short time later he caught the plague and died there, leaving a thirteen year old widow seven months pregnant. Despite Edmund Tudor's premature taking of her and subjecting her almost immediately to a child pregnancy and a subsequent difficult birth that almost killed her due to her youth and small physique and consequently damaging her to the extent that she would never bear more children, Margaret always honoured his memory. She always showed great respect for Edmund Tudor, allowed no-one to think otherwise, and throughout her life continued to name herself Countess of Richmond, the title he had given her and passed on to their son. She had been too young for love and the few months with her husband had been too brief for them to have developed a rapport together so she had been given no opportunity to see how the union might have fared. But she had her son, the only child she knew she would ever have, and from the moment he had been placed in his widowed child-mother's arms he was all-important to her. She had a strongly-entrenched religiosity and was fond of relating the story of how God had appeared to her in a vision, telling her that her marriage to Edmund was divinely inspired and that her son would achieve greatness. Sceptics considered this affirmation to be too convenient for later events and perhaps even near-blasphemous. But it was in her son's interest to enhance the memory of Edmund Tudor, letting no shadow of birth or character cloud it. Cynics recognised the reason and understood it even if they were sceptical.

Margaret was totally absorbed in her son Henry, named after the King to emphasize his royal lineage. Jasper Tudor, now head of the family, had wanted to name his brother's child Owen after their father but Margaret had been adamant, even at 13 years old. He was to be named after the King and other royal Plantagenets, not seen as the progeny of an obscure Welsh patrimony. Dreams of the wonderful destiny she believed awaited him consumed her life to the exclusion of all else. She was convinced that he would one day be

king, though the belief had little to support it for Henry
VI had a son, Prince Edward, to inherit. Also the crown
was now being challenged by the Yorkist faction. The
Duke of York believed the King to be unfit to rule due to
his recurring periods of insanity and believed himself
next in line. Margaret considered the Yorkist claim a
threat not only to the King but to her own ambitions

In the year of 1458 the vicissitudes of the civil war
were in full flow and usurpations and conspiracies
ruthlessly accomplished. Margaret's year old child with
his dangerous inheritance had to be protected at all
costs. The child-mother knew he must be secluded safely
while she herself must safeguard her influence and
her vast possessions by another marriage that would
give them both protection. So when her official year of
mourning was over she agreed to a marriage with fellow-
Lancastrian Henry Stafford, son of the powerful Duke
of Buckingham. Unfortunately this meant separation
from her son who of necessity had to be left in the Welsh
fastnesses in the care of his uncle Jasper, whose belief in
the destiny of his nephew was as strong as Margaret's.

Apart from the fact of being separated so soon from
her son, Margaret enjoyed a happy marriage with young
Stafford, not much older than she was. Although the
marriage had been undertaken for political reasons, they
shared a close and happy relationship. Not burdened
with children they were free to enjoy themselves riding
around her vast estates, hunting, entertaining, visiting
the Court. They were constantly in each other's company
and when separated wrote daily letters. Margaret often
thought how happy her life would have been with Henry
Stafford if only her son could have been included in the
family and if they had not lived in such violent times of

war and constantly changing fortunes. The success of the Lancastrian and Yorkist armies fluctuated constantly as people changed sides for preservation and bloody battles decimated the nobility. As each faction gained ascendancy the crown shuttled between Henry VI, whose cause had now been bolstered by his warlike French queen Margaret of Anjou, and the young Edward of York who had taken his father's place as Yorkist heir when the Duke of York had been barbarously executed by his enemies.

When the Lancastrians were victorious Margaret, continuing to call herself Countess of Richmond, was welcomed at court with her husband Stafford and they enjoyed a regal existence. On the contrary when the wheel of fortune turned and young Edward IV claimed the crown they were suspected and sometimes feared for their lives. At such times they lay low on their country estates, busying themselves with the obligations of landowners. However they were scrupulous in showing no outward animosity to the new royal family. They went to court when commanded, showed respect and obeisance to the king and his queen, even though Margaret hated the two of them, and accommodated themselves staunchly to the regime in the knowledge that their safety and their estates depended upon an outward show of support. The cost of this was separation from her little son who otherwise might have forfeited his life in the ruthless and bloody conspiracies surrounding the throne. Though he was never absent from her thoughts, Margaret resigned herself to the separation in the knowledge that he was safe with his uncle Jasper at his castle of Pembroke and that was all that mattered.

Jasper Tudor continued to fight for the Lancastrian cause in Wales from his base at Pembroke and enjoyed considerable support. But eventually Pembroke castle fell to the Yorkists and Jasper was forced to flee for his life. The Yorkist Lord Herbert was put in charge of the garrison there and also in charge of the three year old Henry Tudor. Margaret remembered this as one of the most agonising times of her life, not knowing what would happen to her child, bereft of Jasper's protection. However Lord Herbert and his wife treated the child kindly and he spent most of his childhood with them. Margaret welcomed the news but wished desperately that she herself could have shared these early years, constantly tormenting herself with imagining all the things his foster-parents shared with him while she was excluded from his life, dreading that her son would forget her and look upon them as his real family.

It was six long years before she was able to see him again. Because the situation seemed settled Lord Herbert invited her to visit them at Pembroke castle. For Margaret it was a dream come true but it was a bitter-sweet experience. The nine year old boy had changed beyond recognition and she, his young mother, was a stranger to him. It distressed her to see him more at ease with Lady Herbert than with herself, treating her with the respectful familiarity of a mother. However during the week they spent together Margaret and her son gradually drew together and established a rapport which was never to be broken, even with subsequent separations. When the time came to part she wept copiously and the child put his arms around her. "Don't cry Mama, you must write to me and I will write to you." At their parting she left with the consolation that now he was at least old enough for them to carry on communication with letters.

For two years they were able to do so and the bond between them strengthened. Margaret was able to send him gifts and as he told her of his achievements in his studies and sports she was able to imagine his progress into youth. But then her most terrible fears were revived when Lord Herbert was put to death during a temporary ascendancy of the Lancastrian cause. There was no news of her growing son and no-one had any idea what had happened to him. She was terrified his life was in danger or even that he might already be dead. It was one of the blackest periods of her life and she could not have survived those agonising months but for the support of Henry Stafford and the comfort of her faith which through her prayers and meditations continued to assure her that her son was in God's hands. Then after months of torment she received news from her brother-in-law Jasper that he had Henry back in his care and they were both safe. She wept copious tears of relief but her faith had been strengthened by this confirmation that God had laid His hands upon him and that he had been saved for some great purpose which was his destiny.

A further five years of separation had followed but Margaret had comforted herself that her son was in the safe keeping of his loyal uncle. A new turn by fortune's wheel gave the crown back to the deposed Henry VI and Jasper Tudor decided it was time his nephew should be introduced to the King. He suggested that Margaret should accompany them to the court and in a state of great excitement Margaret travelled to London with her husband. It was only the second time she had seen her son since she had let him go from her as an infant and she couldn't take her eyes from the fourteen year old, taking in every detail. He was tall and gangly with his mother's small eyes, narrow face and high cheekbones but with Edmund Tudor's sandy hair – almost a man. It was a poignant meeting with a necessary formality, even an awkwardness, though the letters that had passed between them ensured they were no longer complete strangers to each other. The poor unfortunate Henry VI looked older than his years, stooped and grey with unfocussed eyes so that the contrast with his young upright half-nephew in his bright attire was even greater. The King tried hard to study him closely and spoke kindly to him. Suddenly he startled all the bystanders by prophesying that one day Henry Tudor would himself be king. Most hearers dismissed it as a temporary lapse of the King's weak mind for did he not have a son who was now 17 years old, (though most doubted that the King was actually his father). However a tremour convulsed Margaret's tiny frame. Jasper's eyes were fixed on his nephew to gauge his reaction but Henry Stafford was looking at his wife. Resplendent in a jewelled crimson gown of velvet and beaver fur with a gold fillet encircling the crespettes that confined her hair he was overwhelmed by a sudden realisation. With a shock of revelation his thoughts clarified into the knowledge that his wife had always visualised herself as the Queen mother and that her obsession with her son's wellbeing could be more than maternal.

Despite the inevitable separation that was to follow, Margaret returned home buoyed by exhilaration. However her happiness did not last for King Henry was once again deposed and imprisoned and young Edward of York crowned Edward IV. The poor mad King died in his captivity, supposedly of his malady but others uttered more disturbing possibilities. When his only son was killed at the battle of Tewkesbury the news was both sad and hopeful for Margaret Beaufort, Lady Stafford, Countess of Richmond. Her son Henry Tudor was now the only surviving Lancastrian claimant to the throne but because of this he was now in deadly danger as Edward of York reclaimed the crown. Edward was a merciful king but the ambitious greedy men around him did not share his benevolence and no competitors would be allowed to live. Jasper Tudor believed the only solution was to flee the country with his nephew so they took ship secretly to Brittany, which had close ties with Wales and shared a common tongue.

Margaret did not know how she could have borne the uncertainties and alarms but for the support of Harry Stafford. Because they had no children of their own her husband was sympathetic to her worries and tried his best to keep her spirits high. She also had the consolation of knowing that the loyal Jasper Tudor, unmarried and childless, could be relied upon to protect his nephew to the uttermost.

Margaret was thinking of her son, as she often did, as she stood by the long narrow turret window looking out over the flat marshy landscape where even the light was flattened to a uniform yellow haze. Her eyes were fixed on the distant coastline of Lancashire but her imagination ranged beyond the uninteresting and uninspiring view to the wild rocky shores of Brittany. Her son's life was in danger once again as King Edward was trying to persuade the Duke of Brittany to extradite him to England, not to be entertained at the court but more probably incarcerated in the Tower, and Duke Francis seemed to be weakening for as an incentive Edward in return was promising to support him against the King of France, the Duke of Brittany's long-standing enemy.

She heard the heavy oak door creak open behind her and turning saw her husband outlined in the archway. But it was not Henry Stafford. He had died of wounds eight years ago after fighting reluctantly for the House of York at the Battle of Barnet. Her dear friend and companion for thirteen years. He had been requisitioned to fight for both the Houses of Lancaster and York and after much deliberation both he and his wife had decided the best option for their own safety and well-being was to choose the side neither of them favoured, judging (rightly) that King Edward had the better chance of success. However both had been unhappy with the choice and both had a foreboding about the battle. Stafford had written his will and after the battle Margaret had sent a messenger to know how he had fared, only to be told the worst.

The man standing in the doorway was her fourth husband, Sir Thomas Stanley, panting a little after the exertion of climbing the twisting stone staircase to the turret room she had claimed as her own for prayer and meditation. It might be a turret room but it had plastered walls brightly painted with scenes from the miracles of Christ and was lavishly furnished, even the prie-dieu had a tapestry kneeling pad and gilded rails. She went towards him, holding out her small thin hands in a gesture of welcome and offering her cheek for his kiss. "I did not know you had returned. How went it?" she asked, unable to keep the anxiety from her voice.

He took the beringed hands peeping from the fur-trimmed hanging sleeves of black velvet. "Well," he answered. "Our fears are ended for the present.

Duke Francis has refused to surrender Henry, even for a substantial reward, and Edward has been forced to retract his demand. The political situation has also changed. Edward wants better relations between England and France and is seeking an alliance with King Louis so doesn't want to jeopardise this by appearing to side with Brittany."

"Thanks be to God," she whispered, seating herself on the oak settle beneath the window, thickly cushioned in rich tapestry cloth, and clasping the gold crucifix hanging from the jewelled belt at her waist. "I am eternally grateful to Duke Francis for offering sanctuary to Henry and Jasper, and for being willing to keep to his promise."

She felt the tears pricking her eyes as relief overwhelmed her. The only signs of emotion she ever showed were in relation to her son. She wondered if she would ever be free from anxiety regarding the son she saw so rarely. It was because he lived only in her imagination that fears often beset her. She knew from his infrequent letters that he found life as a fugitive in Brittany frustrating and tedious. He was twenty five years old now and with no set role to his life. He hunted with the Duke and shared his entertainment but most of his time was spent in the company of his uncle Jasper, riding or walking along the wind-swept Atlantic coast, reading the books both French and English that he was accumulating in his exile, and writing secret letters to prospective supporters. Would he ever be allowed to return to England, she wondered. Not at least until the King died. Edward IV seemed too well established for there ever to be another Lancastrian revival, he was only young and likely to live for many years and when he died there were now two young sons to succeed him. Her long-held certainty that it was divinely ordained that her son should one day be king was unshakeable but at this time she was forced to admit that her faith held little to support it. She knew that others would have given up hope by now and occasionally a shadow of fear brushed the fringes of her consciousness that Henry would die in Brittany and never come back to England but she pushed the treacherous thought aside with renewed prayer and meditation. And despite his seemingly secure position the King was still afraid of Henry Tudor, so much so that he always kept strict, though inconspicuous, surveillance on his mother. Perhaps he could see into her heart and discern her unweakening desire that her son should one day be King of England himself.

"There were no other problems at the court?" she asked her husband, the words encompassing a multitude of situations which he understood. "The King was in good humour?"

"Edward is usually in good humour, especially when he has the merry Jane Shore to entertain him. The only fly in the ointment as usual is the presence of all the Queen's family wherever you turn and the animosity shown them by the King's friends and relations."

Lady Margaret snorted. She did not like the court and despised Queen Elizabeth whom she considered stupid as well as low-born and greedily ambitious, including her numerous family in the condemnation. But it was her duty to spend some time there and she undertook regular visits graciously, hiding her contempt beneath ingratiating smiles that did not touch her eyes and enjoying innocuous conversation spiked with a barbed irony that her listeners did not recognise. It was important for her son's safety and her own that she should appear to accept the validity of the Yorkist court and settle herself into this regime which seemed set for permanence. Her marriage to Sir Thomas Stanley as steward of the King's household had been undertaken with this purpose in mind. It wasn't a love match, any romantic attachment had been with Henry Stafford when she was young though her unconditional love had always been reserved for her son. Stanley was useful to her, gave her protection. He was important at court, trusted by King Edward, he was personable, even handsome, and he owned estates and houses in many different shires. It was however his great castle of Lathom in Lancashire that was his most prestigious acquisition and Margaret thought she might have married him for this alone. Having no love for London and the court she had become enamoured of the great fortress set in the desolate marshland of the coastal plain of Lancashire, itself a distant shire of which the royal family knew little. Here where Stanley's influence was paramount she was almost a queen in her own right.

He came to sit beside her saying, "I missed your company while I was at court." Ten years older than she, he was still tall and straight with a certain elegance. His face was long and pale with a long straight nose and thin lips. His dark brown hair flecked with grey was shorter than the average courtier's and his long narrow beard was becoming grizzled. His grey eyes were intelligent but restless, giving the impression that he was aware of all that was happening around him and of being ready to deal with whatever chance might throw in his way. It was a clever face but with a disturbing shadow of instability. Margaret felt a momentary pang of guilt that she often preferred to stay at Lathom when he was in London but it was quickly assuaged by the knowledge that he liked her to be there dealing with all the business of the estate when he was away. In any case he was continuing, "But it was wiser for you to stay here at Lathom while I intervened with the King on such a delicate matter. He is usually of a mind to accommodate me."

As steward of the King's household Stanley was responsible for the below-stairs management of the court, though over the years he had served the King in a variety of ways and been well rewarded with gifts of land and estates in the north of England and the Welsh marches. He had not always served Edward. He had joined with the Earl of Warwick, who happened to be his brother-in-law at the time, to reinstate Henry VI as King but then had refused to fight for the Lancastrians at the Battle of Barnet where Margaret's husband Stafford had been killed. Like Margaret, he was a master of political expediency. In this they were alike and though their marriage had been deliberately undertaken for mutual convenience they shared enough characteristics for it to fare satisfactorily. Margaret was also grateful that as he was at present in the King's good favour he was willing to use his influence on behalf of her son.

"And the other matter? Did you have opportunity to broach that?" she asked.

He hesitated. "I did suggest a marriage between Henry and Edward's eldest daughter as a means of solving the problem amicably but he was not willing to discuss it, saying only that Elizabeth was too young for marriage at this time. I am sorry I was not more successful with this."

His wife pursed her small mouth but said, "Well there will be other opportunities to pursue this project now you have set the seed in his mind." And she determined to herself that she would not let the idea founder. Now that it seemed her son might not be able to claim the throne in the near future, she had been playing with the idea of arranging a marriage for him with the eldest daughter of the king, Elizabeth of York, because who knew what possibilities this might afford. Especially if Edward were unseated again. Her active mind was already exploring this strategy and she reckoned the queen might not be averse to the proposition. She decided that perhaps she ought to go to London soon and make a show of friendship to Elizabeth Woodville.

"I am glad to see you back safely and I am always grateful for your willingness to serve Henry's cause," she said.

"And I hear you have been busying yourself arbitrating in disputes with my tenants," he said with a half-smile on his lips, "prosecuting cattle thieves and unlicensed hunters." He was always confident that during the times they were separated his wife was quite able to run their estates efficiently. A belief in her extraordinary capabilities, as well as her great wealth, had attracted her to him as a suitable second wife, he having heirs enough with Warwick's sister Eleanor.

"I never regret being at Lathom," Margaret said.

Lathom was to her a perfect setting for her nobility. The great fortress commanded the countryside of west Lancashire, proclaiming its presence for miles around with its nine tall towers rising from the stone battlements, gatehouses with portcullises on four sides and a wide moat surrounding the fifteen acres of fortifications. The forbidding defensive aspect was further reinforced by another nine towers rising from the walls guarding the inner court which housed the Stanley's living accommodation. But within the domestic interior all was luxury and comfort. Sir Thomas had used his accumulated wealth to enlarge and renovate an original ancient edifice into a palatial residence of large halls with soaring roofs, tapestry-hung walls, huge marble fireplaces, glazed windows, carved and painted furniture, chairs and stools cushioned in silk and velvet, canopied beds and candelabra holding fifty wax candles at a time. Dining tables were covered with white cloths and scattered on every surface were artefacts of gold and silver. Margaret's delight was the beginning of a fine library to which she had contributed books of her own. Although the Stanleys divided their time between the court and visiting their other estates in Cheshire, Staffordshire and North Wales, Margaret's favourite residence was Lathom where she reigned like a queen with no-one to gainsay her.

Her marriage to Sir Thomas Stanley had been contracted in some haste when she had again found herself in a vulnerable position after the death of Henry Stafford and she needed to find herself a protector. It was King Edward who had suggested Sir Thomas Stanley, a servant of his, a rich widower with sons, a powerful land-owner in the north of England for he knew that Stanley would be able to keep a careful eye on his wife. Margaret had not been averse to the proposal for she realised she could use Stanley to her advantage as well as securing the King's favour. Although the King negotiated the agreement she ensured that her own wishes were taken into account and while having to agree to Stanley receiving a life interest in her estates she demanded an annual income of 500 marks from his.

Sitting now in the turret room with her husband she was already planning on how to ingratiate herself into the queen's friendship in order to set the seed of a marriage between their two children. She must not be too hasty for that might arouse suspicion. The idea would take time to plant, to water, to bring to fruition, unobtrusively so that no-one, least of all King Edward, might suspect her own personal involvement. But Elizabeth Woodville was not noted for her perspicacity and Margaret was confident she could use her to out-manoeuvre the king. The planning would take time but that did not mean she could not begin the process at once.

"When are we to return to London?" she asked her husband. "I thought you might have stayed there and sent for me to join you."

"I'm afraid that is the other unwelcome news I must relay to you," Sir Thomas said. "There is plague already reported in the City."

"Plague!" she repeated. A shudder of fear shook her thin shoulders. Eight years ago a severe outbreak of plague had taken a fifth of the population and devastated the country.

Reading her thoughts Sir Thomas said, "It has already reached sufficient proportions for people to fear and leave the City if they are able. The court is already moving away so it seems we must remain at Lathom for the present."

Margaret accepted the inevitable. For an indeterminate period her plans must remain only in her head. But she would continue to form stratagems and include them in the prayers and masses she offered up daily.

CHAPTER 6

London

A sudden gust of wind blew a splatter of rain into the room and Bel shivered as she tried to make herself more comfortable on the hard stool while she plied her needle. The girl seated on the other side of the table glanced at her sympathetically as she said, "The hours seem so long don't they. At least it seems as if the plague is abating a little now that the hot weather has passed. Perhaps by Yuletide it will have gone altogether."

Bel sighed. She looked around the small low-ceilinged room. Along one side of the bare plastered walls a trestle table held bolts of linen while on the opposite wall some half-finished clothes hung on tenterhooks. The table in the middle at which the two girls were seated held reels of thread, pins and needles, measuring rods and tapes, scissors, lengths of braid and woven strips, cords, ribbons, and buttons of wood and leather. The floor was stone flagged and had to be swept daily so that no dirt might touch the clothes but though the flags might be clean they were cold to the feet on such a chilly day. There was a large window opening by the work table but without glass and the shutters had to be fastened back during working hours because it was needful to have as much light as possible, but it also let into the room the foul-smelling air from the narrow back alley with its runnel of refuse and on a bad day it was cold.

The front of the mercer's premises was clean and neat with shutters of polished beechwood folded down in the day to form a counter to display his wares and above the door swung a brightly painted sign advertising his trade. The door led into a room paved with red tiles where chairs were set for customers to discuss their needs and tenterhooks held samples of the best merchandise. A door at the back led into the main workroom where the tailors worked in comfort with chairs and long tables, a planked floor, two glazed windows, and shelves and racks to hold all the necessities.

The girls in their less comfortable workplace did not make the clothes but were relegated to the tedious tasks of hems, laces and buttons, interspersed with the sewing of linen shifts and mens' undergarments. Bel had expected to have found her family by now and be comfortably esconced with them but ill fortune continued to shape her life and six months after landing in England she was still in plague-ridden London working for a mercer.

Her journey to England had been without difficulty. Travelling with the wool merchants she had arrived safely in Calais and had taken ship for Dover still in their company. On arrival at the port nestling among the seven white cliffs she found the harbour and streets a confusing mass of travellers coming and going, pushing and shoving for precedence to get permits, arguing and shouting in a myriad different languages, fighting for places on the ships and questioning the amount of taxes they had to pay, while above them on the white cliffs the rugged castle stood sentinel over the entrance to their new country, warning strangers that England was powerful and protected. She was glad of her companions who helped her with the formalities which in her case were brief. She had no goods to be examined nor taxes to pay and on furthering the information that she was on a visit to her relatives, the Malorys of Newbold Revel, she was given a permit to proceed. Being informed that all roads led to London she stayed with her merchant friends as they joined the many companies of travellers making for the capital, considering that this would be the best place to start her journey. The merchants had hired horses at the port and they allowed her to ride pillion with them as she only had her small bag of possessions.

Although not so hot as France, the weather was still warm and bright with only a few spring showers sprinkling the road occasionally, a road that was well-made because it was such a popular route. The scene varied interestingly from France and she was entranced by the flocks of sheep grazing on the downs above the sea, the grassy slopes eventually giving way to small regular fields and trees lacy with late-flowering cherry blossom. The road was undulating but not arduous and passed through many villages and small towns where they were able to find refreshment. They stayed the night at a hostelry in the pretty town of Rochester and the merchants said they were now following the estuary of the Thames though the river could not yet be seen. They first had to cross the Black heath which was unsafe for lone travellers and during night hours but a large party faced no dangers and soon they were able to see the river Thames as they arrived at the village of

Southwark where its gardens stretched along the strand. Bel was told that this was where they were to cross the broad river by the only bridge and she could now see the city of London huddled on the far bank. But people were saying that it was a city with a visitation of the plague and she felt a tremor of apprehension. At the entrance to the bridge the merchants left her and carried on their way in single file, telling her that the city was straight ahead and she could not miss her way.

It was too late to turn back now so over the bridge she must go. She felt lost and alone after being in their company for so long and stood for a time looking at the bridge which was the longest she had ever seen. It was supported on twenty stone arches set on piers through which the water rushed with a powerful force. The entrance onto the bridge was through a stone gateway and she looked with disgust at the rotting heads set on poles above the gate, considering them an inauspicious welcome to the city of London.

"Yon's the Duke o' Clarence, the king's brother, been up there past a year," a fellow said. She averted her eyes, shuddering at the thought that perhaps the war in England was not completely over.

The bridge was crammed with houses and shops huddled together along each side and jutting perilously over the water like drunken custodians, making the passageway between very narrow. It was difficult to push one's way through the noisy throng of people and carts jostling each other to make headway, while a continuous hubbub of strange voices filled the air like a swarm of bees. In the middle of the bridge a peaceful hiatus was created by a beautiful stone chapel and on stopping to admire it Bel was told it was dedicated to the martyred Thomas à Becket. From here she had a view of the river crowded with boats of all shapes and sizes from small ferry boats to tall merchant ships and a little further along was a wooden drawbridge which could be raised when such tall ships wanted to pass. Bel had never before seen such a bridge nor such a river.

Because of the crowded topsy-turvy buildings restricting the view down the Thames and the waterside it was only when she reached the far end of the bridge that the city itself came into sight. She gasped as she was faced with a skyline of countless church spires and bell towers, more than she had ever seen in one place, discovering later that London boasted over a hundred and twenty churches as well as monasteries and convents. The spire of one church was the tallest she had ever seen, soaring into the sky. On her right an enormous four square tower gleamed white in the sun, reminding her of the white stone native to Soissons, and she wondered what it was, its size denoted a palace of some sort. She stood in wonder for a time then jostled and pushed by the throng stepped onto the waterside and tried to decide where to go. She was immediately engulfed in a crowd of noisy street-traders hawking their wares along the river bank, trays of fish, oysters, eel pies. Standing in front of part of the ancient decaying city wall she wished, not for the first time, that she had Renard to accompany her in this strange heaving city, so much bigger than she had envisaged. She knew some English but the deafening clamour of unfamiliar accents confused her as she was unable to distinguish words in the unceasing flow of noise accompanied by the clanging of bells. She saw people making their way up a steep earthen alley between some timber warehouses so deciding to follow them she soon found herself in a warren of narrow crooked streets. Even though the sun was shining it was dark because the upper storeys of the timber and thatched houses overhung the street so that they were almost touching. For the first time in her long journey she was alone and remembered Renard's warning. Perhaps she had been foolish in undertaking such a mission on her own. She had only a little money left and did not know where Warwick shire was nor how far distant. It was a priority to find an inn for the night so that she could consider her next step.

She was surprised by how many inns and taverns lined the dirty streets made more insalubrious by the gulleys running down the middle filled with refuse and sewage, rotting food and dead animals. No wonder there was plague in the city in the hot weather. She wrinkled her nose in disgust and avoided many of the tavern doorways where disreputable-looking people lolled, drunken men and loud-voiced women. She hastened her steps, fearing to look behind her yet not knowing where she was going and she couldn't help remembering her nightmare journey to Reims. This time there would be no Renard to come to her rescue. Then suddenly with the unexpectedness of awakening from a nightmare she turned a corner and came upon an open space where a church stood in the middle of a garden. She could see that the door was open so she made her way through a carpet of sweet-smelling primroses, violets and lavender, the sounds of birds twittering in the trees and the gentle hum of bees making her think she had entered into another world, that she had passed in a moment into a realm of enchantment as in an Arthurian romance. She stepped into the church and was immediately aware of a sense of tranquillity pervading the cool dimness, a calming stillness after the recent hurly-burly. She leant against a pillar breathing in the sweet-scented air and letting the serenity of silence waft over her. Then she whispered a fervent prayer to the Virgin for help, as she had done in the Cathedral at Reims when Renard had miraculously come to her aid. She also said a prayer for him, wondering if he had arrived in Paris and what he was doing. The thought of him lifted her spirits and gave her courage.

When she came outside into the fading sunshine of early evening she noticed what she had not seen before, that the road at the side of the church led into a wider street and a building that appeared to be a monastery or convent. She followed the road as it filled up with timber-framed houses of a better sort until she came across a woman sweeping the front of a building which seemed to be an inn – a timber and plaster frame with a roof of wooden shingles but with a neatly painted door and windows of translucent horn and a sign above advertising 'The Throstle.' Bel considered it a good omen for her as the thrush was a singing bird whose notes were reputed to be some of the most beautiful of birdsongs. The woman looked up, leaning on her besom and panting a little, and Bel judged her to be a kindly person with her buxom figure and flat pale face, like a dough pastry with twinkling black eyes like currants. When Bel asked if she had a room for the night and proffered the necessary coins she smiled welcomingly and opened the front door that led straight into the inn's tap room. The few sleeping chambers were on the upper floor, the only outbuildings being stables and an earth privy, and Bel was led upstairs and shown to a room that was small but clean and light with a casement of horn. It was furnished with a bed and chest on which stood a pewter ewer and basin with a candle, overlooking the courtyard at the back where the smell from the stables was overset by the honeysuckle growing beneath the window.

Thankfully Bel knew that for that night at least she was safe and could rest her body and order her thoughts about what to do next. For she now had another problem. She had missed her monthly flux and felt sick every morning. She was fearful that she was with child by the man who had violated her and the suspicion filled her with despair. If it were true how could she carry on her journey to find her grandfather's family. How would they react to a stranger arriving at their door, pregnant and unmarried and claiming kinship with them, and also travel would be more difficult in her condition. She was desperately hoping she was mistaken in her fears and that the absence of her signs might be due to the rigours of her journey and the unfamiliar pattern her life had taken. But she thought it might be better to stay in London until she knew the truth even though she was frightened by stories of the plague. However that meant she must find some work for the present in order to support herself.

The following morning she asked the innkeeper, a widow by the name of Betty Trimble who was carrying on her husband's trade, if she needed any help with the inn or knew anyone who was seeking a servant. Betty looked her up and down and liking what she saw said, "As a matter of fact I am in need of a serving girl. My niece has been helping me but with the plague increasing in the city she has decided to take herself off to her kinsfolk in Kent. You're not afraid of hard work are you? Cleaning the rooms, serving the customers, helping with the cooking. I can't pay you much but you will have your board and I can spare a few pence a week."

Bel smiled winningly and impulsively hugged her benefactor, thanking the Virgin again for her protection.

Betty grinned, half in embarrassment. "You aren't English are you? Is it French? We get quite a few French merchants so you will be of help in dealing with them."

Bel thought wryly that she had never envisaged working as a servant in an English inn but was glad of the money and the opportunity to have somewhere to stay for a time.

She didn't mind working for Betty who was an industrious but friendly mistress, full of chatter and gossip which, together with her homely dishes, pleased her customers. Listening to the gossip, which was often about the problems the long civil war had caused or the latest casualties of the plague, Bel improved her English but wondered about the cheerful resilience of these Londoners beset with so many misfortunes. She found the Throstle a welcome refuge from the strange confusion of London and the dangers of catching the plague sickness and didn't like to wander far but her duties included shopping for Betty in the many markets - the busy Cheap, the fishmongers of Billingsgate and the butchers of the Shambles. She was still afraid of the noisy streets and the confusion of strange accents and found the shopkeepers hard to understand with their quick mode of speech. She shuddered at news of the plague victims and was always glad to hasten home but sometimes she would linger to visit the many churches, especially St. Paul's whose unique 500 foot spire had first caught her attention from the bridge. As her confidence increased she began to explore the sights of London. There were many green spaces and gardens amongst the busy streets, especially those belonging to the monasteries and the Knights Templar and she would often rest there for a time. She avoided the tenements and hovels of the poor but admired the great Halls of the guilds – the Goldsmiths, Silversmiths, Mercers and Vintners – and the magnificent mansions of the nobles along the riverbank, as fine as anything she had seen in France though the great Savoy palace was now a burnt-out shell. Betty told her it had been the magnificent residence of John of Gaunt but had been burnt down by rebels who opposed his wealth and power. If it hadn't been for the dread of knowing definitely she was with child she could have been quite happy. But the second month had now passed without the reassurance of her cycle. She did not know how she could bear to give life to the product of such a brutal liaison. If Renard had not refused to sleep with her on the night she had offered herself to him then she might have believed the child to be his and that would have been much worse. She shuddered to think that she might have accepted as his love-child this monster's progeny and thanked God for Renard's integrity. Yet how she longed that the child could have been his. She would have borne the waiting joyfully and lavished on the child all the love she could not give to him. Instead the daily realisation filled her with horror and she despaired of the future.

The loose brown gown that Renard had stolen for her in what now seemed to be another existence hid her condition for a long time. But Betty was observant and one day she made mention of the fact.

Bel began to cry and stammered, "Please don't think the worst of me, I am not a drab. I was taken by force by an unknown man when I was in France."

The innkeeper's dough face was full of compassion as Bel told her the whole story. However she said, "I am so sorry but you cannot stay here. The work is too hard for you now in your condition and though I regret to say this, I cannot have our respectable customers thinking the worst of my house."

Bel sniffled as she murmured, "I do understand. I thank you for giving me work so far."

Betty thought for a moment then said, "We must try to find you some light work until the child is born and then you can decide what to do. Can you sew?"

Bel shrugged. "I don't know," she said. "I used to repair my clothes and my father's when necessary but that is all."

"I'm sure you could manage," Betty said. "Listen, my cousin is married to a tailor who works for a mercer in Cheapside, Master Hawley. I reckon he would be glad of an extra pair of hands, his business is growing apace. You would be seated all day and working away from his customers. Leave it to me and I'll see what I can do."

So Bel had found herself working in the back room of Master Hawley's shop together with young Agnes Lightfoot. The room was cold in the November weather, her eyes were sore from having to do small neat stitches all day, and her ungainly body ached constantly as she tried to shift her weight on the hard stool. It had been even worse during the hot summer. The sickness had swept through the city with devastating consequences as each week had brought more victims, houses and shops isolated and plague pits being dug for the dead. Fortunately Master Hawley's residence had escaped contamination, and mured in the back room all day with little contact with anyone else the girls had been relatively safe. But sometimes when her mental torment was particularly severe Bel had wished she would die then she would not have to face the future. She would not have welcomed a lingering death with the lengthy symptoms of postules, fever and incipient madness but sometimes the plague took people immediately, falling down dead as with a lightning bolt. But then an image of Renard would intrude into her mind – his kindness, his mischievous smile, his quick wits and movements, the beautiful music he could produce - and she would realise she wanted to live in the vain hope of meeting him again some day even though this seemed impossible.

"At least the plague is lessening a little," Agnes repeated. "And you have your baby to look forward to after Yuletide."

Bel said nothing. She wondered what would be Agnes's reaction if she said, "I am going to kill it." For that is what she had decided to do. No way was she going to keep an offspring of that evil man, a constant reminder of his violation, a constant fear that his evil might be reproduced in his spawn. All she wanted now was to be rid of the burden inside her. She hated her swelling body, her clumsiness, the constant aches and cramps without having the joy of a child to make it all worthwhile. She thought the birth might happen around Candlemas but first she had to endure Yuletide.

Master Hawley was a fair enough master. He expected them to work hard and produce good workmanship but he was not too severe. She and Agnes lived in his household as did the two apprentices. They were fed and shared an attic room. Under normal circumstances she would have joined in the Yuletide festivities together with the other servants but Mistress Hawley was not willing for her to reveal her condition to guests and kindred so she had been ordered to keep to her room. Bel grieved that people thought her immoral but did not mind the injunction for she was desperately tired and intended to sleep for a great part of the time while the remainder could be occupied by reading and playing her treasured flageolet which Renard had bought for her birthday. She had no-one to buy her Yuletide gifts but had bought a bone comb for Agnes.

However Betty Trimble had not forgotten her and invited her to partake in her own simple celebrations at the Throstle Inn. "I have invited some friends to share our Christmas feast and I have told them that you are a distant cousin who has recently lost her husband," she confided, smiling at the conspiracy.

So Bel put some new trimmings on the old brown gown and in the hall of the inn, decorated with holly and ivy and with a Yule log burning in the grate, enjoyed roast goose and mincemeat pie followed by plum pudding and gingerbread. Instead of the usual ale there was spiced wine and Betty's homely friends got very merry. They played games of forfeits and sang loudly, and Bel was able to take part in the entertainment, singing or playing her flageolet to everyone's delight. Despite feeling encumbered by her increased weight, in actual fact her slender body had not changed too much, concealed largely by her loose gown, and the friendly strangers had accepted Betty's story. On Christmas morning before they went to Mass at the nearest church Betty had given her some home-made marchpane while she had used some of her little stock of money to buy the innkeeper a piece of good linen from the mercer's to make herself a new head covering. She herself had had to adapt to covering her black curls with a length of cloth, either as a turban or knotted at the back, as was the English custom. England was unlike France and only whores wore their hair loose, so in her persona as a married woman Bel had to sacrifice her vanity.

Christmas had been a pleasant day and Bel fell asleep in her old chamber at the Throstle feeling almost happy. The inn was open again for business on the following day but the twelve days were still kept with some semblance of celebration and on Twelfth Night the inn was alive with drinking and singing and dancing in an haphazard fashion. Betty had made a cake and the inn's customers each bought a slice, those who obtained the pieces containing the pea and the bean receiving the authority to rule the boisterous company for the rest of the evening and commanding what they would.

The following day Bel had to return to the mercer's as she needed the small amount of money she earned there. As soon as the baby was born she intended to begin her journey to Warwick shire and she knew she would need money for the journey and for the purchase of a new gown in which to meet her relatives.

"You can come back here to have your baby," Betty had said. "I have a friend who is skilled in such matters and often acts as midwife to our neighbours and I will get her to tend you."

Bel was moved by her kindness and thought again how her prayer to the Virgin had brought her a helper for the second time. Her mother used to talk about guardian angels. Then a wave of shame washed over her as she realised how she was going to betray the Virgin's care of her. For she had never wavered from her intention to kill her child when it was born. She had decided she would put a pillow over the infant's face when she was alone and resolutely banished from her thoughts the image of the Madonna with her child in her arms. But she was ashamed that Belfiore, daughter of Gianni le Chanteur, was planning to become a murderess and how violence had claimed her life in the past year with the death of her father and her violation.

The burden, as she called it, refusing to personalise her affliction, announced its delivery the week after Candlemas on a day of February sleet and rain. Bel was glad it was not on the day that the Virgin had taken her own child to the temple to be blessed. She made her way to the Throstle Inn with great foreboding and fear but thankful that her ordeal would soon be ended after so many long months of mental suffering. The physical agony however was much worse than she had ever imagined, despite all the stories she had been told. Betty comforted her between her tasks, giving her draughts of vervain, pennyroyal and raspberry leaves but the hours passed excruciatingly into the next day. When the midwife was called at last she anxiously examined Bel's feverish tossing body and talked in low whispers to Betty. Bel tried to distance herself from the pain consuming her by imagining she was back in France, entertaining in some noble's great hall with her father or walking the tree-shaded lanes of Champagne with Renard. She was not aware when her visions melted into hallucinations and as she lost consciousness she lapsed into French, speaking words that were fortunately incomprehensible to the bystanders.

They told her afterwards that they feared she would die. All she remembered was screaming and then the pain ending abruptly as if a door had been shut. She lay trembling on the bed soaked with blood and sweat, not able to believe that the agony had passed but conscious only of a lightness in her belly and a numbness between her legs that would soon manifest itself into a different kind of pain.

"I'm sorry but your child is dead, it was a boy," the red-faced midwife said, her harsh voice attempting to give some sympathy.

Tears rolled down Bel's face and she began to sob, though all her weary body could produce were gulps of shallow breath.

"At least you are still alive," the woman said, misunderstanding her reaction. "It was too long a time, two days, and you were too small for the task. *You* are lucky to be still living."

Tears continued to roll down Bel's pale cheeks but they were not tears of sorrow but of relief that it was no longer needful to take the step she had planned. God had been merciful to her. The Virgin had pitied her despite her sinful intentions.

"Would you like to see the child before we take him away?" the midwife asked, hoping nonetheless that she need not show her the misshapen form. She was relieved when the girl shook her head. Bel experienced no feelings of regret or pity. To her the product of her violation had never been anything more than the original act, a hateful invasion of her body. The midwife misunderstood, believing she was still suffering. It was too soon to add to her grief. Later she would tell her that the damage done to her body would make it impossible for her to bear more children.

CHAPTER 7

Newbold Revel

Bel was at last on her way to find her mother's family. Despite the difficult childbirth it had not taken her long to recover because she was young and strong. She had returned to Master Hawley's workshop for a time in order to earn a little more money to see her on the way and to wait hopefully for the weather to improve by Eastertide, for February was still too cold and wet for a long journey. She also thought that he might be of help to her. She knew from the mercer's conversation that Warwick shire was one of the most important wool-producing regions in the country and that wool merchants from there often came to London to transact business. Bearing in mind Renard's warning about never travelling alone and remembering the kindness of the wool merchants in whose company she had travelled from Amiens, she surmised there must be someone going that way who would let her accompany them and that Master Hawley might have such information.

So it happened that she was introduced to a wool-merchant who was travelling home to Coventry with a group of fellow-businessmen, several of them accompanied by their wives. He agreed that she would be welcome to join their company, the only proviso being that she would have to ride. Bel had enough money saved to be able to hire a palfrey from a livery stable and pay for lodgings on the road but she had intended to buy herself a new gown in which to present herself to her relatives. Now she knew that was impossible. She would have to continue wearing the old gown, no longer nut brown but an uneven colour of dark honey with much washing. But she had her fine gown folded carefully in her bag for later.

Her leave-taking of Betty Trimble was emotional and she had to promise the inn-keeper to visit the Throstle if she ever came back to London. Then Betty pressed upon her some of her newly-baked gingerbread to eat on her journey. Bel left the Throstle Inn and its welcome shelter with some regret but with a growing sense of excitement at the prospect of reaching her goal, while a renewal of the plague sickness due to the warmer weather increased her eagerness to be away. Master Hawley had also bade her farewell with expressions of regret and invited her to choose some new laces and a girdle as a present. The blue cords now adorned the honey-coloured gown and as the dress had shrunk considerably with several washes it skimmed her waist and hips emphasized by the low-slung belt of plaited blue wool. With her blue cloak she looked respectable enough when she joined the group of a dozen travellers waiting at the appointed inn in the chill of early morning. They were all plainly dressed for riding in warm cloaks of wool or leather with woollen caps and leather boots, full panniers strapped to their horses. Besides the eight merchants and a few women there were three loaded baggage carts, on each of which were two guards in chainmail and steel helmets. Bel felt a surge of excitement as she surveyed the noisy innyard, bustling with the activity of stableboys and travellers accompanied by a cacophony of restless snorts and shouted commands. Rather inexpertly she mounted her pony and the little cavalcade left the inn, the horses' hooves clattering on the cobbles and sliding a little on the straw. The pale sun was already glimmering through the clouds and it promised to be a dry day with a fresh April breeze lifting Bel's hood from her curls and ruffling the trees sprouting green with new growth and awakening blossom.

The leader of the group was called Humphrey Meadowcroft, a thick-set man of about fifty years old with grey curly hair and bushy beard, dressed plainly for travelling but with an obvious air of substance about him. He was also loquacious, relishing his position as leader and most important merchant, at least in his own opinion.

"Never travel with any signs of wealth about you," he said to Bel approvingly and she smiled inwardly as she realised Humphrey thought her plain attire such a stratagem. "I never wear rings or chains when I am travelling and my best attire is packed away in my chest, only for wearing in London." He had been impressed by Bel's account of going to join her kinsfolk, the Malorys of Newbold Revel. "An ancient family and well respected in the shire," he said, and introduced her to his wife as a travelling companion.

Philippa Meadowcroft was some ten years younger than her husband, a comely woman with a fair freckled face and fair hair peeping from a close-fitting cap of grey felt set on a broad stiffened band. Her mulberry serge gown was adapted for riding side-saddle, tucked into a belt at her waist to reveal short boots of soft leather and thick wool stockings. She was of a cheerful disposition and liked to chatter, twittering constantly about their visit to London and their neighbours at home which relieved Bel of any need to talk more about herself than necessary while the stream of anecdotes kept her interested for the long periods of time on horseback. Apart from the discomfort of riding, to which Bel was unaccustomed, the journey was largely without problems. Robbers scrupled to attack such a number travelling together, especially with armed guards to protect the baggage and the chests of money they had acquired from their business in the city. The spring air was welcomingly fresh and clean after the smoke and stench of London with only the occasional April showers which never gave them a real drenching. The road to the important city of Coventry was a main thoroughfare and well-travelled and though unpaved and stony for much of the way the mire of winter had dried out and the dust of high summer had not yet filled the remaining grooves. They were able to make a good pace, overtaking the lumbering ox-drawn carts of produce and only being overtaken themselves by messengers on fast horses. Bel found much to interest her in the novelty of the English countryside, the huge open fields divided into strips and growing wheat, oats and barley, the open commons where sheep grazed and the interspersing patches of woodland. The peasants working in the fields and their villages of thatched-roof cottages seemed more prosperous than in France. Occasionally Humphrey Meadowcroft would ride with them and then he would regale Bel with stories of the lawlessness occasioned by the long civil war, pointing out some places where great disturbances had occurred. It was difficult to imagine the bands of armed men terrorising the countryside with plunder and forced enlistment with the pleasant fields now green with new wheat and pasture, cradling peaceful hamlets with smoke curling from the thatch and surrounded by geese and pigs and barking dogs.

At night they lodged in comfortable hostelries and after supper the merchants would take turns to entertain each other with tales of previous travels, suitably embellished with their own prominence and enlivened by amusing anecdotes. Other fellow travellers would contribute their own stories and exchange news. When Phillipa heard Bel singing quietly to herself as she rode she suggested that she sing for them one evening and she accepted happily, singing French songs and playing her pipe which surprised and pleased them all.

On their last night's lodging before reaching Coventry, Bel was seated beside Philippa at the long table where they were being served their evening meal of roasted pork with beans and cabbage and oatmeal bread. The merchant's wife laid down her knife saying, "Well Belfiore it would seem we shall soon be parting company. We shall be making for Coventry while you will continue for some twenty miles or so to Newbold Revel. But I know Hugh Ruskin is travelling on to Market Harborough which is on the same route so you will have his protection for a little longer." Then hesitating a little she asked, "Tell me my dear, do you have any better clothes to greet your kinsfolk?"

Bel had seen evidence on the journey of Philippa's frankness of speech and accepted it as part of her unpretentious manner but she found herself blushing. Although she had seldom given away personal information she was aware that occasionally she might have revealed more than she had intended and said defensively, "I have a very fine gown in my bag."

"But not suitable for arrival at the manor?" Philippa surmised, pursing her lips. She looked critically at Bel's attire then said impulsively, "I don't wish to offend you my dear but I think I can find something better for you. If you won't object to my meddling I have a solution. Come to my chamber and see what I propose."

Bel felt embarrassed and mumbled something apologetic but not wishing to disappoint her companion she allowed the merchant's wife to lead her up the inn's staircase to the chamber she was sharing with her husband. Philippa immediately began rummaging in one of their travel chests saying as she did so, "I have a gown here that is really too tight for me and I would like you to have it, you are so much thinner than I am. It isn't a fine gown, merely serviceable, but I think it might suit your purpose if you would accept it."

She held up a gown of pink wool that had probably been originally a deeper wine colour but was now a delicate shade of rose. It was without decoration but expertly cut so that the soft wool flowed in panels from the hips where lacing led up to the deep curved neckline. The sleeves, tied into the bodice with matching laces, were cut to points over the knuckles, neither too tight nor too voluminous for serviceable wear. The total effect was of elegant simplicity yet it was a gown where the wearer could dress herself without the aid of an attendant. Bel's face showed her longing and Philippa urged, "Take it please, it is no longer of any use to me."

Bel stammered her gratitude, tears starting to her eyes, but Philippa thrust it into her arms and ushered her to the door with cluckings of disparagement, smiling at the young girl's fulsome expressions of gratitude.

The following morning Bel put on the new gown, stroking the soft material with delight and loving the way the folds swung around her as she descended the staircase to the inn's parlour where breakfast was set. Philippa glanced up from cutting slices from the boiled ham on the trencher and a smile of approval lit her face. The dress was perfect for Bel and she could see, as the wearer could not, how the delicate rose shade enhanced her youthful complexion.

When they set off on the last stage of their journey Bel was still wearing her blue cloak but her hair hung loose almost to her waist as she refused to cover it any longer by a linen coif nor force the recalcitrant curls into the heavy plait that was fashionable. She was buoyed up with expectancy, feeling she could fly the rest of the way, free as a bird.

It was well after noon when Coventry came into view and Bel was amazed by the first sight of the city on the horizon. Numerous tall towers and gatehouses soared along the whole length of the encircling red sandstone walls, beyond which could be seen a mass of buildings interspersed by needle-like spires piercing the sky.

"Thirty-two towers and twelve gatehouses," Humphrey Meadowcroft told her proudly. "Coventry is the fourth largest city in England, built on the wealth of the wool merchants. Our guildhall is one of the finest in the country. And we have a unique blue dye for our wool that never loses its colour and is greatly prized all over Europe."

Bel expressed her admiration as was expected, wishing she could see more of the city but yet impatient to be on her own way. She and Philippa parted with affection and some regret that their few days of friendship had ended. However Humphrey was determined to use the opportunity to consolidate the acquaintance of such a notable family and said, "Commend me to your kinsfolk the Malorys, perhaps we may have the opportunity to meet sometime."

Most of the merchants proceeded into the city while Bel accompanied Hugh Ruskin and his servant as they skirted the walls to ride further into the countryside. Hugh was a young man with a freckled face and bright red hair who had made the journey to London on behalf of his father and he had no objection to escorting a beautiful young girl, talking avidly all the way. Leaving Coventry behind they rode through the grounds belonging to Coombe Abbey then through Caludon deer park into arable land and fields with sheep grazing, but once they reached the Smite brook the land became marshy and the paths sodden though interspersed with woodlands. It was a more desolate landscape than they had so far seen and Bel was disappointed by the unexpected barrenness. At the little village of Stretton with its lath and plaster houses lining the main street, Hugh Ruskin said, "This village is part of the Newbold Revel estate, you are almost there now. But we must ride on to Market Harborough. Keep to the road ahead and you will very soon see the manor house."

She thanked them but when they had ridden away into the distance she felt very much alone and afraid. It seemed such a long time since she had started on the journey to find her mother's English family and now she had reached her destination she was filled with trepidation. She had no idea what to expect, how she would be greeted, what kind of people they were, how grand the house would be. For a moment she was filled with foreboding and feared she had been foolish in venturing here. She shivered as she looked at the road ahead for the land looked inhospitable with marshes and woodland, though the day was pleasantly warm and the sun dappled the stones of the path in its fitful hide and seek from behind the fluffy clouds wafted by the light breeze. It was impossible to turn back now that she had come so far on the long and eventful journey so she mastered her fears and pointed the palfrey on the course to which she had been directed.

The flat and marshy plain soon gave way to an expanse of woodland. She felt panic seize her as she found herself enclosed within a thick canopy of trees, recalling her last journey alone in a wood, and in desperation pressed her pony to go faster. However this was not one of the dense French forests, dark as night and redolent with danger. The pale spring sunshine flickered through the foliage, the grass was carpeted with buttercups and ox-eye daisies and a fawn stopped in its tracks to gaze at her with large soulful eyes before scampering away. Calm returned as she came upon a bank of violets and then the trees parted to reveal a manor house ahead surrounded by a moat. Taking a deep breath she set her pony to follow the path to the house.

They continued past a series of fishponds to where a stone bridge led across the moat to a low arched gateway in a surrounding wall. Riding through the arch she could see the house standing within a paved courtyard. It was built of stone, two storeys high with a crenellated stone roof above which soared two chimney stacks. A solid door with iron bars supporting the oak panels stood within a central gable that formed an enclosing porch with a window of leaded glass at the side and another smaller casement above it. Attached to the other side of the house was an older wing, a timber-framed building with a thatched roof. A range of similar outbuildings stood some distance away at right angles. It was not a grand residence but it was the first English manor house Bel had seen closely and she felt a thrill of excitement to realise it belonged to her mother's family. She dismounted and walked towards the formidable-looking door set within the gabled porch. She thought her approach might have been noticed but no-one came so plucking up her courage and trying to still her beating heart she took hold of the heavy iron ring and knocked.

It seemed a long time to her nervous senses before she could hear footsteps, then the heavy door creaked open to reveal a youngish man in what seemed to be household livery, a knee-length blue jerkin over a collarless shirt, brown woollen hose, leather boots loose around his ankles and a blue wool cap on his gingery hair.

He looked enquiringly at her and she said, "I would like to see Sir Thomas Malory," her voice shaking a little.

He seemed taken aback, then recovering himself said in some perplexity, "Sir Thomas has been dead these last ten years or so."

The statement struck Bel like a physical blow. Although she had briefly considered the possibility she had not really given it serious thought in her daydreams, believing in her youthful optimism that all would ensue as she had hoped. This was cruel news after all her anticipation. "I'm sorry I did not know," she whispered, wondering what to do next.

"Would you like to see Lady Malory?" the young man asked.

Bel did not know what to reply. She could hardly explain her presence to his wife as a child of one of her husband's by-blows, a predicament she had not considered. But the servant took her silence for acquiescence and ushered her into the manor house, saying he would call his mistress.

He led her into a broad passage of bare stone. There was a door at the bottom of the passageway and another of solid oak to one side and through which she was ushered. A painted wooden screen blocked the interior from view but he led the way past into the great hall. Then he disappeared through a door at the bottom of the room leaving her alone in the heart of the house. She looked around at her surroundings, fascinated despite the anxiety consuming her. The ceiling was of oak planks criss-crossed by thick oak beams, suggesting another room above. The floor was wood-planked and Bel recalled the woods surrounding the manor. The walls were plastered and painted in an ochre shade but an enormous woven tapestry of martial scenes covered the back wall in front of which stood a long oak table with three high-backed chairs and two carved and fretted box stools. A stone fireplace and hearth took up almost one wall and above it a painted coat of arms was displayed. A box chair was set beside the hearth and along the opposite wall stood an oak livery cupboard on which were displayed plates, jugs and beakers, mostly of pewter but some silver, and behind which was another tapestry of a hunting scene. Beneath the tall window was a long beechwood bench and around the room were several stools of ash and beech wood, square and sturdy with sides of fretwork. There were cushions of woven and embroidered linen and wool, hinting at a woman's industry. The door at the back of the hall opened and Bel turned nervously but it was not a woman who entered.

It was a man nearing forty years old who approached her. He was of average height with a sturdy build evident in his thigh-length belted doublet of embossed brown leather, dark brown hose tightly fitting on his well-shaped legs, the calf muscles visible above his leather boots. A white linen shirt showing above his doublet emphasized the healthy colour of his clean-shaven complexion, sun-browned as if he spent much time out of doors. His hair was dark brown, cut in the current mode with a fringe but with an obstinate wave that refused to follow the fashion of hanging straight to the shoulders. His nose was straight and his jaw square giving an impression of strength and dependability. His deep-set eyes were brown and were studying her with interest and something more. He inclined his head towards her saying, "I am Robert Malory. And who might you be, who has called to see my father, dead since 1471. You are obviously a stranger here. Are you come like some damsel from an Arthurian romance to work some enchantment upon us or lay a quest upon me?"

His levity un-nerved her and she stammered, "My name is Belfiore. I am come from France and that is why I was ignorant of the circumstances."

Her voice betrayed a beguiling French accent and Robert Malory was even more fascinated by this unexpected apparition. When he had come to inquire the business of a woman asking for his father he had not been prepared for the vision that awaited him. The beautiful young girl in a cloak the colour of her eyes, open to reveal a flowing gown which emphasized her slender figure, her creamy skin and rosy lips enhanced by the delicate rose colour, seemed to make the room glow with the promise of warm summer days. Luxuriant black tresses tumbled over her shoulders and as he looked into the deep blue eyes, wide open with apprehension, the sight affected him in a way he had never before experienced.

"Belfiore," he murmured, "beautiful flower. No that is too foreign a name for England. You should be called Rose. Why have you come seeking my father, all unknowing that he is dead?"

His voice was sharp but his expression was not unkind, the square chin and the regular features inclining to fleshiness gave a reassuring impression of solidity and Bel's anxiety lessened enough for her to feel she could be honest. She began to recite the whole story of her grandmother having fallen in love with Sir Thomas Malory when he was a young man in Bayonne and of how her mother Joan, or Jehanne as the French said, had been the product of the liaison."

"So you are claiming my father was your grandfather?" he asked with a quirky smile on his lips.

"Do you not believe me?" she murmured, aghast at the thought.

"Why should I?" he riposted. "What proof do you have?"

"You must know if your father was in Gascony, in Bayonne in the year 1440," she replied.

Robert Malory paused for a moment then admitted, "Yes, he was there, I was a small boy at the time and

I remember him going. His cousin Sir Philip Chetwynd had been appointed Mayor of Bayonne. When he came back to England for a time the French recaptured the province of Gascony and so he recruited soldiers, including my father, to return there. They expelled the French and Chetwynd was reinstated as Mayor. But when they came back to England again, the French took permanent possession of Gascony as you must know."

"So you must believe the truth of what I am saying. While in Bayonne he fell in love with my grandmother, a French girl called Marie-Claire who gave birth to my mother Joan."

"The fact that my father was in Bayonne at that time does not prove anything, my dear Rose. Your grandmother could have been made pregnant by anyone, including any of the English soldiers there, but heard the name Sir Thomas Malory and considered this a likely investment, a knight instead of a common soldier."

Bel was aghast at this defamation of her grandmother, shaking her head vehemently, but she persisted defiantly, "Then how did she know that his home was Newbold Revel in the shire of Warwick, she would not have known such details if she had not known him personally. And if she only wished to avail herself of a rich knight's fortune why did she make no claim on him, on your family. She stayed in Gascony and brought up my mother. She never married. What would be the purpose of her making up a name she had only heard, and such a poor girl would have been unlikely to have heard his name and habitation if he was not known to her personally. It was not a sign of honour to have borne the love-child of an Englishman, not afterwards when the English no longer owned Gascony. It would have been in her interest to invent a French lover if that was what she intended to do."

Robert Malory looked pensive for a moment then said, "Was she given any token, a keepsake, a letter, any documentation that might be recognised?"

Bel shook her head and sank down on one of the stools feeling defeated. "She couldn't read," she murmured. "I never knew my grandmother, I only knew the story from my mother who said she was very beautiful. She said Sir Thomas gave her money to rear her child when he left and it was his wish she be named Joan."

Robert stood looking down at her, still deep in thought. "Why have you come here now when you admit your family never made any attempt to contact my father previously?" he asked. "I think you have invented this story to get what you can out of us, knowing we are a landed family with a long history and a knightly pedigree."

Bel jumped up and faced him, an angry flush on her cheeks and her blue eyes accusing. "That is not true, I would never do that. If I had just picked on you in order to deceive you would I not have known Sir Thomas was dead, would not I have chosen someone nearer London so that I need not have made such a long journey, would I not have chosen a more wealthy family to try and gain some advantage for myself," she cried, gazing around the hall.

Robert Malory tried to suppress the smile that was tickling the corner of his mouth. She was even more tantalising in her anger, the attractive French accent more pronounced.

"My mother died when I was six years old and my father died last year. They always said I should try to find my family in England if I was ever left alone because I have no brothers or sisters and all my relatives are dead. I did not think of the implications, I never thought I would not be believed and, even worse, suspected of being a trickster, an imposter." Her English was good but sometimes she had to pause to find a word and she didn't always pronounce them correctly and Robert found himself being charmed by her passion and the sound of her voice. "I don't want anything, no money or anything. I just wanted to see where the English part of me belonged," she continued, tears starting to her eyes.

Robert took her arm and led her to the bench where he sat beside her. "You might not be so happy with your English heritage if you knew what kind of person my father, your presumed grandfather, was," he said. "He spent a great part of his life in prison for crimes he committed." Bel looked at him with amazement and perplexity in her eyes. "He was imprisoned for robbery with violence, including robbing abbeys and monks, for deer-stealing, for extortion, for rape and for ambushing and trying to murder the great Duke of Buckingham. He fought on both sides in our so-called wars of the roses, first for the Yorkists then the Lancastrians. If Sir Thomas Malory was your grandfather, what do you think of him now?"

Bel was stunned but said quietly, "I would have loved him as my grandfather."

Robert remained silent for a time then said, "So what do you intend to do now, my little Rose?"

"I don't know," she murmured, lowering her eyes and twisting her hands in her lap. She had never thought beyond finding Newbold Revel, never thought that it would end like this.

Robert looked at her sad face and compassion overcame him. "I could give you some money for you to return to London, enough money for you to live for a time, perhaps until you decided to go back to France," he volunteered. Then with a sudden flash of self-awareness he realised he did not want to let this beautiful girl slip away. Whether her story was true or not was immaterial.

"I just wanted to belong," she whispered miserably.

Robert turned her to look at him. "You couldn't really expect my mother to have welcomed you with open arms could you – a product of my father's unfaithfulness. She holds all the rights to his money and property, he left it all to her so she is in charge here at Newbold Revel not I. However we cannot turn you away, it is contrary to all the laws of hospitality. You must stay here at least for a few days. But I will make no mention of your story, I shall introduce you instead as someone who has come to London from France to visit kin and because of the plague in the city you decided to pay a courtesy visit to the house of a man who was known to your family in Gascony. I shall also call you Rose because I think the name becomes you - it is a beautiful flower, it is English, and the pink rose is an amalgamation of the red rose of Lancaster and the white rose of York over which our country has fought for the past ten years and in which conflict my father fought for both sides."

Renard had said that she had been born in the sign of the rose. Bel wondered if this was Robert Malory's oblique way of saying he believed her story but was relieved to know she wasn't immediately being turned away. Robert himself was happy with the way he had temporarily resolved the problem for, though still unsure of her claim, he was absolutely sure that he did not want her to disappear as suddenly as she had appeared.

"It is almost supper hour so you will be able to meet the family," he told her. "I presume you are on horseback so I will have it stabled for the time being."

There was already much activity in the outside passage where the rear door obviously led to the service quarters and soon servants were arriving in the hall with plates, jugs and pewter cups. A tall well-built woman in her sixties was the first to enter. A loose gown of mustard yellow wool clothed her ample figure and her grey hair was almost covered by a linen cap with a stiff turned-up brim and long lappets.

"My mother, Lady Elizabeth Malory," he said, introducing Bel to her with the story he had prepared.

Bel made her a small reverence, and while Lady Elizabeth was courteously accepting her as a guest and making formal conversation she had the opportunity to study her grandfather's wife. Her unlined face had strong contours, the square chin was the same as her son's and her brown eyes were shrewd. She exuded practicality and capability and Bel could believe that Sir Thomas's confidence in leaving her in control of his estate had not been misplaced.

She was followed into the hall by a younger woman and two boys. "My wife, also Elizabeth, and my sons Nicholas and Thomas," said Robert, again making the introductions with the same story. Elizabeth Malory the younger was about the same age as her husband, small and plump as a partridge with a pale face and small eyes of an indeterminate blue-grey. Her day gown of watchet-blue linen had the hem tucked into a belt below her ample bust, revealing an underkirtle of a paler whey, and fair hair was just visible beneath a felt turban of the shade known as milk and water. The eldest boy Nicholas was a young adolescent and had his father's brown hair and sturdy figure while Thomas was several years younger, fair like his mother but thinner. They took their places on the stools set at the table while the women seated themselves in the chairs, Robert leading Bel to his own chair and fetching a stool for himself.

The Malorys were polite enough and interested in Bel's (whom they knew as Rose) story which she constantly had to adapt to fit in with Robert's account, making no mention that her father had been a troubadour but saying only that her family had lived in Bayonne. She could talk freely about her journey through France in a company of merchants (not mentioning Renard) and made out that the kinsfolk she had been visiting in London were the Hawley merchants, with whose household she was familiar. She was not happy about being less than honest but Robert, seated beside her, prompted her constantly and extricated her from awkward questions. He was attentive to her needs during the meal and she began to like him. It was he who declared, without expecting any demur, that she would remain with them for two or three days before returning to London.

Bel was not completely happy that it had not turned out as she had expected, but at least she was settled in what she believed to be her family home for a short while and the Malorys were polite enough even though Robert's wife was reserved. She pushed from her mind all disturbing thoughts about her future and determined to enjoy her time at Newbold Revel. She had been given a bedchamber in the older part of the manor with clean rushes on the floor, a truckle bed with fresh linen, and through the small window of green glass she could dimly see the moat and the fish ponds, like looking through water. She joined the family at meal times where the food was the best she had known for a long time with venison from their deer park and fresh carp from their ponds. She was welcomed by the two women into their comfortable solar on the first floor above the hall, their private domain, for formal conversation which was always accompanied by sewing, both for decorative purposes and for repairing linen. However they were usually occupied in attending to the multifarious tasks of the manor, supervising the cooking, the brewing, the kitchen garden and the orchards, while Lady Malory spent time every day in drawing up the accounts and examined her grandsons' reading and writing after their tutoring by the priest. During this time Bel was free to wander around the estate and loved to walk in the grounds. She had grown to love the place and wanted to think of it as her home, imagining what it would have been like for her grandfather to grow up in such a place and then be its master, imagining what it would have been like for her mother and then herself to live here. She was troubled about what Robert had told her about Sir Thomas's criminal activities and was sure he was mistaken. Why should a knight with such an estate as Newbold Revel be guilty of such crimes? Perhaps Robert had invented this tale in order to dissuade her against believing that Sir Thomas was her grandfather, just as he had invented a story for her. She wanted to ask him again but didn't dare. She wasn't quite sure what to make of Robert Malory. He gave an impression of intelligence and reliability. He was kind to her, but she did not know whether he believed her story or whether he still thought of her as a pretender, only the courtesy of his class allowing her to stay until he could with a clear conscience be rid of her. She wished he could really be her uncle, her mother's brother.

Sometimes Robert would join her on her walks around the estate for there was always something for him to oversee or regulate and once he invited her to accompany him on her palfrey as he rode further. The three days passed all too quickly and regretfully she knew the time had come for her to suggest her departure from Newbold Revel as Robert Malory had stipulated. A great wave of longing swept over her as she surveyed the comfortable manor house, a hive of activity in its own little world, surrounded by the murky green moat and the fields reaching to woodland. She recalled her apprehensive approach through the trees and now she must retrace all too soon her path across the golden carpet of buttercups and wild daffodils, to where, she did not know. The warm spring sunshine had cooled to a chill as a light wind chased dark clouds which threatened rain. Robert had been showing her where he intended to plant some new cherry trees and she was trying to pluck up courage to state her intention of departing when he pre-empted her by saying, "Well Rose, are you ready to leave Newbold Revel tomorrow as we arranged?"

Regret overwhelmed her but she said as brightly as she could, "Yes I will leave. That is what I promised. I am very grateful that you have let me stay so long."

Robert looked at her speculatively, wondering how to phrase his words though he had been thinking about it for some time. "There is of course another alternative," he said and she looked at him in surprise. "You could stay with me. Not of course at Newbold Revel, but our estate comprises several properties across the area. One of them in particular belongs to me, it is in my possession, not my mother's. I could set you up there."

She was taken aback and her eyes were wide as she asked, "What do you mean, set me up?"

Robert smiled. "My beautiful innocent Rose. I mean live with me, be my mistress."

She gasped, "But you are my uncle."

He shrugged. "Perhaps. But only your half-uncle even if it's true, your mother's half-brother. I never met her, we were as strangers to each other. Besides the Pope has now given a dispensation for uncles to marry their nieces, it will be in some great lord's interests no doubt."

Bel felt the world reeling around her as the fish ponds tipped like an earth tremor and the overcast sky seemed to lower.

Robert Malory was serious as he said passionately, "I want you Rose. You are the most beautiful girl I have ever seen. I wanted you from the moment I first set eyes on you. I would keep you well at Saddington where I have a manor, small but comfortable. I would buy you anything you might need. I know I am much older than you but I would do everything in my power to make you happy."

Bel could see the passion clouding his brown eyes and realised she had always sensed something more than courtesy in his regard of her. "You are a married man," she said accusingly.

"Most men with mistresses are," he replied, a tinge of amusement in his tone. "My wife and I do not share a close rapport, do not let that consideration worry you.

In fact we sleep in separate chambers these days as she wishes no further children. She would know nothing of the matter and if she did it would be of little concern to her."

Bel could not believe the two Elizabeth Malorys would be so unconcerned. But the over-riding objection that had shocked her most was that she believed firmly that Robert Malory was her uncle.

"Think about it," he urged, mistaking her hesitation. "What is your alternative? What are you going to do now?"

What was she going to do now? Return to London and find some menial work like returning to Master Hawley's workshop or helping Betty Trimble until she had enough money to return to France? Robert would probably give her money as he had once promised and this would tide her over for a while. But she would eventually have to find work and she was skilled at nothing but minstrelsy which was not a respectable occupation for a girl in England. Even if she returned to France what could she do then? She had no kinsfolk and even there it would be difficult to work as a minstrel without her father or Renard. Her heart ached when she thought of Renard. How she longed to be loved, to belong to someone again. She liked Robert Malory, she believed he was basically a good man. But he was married with children and her mother's brother, even if only her half-brother. It would be impossible to cast aside her feelings of guilt if she betrayed his family and her own. She hadn't replied to Robert's question but he knew she had no answer. He was studying her speculatively, his booted foot braced on a low stone wall. He didn't touch her but she was conscious of his masculinity enveloping her with physical intensity. She liked him, felt at ease in his company, but she was afraid of all the implications of him becoming her lover. Yet she wanted to stay here and it would mean she could stay here on the estate belonging to her grandfather, just as she had always dreamt. She could live in comfort she had never known with no worries about money or what to do next. Temptation was warring with doubts and Robert saw the conflict reflected in her face, in the troubled eyes and the biting of her lip.

"I could take you there tomorrow," he said, leaping on her uncertainty. "I would say I am accompanying you to Coventry and we could go to Saddington instead, it is on the road to Leicester, between the towns of Leicester and Market Harborough. What do you say?" She uttered a little sigh, a sound compounded of fear and longing. "Please agree, Rose," he urged. "Now that I have met you I cannot live without you."

"Can I have a little time to think?" she stammered, frighteningly aware that she was weakening.

He saw it and his heart thrilled but he did not want to lose the advantage and he pressed, "Not too long, don't forget we have to leave tomorrow. You must tell me tonight."

She nodded but her eyes were downcast and she ran back to the manor without looking at him. He watched her go, torn between desire and guilt. He knew it was not an honourable thing to do, to take advantage of her helplessness. She was very young and innocent and had nowhere to go. He had always considered himself an honourable man and had always put his morals above those of his father even though he wasn't a knight and indeed had come to view the ideals of knighthood with some cynicism. But since Rose had made her unexpected appearance in his life he had fallen under her spell with the intensity of a young man in his first love affair and was determined to squash all misgivings in order to keep her. He salved his conscience by vowing to do all in his power to make her happy and give her some of her Malory inheritance, albeit by a morally ambiguous route.

In the solitude of her little chamber Bel stood by the window looking through the opaque green glass to the murky outline of the moat and the surrounding fields merging into dusky woodland. It seemed as if a storm threatened, the dark clouds had grown bigger, almost covering the sky, and the birds had stopped singing, an apt accompaniment to the storm of her thoughts and emotions. Of one thing she was sure and that was that she didn't want to leave this place. The thought of returning to noisy, dirty, plague-stricken London and Master Hawley's shop or even the Throstle Inn was unbearable and even if she had money the prospect of a lone journey back to France was daunting. Robert Malory had promised to keep her in comfort. The thought of sleeping with him frightened her, she had only ever been with men who had violated her. But she liked him. She would have found him attractive if he had been a stranger asking for her hand instead of her uncle and a married man. At least she knew there would never be children from the liaison. A flash of lightning forked the sky and thunder rumbled in the distance. She had no-one to advise her. She was completely alone and she needed someone to be with her.

At supper Lady Elizabeth and Robert's wife politely expressed their regrets at her parting on the morrow and wished her a safe journey. She murmured her thanks, feeling ashamed that she was considering deceiving them and unable to face them with a direct gaze. When they finally rose from the table Robert remained by her side as he had done throughout the meal. It had been an uncomfortable situation as he had tried to make polite conversation and she had avoided his eyes. Now he squeezed her hand unobtrusively to make her look at him. As she lifted her head he already saw the answer in her eyes before she took a deep breath then whispered, "I will stay with you." She noted with surprise that the storm had died away during the meal.

CHAPTER 8

Saddington

In company with Robert Malory, Bel left Newbold Revel the next morning on a spring day fresh and bright after the storm, supposedly on the road to Coventry but when they reached the village of Stretton he took a northerly route.

"The pony is only hired for no more than two weeks. I have to return it to a livery stable if I am not returning to London. When I made arrangements in London and they knew my destination they said I must return it to the 'Green Man' in Coventry after that time," Bel said apologetically.

"Then I shall arrange for that to be done, have no worries. I shall also pay the remainder of your hire. I am going to find you a good horse and teach you to ride properly," Robert said, frustrated by the slow pace.

They rode mostly in silence for another hour or more, Bel nervously contemplating the consequences of her decision and Robert pensive. By mid-morning they had arrived at the small hamlet of Saddington and beyond the huddle of timber-frame houses clustered around a pond Robert turned into a pathway that eventually led to a small manor house. The house was protected on all sides by an encircling wall of beech trees so only when they passed through these sentinels did the building come into view. It was less than half the size of Newbold Revel, built of weathered oak beams closely studded and filled in with brown plaster and with a roof partly of thatched reeds and partly of stone. Though obviously an old house it looked well-maintained and the sun's rays played on the leaded glass panes in the windows, a large one reaching through both storeys to the right of the arched doorway and two small ones on each of the two storeys to the left. There was a small paved courtyard and on one side stood outbuildings of which one was a stable.

As soon as they clattered into the courtyard a young boy appeared from the stable and at the same time the door was opened by a man in a tawny canvas jerkin over a linen shirt with grey woollen hose hanging loosely on his thin legs. He was of middle age with sparse grey hair and thin body but he looked fit and agile with small shrewd eyes in his brown crinkled face.

"Everything is prepared for us, I sent word yesterday," Robert said to Bel.

"But that was before I agreed to come with you." There was a trace of accusation in her tone, but Robert merely smiled as he greeted the servant by his name of Benjamin.

The boy took their horses and Robert ushered her through the door which led immediately into the hall. It was of modest proportions though the roof soared high to where the thatch could be seen between the cruck-frame rafters and the tall glazed window filled the space with light. The stone-flagged floor was strewn with clean rushes and there was a fireplace and hearth along one wall, though the original centre hearth could still be discerned and the hole in the thatch for the smoke to escape had only recently been filled in. The walls were of timber beams inset with wattle and daub but the plaster had been painted with ox blood, as was the stone of the fireplace, and created an impression of warmth. Against one wall stood a pine table, darkened with age, on which were placed pewter goblets with a decorated pottery amphora and a leather ale jack together with a wooden bowl of new apples, a dagger, a leather-bound volume and a chessboard. Behind the table a representation of two knights in combat was painted in gaudy colours on a wooden board. A trestle table with sturdy box stools with cross bars and fretted side pieces stood in the centre of the room and at either side of the hearth, ready set with logs in case the evening turned chilly, were placed two beechwood chairs with arms. The high backs to keep off the draughts were painted red and blue in a squared design. A couple of greyhounds wandered in and settled themselves in front of the hearth and Robert knelt down to pat them before saying, "Come upstairs."

He guided her through a door at the rear of the hall into a passage which led to the newer part of the house, the kitchen and dairy and where a flight of pine stairs, obviously of recent construction, climbed to the upper floor. "The staircase used to be on the outside but I had it moved when we roofed this part of the house with stone," he explained as they climbed up into a spacious chamber. The plastered walls were washed blue as a summer sky with a decorative frieze of red and gold lozenges, and through the open casement wafted a breeze that rustled the lavender and herbs strewn on the floor, releasing their scent. Two large box stools with painted panels and cushions of red velvet were in place on each side of a small table painted in a chequered design of red and black on which was set another book and a writing set together with a wine jug and goblets of earthenware decorated with bold swirls and circles in blue and green. A long oak coffer with candles in pewter candlesticks was set against one wall, behind which hung a gilded wooden board painted with mythological beasts. Although there was no fireplace a brazier was set ready with logs. There were plentiful hooks for hanging things and some of Robert's clothes already hung there. Bel surmised that the richer furnishings in this chamber signified that Robert used it to entertain and do business. However her eyes were drawn to the most striking feature of the room – an enormous bed raised on a dais with four carved posts. A counterpane of red wool woven with a design of fleur-de-lys covered the bed, and hanging on tenters behind the bed-head was a cloth of darker red velvet edged with a wide gold border of heraldic symbols.

"A feather mattress, sheets of fine linen and a fur-lined blanket," Robert said proudly, following her gaze. "There is an anteroom and garderobe beyond. This is my chamber, and now yours." He removed her cloak and then his, then taking her into his arms kissed her gently on the lips. He smelled of wood smoke and thyme, she suspected he had recently washed his hair, and his body felt strong and protective so that she shivered with a mixture of apprehension and excitement. But he said, "Dinner has been prepared for us so let us go and eat."

In the hall the two chairs had been set at each end of the table and they sat facing each other across a distance while they dined on well-cooked meats and home brewed ale served by a young maid, though Bel ate very little through nervousness.

"You must make known each day what you wish to eat," he commanded. "I shall not always be here of course and you will have to spend much time alone but Benjamin is always here to order matters together with the maidservant known as Nan. Another girl comes from the village when needed and there is young Sim in the stable and for any odd jobs that need to be done. I will find you a good horse because you might like to ride to the markets at Leicester or Market Harborough, about an hour's distance. Sim will always accompany you and you need not hesitate to buy anything you need."

She thanked him, saying, "I do not mind being alone, I like to spend time on my own." She was already thinking how much she liked this house which seemed grand by her standards and the fact that it was going to be hers excited her.

As soon as he could Robert guided her upstairs to the bedchamber. He began to unfasten the laces of her pink gown and she realised what she had agreed to. "I am not a virgin," she said and her voice sounded high-pitched. He looked at her in surprise and she hung her head as she cried, "I have been violated more than once. It was against my will. I have never been with a man of my own free will."

Robert paused and when she lifted her head she could see the compassion in his face. Then he said, "And now?"

She swallowed and hesitated. Then realising she had made her own choice she took a deep breath and whispered, "Until now."

She slipped out of the folds of her dress, standing in her shift and shivering.

For a brief moment Robert thought, "*I should not be doing this*." She looked so innocent and there were doubts about their relationship, he probably was her kinsman and in any case he was more than twenty years older than she was. But he was too aroused by her to change course now, he had come too far and she had said she was willing, he had not forced her. He removed the covers of the bed and laid her on the cool sheet then he began to divest himself of his boots, tunic and hose. Within the opening of his shirt she could see the thick dark hair on his chest. He made to lie beside her but suddenly she cried, "You said my grandfather was accused of rape. Was it true?"

Her face was anxious and he was sensitive enough to understand how her mind was working. Sitting on the bed he said carefully, "My father was a very attractive man, attractive to women. He was married to my mother when he fell in love with a girl from nearby Monks Kirby but she was already married and she refused his love. He was besotted with her and one day he went to her house and whether she was willing or not I do not know but they were surprised by her husband. In order to save face and to placate her husband she cried rape and my father allowed her to do so. The husband publicly accused him."

"What happened?" she asked.

Robert replied, "It was as well he was never made to pay the penalty though he was brought to justice. The woman's name was Joan, he always had a liking for the name." The statement hung in the air. Robert did not want to confess that the name of Bel's mother was one factor inclining him to believe her story, he preferred not to remind either of them that he was probably her uncle at the moment he was preparing to make love to her.

Robert Malory had many years' experience of making love and a genuine kindly nature. He took hold of her hands and began to kiss each finger one by one then the palms of her hands and the inside of her wrists, moving along her arm to the crook of her elbow and the hollow of her throat, gently persuading her and all the time murmuring how beautiful she was and how he loved her until her fast-beating heart calmed a little. He stroked the mane of black curls then kissed her eyelids and gently touched her lips. But as his kisses became more passionate and his caresses more intimate she began to whimper.

"Don't be afraid," he soothed her, "I won't hurt you. It won't be as before, trust me. I want to enter into the heart of the rose, lose myself in its petals. I shall teach you to know pleasure, intense pleasure that you will want to repeat time and time again."

Despite herself Bel gradually began to succumb to the delights he was working on her and the shadow of guilt clouding her consciousness began to dissolve. He was an attractive man pleasuring her in a way she had not thought possible as his hands moved with his lips uttering words of love. He laid her on her side and lay beside her as he prepared to enter her, not wanting to revive bad memories for her by pressing his weight on top of her. Her fear dissolved in his gentle embrace and physical excitement grew inside her as she tightened her grasp on the solid flesh of his body, digging her fingers into his shoulders. When she could no longer resist, her surrender washed away all past fears and regrets in an explosion of physical delight. Then he held her close, continuing to caress her, and she lay with her head on his chest listening to his beating heart and feeling safe and protected for the first time since she had parted from Renard.

When finally they dressed for supper Bel felt embarrassed by their changed relationship and found it hard to meet his eyes as he gazed on her. However Robert showed no trace of unease, leading her into the hall, pulling out her chair at the table and serving her himself with food and wine and she began to relax in the unaccustomed solicitude. Afterwards they sat in the chairs by the empty hearth and he began to amuse her with incidents of his early life while she felt drawn to tell him about her life with her father, which she had never before confessed, and he was even more entranced by her history. He refilled their wine cups several times and though she felt pleasantly disorientated, when he led her back to the bedchamber he let her sleep quietly in his arms without disturbing her.

Once Bel had grown accustomed to his lovemaking the summer became a time of great content. She loved the little manor house and began to feel she belonged there as part of her Malory inheritance, even when Robert was absent. She had never had a settled home before and this was the most luxurious she could have imagined for herself. She thought of herself as the mistress of the manor and didn't like to think that maybe there had been others brought to this house of his. One day she couldn't help herself and dared to ask, "Have you brought other girls here?"

"No," he replied firmly. "This is my private retreat. Even my wife has never stayed here. It is where I come to get away from things, please myself, though sometimes close friends will visit. It is furnished and managed to my own personal taste though now I want to share it with you."

Many days he wouldn't come and she began to look forward to the times when she heard the hoofbeats on the stones of the courtyard. When he was in the house she would arrange his meals and play the part of the mistress of the household. In the evening they would sit and talk together.

"I am sorry we cannot read together but my books will hardly be of interest to you, one of them is the history of the hunt and venery and the other is of husbandry," he said. "I will buy you a book that you can enjoy."

But she would tell him stories that her father used to narrate to her and sometimes she would put on her fine gown and play her flageolet and sing to him. Now that he knew her father had been a travelling minstrel and that she used to entertain with him he loved to hear her sing and when she said she liked to play a lute he promised to buy one for her birthday.

"How old are you Rose? Eighteen?" he asked, knowing she could not be much older for even with her eventful life there was an appealing innocence.

"I'm seventeen but in a few weeks I shall be eighteen. My birthday is the twenty first day of May," she said proudly, thinking of how Renard had made the date for her.

"Then I shall buy you a lute as a gift," Robert said, but a shadow crossed her face as she thought of the present Renard had bought for her the year before, a time which seemed so long ago now. Once again she wondered where he was and what he was doing.

Robert was perplexed by her change of expression and said, "Would you rather have a necklet of pearls instead of a lute?"

The smile returned to her face as she replied hastily, "Oh no, I'd rather have a lute," surprised that he should need to ask, and he laughed out loud. He loved her ingenuousness and the absence of greed. As he came to know her well he was compelled to revise his initial opinion that she had thrust herself onto the Malorys in the hope of gain. She would sometimes ride to the town with young Sim to buy merchandise, but only spending moderately on the things she had a genuine need for. It was he who bought her new clothes and fairings. She had never had more than a change of clothes and he loved to watch her face when she tried on a new gown he brought her.

Robert kept to his promise and on her birthday he presented her with a beautiful five course lute of spruce and walnut with an intricately-carved rose ("in honour of you") for the sound hole beneath the nine strings. He had offered to take her to Coventry to watch a joust on the jousting ground but she had refused, remembering her birthday of last year when she and Renard had spent a wonderful day at the Pas d'Armes then entertained at the house of the Bailli. She thought it might revive memories she was trying to forget but which she kept locked away in a separate compartment of her heart, like a jewel in a casket. Instead she played the lute for him, caressing it like a long-lost lover as she found her way again along the strings and frets after a long absence.

Robert had been disappointed that he could not take her to watch the jousting which he loved but said, "I am determined we should celebrate your birthday with something special, my Rose, so next month on Corpus Christi we shall go to Coventry to see the plays."

This relatively new festival of the church was familiar to Bel who had seen religious processions in France but she was intrigued and excited by what would happen here. It also meant that she would see Coventry, as she had wished to do when she first saw the city in the distance as she rode with the merchants.

Early on the June morning they rode to Coventry. Bel wore a new gown of fine yellow wool with hanging sleeves, simply made because Robert had decided her beauty needed no embellishment. She had new ankle boots of kid leather and a padded yellow velvet hat on a broad silk band, from which cascaded her black curls. It had originally had a veil but she had cut it off, being too proud of her beautiful hair to cover it. She had hated wearing linen caps when she had been working in London. She wasn't quite sure of English customs but knew that married women had to cover their hair and unbound hair could be interpreted as wanton but she wasn't married and her position with Robert Malory was ambiguous. Robert wore brown hose and boots beneath a wine-coloured velvet tunic with wide sleeves over inner sleeves of figured brocade. His brown hair waved on his shoulders beneath a soft-crowned hat of murrey velvet with an upturned brim and ribbon streamers which fluttered in the breeze. They looked a handsome pair, though Robert realistically surmised people would think Rose his daughter, especially with her unbound hair. As they rode through the East Gate and across the river Sherbourne into the city centre, Bel eagerly looked around her, fascinated by the obvious wealth of the wool city - the numerous large churches and prosperous shops, half-timbered with jettied upper storeys. The city was indeed as splendid as Humphrey Meadowcroft had boasted. The well-paved streets however were crowded with people and it was impossible to make headway so Robert left their horses in the stable of the King's Head and they progressed on foot.

"The pageant has already started, in fact it probably began about six," he explained as he held her tightly by the arm to push through the crowds. "Come, let's go to the cathedral square where we should have a good vantage point."

On the way he pointed out to her the priory with its tall-steepled church, and the imposing St. Mary's Guildhall that Humphrey had talked about but it was impossible to observe closely because of the crowds lining the street. They were chattering in a crescendo of excitement as the rumble of wheels on the cobbles could be heard. When they reached the cathedral church of St. Michael a waggon was parked on the square, surrounded by a mass of attentive spectators of all ages and classes.

"We have arrived at the Noah play," Robert explained.

Noah was trying to persuade his wife into the Ark but she resolutely refused to enter, continuing with her spinning and deriding his tale of a great flood. The audience was roaring with laughter as the arguments between them increased in volume and scurrility. Noah then tried to beat his wife into submission but she was evading him and returning his insults with gusto. When she spoke directly to the women in the audience, "*We women may curse all ill husbands, I have one, by Mary, that should loose me of my bonds, Yet with game and guile I shall smite and smile and give him his meed,*" they were all shouting with encouragement. The two began to fight to the great amusement of the onlookers until finally the waters got so high that Noah's wife at last consented to get into the Ark. When the wagon rumbled away to its next stopping place, accompanied by thunderous applause, the crowd eagerly awaited the next scene to appear.

All day the waggons arrived at intervals to tell stories from the Bible, moving around the city in a long procession. Bel often found difficulty in understanding the rough country speech which was so unlike the courtly language of the literature she had known but nevertheless she was entranced, amazed at the scenery erected on the wagons - the model of the Ark with blue cloth for the surrounding water, the burning bush, the pyramids of Egypt. Sometimes the action was presented on two levels at the same time as in the Nativity when the angels appeared in the sky above the stable with the Holy Family.

"This Nativity pageant is always produced by the goldsmiths because of the three kings with their valuable gifts. The guilds finance the productions and each guild chooses an episode that has some relevance to their trade," Robert explained. He said that the wool merchants would have produced the play about Joseph and his coat of many colours and Bel wondered if Humphrey would have been involved. She was afraid of meeting him and Philippa, wondering what their reaction might be towards her liaison with Robert and was thankful not to encounter them. By afternoon Robert was getting bored but Bel resisted all attempts to lead her away. Finally however he said, "My dear Rose, I am in sore need of meat and drink so I am afraid you will have to miss one of the most spectacular episodes where the devils drag all the sinners away to Hell's mouth accompanied by flames and lightning. This show will not end until the light fades."

Bel was loath to leave but she complied with his wishes and they made their way back to Smithford street to the King's Head. "If you are too tired to ride back we can stay the night here at the inn," he suggested.

"I'm not too tired, I used to walk for miles in France. I would rather go home, I've had enough of inns," Bel said, and he was pleased with her words, not only because he was loath to publicise his relationship with her if they were seen, but also because she wished to return to what she called home.

The two hour ride brought them to Saddington as the light was fading. As they approached the manor house fireflies sparkled in the bushes to the accompaniment of noisy grasshoppers clicking in the grass, an owl hooted in the wood, and Bel thought how beautiful an English summer evening could be and how much she loved this house that was now her home. Later as she lay in Robert's arms thanking him for a wonderful day, she thought how fortunate she was as she looked back to the summer of the previous year when she had been working in Master Hawley's workshop, afraid of the plague and with the terrible burden of an unwanted child. She still missed Renard and thought of him often as a stray word or memory crept into her mind but Robert was filling her life with the care and companionship she had lost.

The summer passed in a mixture of warm sunny days, frequent showers that enhanced the scent of honeysuckle and lavender, fierce thunderstorms where lightning forked over the beech trees and long balmy evenings when the sun seemed loath to set and she could sit contentedly on a stone bench in the little herb garden, sometimes with Robert, sometimes alone. She was often alone for he could never stay too long but this enhanced the pleasure of his return. She was happy in his company and he doted on her. But she never felt lonely. She liked to wander in the fields around the house or in wet weather sit in the hall or bedchamber playing her lute and reading the leather-bound book Robert had bought for her - a French romance entitled 'Le Roman de la Rose' – "because you are my romance of the rose," he had said. She had never owned a book before and read it over and over again.

She would sometimes make forays to the markets at Leicester or Market Harborough and besides little personal items like veils and laces she would also buy thread to decorate the linen in the house, for although she had never wanted to use a needle again she now thought of the house as hers and liked to put her mark on it. She was also making Robert a gift of a shirt embroidered with his monogram for his own birthday. After all her recent hardships her life had acquired a luxury and security that she had never known. With the thoughtlessness of youth she dismissed his wife from her mind, believing what he had said that there was no love between them. And sometimes the thought would flit into her mind that she was only receiving what was her due as a member of the family, Sir Thomas Malory's granddaughter, not by having to be Robert's mistress as he claimed. But she had grown to like him and she was happiest when he could come to the manor and they could be together. He taught her to play chess and he sometimes let her win, and she liked to hear him talk for he was a man of the world with much experience of life and he told her the Malory history and the events of the civil war. They would often ride out for he taught her to ride competently the horse he had found for her – a strong but gently-natured gelding whom she promptly named Troubadour. And at night she would fall willingly into his arms ready to enjoy the pleasure he gave her. Even in her innocence Bel recognised his expertise and once said to him, "Have you been with any whores, Robert?"

"Not many", he replied. Then he said, "My wife is not of a sensuous nature. She considers she has done her duty by giving me two healthy sons. You have taken me into Paradise, my darling Rose. You have made my life happier than it has ever been."

She tried to get him to talk more about her grandfather and the memories he retained though he was often reticent saying, "I never saw much of him when I was growing up, he was always away fighting and then he spent eight years in prison, much of it in London."

However one night when they were lying in bed together and he was in a mellow mood she ventured, "You told me that the story of Sir Thomas's rape was not quite the truth. What about the other crimes?"

"It's a long story," he said at last, "My father is not an easy character to explain, but you have to realise that he was living through a terrible time of violence and unrest and there was general lawlessness everywhere. For years he lived respectably, was a member of the Parliament and acquired a knighthood, and it's strange that he suddenly began a life of crime for it would seem that he really did do many of the things for which he was accused. One night he went with ten accomplices to batter down the doors of Combe Abbey near Coventry and stole money and valuable ornaments. Then he returned next day with a hundred armed men to do a great deal of damage and steal more valuable artefacts and some arms. Another time he attacked the Abbey of Axholme in the same way. There could have been some dispute with the monks that I am ignorant of, churchmen are notoriously greedy and self-serving, amassing fortunes for themselves."

Bel looked troubled. "It seems strange that he suddenly began to do these things," she murmured, a frown creasing her brow.

"What you cannot understand, my dear Rose, is the nature of those times. I have tried to explain to you the circumstances of the war between the houses of York and Lancaster but unless you have experienced personally the barbarity, the treachery, the overwhelming ambitions of these noble families who stopped at nothing to gain power for themselves, you cannot believe the general lawlessness this conflict unleashed." He paused, trying to order his thoughts. "It's possible that my father, like many others, was trying to raise a private army, both for protection for himself and his estate and to support his own candidates in the struggle for the crown. He was a natural fighter and not the sort of person to stand on the sidelines and wait for fate. It's feasible that he could have asked the monks for funds to support his chosen side in the war and when they refused he took matters into his own hands, knowing how the abbeys amassed great fortunes for themselves. I believe he stole money and valuables for this purpose. He obviously did not steal in order to enrich himself or Newbold Revel for you can see there is no evidence of great wealth there and I can't even afford to buy myself a knighthood. He once took a posse of men and stole a lot of cows and a whole flock of sheep from a neighbour, bringing them to Newbold Revel. Now as you know our house is not big enough to warrant such supplies and again I think they were to feed a prospective army. I could be wrong because, as I said, I was only a small boy and between 1460 and 1470 he was in prison, mainly in Newgate in London. On the other hand his feud with the powerful Duke of Buckingham is a little different."

He had forgotten that she was not familiar with the English nobility and she asked, "Who was this Duke of Buckingham?" having difficulty with the name.

"He was Humphrey Stafford, a great-grandson of King Edward III who caused such havoc in your country of France. The warrior King had several sons and his youngest son Thomas of Woodstock was Buckingham's grandfather, but on the maternal side. Buckingham was a great soldier himself and a mighty magnate. He was known to my father through two sources – one military because he was Captain of Calais at the same time my father was in France, and the other political because they were members of Parliament together for the shire of Warwick. The disagreement between them could have been initiated by either of these factors. Also Buckingham was trying to increase his power and influence in Warwickshire at the expense of landlords like my father and his liege lords, especially the Earl of Warwick. His destruction of the Duke's deer park at Caludon certainly sounds like personal revenge for something. And it cannot have been merely the conflicts the civil war unleased because even before the war started he took a large band of men to ambush the Duke with the intention of murdering him while he was riding through the woods of Combe Abbey. But I know nothing of the circumstances, I was only a boy. Perhaps he was just a criminal after all, this attack was premeditated, my father had collected a large body of men together."

"Perhaps the Duke had done him some great injury," Bel suggested. She reflected sadly how her father had been murdered in Châlons and did not like to think of her grandfather being guilty of such a terrible crime.

"Then I have no idea what it could have been," Robert said.

"Have you never asked Lady Malory, your mother, about his activities," she asked tentatively.

"She always refused to talk about his crimes. It was a very difficult time for her when he was in prison for so long and she had to keep the estate together. During the so-called Wars of the Roses, estates were being snatched and changing possession at the slightest opportunity and she succeeded wonderfully in managing his affairs. So much so that when he died he left everything in her hands rather than mine."

Bel sat pensive, trying to absorb the information and make sense of it and Robert continued, "He was a great fighter, brave and resolute, I was somewhat afraid of him when I was a boy. He did some amazing exploits. Once when he was imprisoned he escaped by swimming the moat and when he was jailed in Colchester castle he escaped by overcoming the guards with sword and daggers."

"Where did he get weapons in prison?" Bel asked, entranced by the story. "Surely they must have taken them off him when he was captured."

"He must either have seized them from the guards or someone must have smuggled them to him, I told you he was an amazing character. When eventually he was imprisoned in Newgate he was considered such a dangerous prisoner that severe restrictions were put upon his guards not to let him escape. I think the fact that he was imprisoned for so long yet never brought to trial was because his fighting skills and his ability to raise large bands of men posed a threat to both the Yorkists and Lancastrians at different times, I told you he fought on both sides. In the beginning he was a Yorkist, being an associate of the Earl of Warwick here in these parts, but then towards the end he fought for the red rose, the House of Lancaster, which was ultimately the loser."

"I don't think he was a wicked man," Bel said pensively, fascinated by the story. "Could I visit his grave?"

"He's buried in Greyfriars in London," Robert answered. "Close by Newgate prison," he answered wryly."

"I wish I could have known him," she said wistfully. "Do you believe my story now, that he was my mother's father and my grandfather?"

Robert thought for a time then said, "Yes I think I do, I know now that you would never seek to deceive, it is not in your nature. I think my father would have been proud of you, Rose." He hesitated then continued, "There is something I would like to show you. It is at Newbold Revel but I will bring it here one day."

The bright colours of summer faded into the muted hues of autumn but the brown leaves of the beech trees still had a glow of red and gold, not yet ready to fall and lie crisply on the ground. The days grew shorter, the morning air tinged with frost and the evenings damp and chill.

Candles were lit early and Benjamin the manservant began to light the fire in the brazier in the bedchamber. Bel now had a mantle lined with fox fur to wear over her gown when she was reading in the evenings and when she was alone she was glad of the fur blanket on the bed. Robert was often busy overseeing the harvest and the gathering in of stores for the coming winter but one October evening when crunchy brown leaves and beech nuts carpeted the grass she heard his horse clatter onto the stones of the courtyard and rushed to meet him.

When he had divested himself of his cloak and hat and Benjamin had served spiced wine they sat by the fire in the hall exchanging news. Then he went to retrieve a leather satchel he had brought with him.

"This is what I promised to show to you," he said, unfastening the buckle and taking out of the bag a huge sheaf of papers bound together with strong cord.

"What is it?" she asked and in answer he undid the cords and handed to her the first page. There was no title and she began to read the words on the page:-

'*It befell in the days of Uther Pendragon, when he was king of all England, and so reigned, that there was a mighty duke in Cornwall that held war against him long time. And the duke was called the Duke of Tintagil. And so by means King Uther sent for this duke, charging him to bring his wife with him, for she was called a fair lady, and a passing wise, and her name was called Igraine.*"

"It's an Arthurian romance," she said.

"It's a compilation of *all* the Arthurian stories ever written, in English and in French, in verse and prose, in history and legend, put together in English for the first time," Robert said. "Nearly a thousand pages. The first time that all the stories of King Arthur and his knights from all the different sources and from different periods of time have ever been put together in one book."

"What a great accomplishment," she cried in amazement. "Where did you get it? Who wrote it?"

"My father wrote it. I have had it in my possession since he died."

Bel was dumbfounded and Robert turned to where a ribbon marked a page in the sheaf of papers he held and began to read, '*this was drawn by a knight prisoner Sir Thomas Malory that God send him good recovery, Amen.*' It's his handwriting. He wrote it during all the years he was in prison."

"Mon Dieu!" breathed Bel. She looked at the neat closely-written script on the paper made of linen and wood pulp, a thousand pages.

They sat in silence for a time as she slowly turned the pages, overwhelmed by the tremendous task the knight-prisoner had undertaken, years of painstaking work alone in his cell with quill and ink.

"He must have had access to all the separate works, French poets like Chrétien de Troyes and English historians like Geoffrey of Monmouth but by what means I do not know. It is unlikely that one person would have had all the books in one library. It would seem that he had several noble friends who were willing to lend him manuscripts," Robert said.

"I did not know he was a scholar," Bel was overwhelmed by the huge manuscript she was holding.

"Oh he was no scholar," Robert refuted her. "In many ways he was a plain simple man and definitely more used to wielding a sword than a pen. He knew French of course from his time in France." He paused significantly. "It is even possible that he could have begun the book while he was in France where French manuscripts were easily available. He tells the story chronologically from the birth of Arthur to his death but it does not mean he wrote it in that order. The tales of the individual knights, Lancelot, Gawain, Tristram, Perceval, could have been written at any time, as and when he found the books."

"If he wasn't a scholar why do you think he suddenly decided to write such a lengthy work?" Bel asked, still amazed by what she was learning.

"The simple answer is to pass his time in prison," Robert answered. "But I believe it was more than that. He had a passionate belief in chivalry, in the ideals of knighthood as a code of behaviour and was immensely proud of his own knighthood, it was the most important factor in his life. Others might consider he did not always live up to it but I think he believed that he did, in his own way and for his own reasons, after all his knights of the Round Table are not perfect and often fall short of their ideals. I think he felt that chivalry and knighthood had been betrayed by the conflict between the houses of York and Lancaster and this grieved him deeply. He began by fighting for the Yorkist cause but then at the end he turned to the House of Lancaster as the rightful inheritors of the Crown. I think, towards the end of the book at least, he wanted to show the dangers of rebelling against a rightful king and bringing disaster on the realm, as happened with Mordred's rebellion against King Arthur."

Once again they sat in silence, the logs in the grate falling into ash with a gentle hiss amongst the embers. Then Bel asked, "What are you going to do with the manuscript? You cannot just leave it to decay or disappear when you are no longer here."

"Yes I have thought about that. I have kept it for eight years but I don't think it should be lost in obscurity. I think people ought to read it. I have considered giving it to Anthony Woodville, Lord Rivers. Do you know of him?" Bel shook her head and Robert continued, "He is the Queen's brother, one of the most powerful men in the country and head of the Prince of Wales's household, a champion jouster and an experienced soldier. But he is also one of the most cultured men in England, a writer of poetry and prose and a patron of literature. He was known to my father through the war and it's possible my father was able to use his library. I think he might be interested in the manuscript."

"Can I read it?" Bel asked.

"I would love you to," Robert replied and she felt she had finally gained his trust. "I will leave it with you." He began tying the sheets together again and placing them carefully in the satchel. "But enough of books, the candles have burnt low and it is time for bed." The candles were guttering fitfully in their holders, casting shadows on the red walls as he led the way up the stairs.

When Robert left in the late afternoon of the following day Bel began immediately to read the huge manuscript written by her grandfather. She read for days, page after page of the neatly scribed manuscript, unable to put it down as she sat by the fire in the hall whilst the October squalls tossed the beech trees and splashed spatters of rain against the windows and down the chimney making the coals hiss. A few of the stories she knew from her father, some of them had been made into songs.

The story of Tristram and Iseult had been a particular favourite and she had once sung a lament together with Renard when they were entertaining at the Bailli's house at the tournament in Amiens. At last she came to the end – *'Thus of Arthur I find no more written in books, neither more of the very certainty of his death have I ever read but that he was led away in a ship wherein were three queens. Now more of the death of Arthur could I never find but that the ladies brought him to his grave which an hermit bare witness. But yet the hermit knew not for certain that it was the body of King Arthur. Yet some men say in many parts of England that King Arthur is not dead but had by the will of our Lord Jesu into another place and that one day he shall come again."*

Tears came into her eyes as she read the end of the story and thought about the man who had written it. She felt a link with him, he had been a minstrel too, telling his stories not in song as her father had done but in words that over the years he had learnt to use with so much skill to convey emotion as much as music did. She had been so engrossed in the story that she had not noticed that she had not seen Robert for several days and he had sent no word that he might be delayed which was unusual. She sat still for a time, her mind still dwelling on times past, of Lancelot and Guinevere who had taken for themselves the religious life as a penance for their forbidden love. She did not think she could be a nun like the beautiful Guinevere even though she had committed a sin with a forbidden relationship.

Suddenly she was aware of Benjamin standing in the doorway from the inner passage, ashen-faced, his shoulders shaking and with tears in his eyes. She rose and went to him asking, "Benjamin, has something happened?"

He found it difficult to speak but at last croaked, "Master Robert is dead."

The words were so unbelievable that they did not register and she looked at him blankly.

"Oh Mistress Rose, Robert Malory is dead," he repeated.

There was a humming in her ears so that it sounded as if the hall was full of swarming bees and she had to cling onto the chair as her knees began to buckle and the floor rushed to meet her. "That cannot be" she stammered. "He is forty years old and always in the best of health. You must be mistaken."

"It is quite true. His horse caught a hoof in a rabbit hole in the rain and stumbled, throwing him to the ground. He fell and broke his neck, dying instantly. He is dead and buried. No-one thought to send us word until now. His mother, Lady Malory, is near to death herself with the shock."

Bel did not realise that the scream rebounding through the hall was coming from her own mouth until the frightened face of the young maid Nan appeared in the doorway. She began to sob, deep gulping sobs that shook her slender frame as the wind tossed the unprotected branches of the trees outside. Then she fell to her knees, folding her arms tight around her body as if to shield herself from a terrible blow. Benjamin stood helpless, wiping his eyes on his shirt sleeve, but Nan realised she was suffering from shock and tried to lift her up into her arms. Bel resisted but finally with Benjamin's help Nan managed to raise her and taking her arm led her upstairs. She tried to persuade her to lie on the bed but Bel shook her head and stood instead by the window, clasping her hands tight and gazing unseeinglyly as her tears blurred her sight more than the rain streaking down the panes. Her whole body seemed torn in two, her heart thumping painfully. She couldn't believe that Robert Malory was no more. She would no more see his strong kindly face, hear his stories, be surprised by his gifts, feel the protection of his body. He seemed to have been taken away from her as strangely as King Arthur. She never saw his corpse and she didn't know where he was buried, perhaps he had been spirited away by three beautiful queens and was enjoying their love in some enchanted castle, ready to return one day. She clutched at the fantasy, believing that somehow one day he would step into the house and take her in his arms. But in reality she knew the sickening truth that he would never come back to her.

Weakness finally drove her to her bed but she continued to cry, remembering how she had shared the bed with him and feeling lost in the space. She had often slept alone there but always with the certainty that he would come eventually. Nan brought her food but she refused to eat, though she accepted the infusion of camomile which the girl thoughtfully prepared. Then as her senses gradually recovered from the shock, her grief was compounded by the terrible realisation that she would have to leave Saddington. She could no longer stay here without Robert's protection. Benjamin had said old Lady Malory was dying. The estate would be in the hands of a thirteen year old boy and whoever would seize the opportunity to control him.

Bel did not know what she would do or where she could go. She had been so happy here, so loved the house and mistakenly believed she was secure for a long time. She realised now how prophetic the name of the place had been – Saddington. She decided she must leave on the morrow before anyone could evict her.

She rose early and began to prepare for her departure. Her face was still red and blotched with crying but she had summoned up all her reserves of strength now that she knew it was inevitable. For a short time, half a year, she had enjoyed living on her grandfather's estate with his son. Now she had to accept that she would never see Newbold Revel again. At least Robert Malory had provided her with supplies for the future. She had a purse of money which he always left with her, a horse, a stock of good clothes, some pretty trinkets, and a precious lute. She began to pack everything into panniers that she could carry on horseback. She also took the satchel containing her grandfather's manuscript. For she now had decided what she would do. She would take it to Anthony Woodville as Robert had suggested, it would be something she could do for him. She would find Lord Rivers, presumably in London, and show him the manuscript. That would be one way of paying her debts to Sir Thomas and Robert Malory and give her a purpose now that she was alone again.

CHAPTER 9

Lord Rivers

Because Bel was afraid that someone from the Malory family might arrive shortly at Saddington she wished to get away as quickly as possible. Also she could not bear to stay in the house without Robert whose sudden loss had shaken her to the core. With the intention of trying to safeguard her grandfather's book to sustain her she made plans to try and find Anthony Woodville, Lord Rivers, whom she surmised would be in London. She now had a good horse to make the journey but needed travelling companions and her thoughts inevitably dwelt on Humphrey Meadowcroft who might have messengers going there, or who would know someone who did. She did not know where his business was in Coventry but as he was an important merchant she assumed that once she arrived in the town there would be someone to direct her so decided to travel there first. She asked the stableboy, Sim, who had often accompanied her to markets, if he would ride with her as far as Coventry. Sim was about her own age, a tall gangly boy with a thatch of unruly black hair that sprouted in all directions and a squint in one of his green eyes, and he accepted eagerly for he had adored Rose, as he knew her, since he had first set eyes on her. They divided the panniers containing her belongings between both horses for due to Robert Malory's generosity Bel now had more possessions. She hung her lute in its bag across her shoulder and Sim carried the satchel with the manuscript. Benjamin watched them go with tears in his eyes after taking an affectionate farewell of her, and Nan was openly weeping.

It was with a sense of overwhelming sadness that she left the place, so aptly named, but everything had been done in such haste that practicality had dampened down her grief. Though she wanted to look back at the house she kept her gaze fixed firmly ahead as they rode through the sentinels of beeches. It would now be only a place in her dreams. Her time here had ended.

The road to Coventry and the entrance through the gates brought back memories of Corpus Christi when she had ridden here with Robert and on that wonderful day had had no premonition that her happy life would so abruptly be brought to an end. However her thoughts were soon forcibly concentrated on the matter in hand as they made their way along the bustling city streets, trying to avoid gossiping citizens and loaded carts impeding their passage.

"The wool merchants have their premises near the Guildhall," Sim volunteered and led the way to where the imposing building stood in the square. He then began to ask around and it wasn't long before they found someone who knew the house of Master Meadowcroft and directed them to Woolrich street. Finding the house as directed they passed through a stone archway and into a courtyard with buildings on three sides. Facing them was a three-storeyed stone house while the range of buildings on either side appeared to be weaving sheds and storerooms. Bel dismounted and rang the iron bell hanging on a rope beside the door which had an intricate pattern of decorative iron. When the door was opened by a man in the clothes of a serving man she gave her name and asked to see Mistress Philippa Meadowcroft. Impressed by the young girl's beauty and affluent appearance he invited her into the house saying he would call his mistress immediately so Bel told Sim to look after the horses and followed the servant. She had hardly time to step into the main hall before there was the sound of running footsteps and Philippa appeared through the door at the opposite end of the room, her excited face beneath the white linen turban flushed almost to the colour of her ruby gown.

"Belfiore, what a wonderful surprise," she cried, going to her with outstretched hands and Bel realised how long it had been since she had heard her real name. Philippa held her at arm's length studying her with interest. Bel was wearing her blue travelling cloak but her head was covered by a close-fitting cap of blue wool edged with a thick band of beaver fur and she wore expensive leather gloves and ankle boots. "I can see you found your Malory kinsfolk," she said approvingly. "But what brings you here? Come and relate all your news."

She led Bel to a box chair beside the inglenook fireplace where logs were glowing and while she went to call a servant to bring some heated wine Bel took the opportunity to look around her. The Meadowcrofts lived in some luxury. The hall had a high collar roof with arched braces, the floor was a patchwork of coloured tiles, the walls oak-panelled with each panel outlined in red giving a chequered effect, and the customary furnishings showed signs of wealth – colourful painted chests and a side board displaying silver, embroidered wool cushions on the benches and the several high-backed chairs.

When Philippa returned she prompted Bel to relate the happenings of the past half-year and Bel began to give her an abridged account. She said only that she had been living with the Malorys, making no mention of her special relationship with Robert except to say that he had died and she wanted to undertake a mission to London on his behalf, in which enterprise she thought Master Meadowcroft might be able to aid her.

Philippa expressed her sadness and surprise at Robert Malory's death and said that although her husband was at present busy sorting and measuring cloth in the store rooms at the side of the house it would soon be the time for dinner to which Bel was cordially invited. She accepted willingly but felt bound to say that she was accompanied by the stableboy who was at present minding their horses which were loaded with her belongings.

"Then he must eat with us also," Philippa said. "The apprentices and my husband's workers always join us for the meal, there is quite a company. I will have someone show him where to stable the horses."

Humphrey Meadowcroft arrived for the mid-day dinner, dressed in a sober belted gown of dark blue wool as befitted his working day though enlivened by a heavy silver chain. He was as surprised and delighted as his wife to see Belfiore and welcomed her heartily, seating her beside him at the table. He listened to a repeat of her account and expressed his condolences at the untimely death of Robert Malory. However he was not enthusiastic about her proposal to ride to London.

"November is not the weather for riding," he said, a comment endorsed by his wife.

"If you do not wish to return to Newbold Revel you could stay here with us," Philippa suggested. "I would be glad of your company, Belfiore, winter is such a tedious time, at least until Yuletide. I can seldom ride out, it is difficult to keep warm or find varieties of food and if we wish to stay up late it costs a fortune in candles."

"To whom does your business refer?" asked Humphrey, ever curious and finding household talk superfluous.

"I wish to see Lord Rivers, Anthony Woodville," Bel replied.

Humphrey showed his amazement and Philippa's brows arched in surprise. "The Queen's brother!" The wool merchant was impressed but said, "How do you know he is in London? He spends most of his time at Ludlow castle in the Welsh marches where he is tutor and guardian to Edward, Prince of Wales."

This was news to Bel and she bit her lip in disappointment. However Humphrey continued, "He will most likely be in London for the Yuletide celebrations so I suppose if you wish to see him it might be as well to go there now for he will not wait until December to bring the young prince from Wales."

"I came to ask if you knew of anyone who might be going to London so that I could travel with them," Bel asked.

"As I said, the winter months are not favourable for long travel, November is usually wet and the roads get very miry," he said. "However there is one possibility. The sheep are mostly sheared in the spring when the merchants buy most of their wool from the farmers but there is a small amount of shearing at this time.

The farmers cannot keep all their sheep during the winter months, there isn't enough grass for them to feed on, so they kill some for the Yuletide feasts but firstly they are shorn of their fleeces and though they are not of the best quality at this time some small merchants buy them because they are cheaper. Swithun Markland is such a one and I think he might be going to London shortly to sell the wool he has bought."

"You should send word to him, Humphrey, and until then Belfiore must stay here with us," Philippa commanded. "I presume your stable lad will be returning to Newbold Revel." (Bel had not mentioned Saddington.) She called the boy from his place with the youngest apprentices and said, "You may return home now, Mistress Belfiore will be in good hands here until she finds companions to accompany her further."

The lad hung his head and said gruffly but obstinately, "I could accompany her."

Philippa looked critically at his thin figure and his working clothes – a brown leather long-sleeved jerkin over a coarse linen shirt which didn't quite cover his skinny wrists, with overstockings on top of his loose-fitting canvas leggings and a woollen hood turned down – but said gently, "I think more than one person would be necessary when travelling at this time, and someone older than you." Noting Bel's more affluent appearance, not to mention her outstanding beauty, she considered privately that it would take an army of mounted men to protect her thoroughly from robbers and worse.

Later in the stable when Sim was unloading Bel's belongings from the horses to take them into the house, he pleaded, "Can't I come with you. I can fight, I'm stronger than I look and I'm not afraid."

"You will still be needed at Saddington," she said. "You cannot just leave your employ. It is a serious offence to leave your master."

"It was Master Robert who employed me. I don't want to stay there without him, in fact there will be little for me to do and when we get a new master he might not wish to keep me."

"Still you are honour-bound to return there," she said firmly.

Philippa was happy to have Bel stay with them for the night, especially when she saw the lute, and persuaded her to play and sing for them in the evening. She was always delighted to do so, singing songs her father had sung and which she had sung with Renard but also a new English one that Robert had taught her, 'Bird on Briar.' Philippa tried her best to dissuade her from another journey, making all sorts of objections like the weather, the discomfort, the dangers but Bel was adamant. Although she enjoyed Philippa's friendship she had no wish to impose herself on another household after living independently for a time and besides she had always been accustomed to travelling.

"Have you somewhere to stay in London until you succeed in meeting with Lord Rivers?" Philippa asked, once she realised her appeals were fruitless.

Thinking of Betty Trimble at the Throstle, Bel assured her that she had.

"And what do you intend to do afterwards?" asked the merchant's wife. She was bursting with curiosity as to what business her friend should have with the Queen's brother but Bel had never enlightened her. She muttered some non-committal reply because she had no idea what she would do once she had entrusted her grandfather's manuscript to Anthony Woodville.

Humphrey Meadowcroft was as good as his word and having sent a messenger to enquire of Swithun Markland he ascertained that the merchant was planning an immediate journey to London with his fleeces, accompanied by two fellow-merchants and their servants. He was willing for Bel to join their company so she made hasty farewells to the Meadowcrofts and prepared to depart. She was loading the panniers onto her horse Troubadour, wondering whether he would be able to manage all of them, when Sim appeared beside her holding his horse's bridle.

"I'll take some of them on *my* horse," he said.

She regarded him sternly. "Have you never been back to Saddington?"

He shook his head. "No. I'm coming with you."

"Have you been here in the stable all this while?"

"I slept here. They gave me food in the kitchen. I'm coming with you, don't say me nay. You are my mistress now Master Robert is dead. I can help you in all sorts of ways, do things for you, I won't need to be paid much. It's too late for me to go back to Saddington now."

Bel made her decision. She was a Malory and Saddington had been her home. She had as much right to employ him as anyone else and she was sure Robert would have approved. It would seem she had acquired a squire of her own, not a very prepossessing one but her own nonetheless. The baggage could be shared between them at least.

As she made her final farewells to the Meadowcrofts she thought to ask Humphrey, "Where is Lord Rivers likely to be found?"

The merchant considered for a while then said, "I think when he is at the court his residence will be in the Tower, at the royal palace there."

So it was to the Tower of London, the great white bastion standing four-square on the north bank of the Thames beyond London Bridge, that Bel intended to apply once she was settled in the city. She was ready to return to London from where, only six months ago, she had begun her journey northwards with so much hope.

On arrival in London and parting from her travelling companions, Bel, accompanied by Sim, went first to the Throstle in Gracechurch Street. Betty welcomed her with open arms, squealing with astonished delight when she walked into the tap room, marvelling at how well-dressed and seemingly prosperous she was and eager to hear all her news. Once again she gave an adapted version then asked the innkeeper if she could provide her with a chamber for perhaps a few days.

"You can stay willingly as my guest without charge," said Betty but Bel refused her generosity.

"I shall pay you the agreed rate. You have been generous in the past when I was in need but I now have the money to pay. I shall also need somewhere for my attendant to stay, perhaps in the stable loft with your own lad, he will lend a hand to whatever needs doing."

Betty agreed willingly, glad of an extra pair of hands, while Sim thought the straw bed in the loft equivalent to Paradise as he realised his dream of seeing at last the great city of London.

Now Bel and Sim were standing on Tower Hill before the first of the three stone bridges across the moat, ready to enter the precincts of the Tower. Sim looked respectable in the plain doublet of bottle green wool with matching hose that Bel had bought for him, with a red felt hat pulled down over his black hair. Bel had chopped it to a semblance of neatness, though she could do nothing about his squint. Still she had a servant of her own and that was something.

The Tower was a formidable fortress encircled by a double range of fortified walls. The first bridge across the moat was guarded by the Lion Tower which led into a courtyard where visitors waited until someone came to enquire their business. When Bel said she wished to see Lord Rivers she was disappointed to be told that the Earl was not in residence but would be arriving for Yuletide in about a week's time. There was no alternative but to return to the Throstle and wait.

She waited impatiently, for there was little to occupy herself, though Sim considered himself in Paradise as he wandered around the great city he had always longed to see, marvelling at the monuments, the many churches and great houses, the noisy markets and the ever-changing panorama of the river. Oblivious to the squalls of rain and chill winds, he loved to go down to the wharves to watch the foreign ships taking home good English cloth after unloading their luxury goods of silks and spices, and was constantly walking the bridge to see the sights from a better vantage point.

As December ushered in darker days, when the curfew sounded too soon after supper and frosts whitened roof-tops and cobbles, Bel prepared to visit the Tower again. She was apprehensive but the impatience of waiting had sharpened her resolve and this gave her confidence. Once again she and Sim made their way across the moat and when they presented themselves in the courtyard of the Lion Tower they were informed that Lord Rivers had arrived from the Welsh marches. Because Bel, beautiful and well-dressed, looked the sort of woman who might be acquainted with the Earl they were told to proceed to the Middle Tower on the second bridge. On arrival there Bel repeated her message and they were subsequently directed across the third and final bridge which was flanked by the two large round bastions of the Byward Tower. This was the last impediment but without more ado they were allowed to pass through into a grassy square inside the inner curtain wall.

Bel and Sim looked around in amazement as they realised they were within the precincts of the ancient Tower of London. The inner curtain fortifications had twelve towers on the battlements but it was the square mass of the White Tower standing sentinel in the middle of the bailey which temporarily halted their progress as they stared in awe at the prison. However built into the curtain walls were ranges of newer buildings with large windows, turrets and imposing entrances. Bel had no idea where to go but the bailey was busy with soldiers and attendants so she boldly accosted an old courtier walking slowly across the grass and asked him where the royal apartments were. Showing no surprise he pointed out a range of buildings overlooking the river and marked by three tall towers, pointing out to her that one was the Wakefield Tower from the doorway of which the royal barge could directly depart down the Thames. When Bel explained that she had something of importance to give to Lord Rivers she was directed to one of the several entrances into the palace.

They passed through a double-barred and studded door into a vestibule staffed by armed guards but when she repeated her business she was given permission to proceed to the Great Hall. She was surprised at how easy it had been to gain entrance and after walking down a long stone passage to another set of oak panelled doors which opened into the hall she was admitted immediately when she said she was of the Malory family, granddaughter of Sir Thomas Malory of Newbold Revel, with a communication for Earl Rivers. She was told to wait amongst the crowds standing patiently with petitions and recommendations in the lofty hall where arras hangings swayed gently in the draughts while a page was sent on his way with a message. After a short time he returned and while Sim was ordered to remain behind she was escorted through the hall and out the other side. There then followed a series of enclosed passages, low doorways, up several flights of narrow twisting stairs and into St. Thomas's Tower.

As she ducked her head beneath the low lintel she found herself in a surprisingly small room where she was faced immediately by Anthony Woodville. Seated in a chair with a gilded high-pointed back he could scrutinise visitors before they had opportunity to study him thoroughly. In front of him was a table with manuscripts and a fine ivory writing set, a quill of which he was just returning to the ink horn from the vellum which still shone darkly wet as he sprinkled the sander across it. Until he looked up and studied her carefully she had time to take in her surroundings. Most of one wall was taken up by a window which overlooked the river and shed plenteous light in the small space. The leaded panes were large and were surrounded by a decorative border of heraldic devices in stained glass of blue, red, green and yellow that cast shifting patterns on the rose-coloured floor tiles. She noted a lute lying on a red-cushioned bench below the window. The other walls were painted in a chequered pattern of blue and green with a gold frieze, and along one wall stood a gilded chest bearing several leather-covered books. She absorbed her surroundings almost unconsciously for in the first instance her gaze was fixed on the Queen's brother Antony Woodville, Lord Rivers, as he rose to greet her.

He was a tall man about the age of Robert Malory, and one of the most handsome men she had ever encountered. His light brown hair was cut straight to his shoulders, his nose was long and straight, his deep brown eyes beneath finely-arched brows were widely-spaced and direct with a tinge of melancholy in their depths. It was a face of strong character, of undoubted intelligence but also of gentleness. Instead of the fashionable short doublet and hose he wore a long gown of crimson embossed velvet over a crisp white pleated shirt, a gold chain belt with medallions encircling his slim waist, fur-lined sleeves hanging down from his slender hands with tapering fingers. Bel felt suddenly overawed by this handsome, wealthy, powerful man. But Anthony Woodville in his turn was captivated by this unexpected young visitor – likeness paying mutual tribute to an instinctive appreciation of beauty. She was wearing a silk gown of deep blue, a darker shade than the cloak draped from her shoulders but the scarlet hem making a splash of colour around her feet. A blue felt hat with beaver trim was perched well back on her head to reveal a cascade of black curls. He was also immensely curious about her.

He seated her in a chair but stood beside her, casually leaning on the desk as he said, "So you are the granddaughter of Sir Thomas Malory, a knight I once knew well."

"My name is Belfiore Lechanteur, my lord."

The name intrigued him, together with the musical accents, but he made no comment. He knew that Sir Thomas Malory, like most English knights, had spent time in France. He waited for her to explain her visit and in the meantime pleased himself by looking at her.

"Sir Thomas's son, Robert Malory, recently died. He had in his possession a manuscript he thought you might be interested in. He was going to give it to you but now he is dead I decided to do what he wished and bring it myself."

At the mention of a manuscript Anthony Woodville's expressive eyes quickened with interest. "What kind of a manuscript?" he asked.

"It is a compilation of all the stories of King Arthur and his knights that have ever been written, poetry and prose, history and legend, all together in English for the first time," she said, repeating the words Robert had used. "It was written by Sir Thomas Malory while he was in prison." Anthony Woodville was thoughtful. "I lent him some books but I thought he just wanted to read them, to while away his time," he said. "This sounds a very interesting project, all the Arthurian material written in English. Do you have the manuscript?"

"It is a thousand pages long, it is rather heavy, I thought I would make certain that you would like to see it first, my lord," she replied apologetically.

"Yes I would very much like to see it," his tone showed his enthusiasm. "Could you bring it to me? Are you staying in London?"

"I am in London for a time. I will bring it tomorrow if you wish."

"At the hour of nine? I will have my servant Griffith await you at the entrance to St. Thomas's Tower, go directly there. I am grateful that you have taken the time to come to me and I am indeed most interested in this manuscript. I look forward to our next meeting."

Anthony Woodville raised her from the chair and calling for his page he courteously bade her farewell, to her embarrassment kissing the tips of her fingers as he did so. She wasn't accustomed to being treated as a lady of consequence. The page led her back to the Great Hall where Sim was waiting for her, standing in a corner and trying to keep out of sight amongst the crowds but avidly watching all the nobles passing to and fro. He was delighted when she informed him that they were to come again on the morrow.

Back at the Throstle, Betty was overcome by Bel's news that she had been received by Lord Rivers himself. "He was very kind and courteous, not at all proud and arrogant. And he was so very handsome."

"All the Woodvilles are handsome," Betty said. "The Queen herself is so beautiful. I have seen her a few times in royal processions through the city. Her hair is like spun gold, as bright as gilt when the light shines on it. It reaches to her waist and she always wears it uncovered apart from a diadem. Her clothes are magnificent, brilliant colours of purple and scarlet, all covered with jewels." Betty's gaze flickered involuntarily to her skirt and bodice of brown fustian, the sleeves of her coarse linen shift rolled to her elbows for working. "I can't believe I have someone living in my inn who has been inside the royal palace and talked with the Queen's brother. Oh Bel you have become such a fine lady and I am so honoured that you should still be my friend."

Her plain dough face crinkled and there were tears in her little bright eyes.

"Don't be silly Betty, I am not a fine lady, my uncle bought me some clothes and I am come on an errand for him, Lord Rivers is known to the Malorys. Fine clothes do not change what a person really is. I have no desire to live in a palace with all the formalities constraining me, nor would I change my place with kings and queens who walk with danger every day of their lives. Do you know I am happiest when I am entertaining, playing music and singing as I used to do with my father," ("*and with Renard*" she thought silently.) "Minstrelsy is my lifeblood, not the blue blood of nobility." As she spoke the words they came to her as a revelation. For a short time she had found pleasure living the life of a gentlewoman with Robert Malory but it was not the kind of life that would have satisfied her for ever. Her Malory blood was only a small part of her inheritance, music and travelling spoke louder. "I have a lute now, I will play and sing in the inn tonight if you would like," she proffered. "I learnt a new English song that will be very apt for the throstle, it is called "Bird on Briar."

Betty accepted joyfully but with a proviso saying, "I will pay you something, your money will not last forever."

Bel knew that was true but said nonchanantly, "I will earn enough with donations. Do you know that one night in France we collected four shillings." She bit her lip as she realised she had never mentioned Renard to Betty.

"By our lady, that would make a feast for all our customers," the innkeeper cried but surmised she was speaking of her father and no further comment was made.

That evening she enthralled the Throstle's customers by playing her lute and singing. Sim had been allowed to join the company and was amazed at his first experience of her music. He had also been confused by the fact that she was being addressed as Bel, though he continued to call her Rose because that was how he had always known her and what Robert Malory had called her.

The following day Bel returned to the Tower with Sim carrying the leather bag containing the hefty manuscript. They received no hindrance and at the entrance to St. Thomas's Tower Lord Rivers' attendant, Griffith a burly Welshman, was waiting as promised. Telling Sim to wait there, he took the satchel and led Bel to the same small study as before.

Anthony Woodville greeted her courteously and seated her in a chair which he had set opposite him at the table. Today he was wearing hose and boots with a high-necked pleated doublet of black velvet studded with pearls. He opened the satchel eagerly and took out the manuscript. For several minutes he was silent, turning over the pages and studying them while Bel watched in silence.

"This is truly extraordinary," he said at last. "May I keep it to read the whole?"

"It is for you to keep," Bel replied. "It is nearly ten years since Sir Thomas Malory died and since that time it has been in the possession of his son Robert. Now *he* is dead but he once told me he intended placing it in your hands so I have done so. He thought that as you have a great collection of books and manuscripts it might be safe with you otherwise it might just be lost or destroyed which would be a great pity."

"Indeed it would, especially as Sir Thomas took so long with this unique enterprise. I can assure you, Demoiselle Lechanteur, that I shall take great care of it. Have you read it?" He took it for granted that a lady like herself could read.

"Oh yes, all of it. It's very good," she said artlessly and he smiled at her enthusiasm. "I wish I could have kept a copy for myself but at least I hold it in my memory. And now my duty is done, my lord." She made to rise, then thought that perhaps she ought to wait until Lord Rivers commanded.

Antony still did not dismiss her and asked, "What are your plans now? Do you intend to stay in London or return to Warwick shire?"

Because he was perceptive he saw a flicker of apprehension in the blue eyes which were the same colour as the cloak she was wearing over a yellow gown with a matching velvet cap on a silk band.

"I shall not return to Warwickshire but I have no future plans as yet," she admitted, realising how often she confessed to not knowing what to do next.

He studied her intently and she felt uneasy, her eyes travelling around the room and coming to rest on the lute lying on the padded bench beneath the window.

It was a very beautiful and costly instrument inlaid with ivory and mother-of-pearl and he saw her gaze linger on it with interest and something more. "Do you play the lute?" he asked, picking it up and handing it to her.

"Yes," she replied, taking it from him and he nodded for her to try it. She began to play, tentatively at first then more confidently as she released the beautiful tone of the instrument, making the sweet notes of a danse royale sound even sweeter. She laid it down regretfully at last saying apologetically, "I'm sorry, I was carried away, it's such a beautiful instrument."

Her youth and natural charm pleased him and he said, "I would like to show my gratitude for the manuscript you have given me and I think I have a proposition that might please you. Is there a place where I can contact you?"

A wave of apprehension coursed through her veins even as she stammered, "I am residing at the Throstle Inn in Gracechurch street." Could it be possible that Anthony Woodville was making the same sort of proposition as Robert Malory – he was the same age, a very handsome man with an appealing manner, but one of the highest nobles in the land. The Earl had no intimation of Bel's fear for he did not realise how little she knew of him. Anthony Woodville, despite being a renowned soldier, jouster, cultured courtier and patron of literature, was a very religious man who had made pilgrimages to Rome and Santiago di Compostella. Besides his manifold gifts he was renowned for his piety and, unlike the rest of the court, for his morality. He had been faithful to his wife and though she had died several years previously he was only now contemplating marrying again.

He said, "I will send a message to you within the next few days if you will stay in London until you hear from me. Meanwhile I thank you sincerely for bringing to me your grandfather's manuscript. I regret I cannot thank Robert Malory but you can be assured I will keep it carefully in his name."

He rose and raised Bel also, bringing her hand to his lips in a formal bow. Then he called for the Welshman to escort her to the entrance to the palace where Sim was waiting.

Bel's thoughts were in turmoil as they returned to the Throstle. She was happy she had succeeded in placing the manuscript in the hands of Anthony Woodville as Robert had wished and was confident that he would take care of the manuscript. She had found the Earl an attractive and sympathetic person but was worried about the proposition he had mentioned and the reward he had talked about. She had had no alternative but to give him her place of residence and it would be a grave insult to a person of his high rank not to wait until he contacted her again. Yet she thought of running away. She considered taking Sim with her and going back to France. But it was the season of Yuletide and Betty was hoping for a repetition of last year's celebrations when she had shared in the Throstle's festivities. She knew Sim would enjoy it and besides it was not the weather for travelling. It seemed as if another period of anxious waiting lay ahead.

Anthony Woodville was reading Sir Thomas Malory's manuscript with pleasure. He was familiar with most of the books the knight-prisoner had used, especially the French ones, and as he continued into the book he was impressed by the manner in which the inexperienced writer had combined all the varied stories into a unified whole to make an absorbing narrative. Such a work deserved to be read and not consigned to oblivion. But he had also not forgotten the beautiful girl who had given it to him.

As the season of Yuletide approached the nobility came from their estates to participate in the royal festivities which as usual were held at Westminster

Palace, the primary royal residence situated on the riverbank west of the city. Two such noble guests were Margaret Countess of Richmond and her husband Sir Thomas Stanley.

There was a huge company amassed in the Great Hall which was the largest hall in England, its three hundred foot length proportioned by the hammerbeam roof soaring so high that flying buttresses had had to be erected on the outside walls to support it. The gathering of the royal family and richly-clad nobles was extensive, the noise of chatter and music echoing around the vast space, the vibrant colours of costly garments and jewels almost blinding in their brilliance. King Edward was his usual affable self, his six foot four inches and blonde hair making him a striking figure even if it hadn't been comple-mented by cloth of gold and the crown he always wore, and he mixed easily amongst his noble subjects laughing and joking. Queen Elizabeth with a gown so encrusted with jewels that she needed her ladies to hold up the hem as she moved, her long silver-gilt hair beneath a diadem hanging past her waist in long plaits threaded with dia-monds, always drew the eyes of even those who disliked her. The two young princes and their four sisters basked in their father's demonstrative pride and the correspond-ing attention they received from his sycophants. But Anthony Woodville was seeking someone in particular and found her walking along one of the arched arcades that formed a passage all around the hall.

"My Lady Countess," he bowed low.

"Lord Rivers," she returned the salutation, holding out her beringed hand for him to kiss.

Margaret Beaufort and Anthony Woodville did not care for each other but always masked their dislike by politeness. Margaret did not particularly hold it against Anthony that he had originally fought for the Lancastrian cause (in which his father and brother had been killed) until his sister married King Edward IV when he had became a Yorkist supporter. She and both her husbands, Henry Stafford and Thomas Stanley, had done the same when survival was essential. But she hated all the Woodvilles because she considered them upstarts and not of noble blood, though she had to concede that Anthony was educated, cultured and religious, attributes she shared and appreciated. For his part Margaret's arrogance was at odds with his own generous gentle nature and he mistrusted her scheming on behalf of her son. He also resented the way she dismissed all the Woodvilles as undeserving upstarts despite their natural gifts, especially as her own royal blood came from a source of bastardy. Yet Anthony was due to marry into the Beaufort clan after Yuletide. His second wife was to be Mary Lewis, Margaret's cousin, daughter of her aunt Elizabeth Beaufort, so there was at present a suspension of their hostility.

The Countess of Richmond barely reached the shoulder of Lord Rivers, even with the tall padded hat of gold brocade with rubies interwoven in the gold thread. Yet the gaudily painted walls of the arcade and the decorative hangings of purple, gold and crimson draped from the arches could not diminish her magnificence. Her long-trained gown in the much sought-after vermilion brocade from Italy, heavily trimmed with ermine, the wide stiff collar of gold tissue over which fell the gossamer folds of voile cascading from the head-dress, should have dwarfed her tiny figure. Instead her regal bearing, the imperious lift of her head and the piercing small eyes gave her a distinction that belied her small stature.

They made courteous conversation for a while, Margaret commending the forthcoming nuptials. Then Anthony said, "A young lady has been brought to my notice whom I think might be of service to you, Countess. She is kin to the Malorys of Warwickshire where she has lost her grandfather and recently her uncle. She is young and cultured, reads well and is skilled in the art of music. Her comportment is modest and charming. She is also French."

Lady Margaret pursed her lips and her mind worked quickly. "Then why have you not suggested this paragon as suitable for service with the Queen, or perhaps even your new wife-to-be."

A half-smile hovered at the corners of his mouth as he said, "She is young and beautiful, Lady Countess." He knew that his beautiful vain sister, now approaching her fortieth year, would not want such competition and he surmised that Margaret would grasp the implication without his having to state it openly. "As for my wife-to-be, I consider she would not welcome my attempts to regulate her household in the early days of our marriage."

"She might also wonder how you came to know the girl and why you should be furthering her interests," Margaret thought, although she knew Anthony Woodville did not have a reputation for licentiousness even though he had been a widower for six years. Aloud she said, "May I ask how you came to know the girl, my lord."

"I made her acquaintance through the provenance of a manuscript she brought to my notice," he replied. Margaret was impressed though tried to conceal it and Anthony seized the opportunity to press his suit,

"I thought the fact that she is French might be of interest to you, my lady. It is her native tongue."

Margaret looked at him sharply. "Yes I like to have my attendants able to read French texts for me with some semblance of accuracy." The dissembling was not lost on Anthony Woodville and she was aware that he recognised this. "Will you send a message to the girl and tell her to come to my apartments in the Lanthorn Tower when Yuletide is done," she said.

Lord Rivers promised to do so saying, "Her name is Belfiore Lechanteur."

He thanked the Countess of Richmond, making his farewells with his usual courtesy.

Bel had heard nothing from Anthony Woodville and was relieved, for the Christmas festivities at the Throstle Inn, though enjoyable, had been overshadowed with anxiety. However she now had to think of what to do, deciding that her best option was to return to France. She was on the point of making preparations when a messenger in royal livery brought a letter with Lord Rivers' personal seal. Trembling with apprehension she opened it and began to read the neat hand.

My dear Belfiore. I hope you are not offended by my presumption but I have taken steps to secure a position for you as a waiting-woman to the Lady Margaret Stanley, Countess of Richmond. I know she will appreciate your ability to read French and play music to her as well as converse about literature, especially French literature. As a member of her household you will live well and be rewarded. If you are agreeable, she has asked that you make your way to the Queen's apartments in the Lanthorn Tower at the royal palace in the Tower of

London and ask for her by name. As you told me you had no immediate plans for the future and you have been left bereaved by your Malory kinsfolk I consider that this could be an ideal solution for you. My kindest regards, Anthony Woodville.

Bel had to read the letter through several times before she fully understood the import. She was being offered a position in the household of one of the noblest ladies in the land, not to do household chores but to play music and to speak French. Tears sprang to her eyes at the kindness of Lord Rivers. He had not merely sent a message but written a personal note in his own hand.

Betty Trimble was overwhelmed by the news. She was sorry to be losing Bel again but wide-eyed at her friend's good fortune. "I can't believe that anyone I know is acquainted with the nobility and the royal household," she stammered over and over again, bursting to tell all the regular clients of the Throstle. Sim was heartbroken at not being able to go with her and Bel was sorry too. However the problem that he would be left without employment was solved by Betty saying that she could use him at the inn and Bel promising that if ever she had need of him again she would send for him.

Then dressing in one of the gowns Robert Malory had bought for her, of good quality but modest, she set off again for the Tower, Sim accompanying her for what might be the last time. It was a new adventure again and she did not know what awaited her in the chain of events that had begun at Newbold Revel with Robert Malory and her grandfather's book that had led her to the royal palace and Lord Rivers.

CHAPTER 10

Lathom

Bel found life with the Stanleys comfortable but stifling once the novelty had worn off. She soon realised that Sir Thomas and Lady Margaret each had their own households and were largely independent of each other so Bel saw little of Sir Thomas and her duties were carried out in mainly feminine society. When Lady Margaret was not occupied with her chaplains (which was often) or attending to the running of the various estates with the steward, the comptroller and the bailiffs, she expected her ladies to read or play music to her or engage in intelligent conversation. When she was otherwise occupied they were not allowed to be idle but had to do needlework, working on altar cloths or panels of religious tapestry or repairing exquisite silver and gold embroidery which she would entrust to no-one else. Bel found the small neat stitches she had learnt to be proficient at in the tailor's shop now worked in her favour though she kept the source of her expertise a secret. The countess also liked her ladies to paint or gild religious statues or decorate devotional books. Sometimes she would allow them to play chess and Bel was glad of Robert Malory's tuition but though she expected skill in the game it was never to eclipse her own. They must always dress well, usually at their own expense though she sometimes would pass on items she had no use for, after first having them stripped of any precious adornment, and occasionally would give them bolts of cloth on special occasions. She held high store by cleanliness and examined their hands and nails, and they must always speak in quietly moderated tones. Bel often felt she was living in a nunnery. She had always been used to masculine company – travelling independently with her father from an early age then for a brief time with Renard and latterly living with Robert Malory. She enjoyed reading French and Italian to the Countess but they were often religious texts, and she loved playing music and singing but it was only within the confines of their small company and she longed to be entertaining a wider audience.

When Anthony Woodville had arranged for her to meet Lady Margaret in her solar in the Lanthorn Tower, the site of the Queen's apartments in the royal palace and which Margaret was allowed to occupy by virtue of her husband's position, Bel had arrived at the now familiar Tower of London with great trepidation. She had dressed in her yellow wool gown overtopped by the mantle of tawny wool lined with fox fur that Robert had bought her, her hair partly covered by her yellow hat, this time with a creamy veil beneath, and Lady Margaret surveyed her with what seemed to be approval. She had been surprised by the Countess's small stature but intimidated by her piercing scrutiny and sharp voice which addressed her in French, accurately phrased but with an English accent. Bel's confidence rose as she conversed in her native tongue and when she was handed a lute and ordered to play some music her nervousness vanished. Lady Margaret herself was satisfied with the girl - well dressed without luxury, modest but without subservience, and possessing talents obviously suited to her requirements. The girl's beauty was no threat to her, she had learnt to ignore and even surmount such apparent competition many years ago. Belfiore Lechanteur had been offered a position as a lady attendant and had begun a new life with the Stanleys.

Because Sir Thomas had many properties in the north, the midlands and the Welsh borders they travelled a lot from one estate to the other and Bel enjoyed these times, travelling from one place to another was something she had always been used to and freed her from the constrictions of a women's solar. Also instead of walking she now had good horses to make the journeys easier. Sometimes she used her own horse, Troubadour, but if the destinations involved overnight stays they would use livery horses or mounts from the Stanleys' extensive stables. Most of the Countess's household hated travelling and dreaded the constant peregrinations to the different properties, the long uncomfortable journeys, the houses cold and damp until they could be aired, the tedious packing and unpacking of chests. But Bel loved to be out on the road seeing the unfamiliar English countryside and relished being released from the confines of hall and solar. The roads were often rough, miry or ridged with frost in winter, dusty and pot-holed in summer, but not dangerous for they travelled in a great convoy of servants and up to a hundred baggage carts transporting beds and other furniture with furnishings and tapestries to make each property equally comfortable. Despite her delicate stature the Countess was an expert horsewoman and enjoyed travelling, the recent gift from her husband of new harness for her favourite horse had greatly pleased her.

They occasionally visited the court and Bel awaited her first visit with trepidation. She was excited at the thought of being in the royal palace of Westminster and seeing the King and Queen but afraid of being socially inadequate and completely ignorant of the procedure. However she need not have worried because the routine was no different from anywhere else when they accompanied the Countess and most of the time the ladies were kept confined at the Stanley's London house on Ludgate Hill and occupied with the same tasks they normally performed. They prepared the Countess for royal visits but were left behind as usually only her chief attendant Ursula Clifford was allowed to accompany her, one of the numerous north country progeny, who had served her long.

Bel however relished the opportunity to be in London again and sometimes managed to escape and see the familiar sights once more. Her companions were shocked that she dared to venture out alone but promised to cover for these short forays in the unlikely event that the Countess might discover her absence and be understand-ably angry at the disregard of polite etiquette. One day she decided to go and visit Betty Trimble at the Throstle Inn. She wondered if Betty might be a little uneasy with her new position but she dressed as simply as possible and armed with an enamelled tin of squares of coloured marchpane she had purchased from a confectioner in the Cheap she took the familiar path to the inn.

Past the church and the monastery and along the wide street she soon saw the wood and plaster building with the painted door and shutters and the sign of the bird swinging from its metal perch. She entered eagerly crying "Betty" but her call was answered by a stranger and the owner of the deep masculine voice appeared from the kitchen – a heavily-built man with a ruddy face and a thick black beard which matched his curly hair.

"Yes what do you want?" he began brusquely, then seeing the beautiful girl in the tap room his tone changed to one of deep respect as his eyes travelled over her with appreciation.

"I came to see Betty Trimble, the landlady here," Bel said, her lilting accent charming him the more.

"She isn't here. She got married and moved away. I'm the landlord here now, Goodwin Greencart at your service Mistress."

A flood of disappointment washed over her and she realised how much she had been looking forward to renewing a part of her past. "Do you know where she has gone?" she asked but the landlord shook his head.

Just then from the kitchen could be heard the scrape of hobnailed boots on the flagged floor and through the back door burst a young man crying excitedly, "Rose! I knew it was your voice."

She looked at the gangly lad with untidy black hair and a squint and cried joyfully, "Sim, is it you. Are you still here?" and to the amazement of the stable lad and the landlord she flung her arms around him and hugged him. "Do you know where Betty is?" she asked him.

Sim shook his head. "She got married again. A tin merchant from the West Country who used to make regular visits to London and stayed at the inn. She went back with him to Devon or Cornwall or somewhere.

She was very excited. I was lucky that Master Greencart let me stay on here when he bought the Throstle," Sim said.

"And I'm sure Master Greencart was also lucky to be provided with your services," Bel said stoutly, looking meaningfully at the innkeeper. "Can you spare him for a half hour while we talk and bring us two mugs of ale."

Sim's face was shining with happiness as the innkeeper hastened to do her bidding and they sat together at one of the tables exchanging their news and reminiscing about times past, a bitter-sweet experience. Bel was happy for Betty's good fortune but sad that an old and valued acquaintance had been lost again. Sim was overwhelmed by this new Rose and her good fortune and found it hard to believe that she still wanted his acquaintance. She promised to call and see him again if there was ever an opportunity, glad that he was still satisfied with his employment. But later as she made her way back along the busy London streets she realised once again that her old life was past. Her sojourn in London was brief for unless the Countess of Richmond had some special business at the Court she preferred to remain on one of their estates.

Bel couldn't understand why Lathom, the rambling stone fortress in the Lancashire countryside, should be the Countess's preferred favourite. The land was flat and marshy to the sea while to the east the landscape comprised low wooded hills with no open vistas and threaded by the murky river Douglas. Scattered around were poor villages and hamlets, there was a lack of large towns and grand mansions and the roads between them were ill-made, twisting and difficult to travel. However Lathom was the biggest and most important of their properties, built as a castle and lavishly furnished so the Stanleys lived there like royalty, by far the most prominent lords in Lancashire to which lesser land-owners owed fealty. When Sir Thomas was absent he entrusted all their business into his wife's capable hands and she was often left in charge there, ruling like a queen in her own realm and enjoying the respect she received.

Listening to her now as she heard some of the complaints and requests of her tenants in her own version of a manorial court Bel was impressed again by the will emanating from this tiny woman, her voice as strong as her purpose and completely at odds with her fragile frame. Seated in a throne-like chair with a high pointed back carved with the Stanley arms, set on the arras-draped dais raised at the back of the great hall, gave her an advantage over the small company of men grouped before her, most of them intimidated by the Countess's regal presence and their imposing surroundings – tapestry draped walls, ornate gilded and painted furnishings, the floor of patterned tiles – such a contrast from their own rough habitations. Besides the clerk writing at his desk, Bel was in attendance behind Lady Margaret, though almost hidden by the countess's high conical headdress with the stiffened gauze veil forming two peaks, ready to do her bidding when required. She was bored by the long discussions on matters she did not understand, not knowing the people or their land-holdings, and her mind drifted with thoughts of her own. During her time with the Countess Bel had grown to admire her qualities but had never ceased to be in awe of her and couldn't regard her with affection, such an emotion would in any case have been alien to her mistress. The Countess treated her servants fairly and provided them with all necessary requirements but all she asked from them was efficiency and loyalty. Bel missed the warmth she had known with her father, with Renard, with Robert Malory, even Betty Trimble. But she was forced to acknowledge that her life had improved on a material level and hardship was now unknown to her. Sometimes she thought about what the future might hold. She did not want to be an attendant to an aristocratic lady all her life for it was not in her nature to be a servant, even such a highly-placed servant. But she did not think anyone would want her as a wife as she could neither bear children nor bring any wealth to a husband, not even a small dowry. Lady Margaret had only been able to bear one child, her son Henry Tudor of whom she constantly spoke with pride, but she had found no difficulty in securing husbands on account of her great fortune and her royal pedigree. Bel supposed the best she could expect would be as a man's mistress again but it would have to be someone she loved, or at least someone for whom she had a liking which might grow into an affection as had happened with Robert Malory. In the two years since his death she had encountered no such men though many had cast longing looks upon her. She missed Robert's affection and disliked her lonely bed but would never relinquish it without at least some mutual feeling. Still she was only twenty years old and her life so far had of necessity been unpredictable so her nature had become attuned to accepting present circumstances and not dwelling on what might happen in the future. Her present circumstances might shift as unexpectedly as had her life at Saddington.

She was jolted from her reverie by the sound of a young voice not showing the customary reverential tone to the Countess of Richmond. She only caught the end of his sentence, "So I wasn't stealing. The cattle belong to us." She looked to where the defiant sound was coming from and saw a young man of about her own age addressing the Countess. He was very tall and slim with blond hair cut to his shoulders, hair so blond as to be almost the colour of the Countess's ivory chess pieces. His clothes were modest brown fustian and a small felt hat was held in his left hand.

The Countess stood and glared at him, a beringed hand appearing from the folds of the crimson velvet hanging sleeves and pointing accusingly. "You know very well, Henry Duxbury, that Duxbury Manor was sold to the Standishes four generations ago to pay outstanding debts."

"The Hall but not the manor, not the demesne," he persisted stubbornly. "Some of the land still belongs to us."

"The Standishes dispute that," she snapped. "Do you think I am not in possession of the full facts."

"Yes I do," he retorted and a gasp of horror whispered around the tapestry-hung hall.

"Refer to me by my title. I do not like your disrespect Henry Duxbury." Her voice was icy.

"My lady countess, I beg your pardon," he murmured, a scarcely perceptible trace of insolence in his voice. "Some of the demesne still belongs to us and the cattle were on our land. The Standishes appropriated them so I took them back."

Lady Margaret pursed her lips angrily. "I will refer the matter back to Master Standish," she said. "Meanwhile stay out of trouble or I shall have you committed to the Assizes."

The young man looked up at the dais and found Bel's eyes fixed on him with an intent gaze that carried a flicker of admiration. The Countess had turned her back to resume her seat and he winked impudently at Bel.

"Do not involve yourself further in this dispute," Lady Margaret commanded. "In any case it does not concern you, only your uncle as head of the family. I should not be so lenient with you except that you are underage but I will send a message to Master John. Now go from my sight before I change my mind."

"I thank you from the depths of my heart, my lady countess," he said making a low bow, his knee touching the ground.

Watching him with fascination Bel was sure the action was touched with a hint of mockery and her eyes followed him as he left the hall. She felt like laughing but knew she did not dare. The Countess called the next claimant to her.

Bel wondered who the impudent young man might be. He had noticed her and made an irreverent acknowledgement of her interest in him but she knew she dare not make enquiries and dismissed him from her mind, not dreaming that he might soon cross her path again.

The Countess usually allowed her ladies to visit the weekly market in Ormskirk, sometimes entrusting them with commissions for herself. Bel enjoyed the Thursday excursions on horseback to the busy little market town less than three miles from the castle. She usually rode in company with Maud Pettifer with whom she shared a bedchamber and was the closest anyone came to being termed a friend even though she was several years her senior and betrothed to one of Sir Thomas's bailiffs.

It was a fresh April morning and as they rode along the bridleways across the flat marshy fields sprinkled with mallow and wild orchids, their gentle hues of pink and violet contrasting with the bright yellow daffodils dancing beneath the alders, her mind travelled back to her arrival at Newbold Revel. "*I mustn't let myself feel sad on such a pleasant morning,*" she thought and began to chatter to Maud about what they might be able to purchase at the market.

When they arrived in the town it was bustling with sellers and shoppers. Bel had learnt that it was a great privilege for a town to be granted a weekly market for it brought trade to the town, both with sellers who offered goods not usually available on a daily basis and purchasers who came from miles around to take advantage of the fact, often staying overnight in the town and patronising the inns. There were stalls crowding the market place around the cross, along both sides of the four streets leading from there, even in front of the church and in any available space that could be found. Knowing it would be impossible to make way on horseback they left their mounts at the Black Bull Inn on Moor Street and went on foot. There were stalls selling everything it was possible to buy - merchandise to eat, to drink, to wear, to furnish, to repair, to amuse, just to look at with interest - the vendors crying out their wares in loud voices each trying to drown out their neighbours. The town sergeant strode between the stalls and hawkers on foot, keeping constant watch that weights and measures were honest, that foodstuffs were not bad nor ale watered and that the stall-holders had paid their dues. The market constables tried to keep a lookout for offenders who were then dragged away to face sharp punishment at the summary court of pie powder, fined heavily or given some appropriate punishment. It was not unknown for offenders to be made to drink their own sour wine while set in the stocks, the bakers to be bombarded with loaves containing stones to make up the legal weight and butchers have their rotten meat hung around their necks, all to the laughing delight of the customers. Dogs were constantly underfoot, scuttling between food stalls looking for scraps, ragged beggars with caps held out impeded progress by their hobbling passage. The bustling crowds provided opportunity for cut-purses to prey on the full purses of would-be purchasers, and thieves (often in pairs to distract the stall-owners' attention) were taking what they could from the open stalls. The noise was ear-splitting, the sellers crying their wares from every stall and trying to out-do each other, the buyers arguing for a better price, and housewives gossiping with raised voices in order to make themselves heard. The weekly market was an occasion for the whole town to mingle socially, to mix business with pleasure and to relish a few hours away from daily labour.

Bel and Maud wandered around in delight, finally purchasing cloves and ginger for the Countess while Maud chose a yard of green silk damask for a hat and Bel bought an ell of cambric to put ruffles on her shift. They returned to the Black Bull to retrieve their horses before the church clock struck twelve, knowing they must not be late for dinner at noon, the most important meal of the day. The inn was overflowing with customers and as they pushed their way through the crowd to make their way to the stableyard at the back, Bel following in Maud's wake heard a voice address her as "the beautiful girl from Lathom." Turning she saw the blond-haired young man who had incurred the Countess's annoyance, gaily waving a large mug of ale in the air and a smile lighting up his eyes which she now saw were deep blue like her own. He was dressed less formally than when she had seen him at Lathom, his blue wool jacket hugged his chest in a way that suggested he had almost outgrown it, his grey hose were moulded to his long legs and his blond hair poured from a grey felt hat with a stiffened brim but devoid of ornamentation.

She searched for his name and said, "Henry Duxbury?"

"Harry, Harry Duxbury. Nobody calls me Henry except the old dragon. Though I expect a more appropriate name would be the old cow with that horned headdress she was wearing."

She smiled despite herself but felt ashamed at doing so, saying in amelioration, "She isn't old. She's only about forty."

"That's old," he retorted. "And I note you don't deny she's a dragon."

"And do you fancy yourself as St. George?" she queried, tipping her head to one side and looking at him challengingly from beneath her long lashes.

"If only!" he laughed. "She hates me."

"Why?"

He looked at her consideringly. "It's a long story. Let me buy you a mug of ale and I'll tell you."

Bel would love to have stayed but was forced to say, "I must return to Lathom House before noon and my companion is already waiting for me." Maud had turned and was looking annoyed.

"How can you bear to be at the dragon's beck and call every moment of the day," he grunted.

"I haven't always been. I have a story of my own," she said defensively.

His eyes sparkled. "You become more interesting every minute. Listen, do you come to the market every week? I could meet you here next Thursday. We could share a drink and talk but in the Wheatsheaf in Church Street, it's more salubrious."

"I don't come every week," she said cautiously. "I have to have the Countess's permission. Do you come every week? Do you live here in Ormskirk?"

"My home is at Duxbury which is about eight miles away. But at the moment I am living with my sister Ethelreda in Ormskirk which is why the dragon has a hold on me otherwise I would be out of her jurisdiction and I shall definitely be here next week."

"But what if I can't come?"

He shrugged. "Then I shall be disappointed. I'll wait for you in the Wheatsheaf next week."

She could hear Maud calling impatiently so nodded agreement and turned to go.

He called after her, "Hey, you know my name but I don't know yours."

"It's Belfiore Lechanteur," she tossed over her shoulder.

"What a mouthful," he groaned. "Are you French? I thought you weren't English."

She smiled and gave him a wave as she hastened towards Maud who was watching her with disapproval and muttering under her breath. He waved his tankard as he called, "Don't forget next week. I'll be waiting for you."

"You don't want to be seen with Henry Duxbury, he has an evil reputation," Maud complained as they rode back to Lathom.

"Who says? Lady Margaret?" Bel retorted.

Maud sniffed, "You are already being influenced by him. He's always in trouble, one way or another."

Bel refrained from asking her to be more specific, intuiting that the account of his so-called misdemeanours might be prejudiced. She preferred to hear it from his own lips and realised that curiosity about him was largely responsible for her allowing him some further acquaintance. She did not know why she had half agreed to meeting him again except that she was ready for a little more interest in her life. Also she had been amused by his irreverent behaviour to the Countess and wished to know a little more about him. Before she had come to live in the Stanley household her life had mainly been passed in the company of unconventional people.

"Of course I won't meet him again, I would hate to attract Lady Margaret's displeasure," she assured Maud, trying hard to keep from smiling.

However on the next market day she made certain the opportunity arose to visit Ormskirk and couldn't believe her luck when Maud had a headache and stayed at Lathom. Bel took one of the grooms as escort but when they reached the town she told him to go and stable their horses in the Black Bull suggesting he pass his time there as she was quite capable of shopping alone, a proposition he agreed with gladly.

Making a quick round of the stalls to buy the few things she needed she then made her way to the Wheatsheaf, not knowing whether Harry Duxbury would be there. She saw his tall frame as soon as she entered the crowded tap room for he stood head and shoulders above most men and he was obviously looking out for her because he was by her side immediately, leading her to a bench in the corner and offering to buy her a tankard of ale. It was an offer she refused for despite nearly three years in England and time spent at the Throstle she had never accustomed herself to the taste of English ale. The inn was full of farmers and farm workers, talking loudly in their broad Lancashire dialect so it was difficult to have a conversation, the light from the small windows was blocked by the throng of bulky bodies and an overpowering smell of sweat and spilt ale pervaded the dim interior so when Harry had quickly doffed his drink he took Bel's arm saying, "Come let's go into the churchyard, it's impossible to talk here."

She followed him up the incline of Church Street, packed this morning with stalls and customers, to where the little stone church with its steeple blocked the top of the road, the path winding around it and onto the marshes and eventually the sea.

"The church was built at the time my ancestors first came here," Harry said.

"Did your ancestors come with the Normans?" she asked.

Harry laughed dismissively and eyed her mischievously. "No, they came long before the French. They were Vikings and came from Iceland in the 10th century. Ormskirk was a Viking settlement, the town and the church were named after a Viking chieftain, as was my home of Duxbury."

"So that accounts for your very fair hair and blue eyes," said Bel, who had heard of the Viking pirates with their longships.

Harry grinned. "They were great warriors. That is why I am not afraid of the dragon with her so-superior

Norman blood." His voice had a mocking tone. The churchyard was also full of stalls so Harry led her round the back overlooking the graveyard where they found a stone bench. It was a mild April morning, the sun's warm rays carrying a promise of approaching summer, mitigated yet by a fresh breeze that chased fluffy clouds across the milky-blue sky and playfully teased the daffodils carpeted around the graves.

"Tell me about yourself. If you are French what are you doing at Lathom with the dragon?"

To her surprise Bel found herself telling him about her early travelling with her minstrel father and he listened avidly. It seemed natural to be talking easily to a young man of her own age, liberated from the constraining conventions of aristocratic courtesies, an opportunity denied her since parting with Renard. Again she made no mention of Renard nor of her rape and the subsequent child. And although she told him of travelling to Newbold Revel to find her English relatives, she kept secret her relationship with Robert Malory. However it must have been something in her voice when she spoke of him that alerted Harry Duxbury because he looked at her keenly and she found herself blushing. However she did mention her grandfather's manuscript and how entrusting it into the hands of Lord Rivers had brought her to the attention of the Countess of Richmond.

"So you see I am not completely French, I am half Italian and a little bit English though I have lived most of my life in France and French is my native tongue."

Harry was fascinated by his new acquaintance, not only by her youth and outstanding beauty but by the aura of unconformity, an exotic flower in the midst of a kitchen garden. Ormskirk was characterised by a concentration on the mere necessities of life and his own existence was largely monotonous, enlivened only by his misdemeanours.

"Now tell me about your life," she prompted.

"In a moment, wait there," he said and to her surprise he loped off with his long stride, returning a few moments later with two large pieces of gingerbread he had bought from a baker passing with a loaded tray of pies and pastries. He had munched his while she was still nibbling the edges of hers then began his own recital.

"My ancestor was a Viking chief who built a hall at Duxbury. All the people with the name Duxbury are his descendants and we lived at the Hall until just over a hundred years ago. Then my ancestors took part in a rebellion against the most important lord of this area, the Earl of Lancaster and his local favourite Thomas Holland who were oppressing their tenants at a difficult time of war and famine. Unfortunately they found themselves on the losing side and for their actions were imprisoned in Lancaster castle. In order to raise the money to buy their release they sold the Hall to the Standishes of Standish Hall, neighbours of ours, who had not been involved in the rebellion. They were supposedly going to buy it back when they could raise the money but not only have they been unable to do so up to this time but the Standishes have no intention of relinquishing it. However what was actually sold is a matter of dispute. Some of the manor, that is the land belonging to the Hall, was never included in the purchase and though not extensive it is considerable, not only land around Duxbury but scattered in several local places. My uncle John is the heir, the elder brother of my father who is dead, and I used to live with him and my cousin because I am under age, I'm nineteen. Uncle John doesn't like to make trouble, he has an heir and is keen to conserve what he has rather than lose more but I don't believe in letting the Standishes get away with taking our land."

"So that is why you were in trouble with the Countess," said Bel, licking the remains of the gingerbread from her sticky fingers.

He grinned. "Yes I do a little cattle-rustling from time to time. It brings some excitement into my life." He didn't like to admit to his new acquaintance that his life was monotonously uneventful. "If I was still living at Duxbury I would be out of her control but for the last six months I have been living with my sister and her family in Ormskirk." He paused then said, "Uncle John was angry about my last exploit, he considered I hadn't enough to do and was a bad influence on my cousin Ughtred so he sent me to work with my brother-in-law Jaxon, he's a leather-worker. I hate it, stuck in his workshop for most of the day unless I'm buying supplies or delivering goods. I get to go to Chorley or Wigan sometimes but I would like to travel as you have done."

"Yes my life has certainly not been uneventful," she admitted with a hint of complacency in her voice, happy that she could score a point over the irrepressible young man she was beginning to like. "But I think I ought to return to the Black Bull and collect my horse and the groom. As I told you, the Countess insists that we all be present for the mid-day meal."

"Listen," he said, "in just over a week it will be May Day and that is a holiday for everyone. There are always celebrations at Lathom House because Sir Thomas likes to keep his tenants happy by providing feasts and games on holidays. I will come and we can meet – there will be dancing round the maypole."

Bel had seen some May Day festivities in England but had never participated and though the day was also celebrated in France she was eager to see how the English enjoyed themselves so when Harry insisted that the day would certainly not be overlooked at Lathom she promised to see him there.

On her return she said nothing to Maud about the meeting and it gave her a secret sense of amusement to think she was cocking a snook at the Stanley household. She enjoyed a very comfortable life and was grateful to the Countess for giving her employment which was pleasant and not onerous but she did miss the gaiety and irreverence that she had known for so much of her life – entertaining with her father and Renard, the boisterous company of the Throstle Inn, the freedom from rules and regulations. Even her short sojourn with Robert Malory had been unconventional and had given her independence for a time.

She soon found it to be a fact that the holiday of the first of May was eagerly awaited by everyone from the lowest servants to the highest members of the household. It was the highlight of the year and the only holiday many of the country people had until the season of Yuletide. Sir Thomas Stanley arrived from London, eager to present himself to his tenants and neighbours as a benevolent landlord who ensured their recreation was generously provided for. The land in front of the castle where the road to Ormskirk passed by the estate chapel was decorated with banners and flags bearing the arms of both the Stanleys and the Beauforts. So was the scarlet and white pavilion which had been set up and from where Sir Thomas and Lady Margaret would preside seated on throne-like chairs. Around the grounds were stalls set out with casks of ale and simple though plenteous platters of bread, boiled eggs, sausages, pies and cakes of oats and honey for the country people to avail themselves. There was a quintain and archery butts, a booth set for a puppet show, a dais ready for musicians and in pride of place in the centre stood the maypole, 30 feet high and decorated with greenery.

The weather was disappointingly cloudy and chill but this did not inhibit the high spirits of the country folk who arrived dressed in the best clothes they had. The Countess had given all the household a holiday so Bel in company with the other ladies was able to wander freely and enjoy the attractions. There was nostalgia however in her enjoyment as her mind drifted back to the tournament festival she had shared with Renard at Amiens when he had decided her birthday was to be the 21st of May and had bought her a flageolet, three years ago now and she still couldn't help thinking about him. She was standing listening to a group of musicians playing a hurdy-gurdy, a shawm, a rebec and drums, the sound loud enough to carry above the din of the crowd, when she felt a touch on her arm and looked around at Harry Duxbury.

"I don't know how you found me in this crowd," she said, but with an obvious note of pleasure in her voice.

"I thought I would look first amongst the musicians," he said and she was surprised that he had remembered what she had told him. He was wearing a scarlet belted tunic over dark blue hose with a blue peaked cap on his head. He took her arm, "Come let's see what sights there are."

She loosened herself from his grip but otherwise made no demur and they mingled amongst the crowd, Harry helping himself to food and drink from nearly every stall they came to though Bel laughingly declined everything except for some honey cakes. They stopped to watch the puppet play which included a lot of domestic violence but when a performing bear was put through its paces Bel turned away saying she didn't like to see animals being used in this way. However every time they encountered a travelling musician, playing a hurdy-gurdy or singing to a rebec or harp she would stay until he moved on. Harry watched her rapt face and noted how her expression moved between joy and regret. "Tell me about when you were a travelling minstrel," he said and she was only too glad to reminisce, even mentioning something of her partnership with Renard.

"Were you lovers?" he asked. He regarded her enviously, the simple blue woollen gown, the colour of her eyes, flowing over her slender figure and laced at the back to emphasize her waist. She had got up early to make a daisy chain to decorate her lustrous curls, floral headdresses being the custom for young girls on this day.

She hesitated a little and an inscrutable expression touched her face for a moment. "No," she said eventually. "We weren't. We were just friends."

Harry smiled happily though he wasn't entirely convinced. "I'm going to try my luck at the butts, come and cheer me," he said.

To her surprise he performed exceedingly well, most of his arrows flying close to the gold, the bull's eye, and he seemed to be in the running for a prize when the competition ended. "Not too bad considering I'm not using my own bow," he said with satisfaction. "Now I shall try the quintain."

Bel looked puzzled. "Don't you need a horse?" she asked, after having several times watched knights try their skill in this exercise.

"You haven't seen our country version," he laughed. He led her to where a huge crowd was gathered beside a straw-filled sack hanging on a post. A young man was seated on a wooden cart being pulled along by two strong lads with ropes around their waists. As they approached the quintain they increased their speed and the rider armed with a long wooden lance attempted to pierce the sack as it whirled from side to side. The crowd screamed their delight, especially when the sack struck the rider in the face or he fell from his "steed" in his efforts. Obviously known to some of the spectators, Harry was encouraged loudly, and was again successful in the sport, hitting the quintain accurately due to his advantageous height. Enjoying his high spirits Bel thought she had not known such spontaneous pleasure since she had shared the tournament at Amiens with Renard and considered Harry Duxbury would be very much at home in the company she used to keep.

"Can you play a musical instrument?" she asked but he shook his head.

"No, I can't play a note," he replied. "I'm sorry to disappoint you but I have no sense of music at all. It is a skill completely beyond me." A jester passed them in his multi-coloured coat and a pointed hood, shaking his stick with bells and making an obscene comment. "That's what I am, I play the fool and make a nuisance of myself."

She didn't know whether or not to believe him but he dragged her away then to the maypole and insisted they joined the dancing. "I'm going to call you Bella because Belfiore is too foreign and too much of a mouthful," he stated and she sighed. What was it about these Englishmen that they always wanted to change her name. However she considered there was little likelihood of her seeing much of Harry Duxbury even though she enjoyed his company and it was pleasant to be with someone her own age who did not bother too much about convention. She could not evade the Countess of Richmond's scrutiny indefinitely and in any case they would soon be on the move away from Lathom and on to one of their other properties, perhaps even London. They joined the dancers and whirled madly, Harry's arm around her waist, and she was glad she was not wearing one of the ridiculously high padded hats such as were fashionable with noble ladies.

The Countess of Richmond was. Seated in state in the pavilion her headdress of purple silk encrusted with jewels matched her gown under a surcoat of black velvet trimmed with ermine. She had caught sight of her lady-in-waiting dancing with the troublesome Henry Duxbury. Bel was fearful that if observed by her mistress she would incur some censure. Instead the Countess's eyes narrowed speculatively and an expression crossed her face which those who knew her well would immediately recognise as a sign that she was evolving some plan of her own.

The celebrations at last came to an end and the merry-makers began to disperse with the lengthening shadows, many of them unsteady on their feet and Harry proudly bearing a large ham which he had won with his progress at the butts.

"The market again this week?" he asked.

Bel shook her head saying, "I don't know. I never know in advance whether I shall be free or not. Besides I think we shall be leaving Lathom soon and travelling to one of the other Stanley properties, probably to Staffordshire."

His face showed his disappointment but he said, "Well I shall look for you anyway, I shall be in the Wheatsheaf every Thursday until you happen to come."

CHAPTER 11

Travels

The expected visit to Staffordshire did not take place after all because the Countess decided to visit her husband at the court. However she had a reason for the visit more pressing than a desire to see Sir Thomas. Her son, as always, was on her mind in his exile in Brittany. Although her belief in his royal destiny had not diminished, for that would remove from her life the rock that had sustained her through all the vicissitudes of her existence, she had been forced to recognise that King Edward IV now seemed settled on the throne and had two young sons to succeed him. However still believing that a miracle might occur to clear her son's path, though in what way she was unsure, she was now considering other means to strengthen his claim. The King's eldest child, Princess Elizabeth, was now 15 years old and of marriageable age. She would be an ideal wife for her son because if the two young princes were to die, not an inconceivable event in this age of high child mortality, then a marriage with the heiress would ensure that Henry Tudor would be the most likely claimant to the throne. She had confided this thought to no-one, least of all her husband, but she looked upon the idea with increasing enthusiasm. She knew that the King was not likely to support the idea for he favoured a marriage alliance with France. So it was the Queen she must work on. Elizabeth Woodville was not agreeable to a French match because this would mean being parted for ever from the daughter she loved and wished to keep close to her, for with all her faults she was devoted to her family, the Woodvilles had strong family ties, so Margaret Beaufort wished to take advantage of what she considered an opportune moment. The Countess and the Queen had never been close associates, Margaret disliked all the Woodvilles, but she decided that now was the time to alter this situation and show friendship. Queen Elizabeth was not known for logical or consistent thought and was easily manipulated into schemes. And because her husband the King was devoted to her (and generally too lazy to oppose her) Lady Margaret knew that if she could convince Elizabeth enough then she would eventually be able to persuade Edward to her will. So striking while the iron was hot she decided to pay a visit to the court, as always using Sir Thomas's presence there to justify it.

Taking with her a small number of her household she chose a surprised Bel to be part of the company when the ubiquitous Ursula Clifford was stricken with a congestion of the lungs. She was given money for a new gown and an appointment with the tailor, much to the envy of Maud Pettifer although her rancour was mitigated by the thought of her forthcoming marriage. Bel was excited by the thought of visiting London again. And when Lady Margaret informed her that she would be accompanying her to a feast at the palace of Westminster she looked forward to seeing the King and Queen of whom she had heard so much, and also perhaps encountering Lord Rivers again. Her excitement was mixed with apprehension about the correct protocol necessary but she consoled herself with the fact that she had many times experienced feasts of the nobility, even if in a less exalted capacity.

Standing beside the Countess of Richmond on the appointed evening she marvelled at her first sight of the Great Hall of the palace of Westminster with its soaring arched beams hung with flags and banners, its arcades draped with embroidered silk panels, exquisite Flemish tapestries in dazzling colours and huge multi-paned windows of coloured glass. The total effect was of brilliant colour - scarlet, purple, green, gold - all illuminated by a thousand wax candles in many-branched candelabra hanging from the beams, and cressets and torches in sconces along the walls. Equally rich and glowing were the clothes of the nobility in the richest of fabrics – velvet, brocade, satin, Italian silk, fine linen from the East, cloth of gold – all lavishly embroidered and sparkling with jewels. The men paraded their splendour as ostentatiously as the women, vying with each other for prominence. Musicians strove to make themselves heard above the laughter and talk of a thousand voices. Bel tried to see the King and Queen but it was difficult in the huge press of glitterati. Every now and again she caught a glimpse of the King as he towered above the company with his great height, the crown on his fair curls casting off radiant beams, his loud laugh tearing through the throng. The Queen was much smaller and Bel strained to see below the glittering diadem on the distinctive white-gold hair. She followed in the Countess's wake as her mistress moved from one noble acquaintance to another, standing silently beside her but drinking in the scene with avid fascination. Even in that splendid company Lady Margaret was difficult to outshine in black so covered with gold embroidery that it was difficult to see the silk beneath and her small frame weighed down by a tall butterfly headdress with stiffened gauze veils. Bel was quite oblivious to the fact that in her simple gown of seawater silk which flowed around her slim figure from a high waist and low neckline, a short transparent veil on a fillet of silver wire revealing her black curls, she did in fact outshine her mistress. Instead of jewels her youthful loveliness provided all the sparkle, and the gown flowed around her like a sea goddess emphasizing her graceful movements so that despite being inconspicuous all those who caught a glimpse of her afforded her a second glance.

"Stay here and wait quietly for me, I wish to speak with the Queen alone," the Countess said and left her to approach Elizabeth who was circulating around her guests. Bel watched her go and saw the two women walk towards a pillar where they made loud protestations of friendly greetings. She retired to the back of one of the arcades where she could continue her observance unnoticed.

Suddenly she was interrupted by a loud voice speaking in French, "Le Diable, quelle miracle! C'est la petite putain de ce bâtard d'un ménestrel de Courcy-le château-Auffrique." To her horror she looked up into the face of Hugo de Maurignac. His big burly figure was blocking the lig ht but there was a leer on the heavy-jowelled face and the dark eyes glittered with malice. A short-waisted crimson doublet and matching tight-fitting hose clung to his strong physique and jet-black hair showed beneath the tall hat of black velvet, heavily padded and draped with rolls of silk, which increased his height. Bel felt suffocated by fear as he hemmed her in by the pillar. She was unable to flee but even if she could she was immobilised by fear. "Tiens, tiens, que nous faisons l'épate," he mocked, putting one hand on her breast and the other on her thigh. "As-tu trouvé un patron riche? Quelqu'un beaucoup plus important qu'un pauvre polisson bien sûr," he sneered. She looked around desperately, hoping someone might see and come to her rescue but all were busy with their own affairs and besides this encounter of a lusty courtier and a beautiful maiden was a common occurrence in gatherings such as these. He saw her desperate searching around the crowds and spoke in heavily-accented English, "Shall I tell these people where I last saw you, singing and dancing lasciviously with your lover, a common troubadour. I don't know why you are here in the royal presence but I'm sure that if they knew your history then you would not be so welcome." He pulled her against him and the jet buttons of his doublet dug into the thin silk of her bodice.

"What are you doing here?" she whispered, unable to say anything more.

He laughed triumphantly. "Not under false pretences. I met King Edward when he came to France to make an alliance with our King. We fared well together and he gave me an invitation to visit him at the court and be part of his bodyguard. He admires my martial skills."

"I am now a servant in the household of the great and noble Countess of Richmond," she said defiantly.

"And does this great and noble countess know of your disreputable past?" he grinned. "Shall I inform her of my personal knowledge, elaborating of course my personal knowledge of you."

A shiver convulsed her for she knew beyond any doubt that what he said was true, that this would be the end of her service with Lady Margaret and indeed with anyone else of note. He might be tempted to do it publicly and shame her in the midst of this royal gathering.

He saw her uncertainty and lowering his voice whispered, "Give yourself to me and I will keep silent. Otherwise....," his eyes were dark with lust and menace. "Is this man troubling you, Demoiselle," a quiet voice interrupted, a voice she recognised but could not put a face to.

Hugo de Maurignac spun around and she could see her deliverer now in the tall figure of Anthony Woodville, Lord Rivers. The brown eyes in the handsome face showed both concern and severity and she was aware once again of the mixture of gentleness and strength in this powerful man.

Hugo de Maurignac breathed deeply then said with an effort, "I was merely paying my compliments to a beautiful maiden, my Lord. A maiden I met once in France so she is no stranger to me," he added defiantly.

Anthony saw the stricken look in Bel's eyes and smelled the scent of fear.

"Are this man's advances welcome to you?" he asked her.

She shook her head and whispered, "No, my lord."

"Then I suggest you take your presence elsewhere and trouble this lady no more," he said to de Maurignac. "If I find you approaching her again I shall take strong measures." His voice was soft and devoid of malice but there was steel beneath the velvet and the Frenchman knew it. He knew that Lord Rivers, the Queen's brother, was the most important man in England. He was not a man to cross.

Seething inwardly he made a low bow, first to the Earl saying, "I crave your lordship's pardon and bid you farewell." Then he made a slight bow to Bel with the words, "My compliments on your beauty, Demoiselle, and farewell also to you." Then he turned and pushed his way into the crowd.

Bel was shivering and Anthony took hold of her arm and led her to a marble bench against the wall in a corner of the arcade.

"Thankyou so much, my lord," she said looking up at him with devotion. As usual he was dressed less flamboyantly than the rest of the royal family, richly but discreetly, his black velvet tunic and hose devoid of ornamentation apart from gold buttons and a gold chain and medallion, a brimmed hat with brooches revealing his shoulder-length thick brown hair. He stayed beside her for a time until he was sure her fear had dissipated. He was aware that something lay behind the encounter and that there was some mystery in this beautiful girl's past but he had been alerted by the stricken look in her eyes like a hunted fawn at the mercy of her pursuer.

"Are you happy in the service of the Countess of Richmond?" he asked.

"Yes I am, my lord. I am very content and grateful for your generous offices in finding such a place for me."

"I read all your grandfather's book and it gained my interest and my admiration. I intend eventually giving it to William Caxton, do you know of him?"

She shook her head and he continued, "I knew him when I was in Bruges where he had a printing press. Now he has set up such a one in London in St. Paul's yard. He has printed several books," (he didn't say that Caxton's first printed book had been Anthony's own 'Dictes and Sayings of the Philosophers') "and I think he might be interested in Sir Thomas Malory's Arthurian tales."

"Does this mean it might be printed?" she asked breathlessly.

"Perhaps," he replied warily. "It is a long book and printing is a lengthy business but I believe it is worth the reading by many people."

"Thankyou again, my lord," she said, but he replied, "No my thanks are to you, my dear, for bringing it to me in the first place and for entrusting it to me."

They were still seated together when Lady Margaret returned to reclaim Bel for her service. She was surprised to find her attendant seemingly so close in Lord Rivers' favour and studied her consideringly, her fine brows arched.

They both rose and the Earl and Countess greeted each other politely before going their separate ways. If it had not been for her knowledge of Earl Rivers' acknowledged morality she might have suspected him of being enamoured of her young attendant.

It took some time for Bel's spirits to settle into equanimity again and the shock of the encounter to pass. Inevitably the unexpected meeting with Hugo de Maurignac had brought Renard to her remembrance again and she thought of their time together on the road through France. This time it had been Anthony Woodville who had been her protector. She was eternally grateful to him for rescuing her from the evil de Maurignac whom she knew with certainty would not trouble her again; for believing in her grandfather's book; and for finding her the position with the Countess of Richmond and the entrée into a life she never dreamt of. In her mind he was the parfait gentil knight and that night she dreamt of him. Then somewhere in the dream he metamorphosed into the figure of Renard de Bourgonville and when she awoke she found there were tears on her face.

When they returned to Lathom the Countess of Richmond was well satisfied with what she had achieved on her visit to the court. But she realised she must continue to nurture the idea in the Queen's mind and though Lathom was her preferred residence she must not leave it too long before she joined her husband again at the court.

It had been two months before Bel could renew her acquaintance with Harry Duxbury for the journey from London took a week and incurred many stops along the road. His face was alight when he saw her weaving her way through the drinkers in the Wheatsheaf and putting down his tankard he went immediately to meet her. "You have been away a long time," he said reproachfully. "I've missed you."

"I'm not in a position to rule my own life. I am only a servant and must do as I am told," she smiled, feeling a shaft of pleasure at his welcome. He led her eagerly out of the back door and into the orchard beyond where they sat on a bench away from the crowds milling around the stalls in the streets and exchanged news.

"I am not leaving Lathom House again immediately. The Countess does have more business in London but she is not taking me, Ursula Clifford has improved and she has some duties for me to perform here in her absence," she informed him.

She did not admit she might have some free time but Harry picked up on the implication and said, "Then you can come and see my real home at Duxbury."

"That doesn't sound like a feasible proposition, Harry," she replied doubtfully.

"Of course it is, I will get my Uncle John's permission to invite you to dinner."

"How far is it?"

He gestured vaguely, "A few miles. I will come and collect you and return you back to Lathom afterwards. It's a pleasant enough ride and Duxbury is well situated in woodland by the side of the River Yarrow."

Always eager for travel and new places and even now not accustomed to a settled routine Bel promised to consider it if the Countess should depart as promised.

It was at their regular rendezvous at the market during the following month that she was met by an excited Harry Duxbury. "I heard that the Countess has left Lathom. When can you come to see Duxbury, I will ride to Lathom and we can go together."

His enthusiasm was infectious and Bel agreed a date and time for the following week. She had her own horse Troubadour in the castle stables and she informed the relevant people that she would be absent for the whole day on a personal errand for the Countess to one of the neighbouring gentry. Harry had told her to imply this was to the Standish family, saying they were more likely to be acceptable than the Duxburys, and Bel had no compunction in doing so. She was grateful to the Countess for granting her congenial employment and a comfortable existence but felt no particular devotion to her, while her peripatetic existence with her father had not nurtured a sense of awe to the obligations of the nobility. Both he and Renard had always considered that as entertainers they were granting a privilege to those who wanted them in their service and their special gifts put them on an equal footing with anyone, no matter how high-born. She looked upon her employment with the Stanleys as temporary and though she could think of no alternative at the moment she hoped one day to return to France. She often thought longingly of her partnership with Renard de Bourgonville and fantasised that one day, miraculously, something similar might happen again. She never acknowledged that her wished-for miracle had as much substance as her mistress's and that in this they shared a bond.

She informed the steward of the household of her absence at dinner and the mistress of the maids, Dame Matilda Perkins, of her absence in the solar, each of them accepting her explanation without demur, but she made no mention to anyone of her association with Henry Duxbury, assuring them only that she was being accompanied by one of the many grooms of the stable knowing that they would not check on the fact.

At the appointed early hour she trotted casually through one of the side gatehouses across the moat and onto the Newburgh road in the opposite direction to Ormskirk. The two guards looked up briefly from their surveillance of two farmers entering with carts loaded with grain, giving her a brief nod of acknowledgement. On the stony road leading to the little nearby village she found Harry waiting impatiently for her and he viewed her with appreciation in her yellow gown hitched up at the side for riding, her hair in a long plait under a wide-brimmed conical straw hat which tied under her chin. Before they reached Newburgh he turned off in a northerly direction and led the way through little hamlets then avoiding the mosses turned west through fields of grain and pasture. Harry's few miles turned out to be about ten but it was easy riding in the warm June sunshine. Bel as always enjoyed the countryside and she had never explored the area around Lathom apart from going to Ormskirk market or accompanying the Countess on her regular attendances at St. Laurence's priory situated between Lathom and the ford at Burscough. After an hour and a half the terrain became wooded and there were glimpses of the River Yarrow. Harry pointed ahead to where a building could be seen amongst the trees and as they rode nearer they could hear the river splashing over the stones. They came into a clearing where stood a lofty three-storeyed building built of stone with a tower at one end. It had obviously been built for defence for the windows were small and the iron clad door out of proportion to the frontage while it was surrounded by a wooden stockade. The river burbled merrily close by, running clear over the stony bed and throwing up sprays of effervescence into the air.

"So this is your home, Duxbury Hall?" she said surveying it with interest.

"No," he scowled, "this is Duxbury Hall but not my home now. It belongs to the Standishes. Sir Edward Standish and his family live at Standish Hall but they let this to a cousin of theirs. This was the original Hall built by my Viking ancestors but it has been rebuilt and altered. At first it was just a timber building with high roof beams and a central hearth opening in the roof, the chieftain's Hall where he lived with his family and retainers and where everything took place in just the one huge room. Then over the years it was rebuilt in stone and more rooms added as well as the tower for defence because raiders sometimes came down from Scotland. But after being involved in the Banastre rebellion against the Earl of Lancaster my ancestors were imprisoned as I told you and in order to raise the money to purchase their release they had to sell the Hall to their neighbours the Standishes."

"Could you never get it back?" she asked.

He scowled again. "We should have. It was supposed only to be temporary. Some time later one of my ancestors married with the Standishes and this alliance was supposed to unite the two families. It's a complicated story but it ended up with the Duxbury heir a child, his Standish grandfather administering his estate and never giving it back to him when he came of age. But they only gained the Hall and the manor, not the demesne which has always remained in our hands and just what belongs to who has always been a matter of dispute."

Bel shook her head in confusion saying, "I find this English law very confusing. So where do you actually live, you said Duxbury."

He gathered up the reins of his horse again saying, "Follow me," going further down the river to where it was shallow and where they were able to cross to the other bank by means of stepping-stones. A little further along they came to what looked like a farmhouse – a low sprawling meandering building of mixed timber, wattle and daub, and stone, with small-paned windows and no sign of an entrance, but a collection of hens and geese pecked around on the grass and a donkey was tethered to a stake on a long rope. Bel followed Henry around the side of the building to a cobbled courtyard where a low carved lintel crowned the door made of planks and nails. A stable door stood open to the side, cows could be seen in the nearby field and the sound and smell of pigs could be ascertained in a pen in the distance.

"This is my home, what was Duxbury farm, but I actually live there," he said pointing to where a pele tower stood on a mound behind the farmhouse. Bel followed his eyes and saw a tall round structure built of rough stone with only small window apertures in the top half. "Come on, I'll show you," he said eagerly, riding towards the tower and leaving her no option but to follow him. "This pele tower was part of the defences against the Scots."

He tethered their horses loosely then climbed the grassy mound and pushed open a door into the interior. "Watch your step, it's dark at first," he warned.

Rough wooden steps climbed upwards and Bel couldn't see the way for there was no light. He took her hand and pulled her up behind him saying, "The bottom floor is just for the animals." The first floor opened out into a large space and a ribbon of daylight round the edges of the closed shutters on two walls gave just enough glimmer to find the way. Harry crossed and opened the wooden shutters and the room was filled with the June sun as it poured through the apertures without hindrance of glass or horn. Bel looked around her. The walls were lime-washed, reflecting the golden beams and the floor was of rough oak planks. In the centre of the room stood a pine table on which were an assortment of wooden bowls, an earthenware jug, a blackjack and a few pewter and wooden drinking vessels.

There were two stools beside the table and underneath one of the windows an ancient -looking wooden settle.

"Come upstairs," Harry said, going further up the staircase. This room was dimmer, boasting only a series of arrow slits around the circular walls which were of rough undressed stone. In the centre was a bed, the old-fashioned sort without a bedstead – a base of slatted wood and rope with a mattress - and a pile of wool blankets on which a covering of animal pelts sewn together had been thrown haphazardly on top. There was a long chest that seemed to be of great age on which more garments lay, and pegs hammered into the walls held various artefacts, a bow, a quiver, a baldrick, a long length of heavy coiled rope and a sheepskin cloak.

"Aren't you cold in winter?" Bel asked, surprised by the lack of comfort.

"I put oiled cloth under the shutters in my living room and my bed is really warm, look at the furs, and the mattress and pillows are of goose feathers, there are lots of geese on the mere."

He looked proudly at his bed, then glanced at her with a look she knew well so she said hurriedly, "Let's go back downstairs."

She led the way and he followed slowly. She stood hesitantly in the lower room but he pointed to one of the stools and seating himself poured from the jug into two of the tankards, handing one to her and when she sipped it she found it a surprisingly sweet white wine. She expected him to explain in more detail his unusual circumstances and some more of the Duxbury history but instead he said, "Tell me about your travels in France when you were a minstrel. I would love to travel."

"Have you not taken part at all in these wars that have troubled England in the past twenty years?"

Harry was pensive for a moment then he said, "You are not English and you have only been here a short time so you can't really understand the nature of these wars. But I too am also too young to have seen much, I was only a child when there was action here in the north, most of it anyway was in Yorkshire on the other side of the country, and as you know fighting has been in abeyance for these past three years since King Henry died. I only know from what I have heard but the great nobles fighting amongst themselves for personal power with the crown as the greatest prize is not strong enough motivation for the lesser gentry to leave their lands at risk and chance their lives. What are they going to get out of it?"

Bel thought of her grandfather, Sir Thomas Malory, and what it had cost him to fight for what he believed were the old chivalric ideals of the past. But he was of the knightly class and his fortunes were linked to the great lords so that the outcome was of personal significance to him, so much so that he had fought on both sides.

As if catching her thoughts Harry continued, "My grandfather Henry Duxbury was with the Lancastrian forces at Clitheroe when King Henry was captured there for the final time. People in these parts were, not surprisingly, for the Lancastrian cause as a whole. And when Sir Thomas Stanley married the dragon that pulled us a little closer to supporting the next Lancastrian claimant which happens to be her son, if the war should ever break out again. If it does I will go and fight if I get the chance."

"Which side?"

"I don't know. It doesn't matter to me. The winning side," he grinned.

"Harry, are you up there?" A high-pitched voice came from the base of the tower.

"Hell and damnation, it's Ughtred," Harry responded angrily, "Go away."

"Father says you haven't to go up there. It's forbidden. I'm coming up to see what you're doing."

"Don't you dare," Harry shouted, rushing to the entrance but there were light running steps on the stairs and before he could stop him a young boy was standing in the doorway. He was about eight years old with the same blond hair and blue eyes as Harry, dressed in a good doublet and matching hose of green wool with sturdy leather boots to his calves.

"What have I told you about coming up here," Harry shouted furiously, grabbing him by the scruff of the neck.

The boy looked unperturbed, gazing up fearlessly with his wide blue eyes. "You haven't to come up here anyway so you can hardly forbid me." He gazed enquiringly at Bel who was still seated at the table. "I might have guessed you had a girl here."

Harry gave him a box on the ear then in exasperation turned to Bel saying, "My cousin Ughtred Duxbury."

"Well aren't you going to tell me who the girl is?" he asked impudently.

"Mind your manners!" Harry roared, giving him another thump. "This is a lady. She is no less a person than lady and companion to the Countess of Richmond and she goes by the name of Lady Bella."

Bel felt the urge to laugh and couldn't repress a twinkle in her eye as she held out her hand saying, "I bid you well Master Duxbury."

"And I am honoured to meet you Lady Bella," the boy said seriously, taking her hand and making a formal bow. "Father said I was to meet you and bring you into dinner. He doesn't know you are in the tower but I thought you might be."

"Well go now and don't ever come in here again or I won't let you use my bow or teach you to fight fisticuffs. You know this is my private place."

"And don't I warn you when the Standishes are snooping about."

Harry frowned a warning and said, "Tell Uncle John I am stabling the horses and I will follow you shortly."

The boy scampered off down the stairs and Harry groaned. "I thought we might have got some time alone here," he said, "but there might be opportunity later, my uncle will be occupied with the farm after dinner."

"So is this tower your home or not?" Bel asked, tilting her head provocatively.

"Yes it is. My own place," he said determinedly. "Even though now they are making me live in Ormskirk I come here as often as I can. The Duxbury family live at Duxbury farm where I will take you shortly to meet the present head of our house, my uncle John Duxbury. My parents are dead so because I am under age I am in his custody. He has only the one son Ughtred whose mother is dead. But the pele tower belongs also to us. The Standishes say it doesn't, they say it is part of the land belonging to the Hall but that isn't right, it was built to defend the farmstead at the time when the Scots came down from Scotland in the 13th century and raided Chorley, that's our nearby market town. My uncle won't use it because he is afraid of more trouble in the courts with the Standishes but I have made it my own. Sometimes I put cattle at the bottom and this adds to my privacy and I sleep here whenever I can. My uncle doesn't always know where I am and Ughtred, pest that he is, keeps an eye out for me."

She looked at him with some understanding, recollecting how happy she had been to have a place of her own for the first time at Saddington Manor and how she was now homeless again. As if reading her thoughts he said, "It gives me some independence. I have nothing of my own and would only be heir of Duxbury if something happened to Ughtred, which I would never wish. Come, let me take you into the house."

As they walked from the mound and across the courtyard he said, "Although only the farm is ours now, together with the pele, our demesne is quite wide. Unfortunately it is composed of many small parcels of land in different places, many small villages like Welch Whittle, Heapey, Wheelton, Altham, so it is not easy to manage and most of it is only sheep grazing anyway. The best land is cattle-grazing on the lowlands near the river but the Standishes have appropriated some of it and that is why I am always accused of cattle stealing."

They entered through the door of the main building and after passing through a vestibule with pegs for outdoor cloaks and a rough seat built into one wall for the removal of working boots, Harry led Bel into a long low passageway on each side of which were other doors. He opened one and she found herself in a lime-washed room with a long small-paned window along one side and a long settle against the other. There were a few rush-seated chairs and a massive oak chest, and shelves set into the walls to hold candlesticks and rush holders, drinking vessels, a horn beaker of goose quills and a leather-bound book. In the centre of the room was the fire (unlit) surrounded by a high stone hearth with a corresponding lantern aperture in the roof. Harry continued through the room to another door where there were people. A man sat at the head of a long table with benches set for a meal with the boy Ughtred beside him on his right. Several other men in good serviceable clothes were seated on his other side with obvious farmworkers in working garb at the bottom of the table. Ready to attend to the serving of the meal were two young maids carrying cauldrons of hot stew. John Duxbury rose from his seat as Harry apologised profoundly for the lateness of his arrival and introduced Bel proudly to his uncle. She saw a very tall thin man of about forty years with the Duxbury blond hair a dimmer shade, as if there were a residue of corn dust, his face tanned and leathery as of a man spending all his time outdoors. For his part he saw a very beautiful young girl, elegantly though simply dressed and with a ready smile, and looking sharply at his nephew he ascertained a flicker of triumph on his face.

Bel was made courteously welcome and seated between Ughtred and Harry. Conversation between all the men seemed to have suddenly diminished, partly due to the eagerness with which they all devoured the plentiful meal of home-grown produce but also because of the intimidating effect produced by Bel's unique presence in this homely setting amongst these farm people. Harry made up the conversation by bringing up local news and recent events, in between eating heartily.

After the meal the retainers of Duxbury farm returned to their work and John, accompanied by Ughtred, retired to the other room and allowed some time with his nephew and their guest and where a goggle-eyed maid served them with wine. Then after a courteous interval John excused himself on the grounds of having much work to do which necessitated him riding abroad for a time. He bade farewell with a careful formality to his guest, assuring her of a warm welcome should she ever return to their locality, proffered his eternal respect to the Countess of Richmond and commanded his son to attend to his lessons. On a final note of warning he fixed his nephew with a stern look saying, "I shall have words with you when I return."

"Are you going back to the tower?" Ughtred asked when his father had departed. "Can I come with you?"

"Didn't you hear your father say you had to attend to your lessons. The parson is due tomorrow and you'll be in trouble if you haven't transcribed the verses. And stay well away from me," Harry commanded.

Ughtred scowled and Bel touched him gently on the shoulder saying, "It was a pleasure to make your acquaintance Ughtred and I am sure we shall meet again one day," which brought a smile to his face as he sped away.

Bel had no option but to return to the tower because she had left her straw hat there but when they had climbed the first set of stairs she stopped in the living space.

"Why the hesitation?" he asked. "This is my own place, I've explained to you. The farmhouse is where my uncle and Ughtred live. You are not afraid of being alone with me are you?"

She shook her head emphatically and he moved towards her, putting his arm around her waist and drawing her to him. "We could spend a wonderful hour upstairs," he whispered.

She drew away from him. "I didn't come here for that," she said sternly. "I came to see your home and I have. That is all."

"Don't you like me? I know you have had lovers. What is wrong with me?"

"There is nothing wrong with you Harry Duxbury. I like you very much. But as a friend."

"We could lie on the bed and talk about things. Exchange stories, nothing more. Get to know each other better," he wheedled.

She smiled ruefully. "And would that be all? Do you honestly believe that?"

It was his turn to look dubious now. She sighed and said, "I'm not ready for a lover yet. There's no place in my life for a lover just now. Will you take me back to Lathom. It is a two hour ride after all and I have been absent a long time."

Harry took solace in the fact that she had said "yet" and "just now" and had not completely dismissed the idea. There was hope for the future and his heart quickened. He kissed her lightly on the cheek. Then he said, "Yes we will go back to Lathom if that's what you wish."

They collected their horses and crossed back over the Yarrow brook. As they were passing Duxbury Hall a figure came out of the stockade and blocked their path. Harry drew on the reins and leaning down said scornfully, "What do you want?"

"A word with you Harry Duxbury." The man was some years older, nearing thirty, thickset and muscular with brawny arms and chest straining against the quality doublet of russet wool. He was handsome in a carnal way, square chin, big nose, bushy eyebrows with a thick crop of chestnut curly hair. He seemed not to notice Bel as he said, "I believe you are occupying the pele again. Well let me give you fair warning that if I ever find you there, together with any of our milch cows, then before I file an appeal against you in the manor court I shall thrash you out with a horse whip."

"You and how many others?" Harry said scornfully, leaping down from his horse. "Before you ever got near the pele I would have an arrow in you."

"Planning murder now are we?"

"If it means keeping what is mine, yes," said Harry recklessly. "The pele is our property, the milch cows are on what is lawfully speaking our land and therefore our property."

"It is our land lawfully settled and documented accordingly. Your uncle has accepted this and it is time you did so. I'm afraid you must accept you are a landless wastrel, Duxbury, all on account of your forbears being stupid enough to involve themselves in rebellion against their lords." He noticed Bel for the first time and after a stupefied gaze collected himself sufficiently to sneer, "It's a pity you haven't anything better with which to woo a fine lady."

He was looking at Bel so he didn't see Harry's punch coming. His fist caught him full in the face and one that followed on the side of his head felled him to the ground.

"Take that for an earnest Rafe Standish and if you ever come near the pele then doubt to walk away with your life. Come on Bella, let's be on our way," he said leaping on his horse and taking hold of Bel's reins. As they rode away, Rafe Standish sprang to his feet, nursing his jaw first then trying to wipe the dust off his doublet and shouting furiously, "You will pay for this, Duxbury. I'll make formal complaint and bring you to justice."

Harry kept hold of Bel's reins as they rode beyond sight of Duxbury Hall and through the woods. "That as you might have guessed was Rafe Standish," he muttered.

Bel was looking troubled. "Should you have done that? And threatened to kill him too."

"My mouth is too big," he admitted ruefully. "No doubt my uncle will soon learn of it. And the dragon too when she returns to Lathom."

They rode in some gloom for a mile but then their youthful spirits reasserted themselves, Harry saying, "He probably won't carry out his threat, he doesn't demonstrate himself a hero when he tangles with me," and when they reached Lathom they both voiced their satisfaction with the day. Bel even made vague promises to repeat the excursion another time if the opportunity ever arose.

Harry's optimism that Rafe Standish would not make complaint to John Duxbury was ill-founded. He hadn't been long back in Ormskirk with Ethelreda and Jaxson before his sister informed him that their uncle was very angry with him and he was warned yet again not to make use of the pele tower. He wondered if there would be further repercussions from Lathom House when the Countess of Richmond returned.

CHAPTER 12

Calamities

One day Bel had been in the company of the Countess of Richmond as she made one of her regular visits to St. Laurence's Priory which was situated only two miles or so from Lathom House amongst the quiet flat fields on the way to Burscough. The Countess often rode there to talk with the prior in his splendid house and spend time in prayer and meditation in the magnificent church with its many altars, stone carvings, stained glass mullioned windows and glazed floor tiles. The priory was a rich and extensive complex, well-endowed by royal subscription and patronised by the Stanleys. Beside the church was an equally richly-decorated chapter house, lofty stone-arched cloisters, several buildings for the monks' use as well as a guest hall and bedrooms for guests, a hospital, and the prior's house. Even the great tithe barn had a finely-timbered roof. Lady Margaret liked her ladies to accompany her with an escort of male servants and Bel always enjoyed a visit there. Inside the priory church was peace and tranquillity but outside in the yards and gardens there was always much activity with the monks busy about their tasks and guests enjoying their hospitality. After the Mass they were usually entertained in the prior's grand house which was as richly furnished as any nobleman's and where they were served with excellent French wine and newly-baked cakes of honey and almonds. Lady Margaret was talking with the prior when suddenly they were disturbed by a rider hurtling at speed into the priory precincts bringing news that a messenger had arrived from London with an urgent message from Sir Thomas and asking that Lady Margaret return at once to Lathom. Trying not to show her anxiety, the Countess collected her ladies and made to return home. Bel however discovered that her horse Troubadour had a stone lodged in its hoof. The Countess told one of her menservants, Daniel Rigby, to stay with Bel and see to it and to follow them later as she had no wish to delay.

There was a smith amongst the servants of the abbey and after it was done Bel decided that it would be better if she walked her horse home as it was only a couple of miles and she had the accompaniment of Daniel who gave his agreement. They made a leisurely stroll through the fields so it was some time later when they entered the precincts of the castle. On entering the first barbican across the moat she felt an undefinable air of unease, a tremor in the air as if a storm threatened though the sky was a uniform blue with only wisps of cloud. The courtyards seemed more than unusually busy and all the way into the entrance to the Stanley apartments there were clusters of people and a buzz of talk like a swarm of bees. Daniel frowned and looked at her enquiringly but he volunteered to take her horse to the stables with his own and she entered the house alone. It was only when she opened the door of the maids' solar that she was swamped with cries of "The King is dead."

She stopped short on the threshold, disbelieving, but the clamour continued from all sides as each of the Countess's ladies tried to be the loudest and she was bombarded with shrill rapid speech. She felt as if she had walked into the middle of someone else's dream. King Edward was over six foot tall, strong and robust and though getting a little stout was as athletic as ever, hunting, riding, tilting, dancing. His hair was golden, his voice loud, his laughter ringing. He had a roving eye and was eager for pleasure, enjoying the good life in all its forms with a large appetite for food and love. He was only 40 years old and larger than life. How could he be dead? He was never ill. There had been no previous talk of any ailments. She struggled to make sense of what they were saying.

"Has he been murdered?" was her first reaction.

"No, he caught cold after swimming."

"He has been dead for a week."

"Sir Thomas has sent word from London."

"The Queen and his six children are devastated."

No-one could believe the news except that it had been relayed by Sir Thomas from the court.

Once the news had been accepted talk centred on what was to happen next. The new king would be Edward's eldest son, another Edward but only twelve years old. After twenty years of internecine strife Edward of York, Edward IV, had brought peace and stability to the land and it had been taken for granted that this would continue indefinitely for the king was in his prime. Now the king was a child again and no-one could but recall how the troubles of the cousins' war had been caused, then further exacerbated, because two kings, Richard II and Henry VI, had succeeded to the crown as young children. Everyone now called to mind the old adage "Woe to the land when the king is a child."

It was obvious that their mistress would wish to return to London as soon as possible for the funeral of the King so all was haste and bustle as her ladies hurried to pack her gowns and jewels. The rest of the household was in equal ferment as preparations were made for the long journey with the best mounts, packhorses and carts but fortunately the weather was good. Lady Margaret ordered all her ladies to be ready themselves for there would obviously be much ceremony at court and she wished to avail herself of as many of her own attendants as she could. Maud Pettifer was grumbling that she did not know whenever she was going to be able to marry Peter Sefton, one of Sir Thomas's bailiffs, but Bel didn't mind going to London again.

"Don't you ever get tired of travelling?" Maud asked wearily and Bel shook her head. "No I like it, I have always been used to it. Travelling was always part of my life. I never knew a settled existence until now."

Although news of the King's early death had shocked her as she recalled her only sight of his vigorous ebullient figure so full of life, it brought to mind also Robert Malory who had died so unexpectedly at the same age and his memory caused her more sorrow than an English king. As a foreigner she was not familiar with England's history so could not share the apprehensions of the natives. Apart from a mild interest in forthcoming events she was content to watch how things would unfold, but although her own life would be unaffected the lives of the Stanleys might well be and she was bound to them. Because the new king was only 12 years old there would have to be someone to rule in his stead until he came of age. The most likely person would be Lord Rivers who was his guardian and had been in charge of his upbringing at Ludlow castle since he was a small child. This did give her a personal interest in what might happen and she couldn't help feeling some excitement at the thought that Anthony Woodville might be king in all but name.

The same possibility had crossed the mind of Margaret Beaufort, with none of the same elation. She was tormented by a maelstrom of emotions – apprehension, hatred, hope – and her unease manifested itself in caustic speech and impatience with everyone, including sharp slaps, while sleeplessness deepened the pouches under her eyes and tightened her mouth. She couldn't bear the thought that the Woodvilles might now increase their power but yet was unable to quench a flicker of hope that this may well serve the interests of her son for most people would not be happy by a reinforcement of Woodville supremacy. She hated not knowing what was happening. It was imperative she joined her husband immediately and got his reaction.

She pressed on with the journey as speedily as possible, riding wildly and for longer hours than usual, impervious to the complaints of her entourage and leaving behind the baggage transport. Lady Margaret was an expert horsewoman with a stamina that defied her small frame and they stopped only when necessary. On the way she paid no heed to gossip and rumour, only interested in what she could hear from her husband at the centre of things.

He was awaiting her at their house in the Strand and dismissing her servants she immediately closeted herself with him before removing her dusty riding clothes.

"According to the will of King Edward he has named his brother Richard of Gloucester as Protector of the realm until his son is of an age to rule," Sir Thomas informed her. "He is now on his way from the north, it took time for the news to reach Yorkshire." Richard of Gloucester's lands were there.

Margaret experienced a momentary relief as she said, "Well at least that has curbed the power of the Woodvilles. It's well known that Gloucester hates them." The initial reaction though was tempered with a disappointment that the Duke's appointment would lessen the chances of her son stepping into the breach. "What is the reaction of the Woodvilles to this news?" she asked.

Sir Thomas grimaced. "Predictable. They are determined not to accept Edward's wishes. They have ordered Lord Rivers to bring the little king immediately from Ludlow.....with an escort of 2,000 men," he added meaningfully. "It is their intention to have the boy crowned immediately, they have proclaimed a date in May. Of course you know that once he is crowned, even if under age, there is legally no need for a Protector. He will rule in his own right."

"Through the Woodvilles," Margaret laughed bitterly. But then immediately her fertile mind went to work again. This would not please the people. The Woodville clan considered themselves too powerful to concern themselves with the will of the people but it was not true that public opinion could be ignored, as events of the past twenty years proved. Perhaps after all this could be the opening for her son to intervene. "What do you think Gloucester will do?" she asked her husband.

"He will certainly react in some way," said Sir Thomas. "We do not know a lot about him because as you know he has always preferred to spend his time in the north where he has lordship. His castle at Middleham has always pleased him more than the court. But what we do know of him is that his loyalty to his brother Edward was paramount, he fought constantly at his side, supported all his policies and was always there when needed. If Edward has named him Protector then it will be a mark of his continued loyalty to do as he is bid. Besides he hates the Woodvilles, blaming them for all the ills of his brother's reign."

When Margaret left her husband to change her clothes she was still deep in thought though her mind was more settled now that she understood the present situation, even if it was unpredictable. At least she now had her husband beside her who could keep her informed of events, Sir Thomas being a member of the King's Council as well as steward of the King's household. However these positions could be uncertain with a change of government. But for the present the Council continued to meet under the leadership of the most important of the nobles, Lord Hastings, and the following day Sir Thomas relayed further news to his wife.

"Richard of Gloucester has left his Yorkshire domains with an escort of at least two thousand men and has ordered Lord Rivers, also on his way to the capital with a reported two thousand in his train, to meet him at Leicester with the young king. Large companies of men! Are they armies? Will Lord Rivers obey? His sister and the rest of his family have told him he must hasten to London to have the boy crowned on the fourth day of May."

"So it's a race," Margaret mused. "If Rivers obeys his family the boy will be crowned before his uncle Gloucester arrives and the Protectorship will be null and void. If the Duke of Gloucester gets to London first then the Woodvilles are defeated."

"The question is whether Rivers will obey family loyalties or the command of the King's brother," said Sir Thomas.

"I don't like any of the Woodvilles as you know but Anthony is the best of them," Margaret said. "He has never shown any political ambitions nor desire for power, even though he has been invested with it. I think he will obey Gloucester and hand over the boy to him because he is a man of honour and that is what the late King commanded."

"Well we shall have to await the outcome," said Sir Thomas.

Margaret looked at his worried face and asked, "Where will you stand?" She was well aware that their fortunes had rested with King Edward and his Woodville family. If the Woodvilles were defeated in their plans then her husband's positions as steward of the household and member of the Royal Council could stand in jeopardy.

Sir Thomas Stanley paused then replied, "I shall see who are the victors."

Bel and the rest of the Countess's ladies were not aware of what was happening except as they heard rumours from the other servants but it was undeniable that the City itself was in a state of excitement, crowds gathering in the streets and inns to discuss the sudden turn of events. It was given out that the new king, Edward V, was to arrive in London soon and that he was going to be crowned on May 4th, not much more than a week off.

"I hope we shall be able to see him," Bel said. "Do you think the Countess will let us out to watch."

Their mistress had spent much of her time closeted with her husband but even so she had not left them to their own devices but kept them busy with what they considered unnecessary tasks of sewing, copying and embroidery, though most of the time they just chattered amongst themselves and spied through the windows on important visitors who called on the Stanleys. The Countess had never talked to them of politics or matters of state, Ursula Clifford being the only one she sometimes shared news with and it was Ursula, not usually known for communicating information but unable to keep this startling information to herself, who told them the latest happenings. Lord Rivers had obeyed the Duke of Gloucester's command and met him at Leicester. He had however not brought his young nephew with him but left him at Stony Stratford together with his large company of armed men on the grounds that there would not be sufficient accommodation for them all at Leicester and that Stony Stratford was closer to London. Richard of Gloucester, accompanied by his friend and adviser the Duke of Buckingham, had accepted his explanation and welcomed him and they had wined and dined amicably together that evening. But when Lord Rivers had retired to bed in the inn he was rudely awakened in the middle of the night and arrested together with his companion, his other nephew Lord Richard Grey, son of his sister Elizabeth through her first marriage. They were accused of trying to subvert the law of the land and of kidnapping the young king for their own purpose. They had been sent under armed guard to be imprisoned at one of Gloucester's northern strongholds. The ladies were agog at this latest news, chattering excitedly and relishing the opportunity for some vicarious excitement in their ordered lives.

But Bel was horrified at what had happened to her beloved Anthony Woodville. "He did what he had been told to do. He was acting honourably as always," she cried in some distress.

Her companions lost patience with her constant questions about what was going to happen to him.

"Well if he's been imprisoned in a northern castle there isn't much hope for him is there!"

"He's a Woodville so that will be enough to condemn him."

"What is it to you anyway. What happens to the nobility doesn't concern us and you are not even English."

This was an attitude expressed also by the Countess when Bel, overcome by the news, dared to face her mistress's anger by asking her what would happen to him. Lady Margaret looked at her with undisguised disapproval, shocked by her forwardness.

"Of what interest to you is the fate of Anthony Woodville?" she barked. "Keep to your own concerns, Demoiselle Lechanteur."

"He spoke for my position with you, my Lady," she stammered.

"The Woodvilles are all doomed anyway," the Countess snapped. She broke her usual custom of never chatting with her servants because she was so exhilarated by the news that she wanted to say it out loud and cried triumphantly, "The King is now in the care of his uncle the Duke of Gloucester and taken completely out of the hands of his family. The Queen has sought refuge in sanctuary at the abbey of Westminster together with her other children, and her brothers have fled the realm, though not without taking much of the King's treasure with them."

Bel did not know what to think but knew that she could speak no more to the Countess about her anxieties for Anthony Woodville.

The Countess herself was still in confusion. Her exhilaration at the downfall of the late Queen and her numerous family was overshadowed by the knowledge that with the capable and popular Duke of Gloucester in charge of the little king and his position as Protector of the realm assured, there were dwindling opportunities for her son. The Royal Council under the leadership of Lord Hastings and of which Sir Thomas Stanley was a part, unanimously decided to support Gloucester.

On Sunday May 4th, the day the Woodvilles had planned for the coronation of the young King, a glorious cavalcade rode into London. As the royal procession rode down Ludgate Hill they were met by cheering crowds packed tightly in the narrow streets and on the city walls to the accompaniment of loud pealing of bells from the many churches. Bel was with the other attendants of the Stanley household as they saw the King greeted by the Mayor and aldermen of the City in their scarlet fur-trimmed robes, followed by a long line of the leading citizens in their finery. The young King was clothed in blue velvet and though overawed by the press he waved and smiled, albeit nervously. On his right rode Richard Duke of Gloucester, all in black. On his left rode the Duke of Buckingham, an unfamiliar figure to most people even though he was the only other royal Duke in the kingdom. Though descended four times from Edward III, including through the Beaufort line, he had never come into prominence during the previous reign, avoiding power and state offices and remaining quietly on his estates in Wales and the Marches. His family had been Lancastrians and both his father and grandfather had died fighting for that cause but as a young boy he had been put in the household of Queen Elizabeth who had married him at the age of twelve to her sister Catherine Woodville, against his wishes as he considered her birth greatly inferior to his own. Now, out of nowhere, he was seen riding at the side of the young king and his uncle. Nearly 30 years old, the same age as the Duke of Gloucester, he could not be more of a contrast. Big and burly against the Duke's small slight figure, his face florid and fleshy against the Duke's pale delicate countenance, protuberant eyes and short curly hair against Richard's brooding dark eyes and raven black hair cut straight to his shoulders. People wondered at his presence but thought no more of it.

"The King looks so little," said Agnes Paniker, one of Bel's companions as they craned their necks to see the procession pass.

"I think he looks afraid," Bel said.

"Well it is rather a daunting prospect for a twelve year old," Agnes commented. But Bel's sensitive nature was imagining how lonely the boy must feel, snatched from the body of his family, separated from his beloved uncle Anthony who had shared his life since he was a small child and thrust into the care of another uncle whom he had never known and was a confessed enemy to his mother, his brothers and sisters and his maternal uncles.

The people of London however seemed satisfied, from the highest to the lowest, and there was little dissension heard. The majority only wanted a peaceful succession from one reign to another and the prospect of continuing stability without the threat of further armed conflict, a hope that seemed set for fulfilment. Sir Thomas and the Countess were relieved when Richard confirmed Stanley in his previous position as steward of the royal household and it seemed that, apart from the removal of all the Woodvilles, little change was to be made from the old regime. From his sessions with the Royal Council Sir Thomas was able to relay that with the inclusion to their ranks of the Duke of Buckingham they were to carry on as before and the Duke of Gloucester had gained the confidence of the City by announcing that the young king would be crowned as Edward V in June, much earlier than had been expected.

Then came the news that Anthony Woodville, Earl Rivers, had been executed at the Duke of Gloucester's castle of Pontefract together with his nephew and companion Sir Richard Grey, his sister's son by her first marriage. The Countess's ladies were seated in the parlour with their various needlework when someone happened to mention the fact while making general conversation. Bel dropped her tapestry on the floor and stood up, her eyes wide, gasping in horror. Suddenly she started to scream, a wild primeval shrieking that startled her companions into stopping their own work and staring incomprehensibly at her. She was hardly aware that she was screaming, it had been an involuntary action caused in the first place by shock as when she had heard that Robert Malory was dead and she was unable to stop. The ghastly sound brought the Countess of Richmond into the room and the ladies trembled with fear at the look on her face as she entered the chamber. Her voice was stentorian as she cried, "What in the name of our Lady is going on here."

Bel's screams had now sunk to huge gasps as she fought for air, her hands clutching at imaginary support. The Countess strode towards her and slapped her face, one of her rings grazing her cheek. "Make an end of this hysteria at once," she cried. "How dare you make such an exhibition of yourself. What is the reason for this appalling loss of control?"

Bel's panic attack had now turned into floods of tears and she was unable to answer but Agnes Paniker replied hesitantly, "Someone mentioned Lord Rivers's death."

The Countess took hold of Bel's shoulders and shook her saying, "And what is the death of a traitor to you?"

"He was kind and good. He did as he was told, he was bringing the King to the Duke of Gloucester."

"What do you know of politics?" the Countess stormed. "He was on his way with two thousand armed men to deliver the King to his mother and her family, to have him crowned and thwart Gloucester of the Protectorship. Richard Grey was aiding and abetting him. They were found guilty of treason and justifiably beheaded."

Grief made Bel bold and amidst her tears she continued to contradict the Countess, "He would never be guilty of treason, it is not in his nature. The Duke of Gloucester just wanted to be rid of him because he was a good man and because he was beloved by the King, unlike the Duke."

There was a concerted gasp of horror from the ladies listening with nervous fascination and the Countess spoke now in a voice of icy anger, "How dare you speak in this way of the Lord Protector and defend the Woodvilles. At this time this could be construed as treason if you were English and not French and as it is such views could bring disaster upon us all. I dare keep you here no longer, you will return to Lathom."

"My grandfather's book, what will happen to my grandfather's book now," Bel sobbed, seemingly impervious to the Countess's words.

"What book? What are you babbling about?" cried her mistress impatiently. "You will go to your chamber now and prepare to leave for Lathom immediately. My servant Reginald Bray is returning there early on the morrow and you will accompany him and await my return." She pushed Bel rudely through the door and with harsh words to the rest of her ladies to watch their tongues and learn from this mise-en-scène she left them to chatter amongst themselves. They were subdued by their mistress's anger and puzzled by their companion's unbelievable behaviour.

"I've never seen anything like it. I can't understand why she lost her head like that, going completely mad."

"She's French, they are all volatile."

"Do you think there was something between her and Anthony Woodville?"

"That's unlikely. When could she ever have been in personal contact with him."

"But she's full of secrets. She never talks about her past like we do. We know nothing about her before she joined Lady Margaret's service."

None of them were particularly fond of Bel, some of their aloofness attributed to the fact that she was foreign and different to them, but there was also a certain amount of jealousy for her exceptional beauty and her talents so there was no great regret that she was leaving them. They were all of the concerted opinion that they were glad they did not have to undertake the long hard journey north and they much preferred the excitement of London to the dreary fastness of Lathom.

Bel however was glad to be going. She was incredibly sad and cried herself to sleep recalling Anthony Woodville's kindness to her. A shadow had fallen over the celebrations of the new reign. But who was king and what happened had no personal significance for her. She couldn't wait to leave the City and get back to the peace and quiet of Lancashire. And she looked forward to seeing Harry Duxbury again with his simple life and his comforting friendliness.

CHAPTER 13

Travelling Players

As usual Bel did not mind the long journey northwards which gave her time to settle her thoughts and she found Reginald Bray, one of the Countess's oldest and most trusted servants, an agreeable travelling companion. A man of middle age, small and sturdy with grey hair curling below his ears and a face lined with creases of good humour, especially around the shrewd grey eyes, he was an interesting conversationalist with a lot of anecdotes about his many travels on behalf of the Stanleys. She learnt more about the lives of her employers and in return she told him some of her own stories about her early travels in France and he enjoyed listening to her. After a day on the road when she felt comfortable in his company she asked him if he knew more about the death of Lord Rivers.

"He wasn't expecting to be so dealt with. He was puzzled by the Duke of Gloucester's volte-face after being so agreeably met and entertained. But even while in imprisonment in Yorkshire he had no intimation that he would be put to death. When the announcement finally came it was a shock to him. However he dealt with it with his customary fortitude. He had a strong personal faith and it consoled him now. He made his will, paying all his debts and leaving considerable amounts to the poor and charitable foundations. He asked that any wrongs he had unwittingly committed should be put to rights. He wished that his nephew, the young king, should be made aware of his love for him and be carefully kept. His greatest sorrow was for his other nephew Sir Richard Grey and he asked that they should be buried together in Pontefract where they were to be put to death. The night before his execution he spent writing poetry. On the scaffold he behaved with inspiring courage, devoid of any show of anger or desire for vengeance. When they removed his shirt for the beheading they found he was wearing a hair shirt beneath his fine clothes."

Tears filled Bel's eyes as she imagined the scene. "That fits so well with what I knew of him," she whispered. "Thankyou for telling me the details."

"He was the best of the Woodvilles," Richard Bray said. "He could have been a changeling he was so different. In the end he had no-one to speak for him."

I'll remember him, Bel thought. As soon as she could she would go to Burscough priory and pray for his soul. But she wondered what had happened to Sir Thomas Malory's manuscript, whether Anthony had managed to put it into the hands of the printer he had called William Caxton or if nothing would be heard of it again.

No-one commented on her early return to Lathom, all believing Lady Margaret had some tasks for her so she realised she would have much time on her hands. As Thursday was the morrow she decided it would probably be possible to see Harry Duxbury at the market so she rode over to Ormskirk. There was no sign of him however in the Bull's Head or The Wheatsheaf or amongst the market stalls. She finished her shopping and decided to go into the church to pray for the soul of Anthony Woodville, laying surreptitiously on the altar a bunch of rosemary she had bought from an apothecary's stall, rosemary for remembrance they said. It wasn't yet time to go home and remembering that Harry had once told her that his sister lived in a house off Moor croft behind Moor street she decided to see if he was there.

Asking for Ethelreda in the neighbourhood she was directed to a substantial double-fronted house with a burgage plot, built of wood and plaster but on a stone foundation. On either side of the central oak door were small-paned glass windows. There were two other small casements of horn just visible beneath the overhanging thatched roof. She seized the iron ring on the door and gave it a resounding bang and a short time later the door was opened by a woman carrying a baby with another small child clinging to her blue linen skirt. Bel had no need to confirm her name because her resemblance to Harry was striking. Several years older than he, she was tall and thin with the same white-blonde hair tied in a knot, the blue eyes and fair complexion.

"Yes?" she said abruptly and Bel intuited she was harassed as the wailing of another child could be heard from inside the house.

"I'm looking for Harry Duxbury. Is he here?" she stammered.

"No he isn't," she replied brusquely.

"Do you know where he is?" Bel asked, somewhat intimidated by her waspish manner.

"Yes I know where he is," she snapped. "Oh yes, I can tell you where he is. He's in the jailhouse at Preston, that's where he is."

Bel was shocked and could only manage, "Why?"

"For brawling with the Standishes as usual, even threatening murder. You would think he would learn but no, he can't let be," his sister's voice now held a weary resignation. "You're his French friend from Lathom House aren't you. He talks about you. But in the name of all the saints I don't know why you bother with him."

"He's my friend," she said. "He's bored, that's why he gets into trouble."

Ethelreda studied her carefully then said, "Well Jaxon has tried to help him by finding him some work so he ought to be grateful instead of getting into mischief and getting us all a bad name. This time he's gone too far because our uncle John has washed his hands of him, says he hasn't to go back to the farm because he's a bad influence on Ughtred so that means I shall be burdened with him indefinitely." She scowled, reminding Bel even more of her brother.

Bel was worried and asked, "What's to become of him?"

Ethelreda shrugged saying, "They would let him out if somebody would pay his fine and some person in authority would vouch for his behaviour but neither our uncle John nor my husband Jaxon will do so, not for a time anyway, they are determined to teach him a lesson and besides we can't really afford."

Bel sighed, thanked Ethelreda and turned to go.

"I'm sorry," Ethelreda said, "If you come and ask next week I might have some news for you."

Bel returned to Lathom deep in thought. If she had some money she would pay his fine. But the only way she could ever earn money was by entertaining which was not possible now. If only she were a man she could travel from place to place finding work easily like her father and Renard. Once again she relived the time she had spent with the young minstrel, they could always find opportunities within a day's walking, some of them better than others. A large town offered many good inns and perhaps the houses of important people but even a village usually had one inn that would be glad of a minstrel for the night, even if the only remuneration was a few pennies and accommodation in a loft or stable. She wondered as she often did where Renard was and what he was doing. Had he found another companion?

The days were long at Lathom with little to do and she occupied herself with thinking of means to get Harry back, at least he offered some diversion and she didn't like to think of his exuberant spirit confined in the gaol, under what sort of circumstances she had no idea but knew they would not be pleasant. If only she could find some way of entertaining and getting some money but there were few families around Ormskirk of the status of the Stanleys, the manors were small and rustic and there was no way she could travel a long distance alone. Even on horseback it was not safe and besides who ever heard of a travelling minstrel arriving on horseback.

The other problem she thought she might be able to resolve. One day when she had been called into the comptroller's office to help one of the clerks with copying out some accounts as his assistant was suffering from problems with his eyesight, she had seen the great seals with the Stanley crest. She was sure she could manage to stamp a piece of parchment with some indecipherable script that might pass for a recommendation from the Stanleys.

One day she was sitting in the ladies' solar reading the Countess's copy of "La Queste del Sainte Graal" and thinking of Sir Thomas Malory's great accomplishment of translating all the separate Arthurian romances into the English tongue and making them into one whole book, wondering again what had become of it with the death of Lord Rivers. One wall of the solar happened to be painted with an Arthurian scene, the knight Ywaine with his lion. Suddenly her attention was diverted by a loud commotion in the courtyard below and putting down the volume on the little coffer with brass locks and a lid painted with red roses, she left her chair and went to look out of the window. Kneeling on the wainscotbench she opened the casement and saw a motley group of people with a laden cart pulled by a workhorse. Dressed in an assortment of ragtag clothes, parti-coloured hose, jerkins and doublets of various materials and colours patched together, fantastic hats with feathers and bells, she recognised them as a troupe of travelling players, especially when one of them began to bang the drum hanging on a cord around his neck. The steward, accompanied by other members of the household, had hurried out to see what the commotion was and was promptly accosted by the leader of the troupe, a tall thin man wearing a voluminous cloak of faded crimson velvet, who made an exaggeratedly low bow as he swept off his broad-brimmed feathered hat to reveal a shock of bright red hair. Bel was smiling delightedly but couldn't hear all of the conversation, only the odd word about entertaining and obviously sounding the praises of his fellow actors as he swept his hand extravagantly over the company who proceeded to make their own obesiances. As the steward shook his head and disappointment crossed the faces of the actors she understood that he would be telling them that Sir Thomas and Lady Margaret were not at present in residence. He did however offer them some refreshment and told them to make their way to the kitchens.

When they returned to the courtyard to harness the cart again, Bel was waiting for them, peering curiously into the cart laden with costumes and properties. She could see a tarnished golden crown, swords and bucklers, angels' wings, a long grey wig, devils' horns, various musical instruments and trestles and painted cloths. She couldn't resist the opportunity to talk to them as fellow-entertainers. Other servants had gathered to watch them depart, glad of the unexpected break in their daily routine, but they merely stood and gaped. Bel however approached the leader and introduced herself. He was surprised at being accosted by a beautiful young lady of the household and spoke deferentially to her but Bel was soon laughing and pouring out her story about being a travelling minstrel in her former life. "I hope that one day I shall be able to resume my old life because that is what I like best and I look upon my stay here as only temporary."

The players gathered around her, entranced by her beauty, her vivacity, her lilting accent and the story of some of her experiences. "Would you really change your life of luxury here for a life of hardship and uncertain fortunes on the road as we know it?" one of them asked, shaking his head in bemusement when Bel said she would.

The leader, who introduced himself as Pell, told her that they were on their way to Standish Hall where there was a celebration for the birth of an heir but as they had come from Preston they had made a diversion in hope of also being able to prolong their time in the area by a visit to Lathom House.

"What will you do now?" she asked.

Pell shrugged resignedly. "We shall lose a night's pay and probably accommodation so that will mean we shall have to find a barn or a hedge to sleep tonight," he said. "But we hope we shall more than make up for it on the morrow. It is likely the Standishes will be in good humour for the birth of a son and heir and will be correspondingly generous. Also because we shall be able to arrive there in the morning we shall probably be able to give two performances, one in the afternoon and one in the evening."

Bel wished them good fortune and watched them depart, merry and singing as they prepared to take the steep road over Parbold Hill towards the little town of Standish. When they had gone however she stood for a time deep in thought and didn't go back to the romance of the grail. An idea was brewing in her mind. She thought about it carefully all night until she was sure she had planned it to perfection, unless some unpredictable circumstance intervened.

Very early next morning she dressed in an old linen gown of orange-tawny. The colour symbolised prudence but she knew she was being reckless rather than prudent. She went to collect her horse Troubadour from the stables and in the leather saddle bag put her entertaining gown, a little shabby now but still eye-catching, her flageolet and bells. Across her back her lute hung on a cord. She mounted her horse and set off, grateful once again that Robert Malory had taught her to ride well. She expected to catch up with them somewhere on the road between Lathom and Standish and she knew she couldn't miss them in their flamboyant entourage and their noisy companionship.

Sure enough almost at the junction with Langtree she came upon the travelling players and hailed them. They stopped in surprise, crowding around her. After their greetings she told them what she wanted. Although glad to see her some of them were reluctant. Especially when she demanded a share of the money they would earn.

"We already have our programme, we cannot change it."

"We know our parts and it would be difficult to include someone new."

But others said, "Most of our playing is improvised, we can easily include some extra material."

"I think songs could be put in anywhere and the audiences always like music. If Bel plays and sings it would increase our appeal and therefore we should earn more."

In the end it was Pell who made the final decision. They were to play a much revised form of "Everyman" and some interludes, both comic and dramatic. A beautiful girl who could sing and dance would raise the value of their entertainment and the extra money they would charge would more than cover Bel's share. However all of them were puzzled as to the reason why a girl in comfortable circumstances at a great castle like Lathom should be in need of money.

"I am merely a servant at Lathom, even if a privileged one," Bel insisted. "I told you my wish is to be a minstrel." But then she made the decision to tell them the truth. She would not have done so with anyone else but these travelling entertainers were of her own world with a lifestyle that did not encompass the rules and values of normal society. She told them the story of Harry Duxbury and they were predictably sympathetic and eager to help.

They arrived at Standish Hall with all the commotion of their usual entrance, blowing a trumpet and banging the drum, leaping and prancing and calling merrily while the cart rumbled noisily on the cobblestones of the courtyard. The manor was situated down a leafy lane leading from the highway that joined Wigan and Chorley, set on a beech-shaded plateau with extensive views across the valley of the river Douglas. It was a house of modest size, timber and plaster on a stone base, two-storeyed with a gabled end elevation rising to a third storey. All the windows, two of them oriels, had panes of glass and smoke curled from a cluster of chimneys in the brick-tiled roof. A range of subsidiary buildings seemed to be stables and service quarters and there was much activity in evidence. The central door was of seasoned oak studded with iron bosses but Pell went around the back of the house to where there was another door into the building and where he could ask for the Standish's steward or bailiff. When he returned however he was somewhat disappointed. They were expected for the entertainment in the evening but everyone was too busy preparing the feast for that occasion and there was no time available for a performance in the afternoon.

"No matter," he said briskly, "we shall go and perform in the market place. We probably won't earn much from the townspeople but it will be better than doing nothing and we can use it as a rehearsal."

He had been in this area before so he led his little company back up the lane to the highway, Bel following on horseback, and after half a mile they arrived at the little town situated at a four lane crossroad. The large market place in front of a noble church contained a cross, a set of stocks and a public well and was teeming with activity as the townsfolk did their morning shopping in the surrounding booths and shops. Shouting and hallooing the players strode into the centre space near the cross where they parked their cart and having attracted the attention of the crowd, Pell leapt onto the cart and began to make a speech. He explained their presence and advertised a forthcoming performance in the square at two of the clock, his announcement punctuated regularly by rolls on the drum by a big burly man Bel now knew of as Jake. The spectators roared their approval and promised to pass the word around, eager to take advantage of this rare intrusion into the monotony of their daily existence.

Bel had decided it would be wiser not to participate in the afternoon's performance in case news should be bandied around and someone later might recognise her, also the entertainment would no doubt be vulgar and rumbustious to serve the taste of an uneducated audience. The travelling players were well accustomed to varying their repertoire to suit the occasion. She was disappointed that she might not be able to earn as much as she had hoped but when she told the players that she would remain a spectator they were relieved for much of their rough entertainment was improvised. The clock on the church tower struck noon and as the square began to empty, Pell suggested they adjourn to the adjacent White Hart and get something to eat. Bel however thought it would be wiser not to join their company and said she would go and sit in the churchyard until later so Pell promised to bring her some food and drink.

She was seated under a tree, her horse contentedly nibbling the grass beside her, when the young boy Tim who played the girls' roles arrived with a meat pasty and a wooden cup of ale. A slight fair-haired boy of about thirteen he had a surprisingly strong voice and lingered for a while to talk to her. He told her that both his parents had been players and his mother used to carry him on stage as a baby and then as a small child when there were such parts, but both his parents had died last year in an epidemic of plague in Nottingham.

"A player's life is hard, there are many dangers," he said.

Bel agreed but when she was alone again, sitting in the dappled sunshine beneath the elm and munching the hot pasty, she thought she hadn't been so happy for a long time and even forgot the reason she had undertaken this adventure.

The strident notes of the trumpet and the echoing of the drum roused her from her reverie and leading the horse she returned to the market place where a crowd had already gathered. The players were putting the finishing touches to their performance space. In front of the waggon they had erected wooden poles on which they had draped a once-bright cloth of linen painted with suns and moons and other strange symbols and although the blue, green and gold had faded it was still an effective backdrop. The crowd was large now and keeping to the back Bel found it difficult to see so she mounted her horse which gave her the advantage of height and allowed her to stay well away from the audience. People had climbed on to the cross and the well rim, women had carried stools from their houses and children were sitting on the ground.

The performance was fast and furious, one incident following another with frenetic speed as the players changed costumes behind the cart, altered their voices, fought and tumbled, so that the audience were reduced to shrieks of laughter. Bel found herself laughing delightedly and was impressed by the troupe's energy and versatility. When the performance was ended, while two of the players continued to carry on a conversation between a charlatan and a fool so that the audience would not leave quickly, the rest of the troupe went swiftly around with baskets to collect what payment they could. Some were loath to pay but Pell had cleverly trapped them in a compromising situation and most of them were willing to drop a farthing into the baskets for the unexpected pleasure they had enjoyed.

"About our usual haul," Pell said as he divided the money between the six of them, keeping the odd coin for himself. "Hopefully we shall earn much more than this tonight."

They began to dismantle the curtain and return their costumes and properties to the cart then with Bell following behind them they made their way back to Standish Hall.

The evening was similar to many of the evenings she had shared with Renard and her father. The hall was not a great size, beamed to a collar roof and wood-panelled without tapestries. The panelling was thick and simply cut but brightly painted with patterns of squares and lozenges in red, blue and green. There was a large pewter candelabra hanging from the centre beam and wall sconces at intervals with more candles and torches. The stone floor would normally have been strewn with sweet-scented rushes but Pell had requested a clear space for the entertainment so bunches of lavender and herbs were hung from the beams. The company comprised only about three dozen people seated at trestles at right angles to the centre dais where at a table covered by a white cloth and displaying some fine silver sat the Standish family. Sir Edward Standish was a man of about forty years old, ruddy faced with light auburn hair and beard, his wife Lady Dorothy, small and plump with a rosy face beaming with pride, and beside them sat four small girls. "You can see why he is celebrating the birth of a son and heir," Tim whispered to Bel. Everyone was well dressed in good quality cloth of wool, cambric and some velvet but without the lavish decoration of the court and in a style several years out of date by London fashions. Lady Dorothy was wearing a towering two-horned headdress of the sort that noble ladies had worn twenty years previously. Also on the dais were other family members, brothers and cousins of Sir Edward with their wives and families and to her horror Bel caught a glimpse of Rafe Standish among them. This was something she had not taken into consideration and for a moment panic overwhelmed her. He had not noticed her and she told herself that he was unlikely to recognise her. He had seen her only once briefly and then she had been soberly dressed for riding, her hair braided in a long plait and her face sheltered by her straw hat. Now she was wearing her flamboyant gown with her hair loose and in any case he certainly would not be expecting her amongst this strange company. Nevertheless she determined to keep as far as possible from him and fortunately in the first episode they were to present she was to wear an angel mask and a blonde wig.

A space had been kept for the players in the centre of the diners and as usual they did some tumbling and juggling while the company ate noisily, Jake banging the drum and Bel playing her flageolet and a tabor she had found amongst the properties but keeping in the background. She marvelled at the troupe's dexterity as they juggled half a dozen balls at a time, standing on each other's shoulders on a plank of wood with wheels which every moment threatened to upturn them. When the meal had ended Sir Edward stood and called for silence then on cue a nursemaid arrived holding a swaddled child which she handed to him. He held the child high in the air crying "Behold our son and heir Alexander," and there was loud cheering, stamping of feet and banging of goblets and tankards on the tables. Then handing the child back to the nurse Sir Edward held up his goblet and pronounced a toast which was answered by several of his relatives, including the lusty Rafe and the rector from the church of St. Lawrence, flushed with the unusual amount of wine he had consumed. Then Sir Edward announced the entertainment which was greeted by loud cries of encouragement.

For Bel the evening passed swiftly, as it always did when she was entertaining. She sang and played her lute at intervals during the performance of Everyman and the following interludes, dressed in the cloaks and masks that the actors had suggested. Then she took the floor on her own, retaining a mask of gilded leather, playing her lute and singing then dancing with the bells and the tabor. A silence fell on the spectators who previously had contributed cheers, laughs and impertinent comments to the action and when she had finished the hall rang with spontaneous and lengthy applause.

"Give them a few minutes more," Pell whispered to her and she obeyed as with sudden inspiration she began to sing, 'Lullay, lullay, my little tiny child,' from the mystery play of the Nativity which she had first heard in Coventry and learnt when she had been with Robert. At the close Sir Edward came down from the dais to thank her personally and then to thank the whole troupe for their admirable entertainment that evening adding to his guests, "I am sure you will wish to show your own appreciation to our travellers who have come to share their skills with us on this special occasion," and this was the cue for the actors to take their baskets around the tables and receive tips other than what their host had promised to pay them.

Bel was still feeling exhilarated by the experience, soaring on wings at her success, when to her horror she saw Rafe Standish approaching her, his muscular figure encased in tight-fitting blue velvet, a matching pancake hat on his chestnut curly hair. She tried not to look too closely at him but the small eyes beneath busy eyebrows were not too prescient and it was obvious he had had too much to drink.

"Here is something for you for your entertainment," he slurred, pressing some silver coins into her hand. "How would you like to earn more for further pleasure?"

She took a deep breath then seeing Pell approach her she dared to say, "I will consider it, kind sir, but first I must help my companions to put away our things, it is important my musical instruments are stored carefully."

"I will seek you out later," he said. "I can provide you with better sleeping quarters than the hay lofts you will be allotted."

She made a vague assent knowing that Pell was close by then turned aside to follow the leader to where the others were packing away their belongings ready to carry them to their cart.

"What are you going to do now?" Pell asked her. "We have been given permission to sleep on the premises tonight."

"I shall take my horse and go home, it isn't far, no more than a half hour," she replied.

The others demurred that it was dangerous but Bel was insistent, she was a good rider and could ride fast and she knew the way. It was doubtful if any evil-doers would be abroad in the inhospitable landscape, Parbold's stony hill and the marshlands, no-one ventured this way at night unless they were familiar with the paths . There were no towns or large manors to tempt thieves, only a couple of small hamlets inhabited by poor people. The main hazard would be the pitch blackness but she was sure of the way.

"We have done well tonight, much better than we expected and much of it due to your contribution to our entertainment. Here is your share," Pell said, handing her a bag of coins which felt heavy in her hand. "We have also been invited to return any time we are along this way."

"I am so grateful that you allowed me to join you," she said. "I have had a wonderful time."

All the actors expressed their delight at having her in their company and young Tim said, "I wish you could stay with us and be part of our troupe."

"I would love to do that, honestly, but at this time I cannot," she said, genuinely regretful as she looked around the faces of this motley company with their outlandish clothes and their weather-beaten faces revealing the hardships of their calling. They would sleep rough tonight, be on their way tomorrow to where they could next find a booking, braving the uncertainties of the weather, but they were friendly, generous and most of all doing what they enjoyed most.

She mounted her horse and the players accompanied her up the lane to the highway where they made their fond farewells, Bel promising that if ever their paths should cross again she would be part of their company.

She felt a moment of apprehension as she left them behind but Parbold hill was not far away and all she had to do was follow it to the bottom. From there several paths led to Lathom's great fortress though she intended if possible to keep on the Newburgh road which was well built as a thoroughfare to Burscough priory. The going was slower than she would have liked because of the hazards multiplied by the blackness though she was pleasantly surprised by the full moon in a clear sky and then faint lights in the little village of Parbold so after taking great care to cross the bridge across the river Douglas she arrived safely at Newburgh. She missed the road at the cross but then picked up the other road to Lathom and soon in the moon's pale beams was able to make out the towers of the castle. She gave her name to the startled guard as she clattered across the drawbridge, mumbling some vague reason for her late return, then went to stable Troubadour. She stroked his mane and kissed his face, whispering her thanks for bringing her home safely then crept into the building by one of the back entrances, monitored only by a half-awake guard who wished only to get back to sleep.

Lying in bed in the chamber she shared with Maud Pettifer but which was now her own as Maud was in London with the Countess, she was still excited by the events of the night. How Renard would have been proud of her, she thought. She smiled ruefully. She still thought of him whenever she entertained, always wished he could be there with her, even after such a long time. She wondered where he was, what he was doing, who he was with. She did not know if she would ever forget him even if it seemed unlikely they should ever meet again. So she turned her thoughts to Harry Duxbury. She now had to get him out of gaol. Now that she had counted it she was pleased by how much she had been able to earn this night. It wasn't quite enough but she had a little money of her own saved. It would be a couple of days now before she could get to Ormskirk on her usual market day trip but that would give her time to find an opportunity to steal into the comptroller's room when he was out and press the Stanley seal onto a piece of paper on which she would scribble some indecipherable script.

The following Thursday she was knocking on the door of the house of Ethelreda Duxbury (or whatever her married name was.) Harry's sister was still wearing the blue gown, her blonde hair this time covered by a linen kerchief and with only one child by her side. She was surprised to see Bel, especially when she handed to her a money bag saying, "This is to pay Harry's fine. Can you get it to him as soon as possible?"

"You had better come into the house," she said, opening wide the door.

Bel stepped inside to a passageway the length of the house leading to another door at the back. There was a door on either side of the passage and Ethelreda opened the one on the left which led into a large room with a window overlooking the street. Hanging from the roof beams was a large ham and an iron rail holding some clothes. The floor was stone paved, swept clean without rushes, and there was a chimney with a hearth and ingle nook where an iron pot hung on a chain over the fire. A pine table with a rush-seated chair and a few joint stools filled the centre of the room and there was a large pine chest with an assortment of clothes piled on top. In a corner of the room a baby slept in a hooded crib while another child was sitting on an open staircase at the back of the room.

"What is this?" Ethelreda said, putting the child on a stool and opening the money bag.

"I told you, it's to pay Harry's fine," she said.

"You are paying his fine?" his sister said in amazement, pouring the coins onto the table where the little boy made to grab them, to be stopped by his mother's rap on his knuckles.

"In a way, yes," Bel replied. "I cannot go to Preston but perhaps your husband might. There is also this paper with Sir Thomas Stanley's seal giving their approval for Harry's release."

Ethelreda was stupefied. At last she said, "I will ask my husband to take it to Preston. You make me ashamed that we have done nothing for Harry ourselves. But we don't have a lot of money with three children and I am expecting another. Jaxon is a leather worker, he makes pouches, bags, belts, but he is not from Ormskirk, he came from Chorley so he has not yet built up a reputation for himself here and sales are slow. Things might improve now he will have Harry to help him."

There was an uneasy silence between them then Bel said, "I must go now. I will call again next week unless I see Harry in the meantime."

"Thankyou again," Ethelreda said as they made their farewells.

Bel made her way back to Lathom, hoping that the money would reach Harry after all her efforts. She had missed his irreverent companionship and did hope she would see him again soon.

CHAPTER 14

Conspiracies

In London Sir Thomas and Lady Margaret were finding
things not going as they had hoped. At first it seemed
that Richard Duke of Gloucester was intent on following
his brother King Edward's instructions and changing
little from the previous reign. He had confirmed the
old officers of the King's Council, with the addition of
the Duke of Buckingham, and had promised a June
coronation of the new young king. However he had then
postponed the crowning indefinitely thus prolonging his
own term as Protector. Then the lords, especially those
of the Council, had become increasingly worried about
the growing influence of the Duke of Buckingham.
Buckingham had appeared from nowhere but Richard
had not only made him his close friend and confidant,
but had also enriched him with lands and estates,
many of them taken from the disgraced Woodvilles, and
empowered him with the highest offices in the land. As a
member of the Royal Council he had begun to overturn
many of their policies, proceed with his own agenda with
the support of Richard, and limit the power of the old
members. Stanley together with Lord Hastings, Lord
Howard, the Earl of Arundel and the other nobles began

to realise that they had removed the Woodvilles only to have them replaced by the Duke of Buckingham as the main power in the land, maker of policies and promoter of favourites. Their own influence was waning rapidly and looked set to be extinguished altogether in the Protector's government so they began to make plans to have the usurper removed, holding secret meetings in various places.

One day terrible news was conveyed to Lady Margaret. Her husband and other members of the Council had been arrested and imprisoned on a charge of treason as Richard of Gloucester himself had invaded one of their meetings. Worst of all was the news that Lord Hastings, leader of the Council and King Edward's closest friend and adviser, whom Richard considered to be the leader of the conspiracy, had been taken outside and immediately beheaded.

Margaret Beaufort experienced once again the terror that had often consumed her in the past when the Lancastrian cause had been lost and she and her second husband Henry Stafford had walked a tightrope to avoid the perils of the Yorkist ascendancy. Although she and Sir Thomas Stanley had given their consent to the Duke of Gloucester's appointment and shown their willingness to serve him, the fact that her son Henry Tudor was the only surviving Lancaster heir to the throne still enmeshed her and her husband in suspicion and consequent danger. The Duke of Gloucester had accused Sir Thomas Stanley of plotting against him. He had been influenced by his mentor Buckingham who obviously was intent on removing from power all those he considered a threat to his own predominance. Stanley's friend and associate the Duke of Hastings had been executed summarily without trial. Could the same be meted out to Thomas? Lady Margaret was on tenterhooks and even her constant prayers and intercessions could not save her from anxiety.

Despite her fears, Sir Thomas was soon released and surprisingly returned to his position as steward of the royal household. The Duke of Gloucester was not a vengeful man and always preferred mercy to malice. But he had made his point. He would be swift to act against those he considered his enemies and the Duke of Buckingham must not be interfered with. Relieved beyond measure by her husband's release, Lady Margaret longed to be able to return to the tranquillity of Lathom, to her prayers and meditations, her good works in the neighbourhood, her thoughts and plans about her son. But she knew her husband must remain in his place at the court and she must be by his side in these uncertain times. If she removed herself to the far north she might invite doubts as to her own loyalty.

"I can't believe you did this for me, Bella. Paying for my release."

"I didn't. The Standishes did. Rafe Standish contributed quite a sum," she replied, waiting for Harry Duxbury's reaction.

He had been waiting for her in the Wheatsheaf in Ormskirk and they greeted each other joyfully. Harry looked thinner and he said Ethelreda had burnt his clothes, but he wasn't noticeably chastened, telling her that he hadn't been too badly treated and he had picked up some useful tips for future harassment from his temporary associates.

"You must behave yourself in future," she said sternly.

He ignored this, asking fiercely, "Did you sleep with him?"

Bel turned on him angrily. "Is that what you think of me, Harry Duxbury? Do you think me a whore, is that all I am to you? I wouldn't do such a thing, even for you and if I had known you thought so little of me then I wouldn't have bothered getting you free at all."

He grasped her arm and said hastily, "No of course I don't, it's just that I couldn't think of any way else you could have got the money, especially from that bastard Rafe Standish."

"Well what about my earning it by entertaining? It's what I do. I am a minstrel, well at least a minstrel's girl. Have you forgotten?" She then proceeded to tell him the whole story. He was enthralled and kept shaking his head at her ingenuity.

"Rafe Standish didn't recognise me and he did try to seduce me but he was drunk and he had already paid me then. Oh Harry don't you think it the most beautiful irony that he actually paid towards your release." She began to laugh her bubbling infectious laugh and soon they were both helpless with laughter.

"What about the paper I forged?" she asked.

"They never even looked at it, just saw the seal and waved it away," he replied. "I wonder what further cozenage we could work, you and I together."

"No Harry," she said sternly. "You must think about what you are going to do with your life."

"Well at the moment I have no choice. Part of the conditions of my release is that I have to work on repairing the bridge at Burscough. You probably don't know but there have been forcible subscriptions for the repair of several of the bridges round here which have got into a bad state. And I have to continue to live with my sister because my uncle John won't have me back. I hate it, all those squalling brats. I have to share a bedchamber with them because there are only two upstairs so I can't even have you with me until I can go back to the pele. My brother-in-law Jaxon uses the other downstairs room as his workshop for making his leather goods and that's where I shall have to spend all my time. Although he does use me to collect supplies and deliver goods."

"Well you will be learning a trade," Bel said encouragingly.

Harry scowled saying, "I want more from my life than that. And I want to get back to the pele."

"You have to think of a way to secure your Uncle John's pardon then."

The scowl transformed itself into a grin. "I can see you are just as eager as I am to get back to the pele with me."

She punched his ribs but admitted, "I have nothing to do at Lathom. I always wish to be free of the Countess's demands but really it is tedious with everyone away. I wish they would return from London and then at least I would have some conversation."

"There are rumours abroad that the Duke of Gloucester is taking all the power for himself just as if he were king. But what can you expect when the king is only twelve years old. Imagine Ughtred as king! He would only do what everybody told him to do so that's not surprising," Harry said, adding, "The Duke of Gloucester is thought highly of in the north, he is more or less a northerner himself."

Bel was not interested in England's politics but knew that she hated the Duke of Gloucester because he had murdered Anthony Woodville.

"I'll try to see you as soon as I can, Bella. I only have to work three weeks on the bridge then I'll send to you and we can meet. I'm sorry it can't be sooner," he sighed. "Thank you again for getting me out of gaol."

Bel bade him farewell regretfully as he made his way reluctantly to his sister's house. As she made her own way back to Lathom she was thinking of how she could help him to reinstate himself in the good graces of his uncle. She had no intimation of how fate would take matters into its own hands and weave Harry Duxbury once again into the pattern of her life.

In London everyone was agog at the latest news issued through the mouth of the ubiquitous Duke of Buckingham. It was proclaimed that King Edward's marriage to Elizabeth Woodville had not been legal because he had been already contracted to another woman. It had been discovered that he was previously betrothed to Lady Eleanor Butler, daughter of the Earl of Shrewsbury and newly widowed when Edward came to the throne. He had fallen in love with the young widow (she was a few years his senior as was Elizabeth Woodville), and Bishop Stillington, Bishop of Bath and Wells, told the Duke of Gloucester that he had witnessed their exchange of vows but had been bribed to keep it secret. Betrothal with the exchange of vows had the force of a legal tie and in the eyes of the church was the sanction of a sacred obligation. Under these circumstances the marriage of the King and Elizabeth Woodville was null and void and therefore their children were illegitimate.

The next move to this startling revelation was expected by all and sundry. If the young king Edward V was not the legitimate son of Edward IV then the next heir to the throne was undoubtedly Edward's only surviving brother, Richard Duke of Gloucester. It was the Duke of Buckingham who made the official announcement from the steps of the Guildhall - the Duke of Gloucester was the legal heir to the crown of England and from this time would be known as King Richard III. This was followed by a sermon at Paul's cross confirming the fact, in the presence of Richard and Buckingham, and a subsequent session of the Lords and Commons gave their unanimous approval. There was little demur amongst the rank and file of the populace. Richard was popular and unlike the so-called wars of the roses of recent memory the transfer of a monarch had been achieved without any bloodshed. It was good for the country to have a mature, wise and seemingly just ruler instead of a child of whom little had been seen of late since he and his younger brother had been transferred for safety to the royal apartments in the Tower of London. What would become of them now was uncertain, though it seemed probable that the boys would be returned to the bosom of their Woodville family.

Sir Thomas Stanley and his wife followed the unfolding events as avidly as everyone else. Sir Thomas, ever watchful, kept quietly in the background until it was certain there was going to be no revolt against the newly-proclaimed King Richard then he was foremost with his avowed loyalty. Lady Margaret had followed him with an obvious show of support for the new regime and at the coronation, which was quickly arranged, she carried the train of the new Queen Anne. But her outward demeanour and her inward thoughts were at variance. In her own opinion Richard had no more claim to the crown than had her son Henry Tudor. And the story of the pre-contract contained discrepancies, Lady Eleanor Butler was dead by the time the young princes were born. The chain of events had strengthened, rather than weakened, her hopes for the divinely-ordained destiny of her son. A flutter of anticipation excited her frail form. She would wait patiently and continue to pray that God in his wisdom would make His way clear. And she would say nothing at all on the subject to her husband.

In Ormskirk little was known of events in London and then only scantily. On market days word was passed around that the Duke of Gloucester had assumed the kingship as Richard III. There was little discontent shown. Richard was known as a good man who had spent most of his life in the north where he was popular. When Bel met Harry Duxbury, who had now finished his turn working on Burscough Bridge, they were idly speculating on what they had heard around the market stalls.

"I wonder what has happened to the little prince." Bel wasn't interested in who happened to be king of England but her sensitive nature had homed in on what the young boy must be thinking about his sudden change of fortune. "They are saying at Lathom that he hasn't been seen for some time, along with his brother. People used to see the boys playing in the castle grounds but lately there is no sign of either of them. Perhaps the new king has murdered them."

"Don't be silly," Harry scoffed. "I told you, King Richard is a good man, everybody says so."

"He murdered Anthony Woodville so I don't see why he should baulk at murdering the little prince who might be the right king after all."

"I told you he wouldn't do such a thing," Harry retorted angrily. "He has a young son of his own. And I don't know who Anthony Woodville was or what he did."

"I told you that he found me my place with the Countess," Bel said. "There's news at Lathom that she might be returning soon. I'm surprised to hear myself say that I shall be glad of it." She paused then said hesitantly, "What about you? Why don't we ride over to Duxbury and you can try to make it up with your uncle John so that you can return there."

Harry's blue eyes took on a stormy look. "I'm not going to beg on my knees just to go back. He can ask me himself. I'm useful to him in many ways, not least keeping an eye on Ughtred, scything and chopping and looking after the animals. In fact I'm thinking of going away from here and hiring myself out to someone who will pay me a decent wage. I'm supposed to be working with Jaxon but he pays me hardly anything apart from my board and lodging."

"You are worth more than that, Harry Duxbury. You can read and write and you are clever and strong. Perhaps they might be able to find something for you at Lathom and then we could see each other often." Bel thought she might make some enquiries there.

However on her return she was surprised by some unexpected news. A messenger had arrived from the Stanley's London house with various goods, letters and instructions, and amongst them was a command for Bel to return to the household in the City. She was to ride as soon as possible bringing some things for the Countess and escorted by some menservants and Reginald Bray. Preparations were made so quickly that she was sorry she had no time to warn Harry of her imminent departure. But early in the morning as the little cavalcade prepared to set out she was astounded to see one of the grooms from the stables leading out a horse on which was seated Harry Duxbury, dressed for riding in a leather jerkin and calf-length boots, a close-fitting wool cap on his blond hair.

"What are you doing here?" she gasped.

"God and His saints must know because I don't," he said, but his voice was gleeful and exuberance shone from his blue eyes. "Uncle John received a message from the dragon saying that she had need of me in London to perform a service, no further information given, and I was to ride with the party leaving Lathom immediately. She has probably heard of my sojourn in Preston and wants to fit up some punishment for me."

However Harry Duxbury was in no mind to refuse, no matter what the Countess had in mind for him. If it meant a trip to London, as far away in his imagination as the moon, provided with a good horse and in the company of Bella, that seemed to him an invitation to Paradise. He had always wanted to travel, to see places other than the small towns of Ormskirk, Chorley, Standish and Wigan – the farthest he had ever been apart from his brief sojourn in the gaol at Preston – and now his dream was coming true. To see the great city of London had always been his ambition and one which he never thought he would realise for they said it was two hundred miles away. His uncle John had been suitably impressed by the fact that no less a person than the

Countess of Richmond had some task for him and was inclined to think more favourably of him whilst Ughtred was delighted by the fact that he would later hear all the story of the adventure and it might prove the entrèe for Harry to return home. Harry admitted to feeling a little apprehensive as to what the Countess had in store for him but any nervousness was overlaid by the pleasure of going to London on horseback with Bella and this was worth anything that later might befall him. Bel was puzzled but not displeased by the surprising turn of events.

The little cavalcade were four days on the road riding hard but the two young people found it not too arduous. Bel always enjoyed travelling, especially now after being cooped up in tedious solitude at Lathom while Harry was fascinated by the constantly changing sights of the journey, from the highroads busy with merchants, chapmen, messengers, churchmen with their entourage and farmers taking produce to nearby towns, to little villages of humble cottages surrounded by fields of labourers, and even the solitary stretches through dark woods where stags ran at bay from the horns of hunters, and poachers and outlaws hid from sight. He was amazed by the size of some of the towns they passed, like Coventry whose walls and church towers brought back to Bel painful memories of her journey to the Malorys at Newbold Revel, but nothing compared to his first sight of London as they rode through Bishopsgate and into the City. His eyes travelled from one great building to another, one church to another, his ears assaulted by the noise of shouts, cries of street vendors, bells, carts, oaths, quarrels, his eyes by the multitude of people in rich clothes or rags and tatters, accompanied by barking dogs and sluggish mules, so many of them that the horses had to push their way through the narrow streets, often having to pause in the press.

When they arrived at the Stanley's house, Bel made her customary way to the maids' chamber while Reginald Bray had been told to convey Henry Duxbury to the servants' quarters where he would be provided with accommodation and told to await further instructions so looking rather bemused he did as he was told. The maids were surprised by Bel's return but denied any knowledge of why she had been called back.

"The Countess has been in an unusual state of agitation, spending more time than normal with her chaplains, in private prayer in her chamber, and regular visits to all the churches," Agnes said.

"She's been up to something, planning some scheme, you can always tell," said Maud knowledgeably. "Though from what I have heard it does not include Sir Thomas who seems totally unconcerned with anything apart fom his duties in the royal household."

The following morning Bel was called to attend her mistress in her private retreat and to her surprise was told to sit on one of the chairs beside the Countess's own opulently draped and padded seat without giving any task to perform. The door opened and to her amazement Harry Duxbury was ushered in by one of the waiting-gentlemen. His customary cocksure demeanour was overlaid by an expression of uncertainty and Bel also felt apprehensive. She feared that by commanding their presence together Lady Margaret must have discovered her association with the young man and perhaps her part in securing his release from gaol which involved dubious actions.

The countess fixed him with a stern gaze but then beckoned him to a stool in front of her and told him to be seated. She paused for a while to intimidate him then said, "I have heard new accounts of your troublesome behaviour Henry Duxbury but in this case I am of a mind to overlook your infractions of the law if you are willing to expiate your misconduct by undertaking a duty for me."

Both he and Bel looked at her in surprise and she continued, "I have a special task for Demoiselle Lechanteur to perform and I require your assistance. She is to travel to France with letters for me and," she paused and said dryly, "having heard of your prowess in the field of physical combat I would like you to accompany her as a bodyguard."

The two young people were now looking increasingly amazed, especially as this was the first Bel had heard of such a proposal.

The countess folded her small hands on her lap and continued smoothly, "The letters and the true reason for the journey are to be known to no-one but the journey of a young Frenchwoman to visit her family will provoke no interest and neither will the presence of a deaf mute to give her protection."

"A deaf mute?" Harry could not help himself from interrupting.

"You don't speak French do you?" the countess asked sharply.

"No, my lady," he muttered.

"The nature of this mission is such that any English person might incur suspicion. Two French people would not, especially one a deaf mute merely there to offer his obvious protection. I know such a constraint on you would be an onerous burden," (there was no humour in her voice), "but now that I have revealed the proposal to you I expect your acceptance."

To Harry Duxbury such a proposal was the stuff of his dreams – to travel abroad and in the company of Bella – and he did not pause to consider the disadvantages and the dangers, of which it must be admitted he knew very little, before eagerly stating his willingness, even to the extent of having to masquerade as a deaf mute.

"You must go immediately because I wish no-one to know you are part of my household and being used in my service. Say nothing to anyone, least of all that you are leaving the country. Take a horse from the stables and make your way to the Red Lion in Guildford, the directions are in this sealed packet with enough money for your needs. Demoiselle Lechanteur will be escorted there later and when you meet she will have the necessary authorisation for a ship leaving Portsmouth."

The countess stood and Harry rose also. She rang a bell hanging from a rope beside the door which was opened immediately. The same gentleman at arms led him out before he had chance to exchange a glance with Bel.

Bel sat stupefied. The countess now turned to her saying, "I expect that as you are in my service you are willing to undertake any appropriate duty that I consign to you."

Bel marvelled that her autocracy had not for an instant led her to consider that she might baulk at such a long and uncertain journey. However she knew she would not have refused. Such an opportunity to return to France with her expenses arranged and her journey planned, with Harry as companion and bodyguard, was too good an opportunity to decline. She might not even come back to England and this possibility over-ruled any misgivings she might have.

"I will give you more details in due course," said Lady Margaret smoothly, "but briefly the import is this. You will carry a message, both verbal and consigned to writing, to Nantes. However you will not travel directly to Brittany. You are going home to visit your relatives in France so you will sail to Le Havre and onto Rouen then go overland from there. Your stay in Nantes will be brief, no longer than two nights and you may return directly to England on a ship from there. Absolute secrecy is essential, no word of this must be spoken to any of my ladies and when you leave you are returning to your family for a time. Is that understood?"

Bel voiced her agreement but when she was dismissed a wave of exultation washed over her. She was travelling again and she was going home to France. From her experience in coming to England she knew it would not be an easy journey, the roads were bad, the sea crossing could be nasty and dangerous, she was being forced to dissemble again, hiding the truth. But it was summer and she would not be alone, she would have Harry Duxbury as she had once had Renard and two heads were better than one. She was young and adventurous and it would be a change from the easy, predictable, often tedious, life in the Countess of Richmond's household that had begun to chafe of late. Her mistress had said the eventual destination was Nantes. Bel knew by now that Lady Margaret's son Henry Tudor was in exile receiving the protection of the Duke of Brittany at his court at Nantes. She wondered what Lady Margaret was sending there that had to be kept so secret.

CHAPTER 15

Brittany

When the coast of northern France came into view in the far distance, a rugged peninsula jutting into the English Channel, both Bel and Harry experienced great feelings of relief. They seemed to have been at sea for a long time since leaving Portsmouth where Lady Margaret had provided them with passports and tickets on one of the larger two-masted vessels exporting wool to France through the port of Rouen on the river Seine. The relatively short distance across the English Channel had taken a long time, the ship rolling continuously in the choppy waters of the swirling currents the vessel must negotiate and the progress painstakingly slow as they were buffeted by contrary winds, all the time the crew keeping close watch for pirates. Even Harry who had so far enjoyed the voyage, eager to see as much as he could with every mile taking him further from Lathom, was struggling to retain his equilibrium while Bel was lying on her bed in the tiny cabin she had been given. It seemed an eternity, the rugged peninsula of coast tantalisingly close on the horizon, before they rounded the wide bay of the Seine into the little port of Le Havre. Then the crew navigated the winding River Seine through green wooded hills into Rouen. As they sailed closer they could see the tall spires of the cathedral rising above the clustered buildings stretching back from the water's edge where many water mills testified to the importance of the textile industry here, using wool imported from England. As the ship manoeuvred into the busy port they experienced an overwhelming sense of relief that they were on dry land at last.

It was a while before the business of disembarking was complete and when finally they stood on the cobbles of the harbour they found it difficult to stand upright, the ground still shifting unsteadily beneath their feet. But Harry was eagerly hurrying Bel onward, slinging her travel pack onto his shoulder as well as his own and crying, "Come, come, let me see what France is really like," as he began to follow others on the road from the harbour and into the town.

"Careful," she warned him, "You are not to speak now remember. Everything must only be said between us when we are alone. Leave everything to me, it is my country and my language so you must trust me. I will keep to the plans we have already arranged."

Harry grimaced. He was going to find this very difficult. He wouldn't even be able to understand Bel now so long as they were in company. But he was too excited at being in a foreign country for the first time to care overmuch at this point. They had already decided they would find accommodation here for the night and explore the town before continuing their journey on the morrow. She had also told him how Jeanne the maid of Orleans had been burnt at the stake here by the English fifty years ago during the long war between the two countries.

"Good riddance to the French witch," Harry had said and faced Bel's wrath and a long diatribe on the courage of the young girl warrior, her devotion to the land of her birth and the perfidy of both the English and the French who had both betrayed her.

Remembering her experiences travelling with Renard, Bel tried to emulate them. She recalled that they were not far from Paris and wondered if he was still there in the city or if he had travelled elsewhere. A pang of regret tore through her heart as she wished he were with her and they were going to earn their night's lodging by entertaining. She decided they must first find an inn for the night before it got too late and all the rooms had been taken by merchants and travellers for whom Rouen was the first stage of their journey as it was for them, but Lady Margaret had provided them with sufficient money to pay their expenses on their travels. She did not know the way and Harry was constantly stopping to gaze in amazement at the tall buildings lining the narrow streets, so different from those in England – timber framed with overhanging storeys but four and five storeys high with gabled attics on top, the timber brightly painted, often in shades of red, and with intricate patterns in contrasting colours on both the plaster and the beams. Through the arches dividing the streets could be seen tantalising glimpses of more splendid buildings and courtyards, the halls of the many merchants with gilded frontages and colourful emblazons for Rouen was a prosperous town with the wool trade. Towering over all was the great cathedral, even from a distance more splendid than anything Harry had ever seen. Keeping the cathedral in front of her as Bel had seen Renard do she soon came upon an inn called 'Le Petit Mouton' on the corner of a side street. It was not large but looked clean and well kept so telling Harry to wait outside she entered and sought the innkeeper. Like most men, the host was entranced by Bel and immediately offered her a private chamber for the night, especially as she was holding livres in her hand, and when she explained that she had a servant who was a deaf mute he complied by offering him a place in the straw in the loft above the stables. Harry scowled but she warned him to keep silent by a threatening look. Later however when they were exploring the town his ill humour dissipated in the excitement of discovering somewhere so strange and exotic to his eyes. They found their way to the magnificent cathedral, which they learnt was called Notre Dame, and after marvelling at the exquisite carvings and delicate tracery of no less than six graceful spires offset by the central square tower they went inside and finding a quiet corner beside a pillar in a side bay of the nave they managed to talk together without being overheard and made their plans for the morrow. They were to hire horses for the next stage of their journey to Nantes, which they had been told would take them no longer than four days, but Harry was still complaining about his accommodation.

"I don't see why I can't share your chamber," he whispered, looking at Bel with the innocent expression she had come to realise usually covered his ulterior motives for action. He was rewarded by a stern gaze although she said nothing.

Next morning however she thought about what he had said. Henry Duxbury was of gentle birth, more so than she was unless she counted the Malorys. He wasn't a servant and it seemed unfair that he should be relegated to the lowest accommodation, cold if the weather should change, no doubt accompanied by rats and fleas and with vulgar companions. She and Renard had shared a room, there was no reason why Harry might not have a pallet in her chamber.

The inn had no livery stables but next day the innkeeper directed them to a friend of his and they hired two mares which they were told were not speedy but had stamina and staying-power and would take them easily the twenty-five miles they had reckoned to their next stop for the night. Harry frowned that the ride would not be as fast as he would have liked but soon cheered when they set off on the road and realised that there was so much novelty to be enjoyed on the route.

When they arrived at Bernay in the early evening they had no difficulty in finding accommodation for the night at 'Le Corbeau'. The innkeeper was uncharacteristically small and thin with a prematurely lined face. He introduced himself as Jacques Legrand and Bel did not know if this was his real name or a witty soubriquet.

"One chamber will be sufficient with two pallets for myself and my companion," she said.

He considered her with shrewd little eyes underlined by deep pouches and Bel guessed what he was thinking. "He is my protector but he is a deaf mute so I do not like him to be alone in case he has difficulty. I have money to pay," she said, untying the laces of her purse and taking out coins which he counted carefully. Bel recalled that as travelling minstrels Renard had had no need to explain her presence in his chamber

Bel thought quickly and replied, "I am on my way to entertain the Duke of Brittany at Nantes and he has kindly supplied us with horses because he wants me there quickly to entertain at a banquet he has prepared for important officials in three days time."

The innkeeper seemed satisfied and Bel thought how quickly she was picking up Renard's habits now that she was back on her home territory. She returned to Harry who picked up their bags and they accompanied the innkeeper to a small chamber on the third floor. Harry's eyes widened when he saw the two pallet beds and she motioned for him to lay their belongings on them. When the door was shut he whispered gleefully, "So you have changed your mind about me."

"No I haven't," she replied sternly in the same soft voice. "You are to stay in your own bed, Harry Duxbury. I just felt sorry for you having to share space with lowly servants, and I thought you might unwittingly give yourself away."

Harry moved hopefully towards her but she put out her hand saying, "But if you come anywhere near my bed you will be back sleeping in the hay loft."

He shrugged, his face displaying his disappointment but as he crawled onto his own pallet his natural optimism resurfaced and he fell asleep dreaming that eventually she would weaken in her resolve.

The journey took a day longer than they had anticipated but they began to enjoy it. Harry continued to bask in the novelty while Bel was happy being back in her native land and speaking her own tongue. They encountered few dangers for there were usually other travellers to ride along with though Harry was frustrated by not being able to understand them. Only once were they surprised by two rough looking fellows brandishing thick cudgels who jumped at them from within a copse and demanded their purses. With a speed that was startling Harry leapt from his horse on top of one of the men, grasping his cudgel and smashing it into his face. After a moment's surprised recoil his companion went to attack Harry only to be pummelled on the head with his friend's weapon and kicked in his most tender parts. Leaving them groaning on the ground Harry returned to his horse saying with satisfaction, "practice makes perfect," as he remounted. Bel knew that Harry liked fighting but after this impressive demonstration of his skills she conceded that Lady Margaret had judged well in choosing him as her bodyguard.

When they came to Angers through rolling green countryside they were within one more day's ride to their destination. The size of the city set on a rocky promontory on the right bank of the river Maine, the castle and the cathedral easily visible above the tall stone walls, proclaimed it as a place of importance. Bel presumed that this was where there would be prestigious inns, promising targets for travelling minstrels she thought wistfully. She knew that she could no longer use her story of being called upon to entertain the Duke of Brittany so close to his domains.

"We shall have to be respectable travellers tonight," she said to Harry. Seeing his disappointed face she continued, "But you can have your own chamber, we have enough money."

Rather than being pleased his disappointment increased.

The cheaper inns in the city proved to be full so it happened that they were obliged to buy accommodation at the large and well-maintained 'Le Mitre' near the cathedral close. For some inexplicable reason Bel decided to wear for supper in the inn the dress that Renard had bought for her. It was shabby now and she never wore it in the Countess's service but it was still striking and her favourite so she had included it in her travelling pack. She left her hair loose, garlanded by a fillet of woven silver wire which the Countess had once presented to her as a New Year gift and Harry was genuinely tongue-tied in his admiration. He had never before seen her so attired and thought with wry humour that it was fortunate he had now become accustomed to masquerading as dumb.

Suddenly there was a noisy interruption as a group of travelling musicians entered, wearing multi-coloured short doublets, parti-coloured hose clinging to their legs and tasselled caps worn at rakish angles. They were carrying lutes, rebecs, a viol, a gittern and a hurdy-gurdy. The host and his wife made no demur so they had obviously been apprised of their coming. They were also warmly welcomed by the inn's customers so it seemed as if they were regular visitors.

Bel watched enviously as they set themselves in place and began to play, noisy and infectious tunes that soon had their audience clapping and stamping. She began to enjoy the music for they were accomplished players though she was just in time to prevent Harry from stamping his feet to the rhythm, whispering, "You are deaf, remember!"

When there was a pause and the musicians took to slaking their thirst, on an impulse Bel made her way into their company. They looked up admiringly as she addressed herself to the hurdy-gurdy player whom she considered the leader of the group, a man of about her father's age with grizzled curly hair and a forked beard, the skin crinkling around his dark merry eyes.

"Do you know of a minstrel called Renard de Bourgonville?" she asked.

He thought for a moment, further wrinkling his lined brow then shook his curly head, "No, I'm sorry, I don't know the name."

But a young lutenist chimed in, "Yes we do, don't you remember the arrogant young pup who had already taken our place at 'Le Chât Noir' in Paris. Damned fine lutenist though with a very extensive repertoire."

Bel smiled. "Is he still in Paris then?" she asked.

The musician shrugged. "No idea. That was more than a year ago. I seem to have a vague recollection of him saying he was moving on somewhere but I don't remember where. What's your interest in him?"

"I worked with him once," she replied.

"Are you a musician?"

"My father was an Italian travelling minstrel and I travelled alongside him until he died. Yes, I call myself a minstrel but I don't have much opportunity at this time, I haven't got my lute with me," she said regretfully.

The young man saw her eyes resting longingly on his lute and on an impulse he handed it to her saying, "Try it."

She almost snatched the instrument from him and began to caress the strings longingly then began to play. The other musicians listened approvingly and when after a few bars she began to sing a gentle love song 'Fammi cantar l'amor' that her father had taught her, the strength and purity of her voice quietened the clamour of the inn. There was a startled silence when she ended, followed by loud applause. She handed the lute back to its owner but the leader, the hurdy-gurdy player, said, "Nay stay with us for a while and sing. You choose some songs and we will follow you."

The evening remained for Bel a great joy. Harry sat and listened in surprise and although she couldn't talk to him her joyous expressions and her occasional nods and smiles to him communicated the message that this was her true life, her metier, the environment in which she was happiest. When it was ended and the group of minstrels were ready to depart, the leader, whose name she had been told was Gaston, said to her, "Where are you bound? We are on our way to play at the Duke of Brittany's court at Nantes, he is holding a feast there in two days time. Would you like to accompany us and join with us for the occasion." They were all enthralled by her talent and knew well that the inclusion of a girl as beautiful as she was could not fail to enhance their entertainment. For Bel it was not only a dream come true to be an entertainer again but a miracle. Here was the perfect occasion to enter the Duke's court in accredited company, without suspicion, without having to invent an excuse. She tried not to sound too eager as she accepted the invitation. Later she told Harry the incredibly good news. "I can't believe there really is a feast there with entertainers," she said, "a stroke of fortune has turned my lie into the truth." She was excited to be among minstrels again, she would be able to complete the Countess of Richmond's mission and deep within her soul she thought she might learn more of Renard, even perhaps find him again.

So Bel and Harry arrived at Nantes in the company of the musicians. There was no need to find an excuse to enter the château now, the minstrels already had an engagement at the forthcoming feast so there was no occasion for her to use persuasion and invention. They were both amazed by the château of the Duke of Brittany for it stood in the centre of the city, the gates and fortifications straddling the complex of narrow cobbled streets and ancient houses and the river Loire flowing close by, like the Tower of London she remembered. The châteaux was encircled by thick stone walls with circular corner bastions and beyond the walls other towers could be seen within the perimeter. Huge iron gates led from the street to an arched bridge over the moat and once again she was reminded of London, though when she and Sim had gone to visit Lord Rivers there had been three bridges to cross the moat before they arrived at the inner courtyard of the Tower. Gaston's introduction at the gatehouse enabled them to pass through the walls and into a vast courtyard, the size of the town itself. Now the similarity to London's Tower was even more marked for many groups of buildings were set against the outer walls, their impressive facades towards the courtyard. In prime place was the most noble edifice of all, four storeys high but still with attics in the sloping tiled roof and a soaring tower topped by three slender pinnacles. This was a palace in its own right and contained the royal apartments.

The guarded main entrance was approached by two symmetrical marble staircases curving upwards to carved and gilded double doors but Gaston led his company round the side to a postern gate. There they were given admittance and told to proceed into the heart of the building through a maze of corridors until they reached the service quarters behind the Great Hall. In one of the several kitchens they were given wine and fruit pastries and told to wait until the Master of Revels sent someone to escort them further. Eventually a lackey arrived to lead them to a small chamber near the hall where they could prepare, tune their instruments and change their clothes. Harry was looking uneasy in the midst of these unaccustomed surroundings, intimidated by the ceremony, but Bel revelled in the familiar rituals that reminded her of the past. Her colour was high and her blue eyes sparkling with anticipation though her nervousness was caused not by the prospect of singing and dancing before an elevated company but by the problem of how she was going to be able to give the message to the Countess of Richmond's son Henry Tudor.

When they were called upon to entertain and entered the Great Hall the noise, heat and colour assailed their senses. A crowd of gaudily dressed people in silk, velvet, fur and damask chattered like swarms of bees, tables piled high with salvers of food and flagons of wine were set around the tapestried walls, the light from the hundreds of candles in candelabra and sconces flickering on silver and gold vessels, but Bel's eyes were drawn immediately to the high dais searching for Henry Tudor.

In centre place sat Francis II Duke of Brittany, a man approaching fifty years, thick-set with protuberant eyes and a beaked nose, but Bel's gaze moved immediately to the companion sitting beside him – a tall slender man in his late twenties with sandy-coloured hair of medium length. It was the long narrow face and small eyes that marked him as Margaret Beaufort's son and she knew without doubt that this was Henry Tudor. He was personable enough for his complexion was ruddy and healthy as if he spent much time out of doors. Beside him sat a ruggedly handsome man whom she judged to be in his late forties, his auburn hair flecked with grey and his bronzed face seamed with lines, especially around his alert blue eyes. She judged this to be Jasper Tudor, Henry's uncle, companion and protector.

The musicians entertained throughout the meal and did not expect to be accorded much attention whilst the many rich and varied courses were carried to the table and consumed, so they deliberately chose loud and jolly tunes and Bel sang the merry troubadour song 'A la Fontanelle' which always drew attention. She had demanded that Harry be included in the group in case anything should go wrong so he had been provided with a cap with bells and a fool's stick and told to prance in the background. Unable to protest he had scowled menacingly but Bel laughed and said, "You once told me you did nothing but play the fool."

Much later however when everyone had sated themselves on the dozens of courses that had been offered and the final dishes of nuts, dates, oranges and sugar pastes had been set on the table, attention centred on the group of entertainers. They played more sophisticated music now, songs of the knights of King Arthur and Charlemagne, the song written by Richard Coeur de Lion, 'Ja nuis homs pris,' as well as popular songs from Provence and Italy. Bel sang some of the songs then with sudden inspiration began the English 'Gabriel fram even sent' which she announced was in honour of Henry Tudor. She was aware that she had gained his attention. Then Gaston told Bel to dance and as the music flowed into a slow Danse Royale she began the sinuous movements, the bells on her fingers tinkling as she swayed. The dance of Provençal courtly love was meant to be danced à deux but Bel made every man present believe he was her partner, especially the nobles on the dais for the couple dances were always directed to the Presence. She moved as closely as she dared towards Henry Tudor, practising a manoeuvre to be used later and was gratified to see his eyes linger on her appreciatively.

She waited until the evening was drawing to its close and people drowsily letting their heads droop over their empty goblets. The Duke's court was one of sobriety and there was no drunken brawling but she kept her eyes upon Henry Tudor in case he should make an early withdrawal though she doubted it would be acceptable for him to retire before his host. Then she asked Gaston if she could dance again. Now she knew exactly how she could draw near to the Earl of Richmond and as the dance was drawing to its close she dedicated the movements to him and bowed low before him in a deep reverence, keeping her knee upon the floor but lifting up her head and fixing him with an inviting boldness in her blue eyes. For one anxious moment she thought she had made a mistake but her experience of men in the last few years had proved that few could resist her and she was not mistaken. Henry Tudor rose from his seat and came down to give her his hand. She took it and kissed it then whispered quickly, "I have a message for you from the Countess of Richmond. Diolch i Duw."

His face registered no surprise but at the Welsh password he raised her up and said, "Dawn. The east postern. Alone." Then thanking her for her music he returned to his place on the dais. Those who had any doubts in their fuddled minds about the brief exchange would only surmise a carnal assignation, for though the foreign Earl of Richmond was not known for his peccadillos it was common knowledge that entertainers had loose morals.

The entertainers as usual were given permission to sleep with other servants in the Great Hall once it had been cleared but while they were packing away their instruments a page was sent with a message to Bel. The Duke had said she might sleep on her own in the small adjoining chamber where they had earlier prepared and informed her that a mattress would be provided for her.

"Diolch y Duw," she whispered, "Grâce à Dieu," knowing that this would make her meeting with Henry Tudor easier though Harry was unhappy.

"Anything might happen to you alone. You could be raped. Perhaps that's what the Duke or one of his nobles has in mind."

For a moment Bel shivered but then told him what had transpired with Henry Tudor. "He probably suggested it. It will be much easier for me to slip away to meet him than if I had been with the others in the hall, that would have invited comment."

But whilst agreeing on the convenience he was still worried. "I will come with you," he proclaimed.

"No you mustn't. He said I must come alone. He is always afraid of being betrayed and if you were there he wouldn't trust me."

But Harry privately decided to go and relieve himself at dawn and keep watch from a hidden distance.

Despite being tired to death with the efforts of the night and the consequent excitement Bel couldn't sleep. It was already the hours of early morning and the ante-chamber had no windows so she was constantly alert, creeping regularly to the door to watch the changing sky in a lancet in the passageway. When the first faint streaks of rose threaded the canopy patching now to shades of luminous grey she made her way swiftly to the eastern postern, whose location she had previously registered and which was the nearest exit through the walls. As she approached a dark figure moved from the shadow of the wall and she started involuntarily until she saw the sandy hair visible beneath the hood of the black cloak. There was little conversation. Bel explained her connection with the Countess of Richmond and gave him the message verbally and then the long letter folded tightly within the woven girdle she had worn all the time, the stitching of which she now severed with the small knife she always carried in her belt-purse. He took it then placed it within his own purse beneath the long cloak. Then he said, "I trust you will breathe nothing of this only to my lady mother the Countess. Tell her I am well, all is well, that I thank her, will act upon the information and pray God keep her in His care. Tomorrow you will depart by ship from the river here which will take you directly to Bristol. I will send someone to escort you at the time of embarkation." Then with a brief farewell he was gone.

Bel stood for some time feeling the damp early morning mist envelop her, droplets of moisture dampening the chill of her face within her hood. An emptiness engulfed her. Her mission had been successfully completed but now she must return. Any exultation she might have felt was eclipsed by the knowledge that she must again leave her homeland and her life as a minstrel which for a short time she had retrieved and enjoyed. All the time since she had embarked on this journey she had cherished the hope that she might be able to stay in France, pick up her old life and not have to go back to serving the Countess in the cold damp of Lancashire. Henry Tudor had ensured that she must leave immediately and directly and there was no way she could gainsay his orders. No more travelling through France, entertaining wherever she could. She must now travel to England all the way by sea and the long, uncomfortable, possibly dangerous voyage awaited her.

She heard a voice calling her name "Bella" softly and turning she saw Harry Duxbury's figure materialising from the mist.

"You shouldn't have come, it could be dangerous," she reprimanded him, while at the same time feeling glad of his presence.

"I was worried about you," he said.

She informed him hastily of what had happened including the fact that they were to leave early on the morrow. He pulled his face at the news, wanting the adventure to continue and in no haste to return to the tedious life of Ormskirk.

"Stay here for a time while I return to the castle," she ordered him. "We mustn't be seen together, no doubt Henry Tudor has his spies," and he did as he was told.

It was already early morning and only a short time later a page approached Bel with the news that a ship was waiting on the river outside the walls of the château to take her and her servant to Bristol. Without more ado they were led quickly around the defences to where a flight of steps descended to the wharf. The captain watched them from the deck and meeting them at the gangplank took them swiftly on board. There was little conversation apart from him showing Bel a small cabin on the middle deck and telling her that the deaf mute could sleep in a curtained corner in the stern.

Then returning to the bridge and shouting to the crew to cast off, with a flurry of noise and activity, the ropes creaking and the gulls squawking around the masts, the 'Antelope' began its steady passage down the River Loire heading for England and leaving France far behind.

A lone figure making for the château of Nantes watched the boat go, admiring its speed as it disappeared into the low-hanging clouds. He was young and handsome, a velvet cap perched jauntily on his short dark hair with a thick fringe, his green velvet doublet with nipped in waist complementing well-shaped legs in parti-coloured hose of red and green. A pack was strapped to his back and across his shoulders was slung a lute in a linen bag. He was confident he could find employment for a time with the Duke of Brittany for his fame had gone before him. Renard de Bourgonville was an excellent musician, everyone said so and he believed it himself.

CHAPTER 16

Changes

Bel removed Harry Duxbury's arm from where it lay around her waist saying, "We ought to be going."

"Not yet. It isn't late. By the position of the sun it can't be more than two hours after noon."

"But you know it's going to take us nearly two hours to get back and I'm not supposed to be away from Lathom even when the Countess is not at home."

"I'm sure you can invent some convincing excuse for your absence," he murmured sleepily. "You're good at making things up."

She pulled his hair and raised herself from the sheepskins on Harry's makeshift bed in the top storey of the pele tower. There was a shaft of sunlight coming through the arrow slits and she looked at him dozing contentedly, his blond hair falling over his eyes. With their mischievous gleam curtained he looked very young and vulnerable and she sighed. She wasn't happy about this change in their relationship but it had all happened unpredictably.

The voyage from Nantes had begun well but then in the Bay of Biscay they had been overwhelmed by a terrible tempest. The little boat had been tossed about like a ball in the hand of an angry god, the sky was black as night split continuously by forks of lightning, the howling wind tore the sails and broke one of the masts in two. As the ship lurched and staggered Bel and Harry noted the desperate faces of the rain-soaked captain and crew as they tried to ride the storm, their expressions and shouted commands revealing their fear that they were not going to make it. Soaked to the skin and trembling with fear and cold, Bel and Harry clung to ropes and railings on the deck as they were afraid to remain in the cabin. For once Harry's zeal for adventure had dimmed and he longed to be back in the tedious familiarity of Duxbury instead of facing a watery premature grave while all Bel could think of was that she would never see France again, never again play music and sing, never find Renard.

At last after hours of agony the storm abated and the little ship, broken and battered, found itself miraculously still afloat and not buried in pieces on the seabed. Even so they were not out of danger for it was a known fact that pirates haunted the coast of Cornwall on the look-out for wrecks and disabled shipping and the weary crew could afford no sleep or slackening of their vigilance. The deck was awash and full of splintered timber and Bel took Harry with her into her little cabin to try and get some rest. They took off their soaking outer garments and huddled together on the narrow bunk beneath the damp blankets, trying to get warm in the closeness of their bodies. They were cold and miserable and found comfort in each other. They had thought they were going to die and now nothing seemed to matter except that they were still alive. Their needs now were life-affirming, encouraged by the awareness that they were not yet out of danger. The close proximity of their shivering bodies, their shattered nerves and the need for physical comfort provided all the stimulus they needed to make love. It was instinctive, fierce and brief. It happened only once and at the time they had no regrets and no thoughts about where it might lead.

The ship limped into Falmouth harbour and could go no further. They were a long way from their destination of Bristol. They had been told not to return to London but go to Lancashire, the Countess determined that Henry Duxbury should not be known to be in her service. However the captain, mindful of having to return to Nantes with his story, found a little cog that was going to Plymouth. "From Plymouth there will be vessels heading onwards to many ports," he informed them. So they took his advice, albeit loath to trust themselves again to the sea, and after the mercifully short voyage to Plymouth they rested a night to dry their clothes and make enquiries. Out of the many ships moored there they discovered that a vessel was leaving for Ireland and calling at Chester. Although neither of them liked the idea of another long sea voyage, nevertheless it was preferable to a longer tedious journey by road. Once they had returned around the hazardous Cornish coast the voyage around the coast of Wales was relatively comfortable as the ship kept as close to the coastline as was possible to avoid the often turbulent extremes of the Irish Sea. There were merchants aboard and fur dealers going to Chester, which was one of the most important centres for the fur trade, so there was much genial conversation and the relating of adventures to pass the time, Harry no longer having to keep up his pretence as a deaf mute. But cabins were in short supply and Harry was disappointed at having to share with other men whilst Bel slept with a female servant of one of the travellers.

Nonetheless they were glad when the ship was sailing up the River Dee to land at Chester and when finally they disembarked they felt solid ground beneath their feet again. The Stanleys owned a house in Chester and making their way there they were able to explain their business to the steward and be provided with horses to take them the relatively short distance to Lathom. From there Bel was to send word of their safe return by the next messenger to return to London.

Bel began putting on her gown and seeing that she was intent on making her departure Harry regretfully began to reach for his hose and tuck in his shirt. Bel tied the laces of her front-fastening blue gown and wound the girdle over her slim hips. When Harry had secured his hose to the ties of his doublet he began to pour ale into a cup from the stone jug on the chest but Bel motioned him not to pour any for herself.

"When can you come again?" he asked drinking it down without stopping and pouring out another. After his nephew's commission from the Countess of Richmond, though ignorant of the details, John Duxbury had allowed him to return home again to the farm.

Bel hesitated. It was only the second time they had made love, Harry's youthful impatience so unlike Robert's leisurely courtship, and she knew she should not have let him persuade her. She liked Harry, he was her best friend, but she wanted to keep their relationship as a friendship and wondered if she had now let it go too far. She said, "You know I can't come here often, it's too far to make regular visits. And I won't be able to come at all when Lady Margaret is in residence, you know that. She keeps a careful watch on her ladies. Today was an exception."

"Harry, are you up there?" Ughtred's reedy voice called from below.

With a muttered oath Harry leapt down the wooden ladder two rungs at a time, roaring, "Don't you dare come any further you brat or it will be the worse for you. I'll beat you black and blue."

"Is Lady Bella there?"

"No she isn't. I'm busy making something. Now go back to the house and if you behave yourself I'll come for you later and we'll play Nine Men's Morris."

Bel had followed him down the stairs, more slowly and being careful with her gown on the narrow treads, and now seated herself on one of the stools at the table. The wooden shutters were open and the summer sunlight flowed into the room, flickering on the white-washed stone walls and bringing with it a scent of new-mown hay from the fields below.

"You can see why I can't come very often," she smiled, using the interruption as an excuse.

"Ughtred won't come up without my permission." He seated his tall frame on another stool opposite her.

She put her hand on his saying, "We must be content with meeting most weeks at the market."

"I m not content with that," he scowled. "I thought you had accepted me as your lover now. I love you Bella. Will you marry me?"

She looked around the tower room with its rough walls and spare furnishings, completely devoid of anything that wasn't a necessity and tried not to laugh. Instead she said, "Where could we live? Certainly not here and your uncle would not be willing to have us take up room in the farmhouse."

"I told you we have other patches of land not far away, some with farmhouses. I could rent one."

"Your uncle would not give his consent and you are under age."

"I could wait another year or two. Do you not love me?"

"I am very fond of you, Harry. I do have an affection for you. You are my best friend," she said sincerely, squeezing his hand. Her eyes travelled around the simple room and the stairs which led to the bedchamber on the top floor of the round tower. She could indeed live somewhere like this with someone she loved. If there was someone who shared her heart and soul, someone she could not live without, then she would gladly relinquish all the comforts of Lathom which was little more than a gilded cage.

"I shall have to learn to play a musical instrument," he said with some bitterness. "I think the lute would be beyond me but I can practise my pipe and perhaps learn to play a fiddle. And I can bang a drum." They both laughed and the tension was broken.

They left the pele surreptitiously. Harry knew that he dare not let his uncle know they had been together. John Duxbury was glad that his nephew seemed to have gained the good graces of the Countess of Richmond and hopeful that she might employ him in her service again but was uneasy that the boy was stepping out of his class in his partiality for the beautiful Bella.

They mounted their horses and set off though Harry couldn't resist the temptation to loiter outside Duxbury

Hall in the hope that he might encounter Rafe Standish and pick a quarrel with him but Bel chivvied him on.

"I think it possible that the Countess could find you some further employment when she returns now that she knows we were successful with our mission," she said encouragingly. As for herself, their journey had kindled in her a desire for her homeland and her old life and she was wondering how she could return to France. If only she could find a way to do so but she had little money of her own and could not travel such a distance alone. She had considered asking Harry to go with her and she knew he would leap at it in his reckless fashion. But he could neither share her language nor her music and though he was her friend and she was fond of him she wasn't in love with him. On the outskirts of Lathom they took their farewells with the promise to meet the following week at the market, Harry disgruntled at the realisation that this seemed to be the only form their relationship could take for the near future. However his youthful optimism reasserted itself in the thought that there were plenty fields and woods around Ormskirk that might provide convenient rendezvous.

The Countess of Richmond returned to Lathom sooner than expected and in a most startling fashion that consumed the household with trepidation. She had incurred the fury of King Richard, though expressed in his habitual coldly menacing manner. News had reached him that Henry Tudor was planning to return to England and that his mother had furnished him with information about those who were ready to accept his claim to the throne with details on how to proceed to those areas where he had promise of support. She had also aligned herself with Elizabeth Woodville in a plan to marry the princess Elizabeth to her son.

Richard commanded Sir Thomas Stanley and his wife to attend him at the royal palace and there challenged them with the accusation, saying he had proof of the matter.

"You realise, Sir Thomas, that this is treasonable behaviour on your wife's behalf. And you know the penalty for treason."

An expression of shocked disbelief crossed Sir Thomas's long handsome face while Lady Margaret froze with fear, realising that somehow her plans had been betrayed. She was not afraid of death but death would mean she would never see the realisation of her life-long dream that her son would one day be king. With an inherent sense of self-preservation she vehemently denied the charges. Her husband also denied all knowledge of such conspiracies, his restless eyes moving rapidly, though in his case his denials were sincere.

The King tended to believe Sir Thomas and this influenced his dealings with Lady Margaret. He was a just and merciful man, though he was also aware that to proceed with the penalty for treason towards a woman and such a prominent member of the nobility would not help his reputation.

"You are to leave London immediately and remain on your estate in Lancashire, detained there at my pleasure," he told her. "You will also be deprived of all your fortune, your money and your lands as is requisite with a charge of treason."

Margaret's intake of breath could not be suppressed. Her fortune was her identity and allowed her to live independently and finance her plans. Richard would most likely pass her wealth and estates to one of his favourites, probably the Duke of Buckingham, as was the normal procedure.

Richard eyed her coldly for some time then added, "However I am passing your fortune in all its manifestations to your husband. He will control it and will be responsible for your future good behaviour." He looked sternly at Sir Thomas saying, "From now on I expect you to keep your wife firmly under your control and any further misdemeanours will be laid to your account."

When they were alone the Stanleys could not believe how fortunate they were and how mercifully the Countess had been dealt with by the King. Lady Margaret knew that her husband would keep her fortune safely and though in his name it would remain to all intents and purposes her own, and she realised again how her marriage had been a continuing asset to her. However she was not sure how far she could count on her husband's support in any future plans for he had been greatly disturbed by her actions that could have brought disaster to both of them. He had always trimmed his sails to the prevailing wind and she had almost capsized their vessel. Fortunately he was unaware of her determination to continue conspiring with her son believing that her near-escape would have curtailed her ambitions. However despite the present set-backs she would not relinquish the belief that her son's destiny was to be king, she had lived with it for so long that her strong will had converted a hope into a certainty. To let the assurance go now would be to allow her whole existence to crumble into dust. She did not permit logic to say that Henry Tudor had little right to the crown, no more than had Richard of Gloucester when King Edward's son was heir to his father. In her mind the whole Yorkist claim was false and the true rulers of England were those of the Lancastrian line of which her son was the last survivor. She also dismissed the fact that this line came from a disputed succession when Henry of Bolingbroke (Henry of Lancaster) usurped the throne of King Richard II, or that her son's claim came via an illegitimate inheritance. Or even that Henry Tudor's grandfather had been a humble Welsh squire though his grandmother had been both Queen of England and France. Had she not been told in a dream that she should marry Edmund Tudor and that one day her son would be king, for in Margaret's religious experience dreams were divine manifestations as the Bible and the lives of the saints so often demonstrated.

She had worked hard to build secret support in England for the return of Henry Tudor, not necessarily to take the crown but to make his presence known and to watch at first hand the progression of events. She was devastated that King Richard had discovered the manoeuvre but the King's mercy did not modify her determination to continue in her efforts to bring Henry Tudor to England. So she would bide her time. To be confined to Lathom was no hardship for her. She would enjoy its luxury and the vicinity of Burscough Priory where she could find religious solace, and wait to see what would happen at the court. Talk was that the Duke of Buckingham was becoming too ambitious and people suspected he might be aiming for the Crown himself while there was concern that the young princes living in the Tower had not been seen for a long time. At least she had Sir Thomas in a privileged position to know everything and to keep her informed.

Her household at Lathom did not know the whole story, only by the excited rumours that circulated among servants and messengers. They expected their mistress to be in ill humour but on the contrary her disposition was more cheerful than normal. Only Bel had known moments of trepidation and initially she had feared the worst on realising that her mistresses' forbidden communication with her son had been discovered, wondering if her own participation should be made known. But then she realised that her visit to her relatives in France had no reason to be connected with events at the court of the Duke of Brittany and not even the Countess made mention of it. Bel had felt a little ill-used that her mistress had not thanked her for the difficult mission she and Harry had completed, not even to comment on her obligation to them. Life at Lathom continued in its regular routine.

CHAPTER 17

Invasion

"Well Renard de Bourgonville, will you join the invasion force as my personal minstrel."

Renard did not like the words 'force' and 'invasion'. He studied the unsmiling face of Henry Tudor with his small calculating eyes and thin mouth and wasn't sure what he was proposing. "I am no soldier, sire," he replied.

"I am not suggesting you fight. I like only experienced men-at-arms around me. But to entertain me, soothe my spirits before a battle and celebrate my victory afterwards."

Renard noted wryly he had made no reference to a defeat and took victory for granted. "Let me think about it, sire. I wasn't planning on leaving France," he said.

Henry Tudor, Earl of Richmond, was not accustomed to being gainsaid but minstrels were not a regulated part of society and lived according to their own rules. Renard de Bourgonville was not in his employ, he merely visited the castle of the Duke of Brittany occasionally when he was in the vicinity. But Henry Tudor had been impressed by his skills and wanted him as a permanent member of his entourage. "Let me know your decision as soon as possible, our plans are almost finalised," he said in a tone that had the force of a command, then he walked away decisively to talk to one of his captains gathered in the inner courtyard of the castle of Nantes.

Renard looked around at the preparations being made with groups of soldiers practising their swordplay or overseeing the loading of carts with arrows and powder. He had only arrived in Nantes a few days ago not knowing about the imminent plans for an invasion of England but he had been welcomed as usual, his entertainment being particularly appreciated by the enlarged audience as a respite from the talk of war. He wandered over to where he recognised a young soldier he had made the acquaintance of. Jamie Latimer was cleaning his armour with an oily rag and a bowl of sand.

"What's the point of cleaning your armour when you're going into battle," Renard asked, genuinely curious.

Jamie smiled, "Well met, Renard. I sometimes wonder that myself but it's part of a soldier's discipline. It is important to clean off any loose rust because it would just deteriorate and you can't see what state the metal is underneath, it could have a hole or a deep split which could cost you your life. But you don't take off too much of the surface even if it is rust because it will weaken the metal."

"What exactly is happening here?" Renard asked. "The talk is that the Earl of Richmond is planning on invading England."

"The talk is correct," Jamie replied.

Renard shook his head in puzzlement. "Why? I thought the wars in England were over now and the succession settled with this new king. Is Richmond planning to depose him? And on what grounds?"

"You might well ask, Frenchman," Jamie shrugged, "though I'd better keep my voice down because that's treasonable talk here. It seems that there are a lot of people in England who aren't satisfied with King Richard, though whether that is because they don't like his government or they don't think his claim to the throne is reliable, I don't know. I haven't been in England for some time."

"But what claim does the Earl of Richmond have?" Renard asked. "I've come here to entertain at the Duke's court a few times now and I know Richmond has been in exile here for a long time, something to do with him being on the wrong side when these so-called wars of the roses ended."

"Apparently he is the last of the Lancastrian claimants to the throne of England. But why rake up a new conflict now when the Yorkist side has been safely enthroned for the past twenty five years I haven't the slightest idea."

Renard knew only the broad outlines of English politics and did not know why Henry Tudor should be the last Lancastrian heir. All he knew was that Tudor's grandmother had been the daughter of the King of France, Louis the mad, and had been the wife of the warrior king Henry V who had wreaked such havoc in France.

"Why are you going if you are not sure about the issues for which this army is fighting?" Renard asked again, not understanding the minds of fighting men.

Jamie shrugged his shoulders. "I'm a younger son and there isn't anything for me to do but fight. My father fought for the Lancastrian side in the English wars and

I've been loosely attached to Jasper Tudor, that's Richmond's uncle, since I came of age, my family estate is on the Welsh borders. Jasper's behind this invasion. When we get to England he's relying on reinforcements from his Welsh supporters."

"Will it be a success? Will they succeed?" Renard asked.

Jamie's round face looked uncertain for a moment and he rubbed his snub nose. "This is the second attempt. You probably don't know that an attempt was made a short while ago but the invasion never took place. King Richard discovered the plot and the weather was also against us. There were terrible storms and we were blown off course round the coast of France, battered and broken so we had to return here. The Duke of Brittany was none too pleased, the Tudors have outstayed their welcome as long-term guests. But this time the Earl insists that everything is better organised, the ships are bigger and better equipped and there are plenty of horses, fire power, spare arms. He has been assured of large English support when he lands."

"On what grounds will the English support him if they already have a king?" Renard was genuinely puzzled. "I know the English like fighting but this seems like taking an opportunity too far."

"Perhaps they won't," Jamie said. "It's only what we have been told from sources in England, Richmond's family and nobles whose power has been curtailed by King Richard. Jasper can be relied upon to supply his Welsh contingents but from my own experience it will depend solely on who wins the battle, neither side seems to have a monopoly of right. But to hear Richmond talk he believes himself to be divinely appointed to rid

England of all her ills. His grandmother was the widow of King Henry V and apparently he makes the same sort of patriotic speeches as Henry did to justify himself, but the warrior king was invading France whereas Henry Tudor is invading England, a big difference. And of course he can't guarantee the weather again but as he believes himself to be God's chosen vessel he doesn't really have doubts about this."

Renard didn't know if his friend was jesting or not but he said, "He has asked me to go with him as his minstrel. I haven't decided yet."

Jamie looked surprised but said, "You should think seriously of it, Renard. There will be rich pickings in England if we succeed and Richmond is likely to reward those highly who have been in his service, especially when he takes the crown and becomes king. Our Henry Tudor king of England! You could be a royal minstrel, Renard, with all the profits that would ensue. No more travelling from place to place, hoping for enough work to buy food and a night's lodging, no settled abode or regular income, but a life of luxury."

Renard's eyes were deep in thought but he asked, "And what if the expedition fails?"

"I don't dare think what will happen to Richmond," Jamie confessed, "but you could return to France. As a mere musician (pardon the expression) there would be nothing to stop you and as a foreigner you could not be accused of treason."

When the two had parted with an agreement to meet in the Great Hall at supper, Renard climbed onto one of the walls and sat looking out over the river Loire flowing past the castle. The proposition was tempting. Paid employment for an indefinite time, travel by boat instead of walking, a chance to see a foreign country – England. No doubt when they arrived there would be uncomfortable billeting in an army camp but he was used to uncomfortable lodgings in hay lofts and under hedges when he didn't have enough money for a bed in an inn. He wouldn't be expected to take part in a battle and would probably remain with the churchmen and clerks but if it came to extremity and he had to fight then, despite his words, he was quite capable of defending himself with sword and dagger as he sometimes had to do with thieves and in tavern brawls. He sat pondering for some time, watching the ships sailing up and down the Loire, bringing more men and supplies. And from the depths of his unconsciousness drifted an image that was never far away and needed only the lightest nudging to materialise. Belfiore Lechanteur had gone to England. He didn't know if she was still there or where in the whole of the country she might be, though he supposed London might be a fair guess. There could be the very slightest of chances that he might find her. Since they had separated he had thought of her often, so many casual incidents bringing her to mind – a girl singing or dancing, arriving at an inn alone and wishing she were with him, watching a tournament and wanting to hear her laugh and jump with excitement. He had had different companions on his travels – other musicians, chapmen, preaching friars, run-away servants and deserters from armies – and he had slept with several girls but though her image had grown fainter over time, none could compare with the only real friend he had ever known, the only person who had ever shared his passion for music, and he wished he had never let her go.

The Countess of Richmond was on tenterhooks now that she knew final preparations were in hand for her son to invade England with a large force and challenge King Richard for the crown. Even while in house arrest at Lathom she had been busily making plans to help him through the means of trusted servants and dependants. Reginald Bray had been very occupied carrying messages to and fro. Of prime importance had been secret communications with Elizabeth Woodville to confirm her assent to a marriage between her eldest daughter Elizabeth and Henry Tudor, a project Margaret had pursued for several years, even before King Edward died. As queen Elizabeth Woodville had been non-commital, thinking their reign secure and considering there might be more advantageous marriages proposed for her daughter, perhaps with foreign royalty. Now however the situation had changed drastically. King Richard's disclosure of the pre-contact Edward had made with Lady Eleanor Butler and the consequent illegality of his marriage had rendered her nothing more than Lady Grey and her children with the king illegitimate. The shock had completely destroyed everything she had enjoyed for the past twenty years.

Now living in a small manor she was leasing in Waltham, twelve miles from London, her busy mind was considering any possibility to regain her position. After her first panic-stricken flight into sanctuary in the abbey of Westminster King Richard had dealt with her mercifully, allowing her to live quietly at Waltham while her daughters had been re-instated at court. However she was now only a widow not a queen and although the king had allowed her daughters to return to the court, chiefly to keep them away from her influence, they were merely attendants on the new Queen Anne and no longer princesses. Elizabeth Woodville was desperate to reclaim her previous position and pacing the small rooms over and over she had come to the conclusion that the only way she could do that was by allying herself to the claim of Henry Tudor and consenting at last to the Countess of Richmond's request to engage her eldest daughter to him. It was in her power to make her daughter a queen and by so doing make herself a dominant feature at the royal court again. Of course all this depended on Henry Tudor's successful bid for the crown which could go disastrously wrong. So her compliance must be conditional and she must lie low and give King Richard no suspicion that she was working against him. She had even intimated to the King that her daughter Elizabeth might prove a suitable wife for *him* now that he was a recent widower, (even though he was her uncle) thus hedging her bets on whatever happened in the imminent conflict.

The Countess of Richmond was not aware of the Woodville woman's duplicity, only that she had received her agreement to give her daughter in marriage to her son. The implied condition was that he should make himself king but the Countess was assured of his success, had not she always had Divine sanction for her hopes and plans all these years. This was the final seal on her son's right to the throne. It was the ultimate solution to combine the white rose of York with the red rose of Lancaster and the children of this union would solve once and for all the contending claims of the past thirty years. This patriotic significance was of course not Lady Margaret Beaufort's first consideration, that went no further than ensuring her son gained the crown of

England for himself, but it was a convenient ancillary that would sway the people.

She had also been busy in encouraging current rumours that were circulating among the populace – that King Richard had poisoned his lately deceased queen so that he could marry Elizabeth Plantagenet himself and so strengthen his position, even though she was his niece, and that he had murdered his young nephews because they had not been seen since he consigned them to the Tower. It was political expediency, at which she had become adept over the years, because she did not believe the rumours. It was well known how much Richard had loved his wife, their mutual affection had always been publicly demonstrated, and she suspected that if the boys were dead then it was the Duke of Buckingham who might be held to account. She had to be careful with rumours about the young princes' deaths because this could rebound upon *her*. She was intelligent enough to realise that if the two little princes were a threat to the legality of Richard's kingship then they were equally so with her son's claim. If Buckingham was guilty of murder then she could find herself tainted by it for she had sought his support for her son when the Duke's ambitions had forged a split between him and the King. Tongues would soon start wagging so it was of vital importance to put the blame on Richard in case rumours suggested an alternative explanation.

Her mind was racing with all the possibilities of what might happen. Henry Tudor was not known to the people of England, he had been in exile for so long and kept hidden before this. How would they receive him if the invasion succeeded? No, she corrected herself, *when* it succeeded. She would allow no niggling doubts to disturb her faith. She was relying, like her son, on the massive support the ever-loyal Jasper Tudor could bring from his supporters in Wales and the Marches. But the strain of waiting was beginning to tell and for days now she had been unable to sleep, her temper short and her prayers long.

"And Richard let you leave London and come back here without demur?" she asked her husband. Sir Thomas Stanley had recently arrived back at Lathom.

"Yes I was surprised myself. He knows about the planned invasion and is making all the preparations he can to counter it. I must admit that in view of your own interest in this imminent conflict I thought he would have compelled me to stay in his household. But when I told him it were better for me to return to Lancashire to raise my own force there, he gave me permission to leave."

Lady Margaret pursed her small mouth and asked her husband directly, "And this force you are raising, whose side is it to fight on?"

He turned aside, not meeting her eyes as he replied, "It depends."

The household at Lathom were all aware that some-thing momentous was going on. There were constant messengers travelling between Lancashire and London so rumours were buzzing that the Countess's son Henry Tudor was planning an invasion of England and intended a confrontation with King Richard, though news took almost a week to arrive so was always out of date and often confusing as to the actual facts. But Sir Thomas Stanley was raising a large contingency force and officers were visiting the towns and villages of Lancashire to collect men and arms, some of them men who had fought in the civil war of twenty years ago, many of them their sons.

"I'm going to enlist in Stanley's army," Harry Duxbury reported to Bel the next time they met at the market in Ormskirk.

"Which side are they fighting for?" asked Bel.

"I don't know. I don't care. It's a chance to get away from here and do something exciting." His eyes were shining and she knew he had found life unbearably tedious after their journey to France.

"It's certainly an awkward situation. Sir Thomas is a trusted and important member of the King's household while being at the same time step-father to the invader. He must be finding it difficult to know exactly where his loyalties lie, with his sovereign or his wife," Bel mused, her forehead crinkling in a frown. "There are secret whisperings around the house that he will wait until he sees who is going to be the victor before declaring himself."

"I hope that doesn't mean we shall miss the battle," Harry cried in alarm.

They were sitting in their usual place on the stone bench by the church and Bel studied his eager face. "Are you sure about this, you aren't a soldier."

"I'm sure a lot of the others aren't also. It's a long time since Englishmen were fighting all the time. But we are to be trained at the musters and I can use a bow and a poleaxe. Better than working on Duxbury farm or in Jaxon's workshop."

Bel wondered if it might not be as pleasant as he envisaged. She was also fearful that she might never see him again. Was she doomed to lose all those she had an affection for. If anything happened to Harry

Duxbury she would definitely leave Lathom. Apart from his friendship she had never thought she really belonged here.

Renard de Bourgonville was in the train of Henry Tudor's invasion force, wondering if he had made the right decision after all as his first sea voyage ended in a small natural harbour lined by stone walls on a flat wooded shoreline. As all the men, horses and arms were unloaded Renard waited in company with one of the clerks he had come to know well, his precious lute held carefully in his arms, his travelling pack strapped to his back. The voyage had been without incident for the weather had been good and now the August sun shone warm on the stones of the encircling walls.

"So this is England," he said, trying to steady himself on his feet after the rolling of the waves.

"No Frenchman, this is Wales," retorted Davy Lambert. "This is Milford Haven in Pembrokeshire, Jasper Tudor's territory and known for years as a safe port. The Tudors are Welsh, though the Earl of Richmond is only so when it suits him. He prefers to think of himself as the grandson of a queen and half-brother to a king rather than the grandson of a humble Welsh body-servant. We shall be marching through Wales to gather support, Jasper's men largely. At least they should be better than the rag tag bunch of mercenaries and ex-prisoners we have brought from France."

Renard was still wondering why he had come. The change of scene was welcome but he intended to stay well away from any fighting. Fortunately Henry Tudor had requisitioned him for his own personal household and if things got too nasty he would sneak away and do what he did best. There would be opportunities for finding employment in the many castles and noble houses he had been told about.

"At least if matters go awry for us you can't be charged with treason as you are French and not English," Davy assured him.

The places they passed through on their march meant nothing to him as they were informed they were making for a town called Shrewsbury and then hopefully with greatly increased reinforcements cutting through into the Midland shires. He played his flageolet as they marched, his lute kept safely in its bag over his shoulder, and when they paused to rest or eat the soldiers were happy to have him sing. Davy Lambert taught him a popular English song called 'Bring us in good ale' which always received tumultuous applause.

"King Richard is apparently at Nottingham," Davy informed him. "It wasn't wise for him to stay in London because he didn't know where Richmond intended to land though common sense suggested he would try a Welsh landing place, certainly not the north which is King Richard's home ground. Consequently he chose the Midlands as the most suitable place to keep a watch on all directions, Richard is a good strategist. He is a well-seasoned warrior whereas Tudor has no military experience at all, though I shouldn't be saying this."

Renard was disappointed that it didn't seem as if he would see London but asked, "Does this mean you think we have little chance of success?"

"I'm hoping for the best. Richmond seems confident. He wouldn't have made the attempt otherwise because if he does fail then it will be the end of him. He has too much to lose to make a mistake. Finally it will depend on how much support each of the opposing armies can muster," his companion replied.

At her safe retreat of Lathom, Lady Margaret was consumed with the same thought. Sir Thomas had been ordered by King Richard to bring his large force to Nottingham immediately. Still dithering about his action he told his wife, "I must temporise." He sent word back to the King that he must delay a little while as he was suffering from the sweating sickness.

"Richard will see no reason why you cannot send your force with a substitute commander to lead them," Margaret retorted, still unsure what her husband intended to do and knowing he could not temporise for ever, the uncertainty contributing more to her frayed nerves.

This was a sentiment repeated by Harry Duxbury, chafing to be on his way with the Lancashire force and afraid he was going to lose his chance after all of participating in some fighting.

On the other hand Renard de Bourgonville was becoming apprehensive about a battle as the army plodded laboriously through the midlands of England. He played his music whenever he could and tried to drown out the constant talk of war that assailed his ears from his companions, often wishing he was back on his leisurely peregrinations through France.

Sir Thomas Stanley's procrastination inevitably brought a new message from the King within days.

"What does it say?" Margaret asked anxiously as her husband broke the seal and opened up the missive.

"He repeats his command that I am to come immediately to Nottingham with the Lancashire force."

He paused then continued, "He is holding George as hostage for my compliance."

George Stanley, a young man in his twenties, was Sir Thomas's son with his first wife Eleanor Neville, and his heir. He carried the title of Lord Strange which had come into his possession with his marriage to Elizabeth Woodville's niece Jacqueline.

"There is also a letter from George saying that the King has accused him of conspiring with your son and he fears his life will be forfeit if I do not obey the King's command. I am his surety."

They stood together in silence for a time, both understanding the score. His son weighed against hers. The imminent conflict had now taken on a personal significance for they both loved their sons. For years they had walked a tightrope of political expediency, aiding and supporting each other in order to survive in the fluctuating struggles for power for both of them loved power, privilege and wealth. Now a wedge was being driven between them as their personal circumstances veered in different directions. Margaret couldn't force her husband into sacrificing everything for her but her strong faith compelled her to believe that if her son was destined to be King, a belief she had always held to, then that would be the outcome. Perhaps God was testing Thomas Stanley as he had tested Abraham by demanding his favoured son, only to have him restored to him on proof of his willingness to do so. She was about to suggest this to her husband when he said, "I must go to the King, Margaret."

She was silent for a moment then said, "Go then. The outcome is in the hands of God and we must wait on His Will."

CHAPTER 18

Turnabout

The news soon reached Lathom. The Countess of Richmond was now the mother of the king. Henry Tudor's forces had been victorious over King Richard who had been slain in the battle and the Earl of Richmond was now King Henry VII signing himself Henricus Rex. One of the first honours he had granted was to his stepfather who was now to be known as Earl of Derby.

Lady Margaret set off immediately for London to meet with her newly-ennobled husband in company with a large entourage which did not at the moment include all her ladies. The house was buzzing with rumours. Would the Countess now spend all her time at the court, no doubt Sir Thomas would receive more rewards and important positions. What about those who had fought on the side of King Richard, would they be harshly dealt with? Would this be the end or would the conflict still continue as it had done when the wars of the roses first started? Lathom was too far away from the heartland to either know or fully comprehend the issues. It was difficult for her household, retainers and countryfolk to realise that their mistress was now the most important woman in the land, mother to the King and queen in all but name until King Henry married.

"How she will gloat and flaunt herself," Maud Pettifer said. "She has always prided herself on her noble lineage and her great wealth, now there will be no stopping her."

Few people knew the intensity with which Lady Margaret Beaufort had pursued her ambition for nearly thirty years or the lengths to which she had gone to see it realised. But most people had experience of her pride, her love of opulent show as well as her religious devotion.

"The imminent coronation will put her almost in the position of queen," remarked Agnes. It was now well publicised that King Henry was to marry Elizabeth Plantagenet, the 18 year old daughter of Edward IV and Elizabeth Woodville. "I wouldn't be surprised if the Countess doesn't delay the marriage until after the coronation so that she can have all the glory."

"Imagine what it will be like to have her as your mother-in-law. How I pity the new young queen," said Maud, in a tone devoid of pity. They had all experienced her harsh censure while in her service.

"No doubt we shall be called to London soon," said Agnes. "You must admit how exciting it will be to be members of the royal court."

"I'm not going, I have been given permission to marry Peter at last and he is to stay here at Lathom," said Maud.

"What about you, Belfiore? Are you excited about being a member of the royal court?" Agnes asked.

Bel had contributed little to the excited chatter of the ladies, knowing little of the exact happenings.

She did not know what to think. It would be good to be in London again but was wary of the circumstances. She wanted Harry Duxbury to return, to make sure that no harm had come to him and to hear his version of what had happened to make the Countess's son King of England.

Harry soon made his way home in company with most of the ordinary soldiers who had fought in Sir Thomas Stanley's armed force. They only had to come from Leicester, near where the battle of Bosworth field had taken place. He sought her out at Lathom House, going into the service quarters by one of the back entrances, easily admitted when he declared himself to have fought with Sir Thomas in the battle, and asking someone to take a message to the French attendant Bella.

Bel ran to meet him and he was pleased by the expression of relief that crossed her face when she saw him. She seized him by the shoulders, examining him carefully and saying, "Are you well, Harry. No hurts?"

"A few cuts and grazes, aches and pains," he laughed, "but most of them a result of the walk from Leicester rather than the battle. I have much to tell you, can we walk from the house?"

They traversed the two courtyards and took one of the postern gates that led to the lane where the little stone chapel and almshouses stood. There they sat on the grass in the warm sun while Harry related to her all the details of his adventure. As he described the carnage and horror of the blood-soaked fields it seemed almost a sacrilege to be seated amidst buttercups and daisies, celandines and cowslips with the scent of the briar roses in the hedges.

"We didn't go in immediately when the battle first started. We were held back and told to wait. As the fighting proceeded people were saying the two sides were equally matched but that King Richard seemed to have the advantage. Then Sir Thomas suddenly appeared and ordered us to go and fight on the side of Henry Tudor. There were fifteen thousand of us, fresh, ready for action. We turned the tide of the battle. It was through us that Henry Tudor won the field and became king."

"Sir Thomas's force changed sides? They were supposed to be fighting for King Richard weren't they?"

"They didn't exactly change sides. They didn't fight at all at first but waited to see how the battle was going. But yes, King Richard expected Sir Thomas to be fighting for him and welcomed him warmly when we arrived, saying that he depended on us," Harry said.

"That wasn't an honourable thing to do. To have no loyalty," Bel was shocked. "He was in the King's service. Availed himself of his benefits. He should have followed his lord," she said. Unaware of recent English history Bel did not know how often people had changed sides in the late war of the roses. She had been raised on the legends of Charlemagne and King Arthur and his knights where loyalty to one's liege lord was the first obligation of the code of chivalry. But then a flash of remembrance brought to mind Robert Malory's words that his father had fought on both the Yorkist and Lancastrian sides.

"Another shocking thing was that King Richard was holding Sir Thomas's son, George Stanley, as a hostage for his father's loyalty. Richard could have had him killed, King Henry V killed the hostages at Agincourt, and Sir Thomas was willing to risk this, risk the life of his son and heir." Bel remained silent and he continued, "No doubt he thought his own interests would be best served by being stepfather to a king and for a start he has been made an Earl and is to be known as Lord Derby."

"He was probably more afraid of his wife than the King," Bel muttered.

"Henry Tudor found the crown in a bush and put it on. After Richard's death his body was defiled and treated very dishonourably, they stripped it naked, flung it across a horse and threw it into a pit in Leicester," Harry continued, judging he had better not reveal more of the grisly details to Bella.

Tears shone in Bel's eyes as she said, "I felt some hatred against King Richard because he had Anthony Woodville killed. But no-one should be treated like that and especially a king. And I still cannot see what right Henry Tudor has to be king in his stead."

Harry sighed. "You are not English, Bella. Our kings haven't always ruled by right and the English are not particularly concerned about this so long as he is a strong king who rules with justice and keeps the land in peace and prosperity. Let's hope Henry Tudor, or King Henry VII as we must now call him, does this. My main dissatisfaction lies in the fact that the dragon has now been elevated to such a prominent position, the most important woman in the land. The only consolation is that she will probably not be here in Lancashire very often."

"That means that I shall probably not be here very often either," Bel reminded him and she saw his face cloud with disappointment.

However recent events had strengthened her intention to try and make her way back to France. She did not want to continue as an attendant to the Countess, now lady mother to the King. The court held little appeal for Bel. She did not like the surface glitter of competing wealth, the fighting for rank and privilege, the jealousy of ambitious courtiers and ladies, the insincerity of flattery. She preferred being with people who were straight-forward and honest, who worked hard to some usefulness, who had interesting stories to tell. She found the decorative position of attendant stultifying, a strictly defined ritual of standing in the background, the tasks of sewing, reading and praying as ordained by others and not by personal preference, the mindless chatter and gossip of her companions. She wanted her life to be richer than that, not with luxury but with freedom. The freedom to roam where she willed, to marvel at the beauty of the natural world, to be in the company of those who shared her passions and to be able to give pleasure to others by using those gifts she knew had been granted to her. She had never been drawn to the Countess and her ruthless ambition now repelled her as did the self-serving nature of Sir Thomas Stanley and the ambiguity of the new king. She had no wish to share in the profits accrued by what her unsophisticated personality saw as vainglory.

She began to plan her escape on the same lines that she had made her solitary journey five years previously. She would be able to find someone travelling to London, probably someone in service at Lathom House who would not know her personally, or better still a merchant from Ormskirk – Harry would perhaps know of someone. This time she had her horse. Once in

London she would take accommodation for a time at the Throstle where Sim was still in service and this would give her time to find once again a group of merchants travelling via the port of Dover to France.

Harry's hope that the Countess's elevation would keep her in London and she would spend less time at Lathom was not realised when the news was passed around that she was bringing her son the King to visit their great estate. For years when he was in exile she had written describing the imposing residence and she wished him now to see it at first hand while at the same time demonstrating to the people of Lancashire her close affinity to the Crown. All the nobles and dignitaries of the shire would be invited to the celebrations which would be as never before seen in Lancashire.

Bel confided to Harry Duxbury that she intended to leave before the royal progress arrived.

"You mean you are making an escape?" he said and she agreed, even though the dismay on his face troubled her.

"I need you to do something for me," she said. "Can you find someone in Ormskirk or close by who is travelling to London soon and see if I can ride in their company? Also I was wondering if I could stay in the tower for a day or two while these arrangements are made."

Harry looked amazed but grinned and said, "Yes, why not. I shall have to spend most of the time in the house and on the farm doing my chores but I can make excuses to get away occasionally. I'll make sure we have plenty of food and drink." He made no comment about finding travellers to London, thinking this could be an opportunity to get Bella to change her mind and stay with him.

He was not blessed with the ability to foresee the consequences of his actions and usually acted impulsively and on the instincts of the moment without looking too far ahead.

"I shall not bring much with me for my travels because I won't be able to carry a lot. My own personal possessions are few – my instruments, my two books, my trinkets and fairings. I shall not take many clothes, perhaps two or three gowns with my cloak and fur mantle. I shall leave the rest behind for the other ladies to use."

"No don't do that," Harry said. "Take them to Dame Grice in Ormskirk, she buys and sells second-hand clothes and she will give you a fair price. You will need money for your journey. I'll take them for you if you wish, Ethelreda buys from her and she knows me."

Bel accepted Harry's practicality and agreed, the money would definitely help.

She was feeling excited now and arranged to meet Harry outside the walls of Lathom on the road to Newburgh in the dark of the night two days hence.

Everything went to plan and they rode to the pele tower without hindrance, Harry's horse sharing Bel's saddle packs so they could keep a fast pace. Quietly they entered the tower and unpacked their loads then Harry went to stable Bel's horse in one of the outbuildings well away from the farmhouse, leaving his own close by. He had brought loaves, cheese, bacon, apples and a wineskin. They ate a little but saved most of it for Bel on the morrow because Harry said he must depart early to go to his sister's house in Ormskirk with some leather for Jaxon that John Duxbury had procured from a tanner friend of his.

"I'll see Dame Grice about buying your clothes. Now time to go to bed for an hour or two," he grinned and she allowed him to lead her up to the room on the second floor. As she lay in his arms on the wooden bedstead softened with sheepskins and needing no coverlet because the night was warm, she felt excited at the fact that she was setting off home, perhaps even on the morrow and certainly by the next day. She didn't mind pleasing Harry when they were shortly to part and she had been so relieved that he had come to no harm during the battle. Harry however was blissfully dreaming of other ideas. He had no intention of letting Bella go if he could help it and was busy putting his mind to finding a solution.

When he regretfully roused himself to return to the house before dawn lightened the sky he told his sleepy companion, "Stay hidden all day. You have plenty of food and drink and I will see you tonight, hopefully with some news about the things you wish."

Bel slept late, snuggled amongst the comfortable sheepskins, then leisurely ate some of the food. She found no hardship in staying within the walls of the tower, it was warm, the sun's rays filtered through the narrow window slits and she had books to read, the Romance of the Rose that Robert had bought her such a long time ago at Saddington and a Book of Hours which the Countess of Richmond had belatedly presented to her as a reward for her successful errand to Brittany now that events had turned out well. It was a beautiful expensive book with a cover of dark red velvet and a little brass lock and the illustrations were painted in brilliant hues of vermillion, lapis lazuli, green and gold. She could hear noises from outside as work began on the farm, the shouts of men, neighing of horses and in the distance the farmyard sounds of geese, pigs and hens. For Bel it was a welcome change to the soft footfalls, dulcet tones and surreptitious whisperings of the Countess's solar.

It was late afternoon and all was quiet apart from the neighing of a horse when suddenly she heard footsteps on the ladder leading up to the bedchamber.

She put down her book, wondering why Harry was so early. However instead of Harry she was surprised to see the bulky figure of Rafe Standish standing at the top of the wooden ladder and surveying the room, his eyes finally resting upon her. He stepped into the room and his eyes gleamed as he saw her shocked face, apprehension all too clear in her blue eyes.

"Well, well, what a surprise," he chortled. "I thought someone was here but expected it to be that lout Duxbury." He drew closer to the bed on which she had been lying until alarm had raised her. "It's the travelling player isn't it, I thought I vaguely recognised you with the actors at Standish Hall."

Bel could only stammer, "What are you doing here? This is Duxbury property," as she got up from the bed and stood facing him.

He laughed, "Is that what Henry Duxbury tells you? Well he's wrong because this is Standish property, legally owing to us because of Duxbury debts. I came to talk with John Duxbury but I had a feeling there was someone in the tower and thinking it to be the arrogant pup I thought I would have a word with him first as I have some scores to settle with him. However this is even better. A beautiful girl all alone and she no better than she ought to be, the consort of travelling players." He came towards her and put his hands on her shoulders, drawing her to him. She tried to pull away but he was too strong. He pulled her closer and sliding his hand behind her neck he bent to kiss her hard on the mouth. She tried to resist, keeping her mouth tight closed but he forced it open with his teeth, pushing his tongue inside. Bel felt sick and afraid as she saw the lust in his eyes, his breath coming unevenly, his face more flushed than usual.

He threw her back onto the bed but with surprising agility she jumped off on the other side and stood defiantly, her arms outstretched with palms facing him to fend him off. She wanted to say that Harry was expected soon but thought better of it. Rafe Standish considered her an easy woman and it would not help either her or Harry if Rafe thought they were fornicating together. She was trying to think of an excuse for her being there when Rafe's manner softened and he said wheedlingly, "I don't usually have to force a woman to let me pleasure her. Why don't we spend a pleasant half-hour together, I'm certain you wouldn't regret it."

"You would have to kill me first," Bel said through clenched teeth.

He laughed. "I believe women of your sort like to be persuaded by a little force."

There was a knife of Harry's lying on the old chest and Bel tried to reach it but Rafe was too quick and grasped her arm, throwing her back on the bed. He picked up a candlestick and lit the candle with the accompanying tinder box.

"Lie with me or I might be tempted to do a little damage here," he said quietly.

"You can't burn the tower, it's stone," she cried desperately.

"I won't burn the tower you idiot, it's my property, but this straw mattress and this other rubbish will burn easily," he said sweeping his hand around the few wooden articles. "Henry Duxbury will miss his bow and his arrows and if someone gets left behind in the tower and an accident occurs......."

Suddenly a piercing voice called from below, "Harry, are you there?"

Ughtred wasn't accustomed to not having a stream of invectives in reply so he ventured, "I'm coming up," and before his cousin could forbid him he was running up the wooden stairs two at a time.

Rafe had blown out the candle and replaced it on the chest, caught off balance by the sudden interruption. Ughtred stood looking around the circular room in puzzlement. "Where's Harry?" he asked.

"Coming soon," Bel replied quickly. She wanted to run to the little boy and fling her arms around him but instead she said calmly, "This is Master Standish who came to see him but he's going now. Can you lead him down the stairs, Ughtred, I think he wants to call on your father before departing."

Rafe glowered at her but there was nothing he could do and with the boy watching him he saluted her brusquely and made his way from the tower.

Ughtred returned shortly, too excited at being in the tower with the Lady Bella without Harry forbidding him entrance. "When is Harry coming?" he asked.

"Soon," Bel replied. "But listen carefully to me, Ughtred, I want you to say nothing to Harry about Master Standish's visit."

"Why not? He'll go and fight with him."

"Precisely. And he will get into trouble again. And we don't want Harry to get into trouble do we?"

"No they'll send him away again and I don't want that," Ughtred said. "I did miss him."

"But doesn't he treat you badly?" Bel asked

The boy shook his head vehemently. "He never does. He only threatens. He doesn't mean it."

Bel laughed saying, "You had better go now. And Ughtred, don't tell your father that you have seen me here. Harry wouldn't want that either."

He thought about it for a minute then, not understanding completely but having some instinct about the matter, he gave his word to do as he was bidden.

Left alone Bel could not settle to anything and wandered around restlessly. The encounter had brought back to her the bad memories of the past and she longed for Harry to return. However when he did come she made no mention of her fright and tried to compose herself so that he would not notice she was somewhat on edge. Harry however was too wrapped up with his own news to sense any unease.

"You can't leave just yet, Bella," he announced with satisfaction.

"Why? Haven't you been able to find anyone travelling south soon?" she asked. "It doesn't matter if they aren't going as far as London, part of the way would be sufficient."

Harry did not reply for he had made no attempt at these enquiries. Instead he said, "The dragon is bringing her son the King to Lathom to see their great residence."

"I know. What does that have to do with me? I have left her service."

"To honour the occasion the Prior of Burscough Abbey is planning to put on a mystery play in the grounds of the priory. We do these from time to time, on special occasions like Easter and Corpus Christi."

"Yes I know. I saw a whole cycle of them performed in Coventry one Corpus Christi," Bel said, her mind travelling back to the wonderful day she had spent with Robert Malory.

"I've heard that the big towns perform them for a whole day at Corpus Christi, going all through the Bible from beginning to end. We only do one or two of them, we don't have enough people or enough money, Ormskirk not having its own guilds," Harry said. "We have a priest, Father Peter, who writes them. He is a good man and popular but also very studious. "

"That sounds interesting, Harry, but what has this to do with me? You can't imagine I shall delay my departure in order to watch a Biblical play performed by the townspeople in the Priory. I told you, I have already seen a whole sequence of them performed in the town of Coventry on a grand scale with waggons and tableaux."

"But you are going to be part of this one." Harry delivered his statement with the aplomb of the town crier relating a momentous national event. Bel looked at him in astonishment so he continued, "I have to play the serpent – in the garden of Eden." He grimaced as if he could not understand why he had been chosen for this particular role and Bel couldn't help laughing. However he continued, "I said I would play the serpent if you could play the Virgin Mary."

"What!" Bel was dumbfounded. "I am not worthy to play the Virgin. I haven't led a very good life." She thought of her violations. They hadn't been her fault but in the doctrines of the church even nuns who had been violated were denied the higher ranks in Paradise, Dante's great poem had told her that. Her relationship with Robert Malory *had* been her choice and she thought also of the many deceptions she had made. She couldn't tell Harry this and said instead, "When we are together it is fornication. I am not worthy."

Harry dismissed this with an impatient shake of his head, "Don't talk nonsense, I love you and want to marry you so it isn't fornication. Of course you are worthy. But apart from that we are only acting the parts, not being the characters. What about those people who have to play Judas and Pilate and all the other wicked men, they are not necessarily evil themselves. I told Father Peter that you are the most beautiful girl I know and you have a wonderful singing voice so he is going to include a song for you. Also you can read. That is a great recommendation because most of the people can't read and they have to learn their parts by having Father Peter repeat them over and over. The other applicant for the part of the Virgin is a daughter of one of the burgesses and she is fat and ugly."

"I am not English," Bel said weakly.

"And was the Virgin Mary English?" Harry retorted. "It's all settled, Bella. Father Peter thinks you will be ideal so we are both going to be involved in this presentation and have to rehearse immediately."

Despite her misgivings Bel felt a shiver of excitement. She was going to be performing again in front of a large crowd of people, perhaps even the King. But she had performed for Henry Tudor before, as well as many other nobles in France and was accustomed to entertaining the nobility. It mattered more to her to be giving pleasure to ordinary folk who so appreciated the brief respites from their life of monotonous labour.

"And before you ask how you are going to live in the meantime I have it all arranged," Harry triumphantly disclosed. "I know you can't live here at Duxbury, it wouldn't be acceptable and I don't want us to get a bad name when I am planning to marry you. Dame Grice, who sells the used clothes, has a spare chamber above her shop and you can live there with her in Ormskirk until the play is over. She is also interested in buying anything you have to offer."

Bel sighed as she realised Harry had everything arranged and it was going to be nearly impossible to extricate herself without hurting him more than she was planning to do eventually. She was disappointed that she was not going to be on her way in the next few days but she had been away a long time so what did another week or two matter. It would still be travelling weather as winter was some time away yet. And deep within her soul was a sense of excitement at the realisation she was going to be a performer again. Her fellow actors would be simple people, the ordinary people of the little market town who would have to learn their parts with difficulty but she would have an audience. She was going to have to live in lodgings again but Harry had assured her that Dame Grice was a kindly soul. But nothing was going to deter her from leaving England when Ormskirk's celebration for the King was done.

CHAPTER 19

Jubilate

Renard de Bourgonville was enjoying unaccustomed long-term luxury as a musician at the royal court. King Henry had given him a permanent place in his household and paid him a regular fee plus accommodation and livery. At first he had enjoyed the novelty of his new life. After the success of the Battle of Bosworth Field there were endless celebrations in which he played a prominent part. He had not been a witness to the battle and only picked up information piece-meal from different sources – some lord had changed sides bringing his large force to the aid of Henry Tudor, King Richard had been killed and his body shamefully treated, the crown was found in a hazel bush. He cared little about the details, in fact his knowledge of the English tongue was not sufficient to fully understand the various complexities of the conflict and all that mattered to him at the time was that he had found himself on the winning side. With his usual expertise he had composed lyrics lauding the new king and the success of the battle, inserting the set pieces of knightly exploits from the old legends of Charlemagne and King Arthur that he always made use of in like circumstances. He had quickly made friends with the other court musicians who admired his skills because though he was often accused of arrogance when promoting himself to prospective employers, he was never boastful or less than generous to others of his calling. With his charm and good looks he attracted young courtiers and a large following of ladies of all ages and status, the most important of which he praised in song. Chief of these of course was the young princess Elizabeth who was to become the wife of the King. She was gracious and modest, her face not beautiful but lovely in its tranquillity, her blue eyes gentle, her hair showing fair beneath her hood. Renard thought that notwithstanding her luxurious gowns she showed a natural grace and nobility which the once-Earl of Richmond lacked. However he also had to pay careful attention to the two lady mothers – Lady Margaret, the Countess of Richmond and the ex-Queen Elizabeth, the first expecting reverence due to her exalted position, the second due to her acknowledged (and self-acknowledged) beauty. Renard cared for neither of them, disliking the Countess's arrogance and Lady Elizabeth's blatant sexuality, but he flattered them as he was expected to. However the superficiality of court life soon became tedious to him and the constant rituals and observances produced a monotony of their own. It was like living in a gilded cage and Renard had always been a free spirit, moving on when it suited him, looking for new audiences and new experiences. He liked to explore the city of London, of which he had heard so much while he was in France, but would have preferred to be entertaining in the many inns and hostelries, a different one each night. However in the streets his lack of fluency in English was a disadvantage whereas at the court everyone spoke French.

He was thinking of soon returning to France and taking up his old life. Another few weeks at the court and then he decided he would ask the King's permission to return to his homeland and if it were denied then he would just run away. He had never counted himself to be at anyone's beck and call, serving the nobility when it pleased him and considering the privilege to be theirs not his. One thing that disappointed him was that he had never caught a sight of, nor heard anyone speak of, Belfiore Lechanteur. He knew it had been a faint hope not likely to be realised. She could be anywhere in the country or even have returned to France. He recollected the name of the relatives she was seeking had been Malory, but no-one he asked knew anyone of that name. Still as he wandered the streets of London in his spare time he still dreamt that he might see her and turned round often when he caught a glimpse of a young girl with long black curls.

He was considering how soon to take his leave when it was broadcast that the King intended to fulfil a long-standing dream of his mother's that he should visit her home in the north and Renard was told that he was to be part of the large company. An inveterate traveller he decided he might as well stay a little longer and see something of the north part of England, though he had been told it was bleak and inhospitable. Then after the winter, when the good weather returned in the spring, he would retrace his steps homeward.

It was a four day journey to the north, to a province he was told was called Lancashire, where the king's stepfather Sir Thomas Stanley, now the Earl of Derby, held many manors and estates and was reputed to be the chief landowner and most important person there.

The royal company on horseback rode ahead of all the baggage waggons loaded with the king's personal possessions, his clothes, books, religious artefacts, weaponry and hogsheads of wine. There was no need to bring the customary hangings and furnishings for Renard had been told that Lathom House was as splendidly accoutered as any royal palace, though the new king did bring his enormous gold and crimson state bed. The King and his mother rode together with a bodyguard of armoured knights, followed by Lord Derby and their personal attendants and men-at-arms. Renard and his fellow musicians rode at the back of the procession on poorer mounts that had been left in the stables when everyone else had been supplied but Renard didn't mind as he was no experienced horseman. It was a pleasant enough ride for the weather was fine but not too hot and the roads reasonably good for most of the time, neither too dusty and stony as in high summer nor squelching in mire as with winter's rain. Trumpeters and heralds rode just ahead announcing their arrival and people lined the streets to watch curiously as they came to towns and villages, fighting to grab the coins flung by the King and his mother. In the evenings they stayed in the castles of great nobles where they were lavishly entertained and Renard joined the music.

The castles had originally been mighty defensive edifices but the lords had done their best to make them suitably comfortable for the royal party, hastily replenishing rushes on the stone floors and borrowing hangings, table linen and plate from willing neighbours, but Renard considered them inferior to the French châteaux he was familiar with. When they came to a place which he was told was told was within easy reach of Lathom House they had to be ferried across a wide river, an operation taking some time, and the King was heard to command Lord Derby, "Get a bridge built here, Thomas, as soon as possible." Afterwards the landscape had little interest though they passed through a couple of busy market towns where their arrival caused great excitement as crowds gathered to watch the unexpected cavalcade pass. Then they rode alongside fields of rye, wheat and beans surrounded by wooded low-lying hills interspersed with little hamlets until after a short steep descent the ground became flat and noticeably marshy. Suddenly the towers and battlements of Lathom House reared on the horizon, the surrounding walls seeming to stretch as far as the eye could see, and the jaded travellers were shaken sharply from their tedium by the size of the edifice. Clattering over the moat and across the drawbridge, through two gatehouses and across two cobbled courtyards, the cavalcade came to rest in the heart of the fortress. This was a collection of turreted and gabled buildings, some of them timber but mostly constructed of stone with slate roofs and tall glass-paned windows, many of them mullioned oriels, and the travellers marvelled at the unexpected grandeur.

The interior more than fulfilled the expectation of the first sight of the noble edifice, rooms hung with glowing tapestries of Biblical and legendary scenes, wall hangings of crimson and gold velvet and figured brocades. Sweet-scented herbs mingled with fresh rushes on the stone floors and the plenteous carved chairs, cupboards and chests were painted in bright colours of blue, crimson and gilt and monogrammed with the arms of both the Beauforts and the Stanleys. At the nightly feasts those on the dais at the top of the hall were served on gold and silver plate at a long table covered in white samite and sagging beneath the weight of the dishes and bowls filled to overflowing with diverse meats and huge quantities of fish ("from the mere"), pastries and fruit as well as flagons of the best burgundy. Blazing log fires had been lit in the large fireplaces to offset the chill of early autumn and the riot of colour emblazoned by countless wax candles set in candelabra and wall sconces. From his lowly place at the bottom of the hall Renard could watch and marvel. This was wealth indeed, wealth meant to be demonstrated. These Stanleys must have ruled as royalty here before Lady Margaret's son had taken up the crown. It was all impressive and word was passed around the company by the proud Lathom servants that Henry Tudor himself was so taken with his mother's house that he was intending to create a new palace for himself on the banks of the Thames in London and he planned to have it built on the same pattern as Lathom House.

In the depths of the night Renard got up from the goose-feather mattress on the floor of the chamber he was sharing with other musicians and went to relieve himself. He had been told that all the rooms in Lathom House had feather mattresses and pillows because there was a great mere nearby of more than two thousand acres in size and the home of wild geese. He didn't return immediately. The moon was full and he crossed the courtyard and climbed one of the walls. He sat for a time drinking in the cool night air, welcome after the stifling heat of the hall redolent with wine fumes, cooked food, smoke and sweat. He realised that the faint gleam in the far distance, silvered by the moon's weak beams, was the sea. Soon he would be crossing the sea, a different sea but nonetheless the pathway from this island to his home country of France – and freedom. The opulence was too much, he felt stifled by it. He needed fresh air in his lungs, tree-shaded paths to walk along, the song of birds and the sound of country animals, even the rain on his face. He had enjoyed playing his music as always but most of the time no-one was really listening. He would soon be back on the road doing what he loved best.

Father Peter had never before been so happy with his attempts at making plays from some of the Bible stories for the townspeople to enjoy, both as participants and as audience. Never before had he been blessed with an actor so accomplished and so suited to their role as was Henry Duxbury's friend Bella. Though Father Peter knew himself to be gifted with intelligence and worthy of a more demanding post in the church, he was content to serve in a humble way in a small country town with poor and often unappreciative parishioners because he considered this was his vocation. But he put some of his gifts to use by converting stories from the Bible into little plays which he trained his parishioners to perform occasionally at special festivals of the church. The services of the church, and the Bible itself, were all in Latin and therefore only the priests and officers of the church could understand them. All the ordinary people could do was to learn the prayers by heart and make the appropriate responses, and learn the gospel message from looking at the colourful frescoes covering the walls of the church and the pictures in coloured glass in the windows. It was left to the itinerant preaching friars to give the people instruction in language they could understand and tell them Bible stories and the lives of the saints, interspersed with anecdotes that amused them and made them laugh. So because he believed that the Christian faith should make people happy, put smiles on their faces and help them to pursue their mundane lives with some consolation that God loved them and cared for them, he turned his convictions into little plays. The spectators received religious instruction in a form they enjoyed. Of course he wasn't the only one to do this, many of the larger towns held performances of these mystery plays. Before he came to Ormskirk he was ordained as a priest in Chester and on the feast of Corpus Christi every June they performed a whole cycle of plays, telling stories from the Garden of Eden to the Last Judgement, but Chester was a large town with trade guilds and more resources. Father Peter was less ambitious for it was not easy to find townsfolk who were capable of acting in the plays. Most of them could not read so he had to read them their parts and they had to repeat the words from him and commit them to memory. A lot of people were too nervous to perform in public and some of the more pious citizens were not in favour of denigrating religion in this way, considering it to be sacrilegious. The ebullient Henry Duxbury had been involved before and so had several others, sufficient to supply him with enough characters for the small number of interludes he had in mind for this particular presentation – the Garden of Eden, the Annunciation, the Nativity and some of the miracles ending with the Transfiguration because he wanted it to be a joyful occasion. Because the Virgin Mary was such an important character he had needed a special person, someone young, lovely and with a beautiful voice because she was to sing, and when Henry Duxbury had brought along a friend of his sister Ethelreda he considered it a miracle of its own. The actors had all worked hard, even Henry limiting his usually boisterous behaviour and applying himself with concentration, the craftsmen of Ormskirk had made the necessary properties – the carpenters an apple tree, a manger, the magi's gifts and three pillars; the mercers lengths of blue silk for the water, the virgin's mantle and a winding sheet; the tailor was making a tail for the serpent and a pair of angel's wings; the potters were supplying urns and dishes; fishermen from the mere were giving nets for the disciples; husbandmen were to find straw, a donkey and some sheep. Others were helping with the costumes. It was all very exciting and Bel and Harry were enjoying the rehearsals, Harry relishing the fact that he was able to cajole time off from his work. Most of the townspeople however were apprehensive about performing before the King.

"He might not come to watch," Harry said to Bel. "And besides we have seen him before so we aren't going to be overawed."

"I'm worried about what the Countess will say when she sees me," Bel confessed.

"She might not recognise you from a distance," Harry assured her.

Bel thought that hope unlikely but decided she would deal with it as and when the occasion arose.

On the appointed afternoon, a day of mild sunshine, the little group of unprofessional actors together with Father Peter arrived early at the priory to make their final arrangements and see where they were to perform. The prior had ensured that the monks and the abbey servants had been kept busy preparing the courtyard in front of the church. The stones had been swept clean and the grass verges cut neatly. At one side of the courtyard a dais had been erected for the distinguished guests, draped in gold cloth with the royal banner behind, and oak chairs with arms and high carved backs had been taken from the prior's house and set in place. A space designated for the performance had been arranged in front of a painted screen taken from the church, making a background to the action but also to be used for the keeping of the properties and for the actors to conceal themselves when they were not needed.

People walking from the town and the surrounding villages and hamlets began to pour into the priory grounds hours before the starting time which was to be when the priory bell struck two, jostling to secure a place near the front and seemingly not worried about standing for such a long time. This was an unexpected treat and most of the spectators were as much excited about watching the plays as seeing the King whom to them was as distant a figure as God and figured but vaguely in their thoughts.

The priory bell had struck the second hour when the royal party arrived, their approach sounded by heralds, and everyone pushed and craned their necks as the large entourage made their way to the dais. Many were disappointed by the sight of the King, a slim figure with thinning sandy hair and small eyes set in a narrow face that gave the occasional smile but looked as if it were an effort to do so. They were disappointed he was not wearing a crown and even the ermine-trimmed purple velvet mantle and black hat with brooches did not make up for the deficiency but their familiar countess compensated by cloth of gold and a new-fashioned gable headdress studded with pearls. Now was the time for the performance to begin for royalty could not be kept waiting.

The prior approached the dais and made a long flattering speech of welcome which included a humble thanksgiving that King Henry had deigned to travel to Lancashire, a panegyric to his mother who was a faithful and generous visitor to the abbey and a history of the abbey itself, extolling its importance. The speech went on and on and people became restless, but their muttering and shifting of positions could not halt the prior in full flow, determined not to curtail the speech he had been so long in composing. Then finally his eloquence was spent and drew to a close with a premature apology for the simplicity of the gift the people of Ormskirk were offering to their King. Father Peter raised his eyebrows slightly then with a last encouraging word to his little band of nervous actors gave the sign for the performance to begin. To the loud accompaniment of the banging of a drum and the rattling of a metal sheet, a length of vigorously-wafted white linen appeared above the screen and God, garbed in a sheet with a long white wig and matching beard that reached to his chest, 'descended' from the clouds. The play had begun and the spectators were transported to the Garden of Eden.

Renard de Bourgonville had not intended going to watch the plays. He was not particularly interested in a group of country folk putting on a performance of which he had often seen the like and his English was not good enough for him to understand the broad accents of the locals. However a friend of his, a fellow musician called Otto, had insisted that it would be a pleasant diversion on a sunny afternoon so he allowed himself to be persuaded.

They set out on foot, not being in any particular haste and enjoying the walk of about two miles through the countryside as they talked together. But being unfamiliar with the terrain which included many small winding paths that twisted back on each other around the marshy fields, they had taken a wrong turn which led them a distance out of their way. Consequently the performance had long started when they arrived at the priory and all they could do was stand at the back and marvel at the great number of people crowded together in the courtyard. They stood on the threshold unable to go any further and tried to see what was happening on the "stage" a long way in front of them. They could make out some animals and Otto said, "They seem to have arrived at the Nativity." Then someone began to sing -

"*I sing of a maiden that is makeless,*
King of all kings, to her son she ches."

Renard's blood ran cold and his heart almost stopped. There was only one person who could sing like that, one person with a voice so pure, so true, so rich with emotion. Was he dreaming? He looked around at the crowd of working folk and the stone buildings set in the marshy fields of a little market town in the desolate north of England, far away from London. It wasn't possible. He was dreaming and he blinked his eyes rapidly. But the singing continued –

"*He came all so still there his mother was,*
As dew in April that falleth on the grass."

A tremor convulsed his whole body. He wasn't mistaken and he wasn't dreaming. There was only one person who could sing like that. He couldn't understand how it should be but he knew without doubt that it was true.

He began to struggle through the crowd, inching a little at a time, ignoring Otto's questions and the complaints of people as he nudged them out of the way. As his impatience increased he pushed people aside more forcefully, immune to their annoyance, drawn onwards by the music like Ariadne's thread.

"He came all so still to his mother's bower,
As dew in April that falleth on the flower."

Eventually he was standing only a little way from the stage. The Virgin was seated on a stool beside the manger, clothed in a blue mantle the colour of her eyes and a veil that had slipped partly from her head revealing a profusion of thick curls as black and shiny as jet and she held in her arms a swaddled bundle as she sang -

"Mother and maiden, was never none but she,
Well may such a lady God's mother be."

Renard could not take his eyes from her and his heart was beating uncontrollably, the blood surging through his veins. She kissed the child's face tenderly then she lifted up her head and saw him. For a moment a shadow of uncertainty flickered in her eyes then suddenly an expression of such exquisite joy lit her face that people gasped as if they were in reality witnessing a heavenly revelation. Tears filled her eyes and began to fall on the 'child' in her arms and the spectators who had already been emotionally touched by her beauty and her singing were awestruck as if they were in the presence of the Virgin herself, a moment of intense spiritual awareness that they were to remember for years. She was unaware of the effect she was creating as her joy and her tears were for him alone, for her own miracle. Against all odds Renard had found her.

He couldn't take his eyes from her as the scene continued with the arrival of the Magi, an interminably long scene it seemed to Renard as impatience overwhelmed him. At last it came to an end and the actors disappeared from view.

He knew she would come to him and he waited, the blood throbbing in his veins, his heart pounding. The Virgin's part was done now and flinging the veil from her head Bel ran around the side of the screen as the players were busy changing the scene for the next episode. He ran to meet her. Wordlessly she flung herself into his arms and he held her close to his breast, his lips caressing her hair. Quickly he pulled her away from the side of the stage where they could be seen, though the attention of the audience was concentrated on what was going to happen next.

"Let's find somewhere to sit," he whispered and they hurried hand in hand round the church to the cloister garth where they sat on the grass near the stone cross.

Neither of them spoke at first, just drinking in the sight of each other, their hands linked, their fingers entwined. In those first moments of reunion there was no need for words. There was too much to say, too much to explain and it would take time to reveal everything. It was sufficient at the moment to be together, to know inexpressible joy that a miracle had occurred and they had found each other. It was incredible to believe that the near-impossible had happened but with the wonder came the assurance that they were meant to be together, they always had been, two halves making one whole.

"I've thought about you so often, wondered where you were, whether you found your family and were settled with them. You haunted my dreams and when

I feared I might never see you again I was filled with terror," Renard said at last.

The words reached Bel's soul and she whispered, "You have never really been away from me. Everything I did reminded me of you."

There was so much to say, so much to explain.

"I have so much to tell you," she said.

"And I you. But now is not the time. We shall have all the time in the world to tell our stories. Now I just want to hold you close, so close that we shall never be separated again. I should never have let you go," he said passionately, "but I didn't want to tie you to me when I had nothing to offer you."

"At that time I had to go," she said, "there were things that made it necessary. Now there is nothing to separate us and I want to stay with you."

Renard looked at her carefully and said, "I had already decided not to stay here in England, not even in the King's service. I was making plans to return to France."

Once again he was surprised by the happiness flooding her face. "I had also decided to go home. I was planning to leave after today. I was going to go alone but now I can come with you."

The realisation struck both of them of how close they had been to missing each other, but then simultaneously they were overwhelmed by the assurance that their destiny would not have allowed this to happen. They were meant to be together. He took her face in his hands and began to kiss her for the first time, gently at first then passionately and she responded to his embrace with a surrender she had reserved for him alone. She realised she had found what she had been searching for all her life and that body and soul knew the fulfilment of her destiny. The emotion flowing between them was tangible and they were content to sit wrapped in the joy of each other until a burst of cheering awakened them to the present.

"The plays are finished. I must return and take off this costume," Bel said, touching the blue mantle that covered her white shift. They rose and hand-in-hand returned to the courtyard. The royal visitors had left the dais and were being provided with refreshment in the prior's house. The spectators were reluctantly making their way home and the players were helping to dismantle their stage and pack up their properties onto a cart.

Harry Duxbury came to meet her saying accusingly, "I wondered where you were. Where did you go?" He then became aware that she was holding the hand of a stranger, a handsome young man who despite wearing the royal livery had a foreign air about him with his short dark hair and sun-tanned face.

"This is Renard," she said, keeping her hand in his.

Seeing them together and struck by the expression on Bel's face, Harry knew he had lost her and a pain shot through his heart like an arrow.

"This is my friend Harry Duxbury," she said to Renard and now it was the minstrel's turn to regard the newcomer doubtfully.

The two competitors stood scrutinising each other with some mistrust – the Englishman tall and lanky in his plain doublet and hose, with blond hair straight to his shoulders and the blue eyes of his Viking ancestors; the Frenchman of medium height with short dark hair falling in a fringe over alert grey eyes, elegant in his royal livery.

"Harry, Harry, you were very good as the serpent, I wish you had been in the play longer, I liked that part best." Ughtred's eager voice broke the tension as he burst into their midst in great excitement. "You were good too, Lady Bella, but your part was not so hard as Harry's. He had to leap about and be wicked and you only had to sit and hold a baby and sing." Bel laughed out loud and Ughtred continued, "Do you think Father Peter would let me have the tail and the mask you wore, Harry?"

Harry turned his attention to his excited cousin, "I think Father Peter will want to keep the costumes and properties for the next time he makes a play," he said.

"Then can you make me a serpent's costume, you are good at making things."

"I'll think about it. Perhaps when you are older Ughtred you might be able to play the part of the serpent yourself, I'm sure it would suit you," Harry said.

Ughtred was trying to drag him away and Bel spoke hastily. To Renard she said, "Harry has been very good to me, my only real friend here and I have a lot to tell you about how he has helped me in many ways." Then turning to Harry she said, "I am going away soon, as I had already decided, but Renard and I will be travelling together now."

He shrugged regretfully but managed to smile saying, "Don't go before we have time to say goodbye properly."

"I won't do that," she promised. "We have shared too much and I owe you a lot." She would leave Harry Duxbury regretfully but her life was with Renard de Bourgonville and it always had been ever since they had first met in Reims cathedral. In time she would tell Renard all the events of her life since she left him, the baby and Robert Malory and Anthony Woodville.

He would understand. However she would not confess that on three occasions she had allowed Harry more liberties than she ought to have done. He had met Harry and might believe there was more to her feelings than had actually been the case.

Otto arrived, wondering what had happened to his friend and once again there were introductions to be made.

"We shall have to get back to Lathom before the King arrives," Otto reminded Renard, noticing his reluctance to leave his beautiful companion.

"I suppose you are a royal musician now," Bel commented.

"But not for long. Tomorrow I shall inform the King that I am leaving his service and returning to France, and then we shall go. It's a long story and I will tell you all the details later. But how about you? How did you come to be here in this strange place?" Renard asked.

"That's a long story too that will take a deal of time in telling," Bel sighed. But briefly she explained that she had come here in the service of the King's mother, the Countess.

"We must leave our stories until later then," Renard said. "But where will you go now?"

Bel explained that she had lodgings in the town but had already made arrangements to leave as soon as she could. The two regretfully parted to go their separate ways, Renard to Lathom House and Bel to Dame Grice's more simple dwelling, but with the assurance that they would be on their way to France without delay. Renard joined Otto for the walk back, wanting to sing at the top of his voice and his quick movements almost a dance. Bel walked to Ormskirk in the company of Harry and Ughtred, feeling sorry that Harry was hurt but not able to keep the happiness from bubbling up in her heart.

CHAPTER 20

Fulfillment

"I would like a room for myself and my wife for this night," Renard announced to the innkeeper of a small thatched inn on the edge of a sleepy hamlet. An oak tree on a painted sign illustrated the name and a huge oak stood sentinel beside, its spreading branches touching the thatch and casting shadows on the grass where hens strutted and where their horses, their reins hanging loosely, were already nibbling. Renard and Bel had arrived in the county of Cheshire after crossing the broad river Mersey which was the boundary of Lancashire. They wished to make their journey to London and then Dover as speedily as possible so had decided to ride instead of working as minstrels on the way. Bel had her horse Troubadour and Renard had hired a mount, saying that he had more than sufficient money for the journey with the wages he had accrued from his royal service.

The innkeeper was a buxom dame with a plain country face that creased into good-humoured wrinkles when she smiled, enamoured at first sight of the attractive young couple so obviously in love.

"I guess you be newly wed," she said conspiratorially. "You can have my best room at no extra cost."

While Renard was seeing to their horses and unloading their panniers she led Bel to a long low room beneath the eaves, light and spacious. When Renard arrived with their baggage she was standing looking at the large box bed with a woollen counterpane chequered in red and yellow.

"You told her we were married."

"Of course."

Bel hesitated then said, "When we parted you told me you were married – two different versions. Was either of them true?"

He sat on the bed, pulling her down beside her. "I was lying," he said, "though there was an element of truth. My father was never a count who married me off to a great heiress to save our patrimony, nor neither was he a minstrel and I seduced by an older woman. These are tales that I make use of in my work. My father is a wine merchant who wanted me to follow in his trade. He had me troth-plighted to the heiress of a fellow wine-merchant, an important and wealthy member of his guild, so that our two families could be united in business but the only thing I wanted to be was a minstrel so I ran away. So legally speaking I am plighted to this woman and another marriage would be bigamous until she either dies or breaks the agreement herself, which I always hope for. I am sorry."

"It doesn't matter. I am not interested in marriage. I just want to be with you for the rest of my life," she said.

"Are you sure about this, Bel?" he asked. "I can't offer you anything – no home except where we stay every night, sometimes in comfort, sometimes less so, sometimes even in the open air; no money other than what we earn ourselves; no possessions except what we carry; no security."

"I want nothing except to be with you and for us to play music. I have tried other ways of life but they did not satisfy me for long. This is the way of life I have been used to from a child and from the moment I met you I have loved you. To share my life with you is the greatest happiness I could ever have."

"Then we will be handfasted. We will bind our selves together in the old way," Renard decided.

"There is something you should know first. I can never have children," she said sadly and told him the consequences of the rape.

Renard's heart was suffused with pity for the suffering he had been ignorant of and kissed her tenderly. "We don't need children, we are sufficient in ourselves, just you and I. I am sorry if you would like to have been a mother," he added, remembering her holding the child in the play, "but children would not suit our way of life." She would have liked to have borne his child but since it was not possible she acknowledged that he spoke true. He took hold of her hand and said, "I Renard de Bourgonville take thee Belfiore Lechanteur as my heart's love from this time forward until the day of my death. Now you do the same."

Wide-eyed and stammering a little she repeated the words for herself.

"Now we must give ourselves to each other," Renard said.

He began to undress her and laid her on the bed, pausing for a moment to drink in her beauty. Then he was beside her, his own clothes quickly discarded, and their bodies were fusing together as if all their life this was what they had been seeking – two halves of a whole. There was no foreplay this first time, just a desperate longing to be united that suffused them with desire so intense that moved from sweetness through profound joy to almost unbearable ecstasy. Bel thought she would die of happiness and when she looked at Renard she saw tears in his eyes. All night they held each other close, their eyes drinking in every beloved detail of face and body as they renewed their lovemaking, unwilling to be separated.

During the hours they lay in each other's arms they related their past experiences and Bel held nothing back. Renard shared her suffering for past tragedies and realised how easy his own life had been in comparison. They were amazed to discover they had nearly missed each other in Brittany.

"Fate gave us another chance," Bel said contentedly, snuggling closer in his arms.

"Our destiny was always to be together, right from that first opportune meeting in the cathedral at Reims," Renard said.

Their minds drifted back to that cold uncomfortable night when they had shared a stone bench, anxious about the morrow. Now they were lying wrapped in each other's arms in a comfortable bed, troth-plighted and awaiting the dawn when they would be on their way again, each mile bringing them closer to home.

When they arrived in London Bel took Renard to the Throstle Inn while they sought out company for the last stage of their journey to Dover. Once again the inn brought her good fortune. That evening there arrived a group of students on a visit to see the sights of Italy with their tutor and some servants and they were only too happy to have Renard and Bel join with them as far as the port. With great regret Bel knew that she must soon be parted from her beloved Troubadour and was worried about what might happen to him in the hands of a new owner. Then in a moment of inspiration she decided to give him to Sim who was still working at the inn. Sim had helped her care for the horse from when his master Robert Malory had first bought him for her, he knew the horse well and was fond of him. When Bel told him that she was giving him the horse as a farewell gift his joy knew no bounds.

"You have always been so good to me, Rose," he stammered with tears in his eyes. "Since Master Robert died you have done so much for me."

"And you helped me too, Sim, when I had need of it," she assured him. "Are you happy here?"

"I love London and I am content for the present here at the Throstle," he replied. "I miss Betty Trimble but Goodwin is a good enough master. Though someday if I can save enough money I would like to have my own inn."

"Then hold onto your wishes, Sim, they sometimes come true," Bel said.

She was glad that her final leaving of the Throstle Inn had seen some happiness.

Her leave-taking of Harry Duxbury had been tinged with sadness. But after his first disappointment at losing Bella, Harry had been consoled by an unexpected turn of fortune so incredible that all else had paled into insignificance. The King had recognised him in the performance at the priory and had called him to his presence.

"He recognised me from our journey to Brittany and when I told him that I had fought in Sir Thomas Stanley's company at Bosworth field he offered me a place in his service," Harry had related to Bel, his natural exuberance at bursting point. "He said he liked men about him who were resourceful and loyal and since I was a countryman with a knowledge of horses and hunting I could serve with his personal grooms. So instead of Duxbury and Ormskirk it's London and the court and no doubt a lot of travelling."

Bel was happy for him but said, "What about your Uncle John and Ughtred?"

Harry grimaced. "Ughtred was upset at first but when I told him I would come home from time to time and tell him wonderful stories he rallied somewhat, and then he realised he could make himself important by boasting that his cousin was in the King's service. Uncle John and Ethelreda were both pleased that at last I had been given something worthwhile to do and proud that it was to be in the royal household. And Rafe Standish was green with envy. Who knows, I might even be a knight one day." Then he said, "But I shall miss you Bella. We shared some wonderful times together and I had hoped for more."

She pressed his hand saying, "You will meet a lot of girls in London, girls who are more suited to you than I. You will marry a girl who will be satisfied to keep your house and bear you children as I never could have done, heirs that perhaps one day will help to recover your inheritance."

The promise of a new life salved his loss, for Harry could never be downcast for long and he was on the point of having a long-held dream fulfilled – travel and adventure. When they finally parted it was with good humour, Bel kissing Harry affectionately and Harry and

Renard shaking each other by the hand and wishing each other good fortune.

Now it was time for Bel and Renard to leave London and head for Dover where they could take ship for France. Bel was retracing her steps but this time in the company of her love for whom the sight of the white cliffs would be a new experience. In their shelter within the bay would be a ship to take them home.

It was their last day at the Throstle Inn and Bel recollected with bitter-sweetness her first arrival there and remembered with affection her old friend Betty Trimble. Renard had no such memories and had walked into the City saying he had some business to finish and Bel surmised he wished to take a last look at some of the sights. When he returned his face held an expression of excited anticipation though there was also an air of mystery about him and he was hiding something behind his back.

"What have you been doing?" she was compelled to ask.

With an undeniable flourish he presented her with what seemed to be a book saying, "I have a gift for you." It *was* a book, a large leather-bound volume.

"You always bought me presents," she said, remembering the flageolet which she had treasured so dearly and had always seen it as a good luck emblem. But she wondered what kind of a book, and such a large one, he could have bought for her. Then as she took it from him she saw the inscription on the cover 'Le Morte Darthur by Sir Thomas Malory' and gazed on it in astonishment.

"My grandfather's book," she stammered, tears welling in her eyes.

"Yes William Caxton the printer who has a shop in Westminster has printed it. Now anyone can buy a copy and read it. They can print as many copies as people want," Renard explained.

Bel was overwhelmed. The book would not now lie forgotten. All Sir Thomas's lonely hours in his prison cell were not wasted but would provide pleasure for countless people. How Robert would have been pleased, and Anthony Woodville who had kept his promise and put it in the hands of William Caxton. She had fulfilled Robert's wishes by taking it to Lord Rivers and by so doing had helped to fulfil what must always have been Sir Thomas's hope that in time to come people would read his book. She felt so proud to have been part of this enterprise, so glad that she had made the journey to take it to Lord Rivers. May God rest his soul, she thought sadly.

"It is one of the very first books to be printed in the English language so Caxton must have realised the great worth of the manuscript and have confidence that many people will want to buy it and read it," Renard said. "He does after all run a commercial business."

Bel looked at the book cover and the title. "It never had a title," she said. "Caxton must have named it so. But he hasn't titled it correctly and also the death of Arthur is only the final part of the book. It is much more than this, more than death but about life and service, honour and loyalty and great love."

She began to turn the pages and came upon the story of Elaine of Astolat. Her eyes moved along the page – "*Why should I leave such thoughts? Am I not an earthly woman? For my belief is that I do no offence, though I love an earthly man, unto God, for he formed me thereto and all manner of good love cometh from God.*

*And other than good love loved I never Sir Launcelot.
And I take God to record I loved never none but him nor
never shall of earthly creature."*

Launcelot did not return Elaine's love but Renard
loved her as she loved him.

"Thankyou my dear love for buying it for me and for
understanding everything I told you about it. Do you
remember when we first met you asked me if I knew the
story of King Arthur and his knights. We can read it
together while we are travelling."

"He was a minstrel in his own way, telling stories in
words instead of music but entertaining people as we do.
A fine inheritance my darling Bel," Renard said as he
took her in his arms and they held each other close.

FINIS

Historical Note

All the nobility and royalty are real historical personages and I have kept to the facts of the events as they were reported. Bel and Renard are my own inventions as are the minor characters. The Duxburys were a real family.

The facts of the life of Sir Thomas Malory and the MorteDarthur are true. Robert Malory died unexpectedly at the age of 40, causes unknown. Bel is my own invention.

Henry Tudor did visit Lathom House and planned his new palace of Richmond in the same style. This event however occurred several years later in his reign and I have anticipated it for the purpose of my narrative.

All the music mentioned is authentic from the period.

Lightning Source UK Ltd.
Milton Keynes UK
UKOW04f0304231015

261185UK00001B/1/P